KNIGHTS ON THE GRAVEYARD WATCH

T. B. Pasko

coffeetownpress

Kenmore, WA

coffeetown**press**

Coffeetown Press books published by Epicenter Press

Epicenter Press
6524 NE 181st St. Suite 2
Kenmore, WA 98028.
www.Epicenterpress.com
www.Coffeetownpress.com
www.Camelpress.com

For more information go to: www.Epicenterpress.com

This is a work of fiction. All characters are creations of the author's imagination.

Knights on the Graveyard Watch
Copyright © 2025 by T.B. Pasko

ISBN: 9781684923205 (trade paper)
ISBN: 9781684923212 (ebook)

LOC: 202495255

Printed in the United States of America

This book is dedicated to those that patiently read through my early drafts and believed there was an entertaining story buried within. Thank you to my test readers: Angela, Ralph, Nanci, Paul, Dan, Missy, Jamie, Teri, Jennifer. You gave me hope. A special thanks to my family for dealing with me throughout this period; Cayce, Amanda, Tracey, Isley and of course, Tyler, the highly skilled international traveling barista. To my agent, Eric Lincoln Miller, thanks for taking on a nobody and making me believe. Finally to Joseph Wambaugh, a true pioneer in police fiction, thank you for your amazing books that got me interested in police work and writing.

Acknowledgments

I want to acknowledge Maggie Tomaro for her support, encouragement and endless supply of red pens. Without her assistance this project would have withered and died. I would also like to acknowledge the assistance of Samantha Simcox, for casting the first technical eye on this work and helping me with the mechanics of storytelling.

Part I- The 7th Precinct

Prologue - August 1990

"Buck, you're up. We got a juvenile, snatched from his driveway. Cory Michaels, white male, thirteen," Detective Sergeant Stafford stated, dropping the case note on the desk before quickly departing. Minimal contact with his surly subordinate was always Stafford's goal.

Detective Bill "Buck" Foster put his uneaten bologna and cheese sandwich back in its plastic bag and rubbed his forehead in disgust. He ran his hand across his buzz cut, slinging sweat onto the wall behind his chair. The desk fan whirred steadily as it recirculated the stifling air. *No air conditioning again? Why don't they tear down this shit hole if they aren't going to fix it?* Foster glanced at the water-stained ceiling tiles and blistered green paint that covered the walls. Phones rang incessantly in the background adding to his throbbing headache. The putrid odor of urine and vomit drifted in from the holding cell down the hall. A transfer was long overdue.

Foster checked the bulletin board daily for openings in other precincts. Any place was better than the 7th Precinct. *Lucky 7 my ass. Bad victims, no witnesses, dead end cases. Fuck this place. At least it's dayshift.*

Foster grabbed his sport coat off the chair and threw it on, covering up his sweat-stained dress shirt.

Fifteen minutes after he walked down the crumbling steps of the dilapidated 7th precinct, he wheeled his battered, unmarked Ford to the curb behind the police car at 1432 Balsa. The center of what the uniform cops called "The Woods," an apt moniker for a cluster of streets in the dirt-poor district named for trees.

The car continued to sputter as he walked towards the nearest uniformed officer. He glanced at his watch and let out an audible whistle. *Three thirty already? Can I stretch this into two hours of overtime?*

"Hey Buck," Sgt. Blevins greeted the veteran detective with a genuine smile. "The heat is something this year." Foster ignored the earnest attempt at pleasantries from the sergeant.

"What do you have?" He snarled in response.

"Michaels, Cory. White male, thirteen. Last seen bouncing his basketball in the driveway around 1445 hours by mom. Mom is Heather Conway, white female, twenty-nine. A few minutes later the ball was in the street and Cory was gone. Widow across the street saw Cory talking to an unknown male in the street. She looked up and they were both gone." The sergeant finished his monotone update, closed his notebook and placed it into his uniform breast pocket.

"Who's doing the report?" Foster asked, glancing across the street at the elderly woman rocking gently on a porch swing.

"Collins is handling the report and talking to mom inside. You want to talk to her or the witness first?"

"What's the vibe on this?" Foster paused to wipe dripping sweat from his face with a faded handkerchief. "Mom a junkie? Baby daddy drama? Domestic history here? Is the kid a shit bag? Any creepers in the neighborhood we know of? You check for registered sex offenders yet?"

"Buck, not everyone is a piece of shit," Sgt. Blevins chided before continuing, "Mom has no priors that we know of; still checking on her current boyfriend. The kid has behavioral problems. He's on meds for ADHD. Suspended twice this year for violent outbursts in class and fighting. The family has no history or open cases with Children's Services, as surprising as that sounds. Ran away twice in the last six months."

"Wonderful," Foster mumbled.

"Mom swears Cory wouldn't leave the driveway; he knew he was grounded over some homework issue. Honestly, we would probably dial all this back a bit, but the neighbor saw the kid talking to an unknown male and, poof, he is gone. We gotta cover our asses, that's why I had them notify you," Blevins finished.

"I get it," Foster said as he wrote furiously in his notebook. "I'll do the follow up. Get me a copy of the report as soon as it's done so I can add it to my case file. We'll treat it as an abduction. Get him entered in the system as a missing-slash-abducted ASAP." Foster turned and headed across the street to the witness's house.

"Ma'am, I'm Detective Foster with the Port Isley Police Department, I need to chat with you for a minute about what happened earlier."

Foster extended right hand and she shook it gingerly.

"Eunice Gulford. Would you like to sit?" She motioned to a rusting steel chair next to an upside-down orange milk crate topped with an overflowing ashtray. Cigarette butts and burns marred the floor by the chair. *She sees quite a bit.* Foster sat down as both of his knees cracked with his descent. He took out his notebook and pen and haphazardly flipped until he found the page with today's date.

He began to write and talk.

"Eunice, how old are you?"

"I'll be 83 next month. I've been here for the last 27 years," she offered proudly. He followed up with several perfunctory questions before getting to the incident.

"What do you know about the kid across the street?" He asked, nodding towards the wood sided, light blue bungalow with a broken screen door.

"He seems like a rambunctious boy. I've spoken with him only a few times, but he was always pleasant to me. He swears a blue streak at his mother though. I don't know much about his mother; she comes and goes at all hours. I think she has a boyfriend now; a young man has been coming around the last month or so. He did cut the grass finally," she paused to light up a Marlboro. She exhaled and started to speak before Foster held up his hand.

"What did you see this afternoon?" He asked, gently redirecting her rambling.

"I was reading the paper, right here, like most days and I looked up when I heard the ball bouncing. The boy was just kind of walking up and down the driveway bouncing the ball. I looked up again when the ball stopped bouncing. That's when I saw the man talking to the boy at the end of the driveway."

"Did you see him get out of a car?" Foster interrupted.

"No, I looked up and he was just there," she pointed to the edge of the cracked concrete drive before continuing. "I didn't hear any car. I don't know where he came from."

Foster looked up and down the street. There were only two cars parked on the street on this block and neither looked operational. He stopped writing, turned back Eunice and nodded for her to continue.

"I saw them both smiling and talking casually. I got the impression they knew each other, so I went back to reading the paper. I saw them a minute or so later when I glanced up. I dropped my lighter about then, reached down to get it, and when I looked up, they were both gone."

"Were there any other cars parked on the street at that time?" Foster pointed at the two cars parked on the block. Eunice shook her head vigorously.

Foster leaned forward slowly and tapped the floor with his right hand before bringing it back up to his lap. "So, you picked up your lighter, and looked up again, maybe ten to fifteen seconds later and they were both gone? You didn't see another car, or hear one drive by? Did you hear any yelling or screaming?"

"No, not a thing," she said as she blew out a mouthful of smoke. "Isn't that peculiar? Someone can just disappear?"

No, they can't. I'm hoping he isn't in the basement of his neighbor's house in five separate trash bags. I'm pretty sure you dozed off for an hour or so, based on the cigarette burns on the floor, and would have slept through a 747 landing on the street. And yes, I noticed the three empty vodka bottles under your porch swing.

"He probably just ran to a neighbor or might have darted between the houses," he said casually as he continued writing in his notebook. "Can you tell me what the man was wearing? What did he look like?"

"He wore blue dungarees and a white t-shirt. He was very tall and thin."

Christ, who says dungarees anymore?

"Taller than me?" Foster asked standing up.

"Oh yes, a good bit."

He held his hand slightly above his head to indicate about six feet.

"A bit taller than that."

He jotted down some notes. Six-foot to six-three, thin to medium build, 175 to 190 pounds.

"Was there anything unusual about him? What kind of hairstyle? Was he white or black, if you could tell?" He continued scribbling as Eunice lit another cigarette.

"He had really neat hair, parted on the side, very short. Brown hair. He looked white to me, maybe around thirty years old. Very neat looking, clean, not the sort of riffraff I normally see in these parts," she said as she exhaled a cloud of smoke. "Oh! Oh! He wore a very shiny watch on his right wrist. Very shiny metal band. What happens now?" She asked in earnest.

"We are going to check out the neighborhood and talk to anyone we can and, hopefully, they saw something and we can track Cory down," Foster said, wiping his brow as he glanced down the street.

Foster thanked her and walked down the wooden steps and stopped in the weed-choked yard. He watched as officers scampered back and forth canvassing the neighborhood. Despite the oppressive humidity, he felt a chill across the back of his neck.

Yes, Eunice, this feels peculiar.

Rumbles of thunder sounded in the distance, heralding the approaching storm.

Chapter 1
Happy Birthday, November 2024

Officer Danilo "Dan" Venko slowly opened his eyes to the digital strains of "Flight of the Valkyries," the alarm on his flip phone. Diablo, his fat, over-sized cat, leapt onto his chest with amazing agility for a girl her size. She purred robotically as he stroked her white fur. He scooped his hand under her and gently placed her on the floor.

Venko gingerly rubbed the scar on his repaired left shoulder, his joints aching in the damp November air. He opened his phone and saw the message from Sarah:

"I know you turn off the sound when you nap. Don't forget to feed Diablo before you leave. Please throw out the pizza that I know is still in your fridge from last week. Ha ha. And don't wear that black ARMY t-shirt for a third straight day. Catch up with you tomorrow, SS."

He smiled a broad, warm grin and struggled with the numeric keypad before sending "OK."

You forgot to remind me to inhale and exhale.

She immediately texted her reply:

"One day very soon you have to get a smart phone. I know it took you five minutes with your sausage fingers to bang out 'ok' on a numeric keypad. LOL."

He surveyed the studio apartment, the light from the desk lamp barely enough to see as he walked to his desk. He bent over and picked up the stack of books Diablo had knocked off the top of the bookshelf. In a fleeting moment of organization, he stacked them in two piles, one for Hemingway and one for Wells. He stared at Diablo, who was now circling his feet and mewing furiously.

"A few more pounds and you won't be able to make that leap," he scolded. Venko looked around the apartment and tried to figure out what else Diablo had explored in the two hours that he spent fitfully napping. The Army photos were still standing on the desk by the laptop and the blinds on the window were not shredded. That was good. It was a real headache to replace the last ones. The remote was on the floor next to the overstuffed chair. She hadn't played hockey tonight. Several books remained scattered on the old coffee table. The TV was slightly askew in the entertainment center.

Sarah is right, that twenty-four-inch TV looks ridiculous on the giant stand. Why do you go back there Diablo? A little catnip stash?

Diablo thundered into the kitchen at the sound of her metal bowl clanking on the cold wooden floor.

Yeah, I know you haven't eaten in what, three or four hours? Do you know how lucky you are?. He put in a Who CD, and headed to the shower.

He dried himself quickly and put on black boxer briefs. His thighs stretched the cotton. Venko took a deep breath and exhaled through pursed lips. He stared in the mirror. His once black hair was now thoroughly streaked with gray. Hard lines edged his blue eyes above a thin straight nose that had been bloodied many times, but not broken. Venko tilted his head back, his jawline was still clearly defined, despite a hint of jowls forming around his chin. He could see the definition in has arms and shoulders had started to fade. Several of his knuckles were gnarled and arthritic, the result of thousands of punches thrown by a midnight police officer over the last twenty-three years.

He grabbed a handful of fat on his belly and sighed deeply. *Okay, six-one, 220 pounds really isn't too bad. Alright, it isn't bad for a twenty-one-year-old college linebacker, not so much for a forty-nine-year-old street cop. Who am I kidding, I am fat.* He looked in the mirror again. *I know, I know. I'm closer to six-foot than six-one.*

Venko grabbed the disputed ARMY t-shirt off the chair and squeezed his shoulders into the faded, black cotton. He opened the wardrobe door and put on the rest of his polyester uniform. Diablo began to circle him as he sat on the coffee table tightening his boot laces.

"Yes, I'm working tonight, you know the routine. Watch whatever you want, but no guests over," Venko said to the circling feline. Diablo was not amused and continued pacing.

The worn leather gun belt seemed to be shrinking as he struggled to fasten it. He glanced at the clock. Just a little behind. He slid on his duty jacket, gloves and black knit cap.

As he locked the door, he could smell strong coffee. Anna Rosales sat on a padded folding chair next to a small bistro table in front of the fire escape window. Her sightless, milky eyes turned towards the sound of the keys. She smiled as he approached.

"Danilo, I made you coffee tonight. It's very, very cold out," she said with a thick Puerto Rican accent.

"You always do, Miss Rosales, thank you. You shouldn't sit in front of this drafty window. I know you like to hear the city outside, but this damp, cold air isn't good for you," he said as he spied the red thermos.

"Danilo, how is your lovely lady friend? And I noticed your hip is bothering you again. Please see a doctor soon," she said, ignoring his warning.

"Uh, she is just fine. And how…" he trailed off awkwardly.

"Just because I can't see, doesn't mean I don't see," she tilted her head up towards the sound of his breathing.

He studied the vacant eyes and the freckles across the bridge of her nose. Wisps of fine, grey hair poked out from the yellow, floral head scarf. She wore a thick, pink cardigan over a faded blue blouse. He knew she had to be at least seventy but probably closer to a frail, seventy-five. As far as he knew, she lived alone in the studio apartment behind her chair. She seemed to get around fine and never had visitors. Venko felt sorry for her and always set aside ten minutes to sit at her makeshift fire escape bistro for coffee. He wondered what she would do if he ever left the midnight shift and worked days.

She reached out and patted his left wrist, near his watch. "Please, sit for a few minutes."

He smiled and sat in the tiny folding chair, his mass completely engulfing the chair. He opened the thermos, inhaled the aroma deeply, and poured a cup of coffee.

"That's better, you look much better when you smile like that. You've always wanted to ask so many questions but never have. You exhale through your nose when you smile. If you wondered how I knew." She replied. "You are a good man Danilo."

He sipped the strong coffee and she continued.

"Could you pick me up a gallon of whole milk, a loaf of wheat bread and two cans of black beans tomorrow?" Rosales asked, sliding an envelope across the table.

"Sure, as always," he responded and picked up the envelope from her and placed it in the back pocket of his uniform pants.

She spent the next several minutes talking about when the ground floor market used to be a real drug store with a soda fountain and small diner. She heard the watch as he turned his wrist to see it.

"Go now, and be careful, this is a different place now."

He capped the thermos and stood.

"Danilo, Danilo," she called as he started down the four flights to the sidewalk. She waited until she heard him stop. "Please put on a clean t-shirt tomorrow."

• • •

Officer Venko enjoyed walking to work in the cold crisp air. His apartment was in a working-class section of Port Isley that clung to life with a few open businesses. The place was about the best he could afford on a police officer's salary. Twenty years ago, he briefly considered jumping to a higher-paying department. Pittsburgh, Harrisburg, and Philadelphia, had snagged a few of his fellow officers, but when it came down to deciding, he just didn't want to relocate. After all, money wasn't everything. He liked Port Isley and the unpredictable weather Lake Erie brought. It was home.

He bounded up the crumbling, concrete steps thirteen minutes before the 11 p.m. roll call. He pulled the brass handle and immediately felt the warmth inside the four-story 7th Precinct building. Harsh light lit the dingy industrial green paint. Old wooden benches lined the walls. On the far-left wall were framed photos of officers from the 7th Precinct that were killed in the line of duty. Eight photos spaced neatly apart. The last photo chronologically displayed on the wall, was of Narcotics Detective Jessica Sullivan, shot and killed during an undercover drug deal thirteen years ago.

The perpetually out of service elevator was at the back corner. The well-worn stairs were at the center of the foyer, and the information desk, to the right of the stairs.

The information desk stood on a raised platform with a half door at the rear, for the desk officer to enter and exit. The front of the desk had a large sign that read: *"Welcome to the 7th Precinct. Precinct Commander-Captain Brian Sellers."*

The sign had a photo of the smiling Captain Sellers just below the lettering. Because of vandals, possibly even some police officers, the complete sign was covered in Plexiglas that was bolted to the front wall of the information desk. Captain Sellers' name plate had been frequently removed and remounted to various stalls inside the third-floor men's room. The picture was often hilariously captioned and routinely enhanced with markers. The Plexiglas, and recently mounted camera on the opposite wall, had kept the vandals at bay for the last several months.

"Happy Birthday, Dan," the smiling desk officer called to Venko.

"Again? Dex, they did it this year too?" Venko asked sheepishly. Officer Samuel "Dex" Mitchell motioned Venko closer. He walked up to the front counter, carefully stopping at the blue line painted on the floor two feet in front of the half wall. A sign at each corner of the counter warned: *"Do not cross the blue line."*

The thin, black man smiled and motioned him towards the rear entrance. Dex shook Venko's hand with gusto as he came through the entrance. His uniform was impeccably creased, and his shoes were polished to a mirror finish. His shaved head and smooth dark skin made him look ten years younger than fifty-two.

Venko stared at the four six-packs and five twelve-packs, a mix of domestic and imported beers, stacked neatly by the half door.

"It's been seventeen years, I can't believe people remember," he said with a grin.

"More will trickle in, I'm sure. It's respect for you. That and hatred for Sellers. Even Central Precinct snuck in and dropped off a six of Guinness. That's from administrators and bureaucrats! Enjoy, maybe hold some training at the park after shift?" Dex asked.

"Good call," Venko replied and paused, shaking his head. "All this over one punch. I consider that fair since the son-of-a-bitch broke my thumb in the academy."

The animosity between Venko and Sellers started shortly after they were hired in the same academy class. A month into academy training, during half-speed handcuffing drills, Deputy Chief Lindley came in to observe. Unfortunately, Venko was Sellers' partner that day. Seizing the opportunity to impress the deputy chief, Sellers went full speed, slamming Venko face first onto the mat. The sudden, jarring move fractured Venko's thumb. Venko grunted in pain and sprung to his feet, shoving the taller Sellers with enough force to send him sprawling into a pair of recruits ten feet behind them. Instructors and recruits grabbed Sellers as he made a transparently pathetic attempt to charge Venko.

Venko realized he had almost reminisced into the start of roll call. "Oops, gotta run, I don't want to be late."

Dex nodded and picked up a clean hand towel from the neatly folded stack on a shelf behind the desk. He grabbed the bottle of Windex and began his nightly ritual. He sprayed the top of the counter and wiped it until it shined. He walked over to the row of fallen officers and with great precision, cleaned and polished each plaque, starting with Detective Jessica Sullivan.

"Dan, I need to see you after roll call," Lt. Cal Swanson called out without looking up from his computer screen as Venko passed by.

"Sure thing, boss," Venko said as he continued down the hall, past the lieutenant's office and into the roll call room. He sat in his back row seat, took a deep breath and tossed his notebook and pen onto the table. He poured a cup of coffee from the thermos and inhaled the aroma.

Sgt. Frank Miller waddled down the aisle separating the six tables where twelve officers sat casually laughing and joking. Miller was "almost five-nine," as he liked to say, and "just a few egg rolls" over two-hundred and fifteen pounds. His girth with a gun belt made the squeeze down the aisle tight. Veteran officers, in unison, picked up their coffee cups as he walked by, knowing a sudden table nudge was always possible. Miller had pale skin, huge jowls and a bushy reddish-blonde mustache. He looked grossly overweight and sloppy but possessed enough street smarts to be respected by the troops. This did not stop them from nicknaming him the "Albino Manatee" which was later shortened to "The Manatee."

Sgt. Miller dropped the clipboard on the podium and started.

"Currently the temperature outside is a tropical twenty-two degrees and with the wind chill coming off tropical Lake Erie, we will dip into the single digits overnight. Having said that, Captain Sellers would like you to be reminded that lunch breaks are thirty minutes and not guaranteed. Should he elect to drive by Molly's, the only open diner on this shift I might add, and see more than two marked units parked there, he most certainly will have you written up. The policy is no more than two cruisers parked outside a restaurant at a time."

A collective groan came in unison. A few suspicious coughs that sounded like "asshole" could also be heard. Miller continued unfazed.

"So, for my sake, and my well-known aversion to meaningless paperwork, please continue to hide excess cruisers in the alley a half-block west of Molly's," Miller paused to make sure everyone heard him.

Miller flipped the page, glanced at the memo and sighed before starting.

"This from Internal Affairs: Officers are reminded that the policy on BWC, body-worn cameras, has been updated. Random audits of BWC footage has commenced for this quarter,"

Miller knew this would draw a comment from the gallery and paused slightly in anticipation.

"Remember Webster defines 'random' as midnight shift in the 7th Precinct, and specifically, the noted crime fighters in Car 1," Officer Rachel Stein interrupted.

Murmurs of agreement bounced around the room before Miller continued.

"You are reminded to activate your body cameras anytime you are on a call or a citizen contact is likely. Failure to do so will result in discipline," Miller rubbed his forehead in exasperation, before turning the page.

"Port Isley Police Department policy states officers will be professional in their interaction with citizens. Profanity is prohibited. De-escalation is the preferred method of conflict resolution." A collective groan came from the audience.

Sgt. Miller stepped slightly to the right and looked down the hall. This was the universal signal that he was going to speak frankly and not in an official capacity.

"Folks, for the last two quarterly BWC audits, I received emails from the desk rangers at Internal Affairs. I was told that these emails were strictly for informational purposes. Right. Anyway, we are leading the league, so to speak, in citizen complaints, uses of force, car chases and policy violations for swearing. Now, you all know my personal feelings on profanity. I, unequivocally, will not tolerate that fucking shit."

Miller enjoyed hearing the laughter and was a master at lifting morale after delivering necessary directives.

"I should point out the obvious, Internal Affairs does nothing for informational purposes. If they have noticed, they are already looking into it. Having said that, Officer Bianchi, the word 'fuck' cannot be a verb, adjective, noun and pronoun. Do your best to substitute an occasional 'sir' or 'ma'am.' The other sergeants and I review all uses of force, car chases and complaints. The lieutenant then reviews them and signs off on them. Captain Sellers then usually sends a dozen or so questions about the incident that we answer before he signs off. My point is, we have no problem with the chases or uses of force and can defend them procedurally. If we cut back on the citizen complaints, maybe we can get off the radar. Honestly, I am tired of this shift wearing a big target." Miller adjusted his reading glasses and sighed.

"Hey Sarge, does anyone realize we work in the busiest, most crime infested precinct and make more meaningful felony arrests than any other precinct? There are very few, 'sirs' or 'ma'ams' at three a.m. Just saying," Stein chirped to a chorus of nodding heads.

"Stein, must you always try and infuse logic into everything," a smiling Miller retorted before starting on the car assignments.

"Officers Martinez, Bianchi Car 1, the war zone. Can we go three nights without a shooting? Vegas says no. Officers Stein, Fitzpatrick Car 2. Officers Niles, Jackson Car 3. Officers Carmen, Stanley Car 4," Miller paused, which immediately put Venko on alert.

He set his coffee down and stared at Sgt. Miller. Generally, the car assignments were run through quickly with minimal commentary from Miller or the gallery. Everyone knew their assigned cars, and unless one partner was on vacation or sick, there were no changes. Venko saw Miller's enormous mustache twitch. Miller caught his glance and shrugged sheepishly.

"Officer Marcus McGhee has transferred in from Central Precinct for the last phase of his field training period. Which means, as you all know, he will most likely be posted here after his probationary period ends. Marcus was out getting a tour of our state-of-the-art facility," Miller paused as chuckles erupted. Miller waved McGhee up to the front of the room. He had been standing in the rear, unnoticed. McGhee strode confidently towards the front table and stood front and center.

McGhee was a lanky six-one, 175 pounds in full uniform. He had the freckles of his Jamaican mother and wore his hair in short dreadlocks, something that wouldn't have been permissible twenty years ago. His African American father had been an attaché at the American Embassy in Jamaica.

"Who is going to train the young Irishman?" Martinez asked, in a terrible Irish accent.

"Jesus, do you not see the irony in a Mexican mimicking an Irish accent in this politically correct world?" Miller asked with a chuckle.

Officer Sal "Jesus" Martinez, earned his nickname from his first field training officer, who repeatedly screamed "Jesus, Martinez, think!"

Miller paused and continued.

"Officer Venko is going to lend his considerable experience and knowledge and guide the young lad through the last phase of his training period."

Venko, processing what he just heard, sank lower in his seat as Miller continued the assignments.

"Officers Venko, McGhee, Car 5, also known as *WW*, warehouse and water district. Officer Hayslip as always, you're driving the paddy wagon otherwise known as the Big Blue Uber," Miller completed the assignments and flipped to the check in patrol section, the list of problem areas for each car to check in their districts. These were commonly known as CIP's.

"Sarge, I am offended by the blatantly racist term paddy wagon," Officer Fitzpatrick yelled, pounding his fist in mock outrage.

"Simmer down, Fitz, go home and slam a Guinness and chase it with a Jameson, like always," Miller shot back.

"Equally offensive, but true," Fitzpatrick retorted, setting off another wave of laughter.

Miller covered the CIP's for each car as well as the names of those with notable outstanding warrants or persons of interest to various detectives. He paused and noticed Fitzpatrick involved in a side conversation with Stein and not writing in his notebook.

"Officer Fitzpatrick, your CIP's?" Miller asked folding his arms across his chest.

"Uh, CIP is Check in Patrol, it's the locations to check through the shift, in other words our hotspots."

"I am familiar with what the acronym CIP stands for, as somehow they did promote me to sergeant," Miller tapped the three chevrons on his sleeve before continuing, "as is everyone else in the room. Now maybe share with the group the CIP's you were assigned tonight," he asked and watched as Fitzpatrick nervously flipped through his notebook.

"Officer Stein, help your partner out," Miller asked satisfied that Fitzpatrick was sufficiently embarrassed and would most likely receive hazing by his fellow officers. Stein rattled off the list of addresses and problems in their district in seconds.

"Thank you Officer Stein for paying attention during roll call. Please strongly encourage your partner to do the same."

He dismissed roll call and the conversations started up as the troops gathered up their notebooks and coffee cups.

"Wait, everyone listen up!" Sgt. Miller pounded the podium until he had everyone's attention. "I almost forgot, happy birthday Dan!"

The whoops and cheers were deafening, Venko felt his face flush as he grinned.

"City-wide gifts in honor of this day have been left at the information desk. If I'm not mistaken, Dan would like to sponsor a tactical training session at the end of shift?" Miller asked.

Venko raised his right fist.

"Let the record reflect, Venko has requested a tactical training session. It appears that we have a quorum. All those in favor of the motion signify by saying aye."

The room erupted in a chorus of "Aye."

"Ladies and gentlemen, the vote is unanimous! There will be beer in the land of misfits. Be safe out there."

The officers again rose and gathered up belongings and began the slow process of starting the shift. Shouts of "Happy birthday Dan," ping-ponged around the room.

"Yo Dan, are you sure you're up to training a rook again?" Officer Hayslip began before segueing into his favorite topic, working out. "I got a good leg regiment and a home brew protein shake that will absolutely kill your quads. Forget that creatine shit.

I mean if your rook is gonna be out there running down mopes, it means you're gonna be out there chug-chug-chugging at some point. Keep it in mind bro! Squat day is Thursdays."

"Appreciate that, Haystack," Venko replied and managed a half smile.

Elroy "Haystack" Hayslip was a giant blonde mountain, formerly a three-year starter at defensive end for the Nebraska Cornhuskers. Five years at Nebraska left him only three semesters short of graduating with a degree in recreation management. Despite four documented concussions, he managed to remain academically eligible during football season. Now twenty-eight, with four years on the job, he maintained a diet and workout regimen that seemed insanely intense to the rest of the shift.

Haystack appeared in a few pre-season games for the Oakland Raiders before separating his shoulder and being waived. While he was an enormous physical specimen, the assistant coach who cut him, stated that he lacked the intellect to grasp the intricacies of NFL defenses. Debate still raged, whether Haystack took the civil service test or his former agent took the test as his proxy.

Every one of his field training officers agreed: Haystack could not write a report that made any sense. He was, however, sincere, friendly and universally liked by everyone. After he lifted a Hyundai compact off a bicyclist during his probationary period, Lt. Swanson decided there would be a place for the six-five, 255-pound behemoth. Transporting prisoners and driving a wagon did not mentally overtax Haystack. His arrival on volatile scenes had a magical de-escalating effect on criminals that his co-workers appreciated.

"Bro, I can talk to the lieutenant if you want. You've earned your keep, you shouldn't have to train," with that Haystack pointed at McGhee, the polyester of his long sleeve uniform shirt straining over his enormous biceps.

"Marley can ride with this here wagon master," he pounded his fist on his chest for emphasis.

"McGhee," Venko corrected.

Stein snorted. "Did you just call him Marley?"

"Sorry bro, you got the Rasta dreads and all, must have been a sub-criminal thing," Haystack offered sincerely to McGhee, who had now walked over to Venko and was waiting patiently.

"The word is 'subliminal,' Haystack," Venko corrected in a gentle tone before turning and introducing himself to McGhee.

"Officer Danilo Venko, you can call me Dan or Danilo, doesn't much matter to me," he said, shaking hands with McGhee.

Venko tapped both of McGhee's shoulders with his ink pen.

"You've just been knighted, from this day forward, thou shalt be known as 'Marley.' Understand that until earning a different nickname, you will be called Marley by the shift. So forget being called Marcus. Hell, it is part of being accepted by the troops. You may also be called, rookie, rook, new guy, NG, trainee and probably dumbass at times. Now supervisors, they will call you anything they like. If you're in some kind of trouble or end up in IA it will most likely be the formal Officer Marcus McGhee.'"

"Fucking a-right! Haystack is a mother-fucking savant! Marley, I love it, that's a classic." Bianchi chimed in and slapped him on the back as he headed out.

"I need to speak to the lieutenant, wait for me downstairs at the information desk," Venko directed the rookie as he stepped into Swanson's office.

"Close the door," Lt. Cal Swanson instructed as he pointed to the padded chair across from the desk.

"One of those talks, Cal?" Venko knew he was permitted this level of informality in private. Normally a patrol officer addressing a ranking supervisor by their first name was strictly forbidden, but they had been friends since attending the police academy together.

"At least tell me why there isn't a better person to train than someone who thoroughly enjoys working a one-man car."

Swanson took a sip of coffee and thought briefly before speaking.

"Look, the last three rookies we put with either Officer Bianchi or Martinez. The dynamic duo came to me last month collectively and said they wanted to stay together and not train this go around. Narcotics is looking at both of them for upcoming vacancies. I'd like to see them go. They are good cops, you know that. Hell, even Captain Sellers hasn't objected to them being interviewed over there."

Swanson glanced out the window and pointed to the parking lot below.

"Hold that thought, you gotta see this. Sgt. Connerly has finally snapped. Connerly from three-to-eleven shift, shares the same police car with The Manatee. We both know Miller's deep affection for Popeye's chicken and Connerly's neatness compulsion. Apparently today was the last day Connerly was going to wipe chicken grease off the steering wheel with baby wipes," Swanson stared with amazement, before resuming. "He parked next to the pole. There can only be a foot between the driver's door and the pole. Hell, Connerly is maybe five-seven, a buck-fifty. How the hell did he get out? With the computer in the center, it would be tough to climb over and get out."

Venko started to chuckle at the apoplectic Miller screaming and circling the car. A roar of laughter could be heard from above. Several members of the three-to-eleven shift stayed over and were enjoying the show from the locker room above.

Swanson doubled over with laughter and tried to speak but couldn't. Venko watched the well-lit parking lot as Miller tried to climb through the passenger side of the car. His chunky legs kicking furiously as they hung out the passenger door, white socks now clearly visible.

"The Manatee is swimming!" Venko declared. With that, Swanson sprayed a gulp of coffee out of his nose and mouth and coated the desk.

The car rocking and leg flailing suddenly stopped, and the horn frantically sounded in irregular bursts.

"Ah, shit," Venko remarked, still staring at the bizarre scene.

"He's stuck," they said in unison as they watched a group of officers running to his aide.

"Uh, you know he is going to kill Sgt. Connerly one day," Venko stated casually.

"Yup." Swanson sat back down and Venko followed suit.

"Dan, I might as well be straight with you. Sellers called me directly when he found out about Officer McGhee coming here. Wants you to train him. With Sellers, his dirty work is on the phone, nothing in email that can be documented. You know how he is. He figured he would fuck up your comfort zone. Seriously though, I would like Bianchi and Martinez to stay together and continue to rack up good stats."

"You think Sellers knows it's my, uh, birthday?" Venko asked.

"Oh yes, every time he looks in the mirror and sees the damage your punch did all those years ago. And to help him remember, someone drew a crooked nose on the Plexiglas covering his picture at the info desk yesterday. Stealthy motherfucker did it in a ski mask at noon, and ran like hell," Swanson paused and smiled. "You will still be the only car in the district without a BWC. You never had one because two extra cameras were diverted to Central Precinct when we started the mandatory program eighteen months ago. Central Precinct always gets what they want, it's headquarters. And, well, because you are you. Yes, I feel more comfortable knowing Bianchi is going to be recorded swearing up a blue streak as opposed to a camera memorializing one of your face punches."

"I am grateful for you keeping me off camera, don't get me wrong. It's just that I haven't trained a rookie since..." Venko's voice trailed off momentarily. "Anyway, what do you know about this kid?'

"Not much, he has bounced around and done well, his last stop was Central Precinct. But that's all unofficial gossip. I'm gonna call in a favor and try to get his file." Swanson shrugged and continued. "My confidential informant still works at headquarters; it will take a lot of favors to get the file copied and out of there. But I'll share what I find out."

A broad grin slowly spread across Venko's face. "Oh my god. You're still hooking up with Fat Fran."

Swanson's face turned crimson instantly.

"She is sturdy, not fat, she played college softball damn it! She is not fat. Besides, how else do you think we get a heads up over here in the 7th every time Internal Affairs is gunning for one of us, or Sellers has a look-at-me harebrained idea he presents downtown?"

Swanson stood and stretched his tall thin frame before opening the door for Venko.

"Go teach the kid something."

Chapter 2
No Snap Chitter Grams

Officer Venko spotted McGhee sitting on a wooden bench, studying his district map as he descended the last few steps.

"You ready to roll sir?" McGhee asked eagerly.

Venko stopped and glanced at what he knew would be problems at the info desk and raised his index finger to the rookie.

Officer Samuel "Dex" Mitchell was seated at a small desk behind the half-wall of the information desk. A very angry drunk was precariously close to the blue line. The drunk was trying to get his car released from the tow yard and was told he had to pick up a release from the information desk. Dex, without looking up from his computer, calmly told the man that he needed to pay his unpaid parking tickets downtown first and bring those receipts, along with his driver's license and proof of ownership, for the vehicle.

And then it happened.

The man stepped across the blue line and slammed his palm down on the chest-high, pristine surface of the counter. This attracted Dex's immediate attention. He shot out from behind the desk and drove the man fifteen feet backwards by the throat. By the time Venko got to them, the man was seated on a bench gurgling helplessly as an enraged Dex was choking him.

"Dex! Dex!" Venko screamed, pulling frantically until the incensed desk officer released him. The drunk sat up stunned, catching his breath.

"He stepped in front of the blue line. Just stepped right across it. He, he…" Dex paused, still furious before continuing. "He touched my counter. He *smudged* it. I can't have that. No, I can't have that. That's why the sign is there. You can't cross the blue line."

"Dex, we will handle this, go relax and clean the counter," Venko said in a reassuring tone, and patted his shoulder. "It will be fine."

Swanson, having heard the commotion, had already descended one flight and was at the top of the last landing.

"We good, Dan?" He called down.

"Yeah, it's handled," Venko added a thumbs up.

Swanson turned and headed back up the stairs, ignoring the bewildered look McGhee gave him.

Dex was already furiously spraying and wiping down the counter when Venko turned to address the very frightened drunk.

"I should arrest you for drunk and disorderly conduct and send you to jail right now."

"That crazy nut tried to kill me, and you want to arrest me?" The drunk yelled, rubbing his throat.

"Sir, I can smell the alcohol on your breath and your speech is obviously slurred," Venko pointed to the sign at the desk. "In case you didn't know, under 567.32 of the city criminal code, unauthorized entry into a blue line area is an arrestable offense. Do you deny penetrating the demilitarized zone and entering within two feet of the counter?"

McGhee rolled his eyes at the non-existent code.

"I'm, uh, officer - I just wanted him to hear me. I swear it will never happen again. Can you give me a break this one time? I swear I'll go straight home," the man said.

"I don't know. If I let you get away with it, where does it end? I mean it is a clearly painted blue line," Venko stated.

McGhee just stared at Venko in amazement.

"Tell you what, I'll put you on probation. No similar offenses in six months and nothing happens. But if I let you go and you violate the sanctity of the blue line again, you'll do nine months in lock up. Understood?" Venko wagged his finger for emphasis.

"Yes, I will walk home right now, right now, thank you, sir."

McGhee started to open his mouth when Venko interrupted.

"Not now, in the car," Venko exchanged salutes with Dex and they headed out the door with the drunk nervously trying to walk in a straight line.

Venko opened the trunk and McGhee dropped a huge, overstuffed backpack into the trunk.

"First lesson, you need to scale back on the war bag. We aren't camping. See what I carry?" Venko dropped in a small black handbag.

"A few pairs of rubber gloves, field test kits for meth, coke and heroin; pens, pocket knife and a backup flashlight. Everything else you need you should be wearing." Venko slammed the trunk on the rusting Ford. They both awkwardly started towards the driver's door.

"Seriously? Day one? I don't think so," Venko said as he smiled and pointed to the passenger seat. Venko notified dispatch they were in service and the pair drove out of the parking lot.

"How many precincts are there in Point Isley?" Venko began the quiz, still memorized from his last rookie.

"Six, there used to be seven, but the 6th precinct was torn down and the 5th and 7th absorbed the officers and territory. The 1st Precinct, or Central, is home to Crime Scene, Detective Bureau, Internal Affairs, Patrol Operations, SWAT and the Training Bureau, also known as headquarters." McGhee responded from memory, in a bored tone.

"I sense you get asked that a lot. Who has the highest and lowest crime rates?" Venko continued.

"Central has the lowest and we, I mean the 7th, has the highest."

"Correct, but just an FYI, 2nd had the lowest crime rate about five years ago. But then Lieutenant Sellers, while at Central Precinct, convinced Major Ellsworth that two grant-funded drug treatment centers and a halfway house were a better fit for the 2nd. As you might expect, Captain Stephens at the 2nd fought against the forced annexation, knowing it would bump up his crime stats. Sellers has a lot of political allies and strong-armed the move."

Venko saw McGhee's puzzled look and explained.

"Sellers was on the promotional list for captain at the time. He was able to convince two businesses from across the state to relocate their headquarters downtown. The drug treatment centers and halfway houses didn't move, precinct boundaries did and their crime stats were then counted towards the 2nd, when the precinct was redrawn. A fact that neither the city councilman negotiating the deal, nor Sellers pointed out at the very media-friendly press conference."

"Seems shady to me," McGhee stated, somewhat unconcerned.

"My point is, Sellers does nothing, absolutely nothing, unless it benefits Sellers. You would be wise to see that, since you'll be here until you can bid out or get sucked up in some specialized unit. Two months after Sellers fucked over the 2nd, he had his promotional interview and somehow jumped two candidates ahead of him on the list, and was promoted to captain. If he gets a chance to screw us over, he will if it means he makes major," Venko concluded.

McGhee was blankly staring at his phone, scrolling through his social media feeds. Venko pulled to the curb and braked hard enough to startle his inattentive partner.

"I don't always work in a one-man car. Occasionally, I get a partner when someone is on vacation. I have one rule inside the car. One rule. Pull down your visor," Venko pointed to the passenger side visor. McGhee pulled the visor down and saw the sign taped to the underside.

"No Snap-Chitter-Gram-ing. Phones in door pocket"

"Sorry, sir," McGhee replied and placed his phone in the door pocket.

"Marcus, I realize I am a fossil that started this job on horseback before cell phones, but you can't see what's going on if you're glued to your phone. I need you to have my back, I have to rely on you. I have to trust you. I don't want your picture or my picture on the wall of the 7th. This isn't day shift at Central." Venko's stare bored into McGhee, and the growing silence ratcheted up the tension.

"I, uh," McGhee started to apologize before Venko cut him off.

"When was your last robbery arrest at Central? When was your last burglary arrest at Central?" Venko saw resignation in his rookie's expression. "Your training officer from Central, what was his daily order at Starbucks?"

McGhee mumbled out, "Cappuccino, two shots of espresso with skim."

"Other than my obvious point about being attentive, you should know the best you can hope for on midnights in the 7th, is Folger's poured from a dirty Bunn-O-Matic carafe at Molly's or the all-night stop and rob at Carson and Wilson Ave."

"Stop and rob?" McGhee asked wide-eyed.

"The generic term for any all-night convenience store," Venko responded without looking over. "You'll pick up the lingo as well, no worries."

The dispatcher's voice interrupted the silence. "Car 5, signal ten at Waterfront Villa's, apartment two."

Venko responded, "Copy, Waterfront number two."

"A ten -" Venko started to ask.

"Fight call," McGhee responded immediately before reading the notes on the screen to Venko. "Rudy Jackson and Brittany -"

Venko interrupted. "Sommers, Brittany Sommers, Rudy is drunk again and she wants him to leave, but not take the car. Yeah, been there, like thirty-seven times or so. Brittany is a stripper at Lucy's, but also a well-known free agent that has in the past, taken her pay for play talents to the motel on Pine Knoll. Rudy is a drunk and her quasi-pimp and will occasionally smack her around. Aside from being there numerous times in the past, I did a short temp assignment in Vice way back, and hooked her up for soliciting."

"Ah, makes sense," McGhee replied.

"Truck seventy-seven will go along with five," Haystack chimed in over the radio.

Venko pulled into the parking lot. As they headed to the door, he could see Brittany looking out the window.

She opened the door and greeted Venko. "I'm so glad it's you this time."

"Until you move out of my district or call during the day, it will always be me, Brittany."

They were walking into the kitchen when an inebriated Rudy stormed out of the bedroom and promptly fell face first onto the carpet.

"Brittany, this is my partner, Officer Marcus McGhee, he is going to talk to Rudy in the living room and we are going to talk in the kitchen."

Brittany smiled at McGhee and he immediately saw the ravages of a methamphetamine addiction. She was missing three lower teeth and the rest were going through various stages of decay.

Brittany pointed to her still bleeding nose and explained that Rudy had taken her tips and she was trying to get them back when he threatened her, and for "no reason" punched her in the nose. Venko nodded and threw in a few halfhearted "uh-huhs" while watching McGhee talk with Rudy in the living room. He immediately noticed Rudy slowly shuffling towards the open door while talking nonchalantly. McGhee was dutifully writing down every word of the statement. Rudy noticed the rookie wasn't glancing up and continued to talk and slide towards the door.

"Marcus!" Venko yelled.

Rudy gave McGhee a shove that sent the rookie toppling backwards over the couch and was off. McGhee darted out the door and was closing the thirty-yard gap quickly. Venko strolled to the open door and was watching casually, when a blue freight train executed a full speed tackle on Rudy.

"Woohoo! Fourth down, bitch!" Haystack pumped both fists in the air, and then lowered them to his trademark double biceps flex.

Rudy never saw the giant defensive end coming from his peripheral or he most certainly would have stopped and ran *towards* McGhee. Rudy lay motionless on the asphalt and continued to wheeze, praying he could coax air into his lungs. Venko casually snapped his phone open and dialed Miller's number.

"Sarge, going to need you out here. We have an injured prisoner," Venko explained as he watched McGhee handcuff the groaning suspect.

"Broken ribs," Venko added.

"How do you know that?" Miller asked.

"Haystack tackled him at full speed."

"Shit, call the paramedics, I'm on the way."

"Baby, Baby, are you okay?" Brittany shrieked as she ran towards the still semi-conscious Rudy.

"Oh, for fuck sake, really Brittany?" An exasperated Venko turned towards Haystack, shaking his head.

"That video is going to be fun to watch," Haystack exclaimed as he held a fist out to Venko. Smiling, Venko looked at the remnants of Haystack's body-worn camera, shattered in four pieces around the prone Rudy.

"Don't leave me hanging, bro!"

With that, Venko fist bumped the glowing Haystack.

"You know, I think we will have to watch the highlights on SportsCenter since your camera is shattered" Venko said in a matter-of-fact tone, pointing to the pieces. "Impact resistant they say, I'd say it's a warranty issue."

"Bro! I'm hosed, that's my second one this year. Any chance we could hornswoggle the lieutenant into believing the camera, like, fell off? Like the magnetic backing lost its magnetic-ism and came off my shirt plate?"

"Horn what?" McGhee asked, confused.

Venko nodded to Haystack, and added, "Let's run it by Sgt. Miller. He's a pretty creative guy."

The paramedics pulled up seconds before Miller arrived. Venko pulled the older paramedic aside and explained the scenario to him and the frowning sergeant.

"Rudy was running down the sideline untouched towards the end zone when Haystack, with a full head of steam, launched a picture-perfect Saturday afternoon tackle, thwarting a sure touchdown."

"Broken ribs, concussion, check," the paramedic recited with an appreciative smile.

"How did he end up in the parking lot?" Miller asked.

"Well Sarge, that's something I need to talk to my rookie about. Also, Haystack needs to talk to you about his camera."

Haystack turned at the sound of his moniker and mustered a timid grin. Miller's mustache twitched slightly and then he nodded knowingly to Venko.

"Officer McGhee, write up the arrest ticket for the suspect, if he doesn't go to the hospital, Haystack will transport the now-compliant gentleman to jail," Miller directed.

Miller took a few steps away and called over Venko for a private conference. "Dan, this is just a tackle, right? No punches or kicks?"

Venko solemnly raised his right hand. "I saw it all, just 255 pounds of mobile fury. Suspect did push the rookie to make his escape, but we aren't going to tack on any cheesy charges. Not after that tackle."

Miller rubbed his chin in thought before speaking. "Thankfully, this use of force counts on Haystack, not you. I'll get an email after I finish the investigation from some Internal Affairs bean-counter giving me the exact number of times that Haystack has had to use force, belch, fart and swear over the last three months. I'll interview the suspect after the paramedics' finish with him," Miller took a few steps towards his car and stopped.

"And Dan, can you please assist Officer Hayslip with his use of force report?"

"C'mon Sarge, Haystack was in college for five years!"

"He attended college, attended," Miller corrected before continuing. "And writing isn't his strong suit. Remember how long it took me to get him to be more descriptive than 'the dude ran and I tackled him.' His second draft was 'the dude ran and when I caught him, I gave him the pile driver smack-down.' 'Pile driver' and 'smack-down' should not be in the police lexicon. Suffice to say, I expect his report to be rife with Venko-istic non-flair."

"Roger that, boss," Venko acknowledged the unofficial directive and nodded.

Miller finished his instructions and sat back in his car and opened the box of now-cold Popeye's. Venko watched as the paramedics checked out Rudy in the back of the ambulance. He noticed the concern of Brittany rapidly fading as she surreptitiously peeked into the supply cabinets next to Rudy, hoping to find a stray pill or two.

"Let's move out, McGhee, you have paper to write and I need a slice of cherry pie and coffee," Venko fist bumped Haystack again before driving off.

Venko pulled into Molly's parking lot and parked next to a rusted, grey panel van. McGhee took the computer from its mount and carried it inside.

"Hey, handsome," Ebony Robinson called out as she grabbed the pot of coffee. He held up two fingers and requested a piece of cherry crumb pie.

Venko took a booth at the window and faced the door. He notified dispatch they were out completing paperwork but would be available for priority calls. McGhee sat down and began typing as Ebony filled their coffee mugs. She had dark skin, a dazzling smile and carried her extra weight well. McGhee noted this as she walked to the counter to get menus.

"Easy there, try to be less obvious. Let me impart a little life lesson, at no charge. Lots of pretty girls are going to smile at you. One day you'll wake up forty years old with a beer belly. You'll put on a pair of jeans and a black tactical t-shirt before grabbing your off-duty pistol in some god-awful belly bag before heading to Wal-Mart. You'll find yourself digging through the discount Blu-Ray bin and suddenly some drop dead, smoking-hot blonde will be reaching into the bin next to you. You'll recognize her as Tiffany, Amber, Krystal, Ginger, or pick your own favorite stripper name. You'll suck in your stomach and give her your best dazzling smile and say hello. She's bound to recognize you because you've been to the strip club a dozen times on fight calls. She always smiles and flirts with you on calls. But today, she looks at you with all the warmth of a fat girl staring at a plate of brussels sprouts before abruptly walking away. That's when the epiphany comes; all those fight calls, all those smiles and flirtatious double entendre were about the uniform. She never saw you, the person in the uniform."

Marcus smiled broadly.

"That happened to you?"

"No! Obviously, it's a combination of many events I've seen and heard, designed to teach you a simple lesson. Besides, I would never wear a belly bag. And in my case, it was a hot cashier, not a stripper. And it was at Home Depot."

Venko sipped his coffee and pointed discreetly at Ebony.

"Ebony is a nice girl, nineteen, in her second semester of community college. Now, you're thinking what Ebony needs is a nice injection of Marley's Rasta-mojo. You're mesmerized by the extra juice in that caboose, and those jeggings are just bouncing about right. But what Ebony needs is about half of your paycheck to help pay for daycare while she works nights and goes to school during the day. She has a three-year-old son and if you sneeze in her direction, she would get pregnant. Marcus, are you catching any of these lessons?"

"Bang waitresses from outside your district," Marcus added a thumbs up for emphasis.

Venko slowly ran his hands through his hair.

"Yes, yes you're on the right track. Actually, you're on a dirt access road that eventually leads to the entrance ramp which will take you to the right track."

Venko turned the laptop and read the narrative McGhee had typed. He mumbled and nodded a few times before speaking.

"Marcus, on the last call, getting a statement is important. But always position yourself between the suspect and the exit. Always, always, pay more attention to what he is doing rather than what he is saying. If you're between him and the door, this doesn't happen."

"I'm sorry, sir, it won't happen again."

"Marcus, this is the last phase of your field training, not day one. Call me Dan. I'm well aware of the fact that you may not have been exposed to some situations in other precincts and on different shifts. I'm not worried, you'll pick it up quickly."

McGhee appeared immediately relieved and sipped his coffee.

"Thanks, sir, er, Dan, and Happy Birthday."

Venko swallowed a chunk of pie before speaking, "My birthday is in June, which is a long way from November. There are a lot of things you need to know about your new home."

"What's the story on the information desk officer?" McGhee asked.

"I'll tell you in the car, I will show you the hotspots in the districts," Venko waved to Ebony for the check. As she dropped the check on the table, Venko introduced McGhee as his new partner. She leaned forward and shook McGhee's hand, gravity pulling her ample bosom forward in her purple V-neck.

"You come back and see me," she said, smiling at him as she grabbed the bills off the table and sauntered away.

Venko held the door for McGhee as they exited.

"I like Marquez or Marqueese," he remarked quietly to McGhee.

"For what?" he shot back, puzzled as he got in the car.

"Baby names, in nine or ten months," Venko quipped with a chuckle.

"Not funny."

Venko drove around and pointed out known spots for drug dealing near the two district bars and Ziggy's Convenient Mart at Carson and Wilson. They took two reports, one for a stolen car and one a burglary in the projects. McGhee wrote well and the reports required few changes. Venko turned to McGhee as he was finishing up the report.

"You asked about Officer Samuel Mitchell, Dex as he more commonly known. I guess you should know, and I'd prefer you hear it from me," Venko began. "About seventeen years ago I trained Officer Jessica Sullivan. She was everything the 7th epitomized: a tough, resourceful, balls-to-the-wall, go get 'em cop. She could run and fight like a wild cat. She loved chasing dopers and making drug arrests. She fed Narcotics a constant stream of drug intel from the 7th. It didn't take Narcotics long before they borrowed her for thirty- and sixty-day temporary assignments," Venko paused and glanced away before continuing.

"Dex, was her partner during those stints and was instrumental in getting her selected to fill a vacancy in Narcotics. She had been on about three years total at the time. It was, and still is, rare to make it to Narcotics in three years. Dex was her rabbi when she went over there."

"Rabbi?" McGhee asked, unfamiliar with the term.

"Rabbi, someone that takes you under their wing, a teacher, a mentor. Anyway, they were great partners and knew how to run sources and CI's, confidential informants. They were both selected to work the DEA task force and were making a huge dent in the heroin trade on the waterfront. They rotated out of the task force and were back at seizing cash, contraband and vehicles, weekly it seemed." Venko tapped the steering wheel in rapid succession for emphasis.

"They worked one particular CI up to a mid-level dealer. Jessica felt she could be introduced by the informant to the dealer, make a buy and work her way further up the organization. She knew it would make a better case and prosecutors generally preferred a detective's testimony to that of a confidential informant. Informants are always reluctant to testify anyway, and most have extensive criminal records. Dex Mitchell was opposed to the idea for several logical reasons. The buy would be in the dealer's apartment on the fourth floor of a shitty apartment building, with lookouts all over the property. Jessica, however, convinced the bosses it could be done. A handful of uniform officers and narcotics detectives were put in plain clothes as carpet cleaners. Since I was Jessica's last field training officer from her uniform days, she insisted I be brought into the operation. Dex and I were put in overalls and assigned to the fourth-floor carpet cleaning detail. We would be the closest back up." Venko glanced at McGhee, who was now hanging on every word.

"As luck would have it, Jessica's undercover car broke down the night before. She grabbed another seized vehicle. It was an old, boxy Audi. It had been repainted and the ridiculous rims and tires were replaced with factory versions. It was painted a generic shade of grey and shouldn't have stood out." McGhee shrugged, and nodded in agreement.

"The guys listening to her wire said everything was going fine. The dealer was more of a wanna-be than an actual player and went by the street name of Two Tone. I can't remember his real name now. He always carried a semi-auto forty-five, more for show. The dude wasn't a hot head. He had no violent criminal history. Just sold dope and had done some prison time at various points in his life. He considered himself a businessman, not a thug. The confidential informant, CI in cop speak, made the introduction and the cash and product were on the table and some small talk was going on between Two Tone's bodyguard and the CI. Two Tone must have looked out the window, because he suddenly asked Jessica about the Audi. Jessica either saw, or felt something was wrong, because she used the safe word over the wire." Venko looked out his window, avoiding eye contact with McGhee.

"We immediately started towards the door when we got the order. For a split second everything was eerily silent and then an explosion of rounds started ripping through the drywall and I hit the deck and started crawling as fast as I could to the door. Dex was running with rounds snapping by his head. He booted the door and was firing. I took a stray round in the shoulder that came through the wall. At the time, it felt like a bee sting, I got up and ran inside the apartment." Venko realized his hands had become animated, and forced them to rest on the steering wheel. McGhee sensed that Venko was reliving the moment.

"I did a tour in Iraq, so I've seen some gruesome things. This was as bad as it got. I remember the head-splitting ringing in my ears and a thick haze of gunpowder you could taste, just hanging in the air. The CI was lying next to the table gurgling through several holes in his chest and throat. The bodyguard was on the floor next to the couch, trying to hold in his intestines through several holes in his stomach. He sighed heavily and died right in front of me. Jessica was on the floor with her gun in her right hand, she took a round to the left temple. Dex was standing over a very dead Two Tone. He had fired every single round from his Glock's fifteen round magazine, into Two Tone." McGhee shook his head slowly, acknowledging his dismay.

"I had gone to clear the back bedroom and by the time I returned, the rest of the backup team was inside. Dex was on the floor with Jessica's head resting in his lap. He was…he was…" Venko stopped and exhaled deeply to regain his slipping composure.

"The round entered her left temple and left a huge hole when it exited on the right side of her head. There was a flap of skin and skull, the size of a silver dollar just hanging down like a puzzle piece. Dex was in shock. He sat there gently trying to put the piece back in her skull. He had her blood and brains all over his hands and overalls. He just kept stroking her brown hair, trying to put her back together again. We couldn't move him away until the medical examiner got there." Venko's hands dropped from the wheel, as he shrugged.

"We later learned that the Audi she grabbed at the last minute was formerly registered to a Shenise Jenkins before it was seized as part of an investigation into her boyfriend, Melvin Lang, two years earlier. As luck would have it, he was also a second cousin of Two Tone. A connection that was never made at the time because Two Tone was in prison during most of that investigation. Unbeknownst to us, Two Tone was a big fan of Audis and had a picture in his living room of Shenise, Melvin and the Audi. Part of the front grille was missing in the picture, the part with the Audi logo. Probably just a minor fender bender at the time. When we seized the car, we swapped out the tires and rims and had it painted, but nobody got the grille repaired."

"Fuck." McGhee muttered, slumping in his seat.

"Exactly," Venko said with a nod, before continuing.

"Department protocol required everyone on scene that day to undergo a critical incident debriefing. Additionally, Dex and I had to go to see the department psychologist for several months. After that we were grilled by the shoot team for a full day. That's a group of detectives, patrol captains and investigators from Internal Affairs, you know, to make sure we didn't violate any chicken shit policy while fighting to stay alive. We also gave lengthy statements, both written and oral, to the prosecutor's office and the law department. Eventually the union stepped in and got them to quit calling us at home with 'one more question.'" Venko drove his right fist into his left palm at the memory.

"I returned to full duty after shoulder surgery and physical therapy, about four months after the incident. Dex wasn't officially cleared in the shooting until about six months later, but he wasn't ready to return yet. He still saw her blood and brains on his hands and shirts. I took him shopping after he burned every shirt he owned on one of his darker days. He saw the stains on brand new shirts. It took months for him to stop scrubbing his hands with steel wool. He absolutely refused a disability retirement. He will not quit. Prior to Sellers coming over as the captain of the 7th, now retired Stephenson was the captain. He was the lieutenant in charge of Narcotics at the time Jessica was killed. When he was promoted and came to the 7th, Dex agreed to come over as his desk officer. Dex is divorced and his only daughter died of cancer three months after the shooting. He has no one; he can't stop working." Venko shrugged, as if he understood Dex's need to do something, anything.

"You'll never see so much as a speck of lint on his uniform now. It's perfectly creased and dry cleaned and kept in plastic until he wears it. The incident you saw at the counter of the info desk tonight, Dex doesn't see smudges and dirt like you and me. He sees other things; things he doesn't want to see anymore. Stephenson understood this and let Dex put up the signs and paint the blue line. Sellers just sees a fit officer in a perfect uniform, the model of police professionalism, and doesn't care beyond that. Dex is much better now, but some days, as you saw, are still a struggle. The desk officers from days and afternoons, keep everything spotless. No one cleans or touches the memorial plaques and photos but Dex. He always uses fresh clean hand towels each night, and a spray bottle of Windex. Hence the nickname, Dex. He is a great cop and would do anything for you. Talk to him, he is a bright, funny guy. Just stay behind the blue line unless he calls you forward, and never, ever touch the countertop."

McGhee sat in stunned silence before the radio interrupted.

"Car 5, signal 37 at 22 Waterfront, front motion alarm. Morely and Sons Manufacturing."

Venko glanced at McGhee, waiting on him to decipher the police code.

"A 37, an alarm," McGhee responded confidently.

"That place has been closed a while. Been in the same family since the late 70's. Finally closed about two years ago. The Environmental Protection Agency finally caught up to them illegally dumping hazardous materials and waste. Bad press and heavy fines finally did the trick. Still a scrapper's dream though, all kinds of junk and scrap metal inside," Venko explained as he dropped the shifter into drive and goosed the pedal, squealing the tires on his turn.

"The building is in the process of being sold. A developer is paying for the alarm monitoring and camera system. No doubt in a few years that whole rundown area of crumbling buildings will become hipster waterfront condos. Nine out of ten times it's a false alarm anywhere down there. Especially this time of year. Lots of wind, stray cats, power outages," the radio interrupted Venko's lecture.

"Car 1 will be pulling up on the thirty-seven."

Venko punched the accelerator and the old Ford roared to life. "The Crime Fighters jumped the call, if we don't get there quick, I'll hear nothing but cracks about being old and slow for the rest of the night."

A panicked voice sounded over the radio.

"Car 1, signal five, my partner is chasing a white male, black, puffy coat and jeans. North from the alarm location."

Dispatch responded, "All units, we have signal five, emergency traffic. Car 1 is in foot pursuit of white male with black, puffy coat and jeans northbound from the alarm, any unit that can assist Car 1?"

Venko grabbed the microphone and keyed it.

"Car 5 is southbound on Water," Venko locked up the brakes when he saw the suspect forty yards ahead coming right at them.

McGhee bailed from the car before it came to a complete stop and was running when he saw both the suspect and Bianchi turn eastbound down the alley. McGhee passed the winded Bianchi with ease and overtook the suspect at the back of the alley. When Bianchi arrived, McGhee had already handcuffed the prone suspect and was pulling him to his feet. Venko jogged up the alley a minute later as Bianchi completed his search of the suspect.

Venko heard multiple sirens converging on their location and notified dispatch the suspect had been apprehended and no further assistance was needed. He hoped he gave the all-clear before Haystack ran any late-night motorist off the road.

"This mother fucker got some jets," Bianchi panted out, still trying to catch his breath.

Stein, Fitzpatrick, Martinez and Haystack rolled up and individually fist bumped McGhee in recognition of his work.

"In five, four, three, two, one…" Venko counted down holding his cell phone out. It rang three seconds later, and he snapped it open and responded.

"Hey Sarge, what's up?"

"Did he give up, trip, or was it more of an assisted surrender?" Miller asked nervously.

"No worries, Sarge, nice and clean. McGhee ran him down, his 160 pounds caused nary a scratch. He was already in handcuffs when backup arrived, preventing any gratuitous pummeling," Venko smiled and the small gathering gave him a thumbs up.

"Copy that, thanks Dan," Miller hung up, relieved he only had one use of force investigation to work on.

At 0630 hours McGhee finished the last of the felony paperwork on the Morely and Sons break in. Venko sent all the arrest paperwork, along with the use of force and prior domestic paperwork, to Miller via the computer terminals on the second floor of the precinct. The pair made small talk with the other officers waiting to be released.

"Dan, will your young greyhound be accompanying you to drink a toast to this infamous date?" Stein asked, smiling.

McGhee, thrilled to have seen more action in one night in the 7th than he had in two months at Central, nodded his head emphatically. Venko chuckled softly, knowing McGhee would be too amped up to sleep for quite some time.

Venko caught a ride to Waterfront Park with Haystack in his giant Dodge pickup truck, the last thing he bought from the salary of his brief NFL career.

Waterfront Park sat directly across from Morely and Sons Manufacturing. A long-neglected park, it was filled with graffiti and the parking lot was strewn with broken glass, condoms and needles. The whole area was in rapid decline and no funding was going to a park no one saw or went to anymore. It was hoped that the sale of Morely, and its eventual development into hip living space, would rejuvenate the waterfront and draw business and retail back into the area. For now, it was a place where a group of cops could go, sit in the pavilion unnoticed at 7 a.m., and drink beer. Venko sat on a picnic table and handed McGhee a Molson's.

"Overall, you did good," Venko stated.

"Thanks," McGhee stated with his gloved hands cupping the beer bottle.

"I could give you a rundown on everyone here, and I'll tell you what's important about each of them, but you'll learn more watching and listening to them. Shall we join the group?" Venko asked as he got up and sauntered over to other officers.

The pair sat on a table next to Officers Bianchi, Martinez and Stanley. Stein, Fitzpatrick, and Jackson sat across from them. Officer Carmen no-showed for an early morning off-duty job. Officer Morris worked the overlap car from 2100 hours till 0500 hours and was long gone.

"Rachel, your fuck buddy is here now," Bianchi chided Stein and pointed to Walter Niles who was chatting amiably with Haystack in the parking lot.

Niles, the twice divorced thirty-four-year-old harbored an obvious desire to make Stein wife number three. Her constant rejections were blunt and would be considered soul-crushing to most men. Niles, who was very broke and lived in an apartment above his mother's garage, was not discouraged easily. The other officers found him odd. His receding hairline necessitated a shaved head, and his sunken brown eyes were always accented by heavy, black circles. He worked every extra job he could find to try and stay afloat. His weight had dropped to an unhealthy level lately and he had been a chronic smoker until switching to vaping two months ago. His teeth were still an uneven shade of yellow-brown. He responded to every fight call as back up and just as quickly would disappear before the paperwork was divvied up. Martinez coined Niles's style of police work as "Vape and Vanish."

"Yeah, that's not happening. I don't want to go hang out in his mother's basement and look at his insect collection." She noticed him waving at her, as did the rest of the group.

"Gentlemen, make room on your side, that dude is not sitting anywhere near me," Stein said, finishing her Budweiser and opened another can with her fingerless gloves.

"Shit, Rachel, what's the worst that could happen? You gotta put the lotion in the basket at the bottom of a tiny basement cell?" Martinez chimed in.

"The Mexican just got Netflix, and now is going to drop pop culture bombs on us," Stanley said matter-of-factly.

"Who?" The collective chant sounded, followed by raucous laughter.

"Who" was the name given to Officer Tim Stanley, a five-year veteran of the 7th. He was five-ten, 170 pounds, fit, but not muscular. In the words of Stein, he looked extremely average, exactly like hundreds of other police officers between the age of 25 and 30--completely invisible. After Stanley's first year on the job, Swanson was reviewing a commendation for Stanley written by Miller. Swanson asked Miller, "Who exactly is Stanley?" Miller pulled up Stanley's department photo on the computer and stated, "Sir, he works for you on midnights." The photo did little to jog the memory of Swanson, so Miller drew up a seating chart for roll call with the names written over the places the officers regularly sat during roll call. The good news for Stanley was that he was often misidentified on complaints as other officers.

"Now Haystack, I could see climbing that tree, but I'd have to try and talk to him in the morning and I just can't get that simple," Stein continued.

Venko thought this was Stein just trying to fit in as one of the boys. Then he paused and thought, *no one can really be that obnoxious, can they?*

Miller walked up and joined the group and was promptly handed a Budweiser.

He raised the can and exclaimed, "Happy Birthday, Dan!"

A chorus of cheers followed. Venko knew much like the last couple of years, he would have to rehash the entire story for those that came to the shift in the last year.

And, as if on cue, Haystack asked, "Bro, you going to fill in your rook on the history of this most awesome day?"

Venko reluctantly told the story.

Seventeen years ago, to the day, Venko and a group of young police officers got together at Nuts and Bolts, a bar owned by retired Sgt. Sal "Tommy" Tomasino. Venko's academy classmates from various precincts gathered there annually, to catch up. Things were going smoothly four beers into the night, when Sgt. Brian Sellers walked in with a couple of city councilmen, two sergeants from Internal Affairs and Lt. Hoyer from Central Precinct. Sellers and Venko were academy classmates. Sellers was brash, arrogant and self-promoting, the opposite of the more reserved, fun loving, Venko. None of the other 80 cadets in the academy class liked Sellers. He frequently mentioned his father, a city councilman, and talked incessantly about supervisory positions he would like to have.

Tommy had refilled the draft beers in front of Venko and his classmate, Calvin "Cal" Swanson. The two clanked glasses and congratulated each other on their five-year anniversary and chatted about where they could go to escape the midnight shift in the 7th. Fellow classmates came and went from the bar, offering some good-natured ribbing to the pair as they continued to talk.

Then Sellers and his entourage walked into the bar, with Sellers taking the stool to the left of Venko. The very drunk Sellers began to loudly hold court with his group. He began to criticize the lack of "spit and polish," of today's officers. He continued bemoaning the lack of discipline and accountability and mentioned a few of the 7th precinct officers he had written up for their sloppy appearance, unpolished boots and non-regulation facial hair.

Since Sellers worked at the Central Precinct, his contact with 7th Precinct officers was limited to when they worked off duty jobs downtown. He never missed an opportunity to do a full inspection on the officers, especially if he was in the company of a lieutenant or a captain from downtown.

Venko recognized a few of the names. He knew them as good cops. He knew what the 7th was like. On any given night, an officer could come in wearing boots with a polished mirror finish. Three calls later, you could run through, mud, water, garbage, salt and snow.

Swanson saw Venko pause, and he instinctively tapped Venko's arm and whispered, "Let it go."

Four beers were good for Venko. After that, things could get a little dicey.

Sellers began schmoozing the councilmen for supporting his plan to divert some of the funds earmarked for equipment in the 7th back to the Central Precinct to add more equipment and investigators to Internal Affairs. This would create an additional supervisor's position, which was without pretense, for Sellers. Hoyer supported whatever position was popular at the moment and knew the power and clout that Councilman Walter Sellers wielded. Having Sellers as an ally would only help his career. The two sergeants from Internal Affairs nodded sycophantic approval to whatever Sellers said. They would occasionally interrupt, with stories of police misconduct they had heroically uncovered.

Venko drained the glass and sat the mug down forcefully. Sellers' group stopped and glared at Venko.

"Have you ever been a real cop? Seriously. When was the last time you did any real police work?" Venko snapped.

Swanson began lightly tugging on Venko's right arm. He waved him off like a pesky fly.

"Venko, the reason you're a police officer and not a sergeant, is because you don't understand the big picture. You don't understand the discipline and integrity the department lacks. You have no vision. It's why you will always be a wharf rat working the 7th on midnights," Sellers retorted.

"Well, Brian -" Venko started, before he was cut off.

"You mean Sergeant Sellers," Sellers corrected loudly.

"Well, Brian," Venko continued without concern. "Integrity? How 'bout a recruit that starts his probationary period at Central Precinct, calls his daddy and magically never rotates to any of the other precincts like every other recruit. Spends three years on dayshift at Central, getting coffee for the majors and occasionally having to work a parade. Wait, did I forget all the schools and leadership training you were sent to, when the training budget is effectively zero for the common folk? How did you not get a commendation for all your combat in the bureaucratic jungle?" Venko followed up his crack with a mock salute.

One of the councilmen started to smirk and Sellers became enraged. Venko continued his onslaught.

"Our cruisers have over 130,000 miles on them. The building is crumbling, the heat and air conditioning doesn't work half the time. We get one officer in return for every two we lose, because some moron like you thinks every specialized unit is more important than the patrolmen that keep this city from erupting in total chaos. And, lest we all forget, you jumped from 37 to 13 on the sergeants' promotion list after you magically produced college transcripts from eBay Online U or whatever scam you pulled to get the college bonus points added to your score."

Swanson was now frantically pulling at Venko when Sellers fired back.

"You don't know the first thing about modern policing. You live in the little cave that is the 7th, answering calls without any overall analysis on how we could improve efficiency. It explains why you are not cut out to be a supervisor. You're not cut out to make the hard decisions."

Venko set his beer down, rolled his eyes and whistled. "No, you are correct. I would not get absolutely giddy every time I wrote someone up for not polishing their boots, or taking a few extra minutes on lunch break, or signing a report with blue ink instead of black ink or whatever nonsensical rules violation you can conjure up. For a guy that is a stickler for professional appearance, how the hell do you know when your boots need polished? Because you sure as hell can't look down and see them."

Venko held up his empty mug for Tommy to refill.

"Ah, shit," Swanson mumbled prophetically.

"Listen, you worthless asshole," Sellers started and leaned towards Venko.

Now a legitimate concern spread across the nearby spectators. This had passed generic ball busting.

"You'll never go anywhere or do anything but grind out an existence on midnights in the 7th. Wherever I am, I'm going to find you and grind you down. When I make captain one day, I'm going to come to the 7th, for no other reason than the pleasure of grinding you down until you quit, or screw up and get fired. I want to be the one that collects your badge and gun."

Venko smiled broadly and set his newly filled mug down. Swanson let go of Venko and sat up, resigned to just watching the show.

Venko turned slowly from the bar, back towards Sellers.

"That's a ton of grinding, maybe if you had ground at home, your ex-wife wouldn't have been the Central Precinct slam-piece. Mind you, I never got in line for that. Far too many shoes were up in that closet. Now I understand why they always sent you to training. They knew you weren't coming home for a week."

Venko saw Sellers clench his right fist, as it rose an inch from his lap, Venko pinned it down with his left hand and threw a straight right hand that connected with Sellers' nose. The popping sound was gruesome. Blood spattered everywhere within three feet of impact. The force of the blow knocked Sellers off the stool and onto the floor. There were a few seconds of silence as the other patrons in the bar tried to process what just happened.

Tommy threw a towel at Hoyer, who with nearby assistance, was trying to help Sellers to his feet. Sellers' nose was grotesquely bent to the right and bleeding heavily. The bloodstain on his blue golf shirt had now begun to creep over his ample stomach. Tommy immediately retreated to the back office and removed the VCR tape from the surveillance system. He efficiently put it in the bottom of a brown paper bag and sat a six pack of Budweiser on top of it. He closed the bag and walked back behind the bar.

Swanson was staring at Sellers in amazed shock. Venko spun his stool back to the bar, and calmly took another swig from his mug. Tommy whistled at Swanson and handed him the brown bag.

"Here is your to go order, time for you fellas to head out," Tommy said and nodded towards the door with a wink.

The pair started towards the door when Hoyer stopped them.

"Just a fucking minute. We need to sort this out."

One of the sergeants from Internal Affairs started walking behind the bar. The unmistakable sound of a baseball bat slamming the bar top echoed through the building. A sudden, eerie silence followed. Tommy's right forearm fluttered as he draped the bat over his shoulder, the faded USMC tattoo now visible across his broad forearm.

"What are you doing behind my bar?" he asked in a menacing whisper.

"There is going to be a formal inquiry into this, I'm going to need to take any video surveillance you have as evidence," The sergeant tried to speak with authority, but failed miserably.

Tommy pointed the bat at Sellers.

"This was a fight; your boy was a little slower and it cost him a straight nose. Nothing more than a fight. The cameras don't work. I leave them up to scare any shithead that is thinking of doing something foolish."

The sergeant was determined and tried to assert his authority.

"Whether it was a fight or an assault is not your call to make. And as far as your surveillance, I think I'll check for myself," he said as he tried to pass once more.

Tommy pointed the Louisville Slugger at the sergeant.

"Son, if you want to look for yourself, you're going to need a search warrant. I don't believe you have one on you. If you really don't think you need one, take another step, and I'll shatter your knee cap."

The group left without another word. The next day, word of the incident spread like wildfire. Officers relished the tale. That night three six packs of Miller arrived at the 7th, with a birthday card for Venko. The birthday greeting was a covert way to acknowledge and appreciate the deed. The tradition was born that day and continued with participation growing yearly as Sellers moved up the ranks and his poor reputation spread.

The inquiry lasted two months. Fifteen officers were there that night, seated at tables away from the bar. Not a single one saw the confrontation. In a testament to Sellers popularity, when Internal Affairs investigators were sent to all the precincts, an additional thirty officers claimed they were there that night and saw nothing.

In the end, after much political jostling and a few phone calls from Tommy, the matter was dropped without any action. The councilmen quietly withdrew support for the transfer of funds and the expansion of Internal Affairs. The 7th Precinct eventually received two new police cruisers and a new maintenance contract was bid to repair the aging building.

"That story always warms the cockles of my heart," Haystack remarked, wiping away imaginary tears.

"Cockles? You are truly an enigma Haystack," Miller stated with a chuckle.

"Actually boss, I'm German and Dutch," Haystack flashed his usual oblivious grin.

Venko slipped away from the increasingly rowdy group at 8:40 a.m. He heard the horn and looked over at the 10-year-old grey Volvo as it approached him.

"I was trying to find a big, dumb Ukrainian to have breakfast with since my pre-trial was cancelled this morning," Sarah Sterling said as she opened the passenger door.

"How did you know I'd be here instead of home sleeping?" Venko asked.

Sarah held up her smart phone with the calendar open to today's date. Venko smiled as he read the notation: "*Not really Danilo's birthday, beers at Waterfront Park 0700 hours.*"

"Like you're going to change your routine?"

She smiled as he closed the door. Venko looked at her appraisingly. The black skirt hugged her muscular thighs and the royal blue blouse was snug enough to have a few gaps at the buttons.

"Glad I meet your approval," she stated from his obvious glance. "My pre-trial was cancelled and I have some time, figured I could pick your brain while watching you eat a bucket of sausage gravy and eggs."

"I would be honored," he responded as she pulled away.

"Happy birthday by the way, you had to tell the whole story again, right?"

"Yup, and I am training a rookie," he added nonchalantly.

"Get out of here! You? Training?" She could not suppress her laughter.

Venko loved the sound of her deep, throaty laughter. He found it attractive when she was still a city prosecutor but never had the courage to pursue her beyond small talk in her office. Sarah quickly moved up to county prosecutor and then a lateral move for more pay, one county over, two years ago. Nearly a year ago, they went on their first date.

At 42, Sarah Sterling was an athletic five-four and carried her 132 pounds well. Her legs were muscular and slightly large for her slim waist and delicate upper body. Her brown hair was worn stylishly at shoulder length and anyone that ever faced her in court, knew the fire of her green eyes.

"I'm assuming you don't want to go to Molly's?" She asked.

"Not at all. I love it when people assume because they see a lot of police cars that the food must be good. Newsflash, cops would eat pine cones if they were half price," he answered truthfully.

"Bob Evans it is then," Sarah said with a smirk.

The waitress smiled at Venko's uniform and seated the pair at the back booth. Sarah automatically took the seat facing the wall leaving Venko the seat facing the door. Sarah knew the cop in Venko would want to be able to scan the restaurant and entrance. She ordered an egg white omelet, dry wheat toast and tea. Venko ordered a sausage and mushroom omelet with hash browns and a side of sausage gravy and biscuits. The waitress poured Venko's black coffee and returned with Sarah's tea.

"Wow, maybe a stick of butter to round out your cholesterol buffet?" Sarah smiled, but said with a hint of concern.

"If the Army and this job hasn't killed me, I think I'm good with an occasional fried orgy," he replied.

"You remember me telling you about Bishop, my robbery case?" She asked while stirring Sweet-n-Low into her tea. Venko shook his head.

"Wally Bishop, tall skinny white dude, meth junkie. Anyway, they got him dead to rights, after robbing John Q. Citizen outside a gas station. Recovered the gun and he had the dude's wallet on him," she explained.

"Wait, like a real citizen victim, not a dope dealer or otherwise mope? An honest to goodness taxpayer with a job, victim?" Venko remarked with intended sarcasm.

"Yes, every prosecutor finds an occasional unicorn. A legit victim, but that's not the point. They linked him to an MP from two years ago, a missing person case," she stopped to sip her tea.

"I know what an MP is," he smiled and put down his coffee as the waitress delivered the food.

"The MP was Dakota Billings, twelve-year-old, white male that..."

Venko interrupted, putting his fork down.

"Lived in the projects in the 7th. A 2017 case grabbed off the sidewalk. I was first on scene and took the report. How is your dude linked?" He asked with genuine interest.

"Initially all I had was the robbery file. I asked for and got the case file on the MP yesterday. When he disappeared two years ago, they looked at Bishop. He had dated Billings' mother briefly and lived close by. Billings was a problem child, kicked out of three schools in the year before he disappeared. Billings stabbed a classmate at his last school and was a frequent runaway. When Bishop dated Billings' mom, there were problems," she paused and pointed to her chin. An indication of a huge glob of sausage gravy stuck to the salt and pepper stubble on Venko's face. He wiped his face and recalled an incident.

"I remember going there several times for fights and loud arguments. The kid was a handful without a doubt. I also had the feeling that Bishop smacked him around. Both Bishop and what's-her-name were smart enough to not let me go any further than the living room. Couldn't snoop for dope or paraphernalia. I knew they were both heavy users, but I had nothing on them. That kid was already gone, no foster home could have handled him. So how is he tied in now?" He asked.

"Glad you asked. At the time of the disappearance, there was very little to tie Bishop to Billings. He was no longer dating what's-her-name, as you put it, and hadn't had contact with the family in at least six months. There was so little to connect Bishop, the judge refused to grant a search warrant for Bishop's residence. Fast forward a few years. Bishop is nailed on this robbery. He still lives in the same cracker box apartment and is suspected in two other robberies. Detectives get a search warrant this time, and find clothes and property linking Bishop to one of the other robberies. They also find an old pair of work boots in the back of his closet. One of the detectives, a smart one, thinks the stains might be old blood drops and calls out the Crime Scene Unit. Long story short, boots are taken, the small stains are blood. They manage to get enough of a sample, and boom, we just got a DNA hit on one missing Dakota Billings," she finished and sipped her tea and waited for his response.

"That's great!" Venko said with a mouth full of biscuit. He nodded to the waitress and asked her for a bottle of hot sauce. He caught the look Sarah gave him full force.

"You're giving me the look, not as intense as the sock-drawer-look, maybe on par with desk-pens-scattered-about-and-not-in-the-pen-holder-I-gave-you look," he smiled sheepishly.

"People should match up socks, not just throw them in a drawer with little regard for their mate. You can't say that all black socks and all white socks can just be grabbed willy-nilly and paired up. They should be put away, connected. But this look, is a 'how are you going to sleep with a belly full of churning spicy cement in your stomach.?' And the pens are a separate obsessive-compulsive issue I have."

"Willy-nilly? Willy-nilly? If I were not to pair them, would that start a donnybrook? Or perhaps a row?" Venko accented his absurd comment by extending his crooked pinky while sipping his coffee.

"You're hilarious, Danilo, and there just may be a fracas!" Sarah held the tea cup with both hands in front of her and gave him a slight smirk of superiority, before continuing.

"All synonyms aside, I got a gut feeling that Bishop isn't the right dude," she sat her cup down and shook her head slowly in thought.

"They have blood evidence in his house, they can prove he knew the kid, they can prove a history of not getting along with either the kid or mom from past reports, and the number of dispatched calls where he was on scene. So why so glum?" Venko cocked his head slightly left when he finished, then reached for her remaining uneaten slice of wheat toast. She automatically handed him a packet of butter, which he shredded open and spread on the toast.

"Here's the thing. Bishop is no mastermind, I don't think he is capable of snatching Billings off the street and disposing of him over the next two years without a single trace, except for a few drops of old blood on a pair of work boots. I mean, he had a violent history and very well could have smacked him around and bloodied his nose or whatever, and gotten blood on his boots. But, had he abducted and killed him, wouldn't you think that he would have gotten rid of the boots? Hell, he is driving the same car. He is wearing the same jacket from a previous booking photo. No one has seen a trace of that kid since that night. No reported sightings, nothing, he just vanished. It doesn't make sense. I don't know how they got the grand jury to indict him on the abduction charge. I'm shocked," She threw up her hands in emphasis.

"So, you're telling me, he was indicted based on a few drops of old blood at his place and prior relationship with what's-her-name?" Venko asked in a calm manner.

He recalled taking the initial report, but detectives took over and he moved on to other calls that were waiting. He was given updates and places to check for Billings over the next several weeks, but the case quickly grew cold, then nothing.

"Well, there was a witness that saw a tall, thin white male with Billings a minute or so before he vanished. And yes, Bishop is sort of tall and most definitely thin, but the witness described the male as clean and dressed nice. On Bishop's best days, no one ever described him as clean. I just don't think it's him and the connection is weak," she finished and sat back in the booth.

It was around 2 a.m. and you know––dark, how reliable is the witness? Do you want me to take a look at the files?" he asked sincerely.

"Yes," she replied with vigor. "The files are in the car!"

Venko realized he had once again been manipulated by the master, and shrugged before mumbling, "OK."

Venko watched her face change to a warm grin as she saw the waitress and two other waiters approach. The waitress carried a lone cupcake on a plate with a burning candle as the trio sang 'Happy Birthday,' terribly off key.

"I called ahead," Sarah said as she picked up the check.

"Of course you did," Venko replied as he took a huge bite of the chocolate cupcake.

Chapter 3
Run rabbit, run!

"You have a week under your belt at the 7th now, so I'm going to quiz you at various points tonight. If you do well, you can start driving tomorrow. We can alternate nightly from then on," Venko instructed McGhee with a noticeable reluctance.

"I'm cool with that," responded a smiling McGhee as he dropped his new, considerably smaller war bag into the trunk.

"From 0200 hours until 0400 hours, we are on a signal 40," Venko paused and waited for McGhee. McGhee had grown accustomed over the last week of the constant barrage of quizzes and questions from Venko.

"A signal 40 is a special detail. We are working with Martinez and Bianchi looking for suspects that have been breaking into the warehouses along the waterfront," McGhee responded.

"I'm glad you're paying attention in roll call. Let's grab a cup of coffee before things heat up. What time do you have?" Venko asked without looking at his watch.

"1133," McGhee responded, then caught Venko's glare and converted the time to the 24-hour clock used by police departments and the military, "2333 hours."

"Scratch that for now, I forgot my flashlight. We have to run by my place and pick it up, I left it in the charger," Venko dropped the transmission into drive and began the short drive home.

As the pair climbed the steps to Venko's third floor apartment, they could hear coughing from above.

"Miss Rosales, are you okay?" Venko asked. She pulled a green afghan tighter on her shoulders and sipped her coffee. A battered portable radio was playing salsa music.

"Yes Danilo, it's the metal. There is metal in the air, I can taste it. It brings bad things. You must stay home, don't work tonight. Stay in 'til sunrise. This is number five," she finished and turned her eyes to McGhee. Venko noticed McGhee looked uncomfortable, even fearful.

"Who is this thin, young man you brought with you, Danilo?" McGhee looked at Venko, who held up a hand as if to say *I'll explain later, don't ask.*

"This is my partner, Officer Marcus McGhee."

McGhee nodded his head, then realizing she is blind and greeted her.

"Hello."

"Marcus, you are young and healthy. Take care of Danilo, he has many things yet to accomplish."

"I will, ma'am," McGhee replied nervously.

"Can I get you anything, Miss Rosales? I have to run in and get my flashlight before heading back to work."

"No, thank you," she responded, her head still turned towards McGhee.

Venko flipped the light switch as they entered his apartment.

"Wow, a one room cave. You decorate this place yourself, Dan?" McGhee asked looking around at the sparse furnishings.

"Why yes, thank you. I think the Spartan motif is quite trendy again," Venko responded, grabbing the flashlight from the charger on his desk. McGhee picked up the picture of a smiling Venko with a group of Army buddies.

"I didn't know you were a veteran," he remarked casually, returning the photo and grabbing the one of Venko's mother and father standing with him prior to his deployment.

"I tried a year of community college, played football as a freshman. Too slow for a fullback and got moved to center. I got tired of getting hit in the head every play, and honestly, the college scene made me restless. I didn't want to spend my entire life in the same area. On a complete whim, over summer break, I joined the Army," Venko looked at the photo taken shortly after arriving in the Middle East and chuckled before continuing.

"The next thing I know, I'm up to my ass in sand and then slogging through the streets of Kuwait trying not to get shot. I liked it so much that I re-upped," he chuckled sarcastically. "The hardest part of all of it was making split-second decisions on whether the people approaching were trying to thank me or kill me."

Venko put the flashlight in his belt holder and grabbed a bottle of water from the fridge after tossing one to McGhee.

"Were you ever wrong?"

"Nope."

At that moment, Diablo decided to bolt from behind the TV and landed with a hiss at the feet of McGhee.

"Shit!" He screamed and fell backwards, knocking the books off the top of the small bookshelf. "What the hell is that? Is that fat thing some kind of mini white tiger?" McGhee asked. Venko chuckled and picked up the large, white feline and stroked her head. Diablo's eyes closed halfway as she purred heartily.

"She is very territorial, you're new, so she had to investigate. She is fine now, you can pet her."

"Nah, man, I'm good," McGhee said looking into Diablo's eyes. He was pretty sure her glare was saying, *Step the fuck off*. "I'm not good with animals," he added as he picked up the books. "You read all these?" He asked looking over the collection of hardcover and paperbacks shoved in every open nook of the shelf.

"Yeah, I started when I was overseas. Lots of downtime, and boredom, I found I could pull a paperback out of my pocket and read just about anywhere. After swapping out and reading everything I could get from my unit, my folks started sending me books in care packages. When I got out and was back stateside, I discovered I really enjoyed hitting the used bookstores. Grabbing a coffee, sitting and reading for a few hours was my decompression. It worked for me. As you can see, I like variety. Science fiction, historical fiction, literary classics and an occasional biography."

"Your mom and dad still around?" McGhee asked, not sure if it was an appropriate question.

"Mom died of cancer ten years ago. She worked at Morely and Sons Manufacturing as a secretary for 20 years before getting cancer. It ate her up. There was some talk of a class action lawsuit; three other workers developed cancer and died. We know there were all kinds of undocumented chemicals being used there and the company got caught illegally dumping chemicals and violating several environmental regulations. But they had high dollar lawyers and proving a direct link to the illness was going to take time and money that no one had. Local law firms refused to invest the time and effort needed for a payout that would take years," Venko shook his head "Dad died three years ago of a heart attack, sitting in his favorite chair watching a Steelers game, beer in hand."

"Brothers or sisters?" McGhee asked.

"Nope, just me. No ex-wives and I have sired nary an offspring to carry on the Venko name," he responded matter-of-factly.

"Even an old dude like you needs someone, you got a lady friend?"

"Why is it when people are 'my age' they have lady friends and not a slam piece or hook up?" Venko laughed. "Yes, I have a lady friend that I occasionally squire about. She is a prosecutor in another county, you'll meet her eventually."

"Squire? You talk funny for a cop, is that what this collection does to you?" McGhee asked as he nervously watched Venko set the cat down.

"Yes, smartphones have destroyed the English language. Everything is abbreviations or text lingo. You want some of that chocolate loving from Molly's? Impress her with a genuine conversation that expands beyond what you see on YouTube or Instagram." Venko finished and opened the door and McGhee headed into the hallway as he locked up.

"We are going to head out now Miss Rosales, it's getting real drafty out here, you might want to head in soon," Venko said softly.

"Don't worry about me, Danilo, but please take no foolish risks tonight. Chaos is in the air. It was nice to meet you Marcus,"

Miss Rosales said and started to extend her right hand, but then cocked her head and extended her left hand in McGhee's direction. McGhee shot Venko a puzzled look and then gingerly shook hands with Miss Rosales.

"It was a pleasure, ma'am," McGhee politely said before heading down the stairs. He was on the third step down when he stopped and glanced back at her. She was shaking her head at him and mouthed "Don't do it." An icy chill ran down McGhee's neck and he hurried to catch up with Venko. When the pair made it out the front door, McGhee stopped and took a deep breath and exhaled the cold night air.

"That lady freaks me out. Is she some kind of witch? I mean, how did she know I was left-handed. How did she know I am thin? Or young, for that matter?" McGhee was still frightened by her last comment and he wasn't about to share it with Venko. *What did she mean by "don't do it?"*

"She isn't a witch and it isn't some kind of voodoo. She is a very nice lady. I try and check on her or chat with her daily. This is an old building, the wood floors creak under my weight, much less under your weight. Your stride length is different from mine. She hears the same patterns daily, hundreds of times. She has never heard your footfalls or the creaks the boards make under your feet until tonight. She undoubtedly heard your Timex ticking on your right wrist, so it was a logical assumption for her to guess you're left-handed. Honestly, it freaked me out at first as well. But I got to know her and got used to her mannerisms. As for knowing you're young, I suspect she, and everyone else in this block can smell the cheap millennial mojo or body spray as you call it, that you douse yourself in. A little Hatchet goes a long way."

"It's Axe."

"Whatever it's called, a short burst is enough, lay off the fogger," Venko stated waving his hand in front of his face for effect, as he got in the driver's seat.

"Nah man, there is something freaky about her, she looked *through* me," McGhee shivered as he finished the sentence.

"Let's grab a cup of coffee at Molly's now, before things jump off," Venko remarked as he pulled away from the curb.

• • •

Ebony waived at the pair as she retrieved the coffee pot and brought over two mugs.

"What's up, girl?" McGhee brazenly greeted her, adding a disarming smile.

"How you doing, Marley?" She asked with a wink.

"Yeah, everyone knows your nickname, word travels fast," Venko stated, sipping his black coffee. "What did they call you when you were training on dayshift in Central Precinct?"

"Token," McGhee replied flatly.

"Oh, that is kind of funny, you have to admit," Venko said with a slight shrug. "What's your story, Marcus?"

"Nothing fancy. Public school, played a little basketball, got in a few fights. Suspended once, curfew and underage drinking arrests, smoked some bud back in the day. Nothing that would keep me off the department. Kind of a lady's man as you might have guessed. My old man took off, so my mom raised me. Older brother in prison for burglary. I decided it might be smarter to go the other way," McGhee stopped and stared at Ebony's ample backside as she passed their booth.

"What about college?" Venko asked.

"I'd like to go, I guess, but I'm not sure what I would study. I'd like to eventually be a detective and work homicides, shootings, stabbings and felonious assaults," McGhee answered truthfully.

Dispatch squawked across their mobile radios and broke the brief silence.

"Car 4 and any car in the area, 911 call from 344 Birch Circle. Twelve-year-old male taken by unknown white male in front of this location."

"That's in the projects, in the center of the Woods," Venko remarked, then advised dispatch they were en route to the call. Officers Haystack, Stein and Fitzpatrick also acknowledged the call and were responding as back up. Venko threw down a few bills and the pair jogged to the car.

They arrived just over a minute later. A very distraught Wendy Fisher ran from the brick duplex to meet them in the drive.

"He's gone, he was just here, right here and he is gone!" Wendy struggled to get the words out through sobs.

"I am Officer Venko and this is my partner Officer McGhee. We are here to help. Are you his mother?" She nodded to Venko's question.

Venko finished gathering information and put out a description of the missing child over the police radio. He directed the backup units to check the area for the pair on foot or any suspicious vehicles leaving the area. Sgt. Miller pulled up as McGhee was walking Wendy back into the house. The wind picked up and the temperature had fallen to ten degrees, a light snow began to drop. Venko got into the passenger's seat of Miller's car.

"What do you have, Dan?" He asked.

"Wendy Fisher is mom. Child is Gabriel Solomon. White male, twelve. She said she heard him sneaking out and saw him on the sidewalk from her bedroom window. When she got to the door, she saw him talking to a white male by the back of her van parked in front of us. As she was running down the driveway, they walked behind the van. When she got to the van, they were both gone." Venko stopped and rubbed his chin.

"Could they have run across the street through the yard? Would the kid have gone willingly? No screaming or yelling?" Miller asked, genuinely puzzled after surveying the area.

"She said there was no car, no sound, they were just gone. I know, I know, they had to go that way they couldn't have just vanished."

Venko strained his eyes looking down the block. Miller called Stein and Fitzpatrick over the radio and advised them to switch over to an available tactical channel. He switched channels and advised them to start their door-to-door canvas across the street from the Fisher residence.

"This sounds strange, let's go in and talk to her. I'll call the on-duty detective and get him rolling this way," Miller stated grabbing his phone from his jacket pocket.

"Who is in tonight?" Venko asked.

"Bledsoe."

"Shit, not Beans again. Where is Cassie?" Venko sighed.

"She took the night off," Miller responded.

Benny "Beans" Bledsoe was a midnight shift detective that proudly told anyone that would listen he was in his last year and could, and often would, spew the day count remaining until his retirement. His first priority was managing his online retirement portfolio. His cheap suits hung awkwardly on his gaunt frame. He wore thick, black glasses and his pile of unkempt, grey hair made him appear much older than fifty-seven. He earned his moniker by giving unsolicited investment advice every chance he got. His on-the-job effort increased proportionally to the amount of overtime a particular case offered. He routinely scheduled follow-up interviews just prior to the shift starting, or just after it ended. Because, after all, in his words, *it was all about the beans.*

Venko and Miller sat at the kitchen table with the distraught Wendy as McGhee typed the report on the computer.

"Ma'am we have cars out right now checking the area. What we need is more information from you to help us," Venko explained in a soothing tone.

Fisher explained that Gabriel has just been released from youth detention. He had gotten in a fight at school and "defended himself" by stabbing a thirteen-year-old girl. She admitted he had some behavioral issues and would disappear for days at a time. She reluctantly added that his Ritalin had been stolen in a burglary last week and his doctor was reluctant to issue a new prescription. This information caused Miller to glance over at Venko.

Venko quietly excused himself and called Beans and asked for prior calls and criminal history on Wendy Fisher.

"Do you guys really need me out there?" Beans started off the conversation, annoying Venko.

"Beans, the market closed hours ago, nothing will change till tomorrow, no use in just sitting there. While you're still at your desk, look up Wendy Fisher, I need calls and priors."

Beans searched and located two prior shoplifting arrests and two low-level felony drug possession cases that had been dismissed in lieu of treatment. Beans finished his conversation with Venko, grabbed his coat and scarf and slowly headed out. The five-minute drive would take him twenty minutes after he stopped and picked up coffee. By then with any luck, the kid would be back home or found at a friend's house.

"Mom?" The timid voice of Gabriel Solomon called from the back door.

"Gabe!" Wendy screamed and jumped to her feet as the rest of the table sat in stunned silence.

"What's going on? Why are the police here?" Gabriel asked.

"Because you disappeared, where did you go? Who was that man with you?" she asked, nearly shaking him.

Venko slowly walked over to the frightened boy and spoke softly.

"Gabe, your mom called because she said she saw you at the end of the driveway talking to someone. She said you and that person disappeared and she couldn't find you. Now it's maybe ten minutes later and you walk in the back door. Just tell us what you remember."

"I was walking down the driveway, I was going over to Max's house. I saw the man at the end of the drive, and then I was in the backyard and came in because it was cold outside." Gabriel finished and sat down on the torn couch.

He gave his mom a confused look. Venko immediately knew something wasn't quite right. While Wendy wrapped a blanket around the shivering Gabriel, Venko motioned Sgt. Miller into the kitchen for a private conversation.

"Something is off, I'd like to call EMS over to check him out," Venko requested.

"He was gone maybe ten minutes? Not really enough time for anything to happen. Do you believe there was someone else out there? There is something off about all of this, and the kid looks dazed, go ahead and get a squad out here to check him out." Miller finished and walked back to the group.

"What about this report? Should I cancel it, or file it as missing and recovered?" McGhee asked, genuinely perplexed.

"A med unit is coming, add whatever they say to the report then send it," Venko instructed before turning back to Gabriel.

"Gabe, you walked down the end of the driveway, saw the man, and the next thing you remember is being in the backyard?"

"That's right, sir," Gabriel answered truthfully.

Wendy's head snapped around when she heard her son say "sir." She had never heard her son speak in a respectful tone to any of the police officers they had dealt with over the last few years. Venko caught the confused look she shared with her son. It added to his sense of unease. Sgt. Miller also caught the quick exchange.

"McGhee, get a complete description of the white male in the street and list him as a suspect. Pass it on to Detective Bledsoe, whenever he eventually arrives. Make sure he does a facial composite on the computer," Miller directed, then he notified the other units in the area that the child had been recovered but to continue to check the area for any suspicious persons.

"Wendy, can you give me a description of the person you saw in the street, as complete as you can remember?" Venko asked calmly.

"He was a tall white guy, a little taller than you. He wore a black wool-like coat and jeans," She paused. Venko probed for more details.

"Was he thin, heavy, muscular? What about his hair? Did he have a cap? Did he wear glasses?"

"He wasn't heavy or thin, more like fit, but on the thinner side. He was neat, his hair was dark. Brown, maybe? Parted on the side, no hat, no glasses. He was standing by my van, under one of the few remaining working streetlights on this block. He looked too neat, too nice for this neighborhood," she stopped momentarily in thought. "Oh, and he wore a watch with a real shiny, silver metal band."

"Which arm did he wear it on?" Venko asked as McGhee typed furiously, adding information to the report. She paused, trying to recall.

"I think it was his right arm."

Paramedics walked in and nodded to Venko and Miller. They escorted a confused Gabriel outside to the ambulance. Fifteen minutes later, they returned.

"Ma'am, everything appears fine. No sign of any injuries, no frostbite, however he seems to have lost track of ten or so minutes. There is nothing to indicate a concussion or other head injury. We are going to release him to your custody. You can certainly take him to the hospital should he develop any other symptoms," the older paramedic explained before leaving.

Beans walked in carrying his laptop and a cup of coffee.

"Is this the missing child?" Beans asked, pointing to Gabriel.

"Yes, Beans, but we need you to do a composite sketch on the computer for the file. McGhee is finishing up the report and will forward it to you in a second, add the composite and anything else you can think of," Miller instructed with a look that said *don't try and blow this off*.

"Sure thing, sarge," Beans responded with a noticeable sigh and opened his laptop at the table.

Twenty minutes later, Venko, McGhee and Miller headed out, leaving everything in the capable hands of the reluctant Beans.

• • •

At 1:45 a.m., Venko pulled alongside Car 1.

"Dude, we were sitting on a good dope house. Nothing personal, but anyone could have come over and helped you on this detail. Fucking break-ins are not our thing," Bianchi explained. "Besides, you got a greyhound next to you anyway, what do you need us for?"

Bianchi nodded at McGhee who was oblivious as he scrolled through social media on his phone. Venko glanced over and quietly noted his partner's glaring rule violation. Bianchi quietly tapped his partner and pointed to McGhee.

"You know, Dan, they never caught the Red Scarf Bandit. If we get him it could be huge. You might finally get promoted to sergeant," Martinez added, smiling.

Venko chuckled. "I guess, since the sergeant's promotion list is still active. What are the odds they pass me over again?"

"Well maybe fucking Sellers dies in a car crash and isn't sitting in on the interview, or you answer every one of his off-the-wall questions correctly this time," Bianchi shot back.

Venko rubbed his stubble-covered chin before answering.

"Nah, I think I'm good right here in the 7th. I've made peace with it."

"Hell, you're practically a sergeant now. We have a good crew of sergeants and Miller is staying, but Sullivan and Jefferson are young and will bail first chance they can, to get off midnights. Which means, another rotation of newly promoted sergeants from outside the precinct. What we really need is a calm, mature presence, such as yourself as a new sergeant," Martinez finished and grinned.

"I realize this may sound blasphemous, but you're full of shit," Venko replied.

"Nah, I tell him that everyday Dan," Bianchi added.

Venko glanced at his partner, preoccupied with his phone, and then back to Bianchi.

"We are going to set up in the 100 block of Waterfront, you guys set up north, around Chester and Waterfront. Go to a tactical channel, let's make it Tac 2. Should only be us, Miller and possibly the lieutenant on this channel. If things go bad one of you put it out on dispatch channel. You got binoculars?" Venko asked.

Martinez reached into his bag and pulled out a pair and showed them to Venko.

"Check."

"Red Scarf Bandit," Bianchi said and extended his fist out the driver's window.

"Roger that." Venko fist bumped Bianchi and pulled off.

Five minutes later, Venko was driving slowly westbound through the alley between Waterfront and Longfellow.

"There! Black jacket, red hoodie running towards Longfellow." Venko stopped the car as McGhee tossed his phone into the door and jumped out. He sprinted toward Longfellow and heard Venko give updates over the tactical channel.

"White male, black jacket, red scarf or hoody, under the jacket, approaching Longfellow on foot."

As McGhee reached Longfellow he heard Bianchi on the radio.

"We see him, northbound on Longfellow, he just cut eastbound on the alley back towards Waterfront."

McGhee cut right and sprinted hard northbound toward the alley. Seconds later he was in the alley, but still couldn't spot the suspect. He paused for a second and slowed to a jog, thinking the suspect might have ducked behind the dumpsters scattered down the alley.

"I'm coming bro!" Haystack chimed in. Both Venko and Bianchi were trying to key their microphones at the same time creating an annoying buzz that prevented anyone from transmitting. Finally, Venko got through.

"Negative truck 77. Stay on the perimeter and we have enough units." Venko tossed the radio microphone onto the passenger's seat and continued to drive slowly up Waterfront. *I should have known Haystack would be monitoring the tactical channel, always looking for adventure.*

Venko quickly grabbed and keyed the radio handset.

"I see him, northbound on Waterfront around the 200 block."

Venko stopped the car and watched as McGhee exited the alley and sprinted northbound onto Waterfront. His grin turned to utter shock as he saw a second, very large figure emerging from the alley trailing McGhee, but gaining on him. Bianchi and Martinez were facing southbound on Waterfront and observed Haystack running with McGhee.

"He turned westbound on Clove Alley back toward Longfellow," Martinez directed over the air.

"I think I see him!" Haystack shouted into his radio as he turned westbound on Clove Alley.

"Marley, you better catch him before Haystack does," a very excited Bianchi chimed in.

An extremely calm voice shattered the electric moment, "I have an apprehension at Clove and Longfellow. All units slow down."

A very panicked Bianchi stopped the car and looked at his partner.

"Dawg, I think that was Lieutenant Swanson," Martinez whispered.

"Fucking ay right it was. Shit," Bianchi responded.

As the units slowly converged on Clove Alley and Longfellow, Lt. Swanson stood against the hood of his unmarked car, arms folded, talking to Sgt. Miller. Officers Bianchi, Martinez, Venko, McGhee and a very winded Haystack slowly walked from their vehicles toward the pair.

"Red Scarf Bandit or White Mike this time?" Lt. Swanson asked the group. Bianchi and Martinez sheepishly looked to Venko for guidance.

"Where is the son-of-a-bitch?" McGhee asked, walking between the sergeant and lieutenant's cars, peering into the rear windows.

"Officer McGhee, there is no suspect," Lt. Swanson started to explain before Venko cut him off.

"Red Scarf Bandit this time. McGhee had his nose buried in his phone and I thought I might just teach him a valuable lesson about keeping his eyes on the street. I enlisted the help of Bianchi and Martinez," Venko stopped and looked at the dumbfounded Haystack. "I had no idea Haystack would be eavesdropping on the tactical channel. I assumed anyone eavesdropping would have heard 'red scarf' and realized it was a, uh, training exercise."

"Bro, this was all bogus?" Haystack responded, crestfallen.

"Haystack, I did the same thing to you four years ago that last time we partnered up! Don't you remember that?" Venko shot back completely stunned. A slow smile crept over Haystack.

"Oh yeah, I remember you telling me it was like running wind sprints after a bad practice. You got me again, bro!"

Sgt. Miller did a slow facepalm as Lt. Swanson turned towards Venko.

"Dan, can we all agree shutting down this little training exercise prevented Haystack from clotheslining the first random citizen he may have encountered, and thus saved the city untold legal and medical expenses?"

"Most certainly sir, I believe McGhee will now leave his cellphone in the door pocket and focus on the streets." Venko caught a quick glance from a furious McGhee.

"Sir, I never clothesline, I always lead with my shoulder and drive through the tackle with my arms wrapped. If you try a clothesline, people can duck under and escape," Haystack explained to an uninterested Miller.

"Dude, you got jets! You'll do well here." Haystack held out a fist to McGhee who turned and stalked off towards the parked cruiser. "Bro, don't leave me hanging!" Haystack called out to McGhee.

"Did he wear a fucking helmet when he played?" Bianchi asked Martinez.

"Would it have made a difference?" Martinez shot back and accepted Bianchi's fist bump.

"Let's get back to work," Swanson ordered, fighting the smirk creeping across his face.

"You heard the man," Miller said as he got into the car, his mustache twitching as he drove away.

Chapter 4

Double Cherry Danish

Venko opened his eyes to the smell of fresh coffee. Diablo glared at the visitor but wasn't concerned enough to move from her spot next to Venko's head. .

"Good morning Dan, I have fresh coffee and a supersized cherry Danish to start your weekend," Sarah said and placed the bag and coffee on the small Formica-covered table.

"What time is it?" Venko asked, pulling on a grey sweatshirt.

"It's the crack of 3:30 p.m.," she said as she sat at the table and sipped her tea. Sarah wore a dark green wool sweater under a waist-length black leather jacket, fitted jeans and black boots.

Venko raised the blinds and gazed out at the cloudy sky. Sunday and Monday were his days off this week, and it looked like light snow today.

"How was work last night? How is your training of the young cub coming along?" She asked smiling as he sat and opened the Danish bag.

"Red Scarf Bandit," he answered with a mouthful of Danish.

"You made that poor boy run for nothing?" She remarked sarcastically.

"These kids today and their damn smartphones. I told him on day one, pay attention to the streets not the screen. So yeah, he needed to run a bit. But then Haystack was eavesdropping on the tactical channel and heard the foot chase, and jumped out of his wagon and took off after McGhee. I put out 'Red Scarf' over the air, yet somehow, he missed that.

He actually said, 'I can see him,' as he was running with Marcus."

"See who?" Sarah asked.

"No one, they were chasing a ghost!" Venko said, throwing up his hands.

"God does smile on the stupid," Sarah added.

"What do I have planned today?" Venko asked half-serious as he filled Diablo's bowl with food.

"Well, I believe you wanted to walk down to Binder's Book Store and have a second cup of coffee while doing some light browsing and discuss your take on the Bishop file I gave you to review," she paused, noting Venko's glazed expression as he sipped his coffee. "The missing kid you took a report on a few years back, Dakota Billings."

Recognition flashed in Venko's eyes.

"Oh yeah, I did look it over Counselor, a pretty weak case. What else am I doing today?"

"You wanted to take a jog in the park around 6 p.m. with me, before cleaning up for a hearty pasta dinner and wine."

She sipped her tea and awaited his response.

"Funny, I don't recall planning any of that," he mumbled as the Danish disappeared with a gigantic bite. "What am I wearing today?" He asked sarcastically.

"Not that sweatshirt," she shot back.

• • •

Binder's Bookstore sat four blocks from Venko's apartment building. The one-story brick building featured both new and used books. It remained viable competition to the large bookstore chains because of its outstanding offering of homemade baked goods, along with fresh coffee and a clean, cozy seating area. A fireplace crackled along the back wall near overstuffed couches and a few small unoccupied bistro tables.

"Hello Danilo," Mrs. Esposito greeted Venko warmly at the counter.

"Good afternoon, Mrs. Esposito, where is Giuseppe today?" Venko asked the co-owner.

"He is at home watching football," she responded. Venko shot Sarah an arched eyebrow that said *I should be watching football, too.*

"Hello Sarah, what can I get you?" She asked.

"Francesca, I'll just have a hot tea, and Danilo will have his usual, black coffee."

Francesca completed the order and took Danilo's cash.

"Danilo, you forgot this," Mrs. Esposito called to him as they headed towards the fireplace. She handed him a white paper bag that he knew would contain a cherry cheese Danish. Venko sheepishly retrieved the bag from a smiling Mrs. Esposito. "You're getting thin Danilo, you must keep up your strength."

"Thank you, Francesca."

Venko smiled and turned towards Sarah's incredulous glare as they walked to the table by the fireplace.

"We're going to have a second Danish are we?" Sarah asked, glancing down at Venko's not-so-flat stomach.

"You heard her, I'm getting thin, I have to keep my strength up." He grinned at her.

"What is it with you and old ladies? They love you," Sarah said.

"Francesca? She was a childhood friend of my mom. They used to play cards every Friday when I was growing up. I can never get away with just ordering coffee here. Besides, you wouldn't want me to insult her by refusing the Danish?"

"No, we can't have that." Sarah shook her head emphatically.

She reached into her large shoulder bag and retrieved the manila folder with "Bishop" written across the top.

"I'm always amazed what you can fit in that bag. It's like your own personal clown car. Just reach below the leaf blower and pull out a file," Venko chuckled.

He stopped when Sarah arched her eyebrows and handed him the file.

"Enough frivolity, I know. Here's what I took from the file. They had small amounts of blood on Bishop's work boots. It appeared old and dried. That blood belonged to Billings. At the time of the abduction, they had so little to link him to the disappearance, that they could not get a search warrant. Yes, he had an occasional relationship with mom, and he was most likely violent to both of them, but that relationship ended months before the kid disappeared. There is nothing to prove that he had been back there around that time. Since he lived nearby, yes, he probably drove down the street. Any valuable data from his cell phone would be long gone after two years. The witness description is not in any way an identification of Bishop, as a matter of fact, he wasn't picked from the photo lineup. Honestly, I'm not sure how he got indicted, and more importantly, I'm not sure how you're going to prosecute this case."

Venko took a gulp of coffee and bit into the Danish.

"His appointed counsel is Coffman, there will be no plea deal unless he gives up the location of the body. That seems unlikely, because my gut is telling me he didn't take the kid, and some haphazard police work somehow got him indicted," she paused, more thinking out loud rather than talking to Venko.

"So, because he's been locked up before, he isn't too worried about the gun and robbery charge. He'll go to trial on the abduction. Coffman will make me an offer on the robbery, though. Something ridiculous to start, but he will end up accepting a couple of years to plead to the robbery. What a mess."

She sipped her tea and looked at Venko who was smiling.

"What?"

"I just like to watch the little hamster run on the wheel in your head. They could always withdraw the abduction charge if they find evidence to exonerate him or discover evidence that points at another suspect."

Venko finished the Danish, and then shot a guilty look at Sarah.

"Did you want half?"

She stared briefly into his blue eyes and grinned wryly.

"No, we can't have you all waif-like, I wouldn't want you to pass out." Venko shrugged in agreement and sipped his coffee.

"I took a weird call last night, attempted abduction of a twelve or thirteen-year-old. Mom swore he was snatched off the street in front of the house. The kid turned up, not even ten minutes later.

Just walked in the back door. No sign of injury to the kid, so-so description of a suspect. A canvas of the neighborhood gave us nothing, no witnesses. Something was just off about that whole call, not sure if mom or the kid was lying, or if there really was a suspect," Venko said as he leaned back and exhaled.

"Well, newsflash, it wasn't my dude Bishop, he is still locked up."

• • •

The three-mile run dissolved into two miles, sprinkled with liberal amounts of walking. The cold air hurt Venko's lungs and his joints ached. He napped for about thirty minutes, cleaned up and was at Sarah's door for dinner promptly at 8 p.m. He stopped at the door and took in the aroma of simmering spices before knocking. Sarah opened the door clutching a glass of wine and smiling.

"Hi, come in. You wore a sweater, for me? Hoodie in the wash?" She gave him a quick kiss and noticed the faint scent of cologne.

The one-bedroom apartment was bright, open and airy. Small potted plants thrived on the windowsill. The furnishings were modern and the framed prints adorning the walls were tasteful. A few personal photos were scattered around the entertainment center. A small bar separated the kitchen from the living room. Venko took off his coat, caught Sarah's glance, and walked over to the coat tree and hung it up before plopping down on a bar stool.

Sarah pulled a Corona from the fridge and slid it down the bar to Venko. He opened it and drained nearly half with his first thirsty gulp.

"Easy there, I have plans for you later," she said with a smile.

She carried a large salad bowl over to the small table and placed some garlic bread on a plate. Within a few minutes everything was on the table and Venko was desperately attempting to get the pasta from the bowl to his plate without any collateral damage to the tablecloth.

"Do you know when the next round of promotions will be?" Sarah asked.

Venko knew this to be her way of gauging his interest in getting promoted to sergeant. She was aware of him being passed over during the last round of promotions. Sellers had been part of the interview panel and had veered away from objective questions on policy and supervision and directed Venko's questions towards subjective topics. Although it was clear to the rest of the panel that Sellers had introduced some of his own questions, they allowed the questions to continue once Venko began to falter. Venko had not prepared for questions on the role of body-worn camera audits and inspections on police efficiency.

Sellers thrived on creating paperwork to document irrelevant minutiae. Creating needless forms and databases enhanced his ego. Supervisors in the 7th were routinely given weekly deadlines to complete exhaustive and worthless audits and inspections. Sellers would then create elaborate presentations to show deputy chiefs how he maintained quality control and professionalism. Sergeants and lieutenants in the 7th, quickly learned that if they were conducting personnel inspections and body-worn camera audits as directed by Sellers, supervisors would never leave the building, ending and starting audits, in an endless cycle. Swanson argued that the midnight shift was primarily composed of the youngest, most inexperienced officers in the department. He felt his sergeants should be in the field and had argued that Internal Affairs' quarterly audits were enough, but Sellers stated that his precinct would do more than the mere minimum.

After the first few supervisors had vacation time taken for not meeting deadlines, the subtle, coordinated push-back began. Swanson met with his sergeants and directed them to enter all the officers' information into Sellers' exhaustive spreadsheet. This included documenting serial numbers for firearms, handcuffs, flashlights, body-worn cameras, and ballistic vests as well as the condition of those items. The sergeants would then rotate the task of copying and pasting the same information into each weekly report. Swanson had two caveats for this process. The officers had to actually be at work on the day of the spurious inspection, an officer on vacation might cast doubt on the veracity of the report.

Sergeants were to require officers to immediately report any lost or damaged police property so the audits could reflect that.

Beating the body-worn camera audits was a more challenging and creative process. Sellers had instructed Swanson to have his sergeants randomly pick one dispatched call a week of each officer on the shift and watch the entire video of the incident. The sergeant was to complete a written review of that call, to include documented policy violations, suggestions for improving citizen contacts, a critique of radio transmissions, and response times. Sergeants were to review their findings with the officer and issue appropriate reprimands or discipline as necessary. Once the paperwork was completed, it was to be uploaded into Sellers' computer audit folder. Since cameras were supposed to be activated during the citizen interaction of any call, videos could last between a few minutes and an hour long.

Swanson met with his sergeants and discussed the type of random videos he would like reviewed. The sergeants passed along this information to the officers, who were instructed to notify their sergeant by cellphone, when they had cleared a call that was worthy of an audit. Initially, this created the inadvertent corollary effect of officers racing each other to be the first on scene to assist a stranded motorist, or other service-oriented call that could briefly showcase their professionalism for that week's audit.

A few weeks into Swanson's streamlined version of inspection and audits, Miller pointed out that the number of policy violations and the audits of strictly service oriented calls were going to skew the numbers drastically from what the other 7th Precinct shifts were putting out. To allow for some statistical deviation, the types of calls selected were altered, but yet carefully randomly selected for their likely positive outcome. Additionally, there was now a monthly verbal reprimand lottery. Sellers' style of supervision permitted almost no discretion on the part of supervisors for handling policy violations and discipline. If he became aware of an incident that was not handled in an official capacity, the supervisor would be cited for failing to supervise and disciplined. If one looked hard enough, nearly every video had at least one minor policy violation. Swanson and the sergeants would get together monthly and select the lucky recipient of this month's verbal reprimand, the lowest level of official discipline. These were usually violations of the personal appearance policy: unpolished boots, torn uniforms, non-regulation facial hair, or most commonly, swearing or otherwise profane language.

The officers took the occasional discipline well, understanding the benefit of the system designed to keep Sellers at arm's length from the day-to-day operation of the shift and to shield the officers from even more ridiculous scrutiny. The common reaction to being summoned to the sergeant's office by the officers, was to shrug, as if to say, "it's my turn."

Officer Venko struggled, trying to decide if he really wanted to put in the effort preparing for another panel interview after the disastrous last attempt. Passing the written test had been a breeze, and the interactive assessment phase clearly displayed he had the practical knowledge to do the job. The panel interview was the last phase of the promotional exam. For decades, it was a chance for the soon-to-be-promoted sergeants to meet the upper management of the department in a relaxed atmosphere and discuss issues facing the department. In the last few years this phase became a chance to manipulate the system. Candidates were now being scored during the interview. Preferred candidates could rack up points during the interview and jump ahead of higher ranked candidates. Non-preferred candidates could be passed over for promotion and plummet down the eligibility list.

Venko knew that Sellers was universally reviled by the rank-and-file officers, but held some sway with upper management, which permitted him to participate in the promotional board interviews and sit in on policy committees. He also knew that Sellers never forgot a slight and would continue to do everything in his power to keep him from being promoted.

He looked at Sarah and answered honestly.

"They will promote sergeants again sometime in the spring after the next round of retirements. Honestly, sometimes I just want to finish out my career driving around the 7th Precinct on midnights. Other days I realize how much work I create for Sellers just by going through the promotional process. He has to work hard to keep me from getting promoted, and I just want to cause him that kind of aggravation."

"You know, besides being a pain in the ass to Sellers, you would actually make a good sergeant. No, no," she raised her hand to prevent his interruption before continuing. "The young officers on your shift really respect you, as do the supervisors. Think what you could teach them. How you could guide them. They need some old school dude to tell them what is what." She smiled.

"I would not be opposed to the bump in my pension," Venko stated, taking a long pull on his second beer. "I just have to figure out a way to beat Sellers or get him booted from the process. Can you imagine Captain Sellers expression if he had to shake hands with newly promoted Sgt. Danilo Venko?"

"I'll help you prepare for the interview. Swanson will give us a list of topics we can study up on. I know he will help you," Sarah said with genuine optimism as she cleared the table.

"I think I'd like to study now for about eight minutes or so," he stated with a mischievous grin.

Sarah turned from the sink with a raised brow. "Eight minutes, feeling optimistic, are we?"

"You always said, it's good to have goals," he replied.

"I would like to counter your offer," she purred as she approached him. "I'm not opposed to ten minutes, with two minutes of cuddling." She finished her sentence and straddled his lap and kissed his left ear.

"Uh, counselor, are you trying to interfere with my ability to negotiate this matter?" He asked, his voice starting to crack.

She slid forward and kissed him deeply. His powerful legs lifted them both effortlessly, and she giggled as he carried her to the bedroom leaving a wake of scattered clothing and breathless murmurs.

Chapter 5
Rock, Paper, Scissors, Chainsaw

Venko's alarm startled him from his nap, leaving him roughly ninety minutes before the 11pm roll call. The last two days were a pleasant haze, but it was Tuesday night and his weekend had evaporated. He rose stiffly and noticed Diablo had no such schedule to contend with. He opened his phone and saw messages from Lt. Swanson and Sarah. He opened Sarah's first.

Be safe tonight. I had an awesome weekend! :) SS

ME2, Venko responded, as fast as his fingers could tap the keys.

He couldn't bring himself to add the smiley emoji. He checked the message from Swanson and grimaced.

Sellers wants to meet with me before roll call. Get the word out, we are at Defcon 1.

Venko knew this meant Sellers would probably attend roll call and most likely address the shift. He rarely refused an open podium and a captive audience. Venko scrolled through his contacts and tried to figure out who could spread the message the quickest. It was already 9:15 p.m. He stopped scrolling at Officer Rachel Stein. No one was faster. He forwarded Swanson's message. Rachel responded less than a minute later.

Fucccccckkkkkk!

Venko knew officers would alter their routine tonight to add time for a shave, polish their boots and check the condition of their uniforms. Several officers would no doubt end their uniform rotation a day or two early.

The uniform rotation generally meant wearing the same shirt and pants for two at minimum, or three days before changing. November in western Pennsylvania guaranteed that there would be salt stains along the bottom of the pants and on the boots. Several officers kept inspection boots in their lockers for just such occasions. These were a second pair of boots kept polished and stored in the precinct locker room. Officers would change before going to roll call, then change back before hitting the streets. In the event officers did not indulge in the second pair of boots, Sgt. Miller kept a squeeze bottle of black quick shine in his desk drawer.

Changing uniform shirts meant moving the badge, name tag and specialty pins to a new shirt. Venko was not a member of the SWAT team and had no other specialty training that was designated by a pin. He did wear his Fit for Duty pin over his right breast pocket. The fitness test had a sliding scale based on age, and he had no problems passing the test.

He took a quick shower. Like most of his male counterparts on the shift, he shaved every other day. However, with Sellers anticipated attendance, he shaved quickly, slicing open a small spot below his nose and on his chin. He cursed, and stuck pieces of toilet paper to the affected areas to stem the bleeding as he finished putting on his uniform.

Venko locked the door and could immediately smell the rich coffee in the air.

"Hello Danilo, did you have a good weekend?" Miss Rosales asked, pouring him a cup of coffee.

"Yes, I certainly did," he said smiling and accepted the coffee cup.

"Sarah is good for you. You walk lighter after seeing her. This is good. You should tell her," she finished and patted his arm gently.

"Tell her what?" Venko asked.

"Tell her that she is good for you."

Venko thought about his brief text response to her and realized he could have elaborated more.

"She knows."

"Does she?"

The words hung awkwardly in the air briefly before he responded.

"I think so, but you're right I could do a better job of telling her."

Miss Rosales chuckled, "Oh I didn't say that, I just helped you discover what you already knew."

"Of course you didn't, I am adding master psychiatrist to your resume," Venko said and grabbed the thermos before pausing. "I never see or hear anyone come visit you. I worry sometimes. Do you miss your family?"

"Oh Danilo, I'm much stronger than I look. I will see them all again one day, soon," she said with confidence.

Venko shook his head and thought about the day she simply would not be in the hall to greet him before work. He wondered how he would react to that day. His gut told him it would be soon. He opened his mouth to speak but she cut him off. It was almost as if she was reading his mind.

"Danilo, be careful. Remember the wolf comes in many forms," Rosales whispered as he stood. She grabbed his arm briefly.

"Keep your mind strong, time is shifting, stay on top of the sand."

Venko responded warmly to her concern, "I will be fine, nothing can keep me from our nightly meetings."

She stared at him and smiled as he walked down the stairs.

He could see the shiny, black, unmarked Ford parked in front of the precinct. Sellers was in the building. He hoped the rest of the shift had gotten the alert. His concern was alleviated when he walked into the roll call room. Everyone was already seated, twenty minutes before shift. Fitzpatrick, Haystack, Bianchi and Niles all had fresh facial cuts, the result of frantic last-minute shaving. Sgt. Miller was quietly in the back, reviewing notes on the clipboard for roll call. His walrus mustache had been trimmed, it no longer crept past the corners of his mouth. The room was somber without the usual loud conversations; most officers were just looking through their notebooks.

Lt. Swanson paused outside the Sellers' office door. He exhaled, as a feeling of dread swept over him. He knocked lightly and was directed to enter. Captain Sellers was seated behind his desk and motioned for Swanson to sit at one of the two chairs in front of the desk. He looked around the office at the photos of Sellers with various prominent business and community leaders. No one loved themselves more than he did. Swanson wondered if Sellers desk was raised or the chairs were slightly smaller. He thought it would be just like Sellers to customize his desk and chair so he could look down on anyone in his office. There would be no pleasantries exchanged, Sellers had no additional spectators and would not have to mask his arrogance.

"Lt. Swanson, I have reviewed the most recent crime stats, I'm seeing some increases in burglaries and breaking and enterings. I'm sure you have reviewed these reports, what action plan have you developed to reverse this trend?"

Swanson didn't need to read the reports to understand what was going on in the precinct. The burglaries and break-ins were tied to the soaring number of opioid addicts living in the poorest area of the city. Swanson wanted to explain that increased patrols and even arrests didn't change the addict's desire for the drug. In other words, as soon as they were released from a brief jail stay, they would go right back into finding ways to fund their addictions. But he also knew that if he tried to explain this, Sellers would dismiss it as an excuse, and tell Swanson once again, that he was only interested in results.

"Well Captain, I am assigning cars to various hotspots nightly, for an hour or two during peak hours. It would really help if we had a detective or two in an unmarked car to do surveillance and set up on a few locations."

Sellers leaned back and steepled his hands. His expression was one of annoyance.

"Lieutenant, people in hell want ice water. I expected more in the way of specifics from your plan. Tonight, I would like you to type up an action plan, include only the resources you control, and show me you can command. I'm not really happy with our detectives right now, and I'll get to that in a minute. If they are free, you can use them."

Swanson tried not to look at Sellers' crooked nose.

I wish I'd have given him a good shot, too.

Sellers's hair had started to recede rapidly in front, his small brown eyes were engulfed with puffy flesh that gave him the expression of a basset hound. The collar of his white uniform shirt was partially covered by a roll of girth from his neck. Supervisors, the rank of lieutenant and above were permitted the option of wearing a white uniform shirt instead of the traditional navy blue. Sellers wanted everyone to immediately notice his distinction in rank and wore a white shirt daily. Swanson measured his response carefully before speaking.

"I'll talk to Detectives Bledsoe and Oliver and see what they have going on currently case-wise and see if they can help out."

Sellers shifted forward in his seat and took off his reading glasses.

"Which brings me to my next point. I read your commander's report and the one from Detective Bledsoe. This Solomon kid is missing for ten minutes, returns and we file an official report? What in god's name is Sgt. Miller thinking? Does he think I need an unsolved attempted abduction on my statistics for this quarter? Come on, Cal!"

Sellers' face had already started to shift to red and would no doubt go full purple before he finished. Swanson decided against attempting to inject logic into the discussion and would let Sellers finish.

"I read the report Venko and his rookie put out. The kid has a history of problems and mom isn't a saint. Don't you think maybe the kid snuck out to get high or meet a friend?" Sellers faced bobbed as he finished the sentence, causing a ripple on the loose flesh beneath his chin.

"Captain, mom insists she saw someone on the street near Solomon and they both disappeared. Sgt. Miller is convinced from listening to mom and talking with Venko and McGhee, that this report is legit. The kid walked in the back door and seemed out of it," Swanson finished calmly.

"Mom is a fucking junkie! This is a no win, pat the kid on the head and say thanks for coming home and don't do it again. Now that report sits on my watch as another unsolved, because let's be honest, we got nothing, and Bledsoe couldn't solve a game of tic-tac-toe. It's not like we can pull the report out of the system once it's filed. Do you have any ambition beyond midnight lieutenant in the 7th Precinct?"

Swanson knew this was a loaded question and answered cautiously.

"If something opened up that interested me, yes, I would consider it. If a promotional test for captain comes soon, I'd consider it. I'm also comfortable right here."

Sellers' eyes seemed to shrink as he glared at Swanson.

"Well if you were ambitious, you would understand that sometimes incidents like this are better off unofficial. Good supervisors don't believe a junkie mom and a juvenile delinquent. In the big scheme of things, the kid will be locked up in a few years anyway. You will come to understand how negative statistics taint your reputation as a commander."

You are the definition of toxic leadership, Swanson thought before responding.

"With all due respect, if we were to handle this unofficially without a report or any investigative effort, and the same suspect snatches up another kid, the fallout would be enormous. That would be frontpage news. I trust the decisions Sgt. Miller makes, and Venko is a pro."

Swanson wondered if Sellers knew that *with all due respect,* was universal cop speak for, *Hey asshole!*

"Speaking of Venko, I have been calling and emailing Central Precinct to get a body-worn camera issued to him and they can't seem to find one or two more cameras for us."

Swanson suppressed a smile and would thank Franny for her continued good work, later.

"For now," Sellers started and slid a form over to Swanson. "I would like Venko to complete a log sheet nightly, starting tonight. Everyone needs to be held accountable for their work product and he can write down the training he provides McGhee and his nightly activity," Sellers finished and then began typing on his computer, an obvious sign that the conversation was over.

"Captain, Venko already completes a weekly, written evaluation on the progress of Officer McGhee. This seems a little repetitive," Swanson finished and knew he should have just walked out when Sellers dropped his non-verbal cue that the meeting was over.

"At what point did I ask for your input? I suggest you go run your shift now."

Lt. Swanson walked into the back of the roll call room and listened as Sgt. Miller was reading off a list of areas for each car to check. Swanson rarely heard Miller affect a humorless, monotone voice, but understood the effect Sellers' presence had on everyone. A minute later as Miller was finishing up roll call, Sellers walked in and stood at the back of the room.

"That's all I have today, Lt. Swanson do you have anything to add?"

Swanson shook his head.

"Captain Sellers, do you have anything you would like to cover?"

Sellers was already walking towards the podium when he answered, "Just a few things."

He looked out at the disinterested faces before beginning. Sellers spoke for twenty minutes on looking, acting and being professional. He went on at great length, about the need for improvement in citizen interactions, and covered last quarters' statistics on complaints, car chases and uses of force. Like dominos, officers began to shift in their chairs until almost all were leaning back with arms folded. Sellers, oblivious to this universal sign of being tuned out, continued.

He finished with, "We can all do better."

What he didn't discuss and was apparent in the quarterly stats report, was the precincts' increase in felony and misdemeanor arrests and a drop in violent crime. The officers knew this and were used to these pep talks that only highlighted the negative. There were no questions when he asked, just like every time he spoke. No one risked a question or comment. To do so could get you marked as a malcontent or troublemaker. Everyone knows Sellers never forgets.

Roll call was dismissed, and officers lingered, gathering up their belongings, not wanting to risk a casual conversation with the captain in the hall.

Swanson tapped Venko on the arm as he was passing and motioned him over to the side of the hallway.

"Dan, the captain would like you to start completing log sheets since you don't have a body-worn camera," he handed Venko one to examine.

"What the hell is this shit? We haven't used log sheets since we put the computers in the cars. If he wants to know what I'm doing he could pull up my identification number on his desktop and list all my calls for the day, the week, the month," Venko snapped back.

Swanson could see Venko's irritation rising.

"Dan, I realize all that. The form is a little more detailed, it asks for specifics on things you reviewed with McGhee on each call, teaching points. It also covers time periods between calls and self-initiated activities."

"Lieutenant, most of those are listed in the weekly Field Training Officer reports. You know that. Stop trying to bullshit me. This is meaningless busy work."

Venko folded the form and stuffed it into his back pocket.

"Bottom line Dan, captain wants them done nightly, most likely until you finish training McGhee."

Swanson noticed all the officers were gone now; an eerie silence filled the hall.

"He doesn't even realize what a complete asshole he is. He comes in here and has an opportunity to talk about the good work being done nightly, the dope arrests that Bianchi and Martinez make, the burglars that Stein and Fitzpatrick grabbed last week. But no, he wants to talk about improving our interaction with citizens, complaints, and meaningless statistics. He should patent his method of killing morale," Venko finished and began walking down the hall.

"We'll get through this Dan, we always do," Swanson said watching him walk away.

Venko spotted McGhee standing at the back of the cruiser with the trunk open as he approached.

"You're driving, let's see what you can do tonight. You'll handle calls, I'll step in if you start to do or say something stupid, but I'm only here as a life jacket. The captain has created a new form for me to fill out, more useless busy work," Venko said as he threw his bag in the trunk.

"Roger that," McGhee responded, eager to prove he was up to the task.

They drove in silence for the first ten minutes, cruising by mostly abandoned strip malls, save for check cashing businesses, furniture rentals and liquor stores. Venko flashed back to working with Swanson many years ago. Swanson had coined the term "trilogy of decay." Venko and Swanson had unscientifically determined that once those three businesses opened in the same area, it signaled the beginning of an economic collapse. Venko smiled briefly.

"What the fuck?" McGhee shouted as a red BMW 535 blew the stop sign and turned northbound in front of them, causing him to tap the brake.

"Don't light them up just yet. I'll run the plate first and see what we have."

Venko said before typing the license plate number into the computer.

"Yeah, we see you too," McGhee stated, noticing the couple in the back seat frantically turning back and forth from the driver to McGhee.

"Oh, someone is drunk," he added, noticing the speed had dropped to 19 miles per hour.

"The car comes back to Travis Anderson, white male, 24. He lives in the fancy-schmancy new apartment building downtown. The Wingnut. New beamer," Venko finished and unbuckled his seat belt.

"The Wing-Lutz," McGhee corrected with a laugh, as he turned on the overhead lights and pressed the siren.

The car came to a slow stop, gingerly bumping the right curb before coming to a complete stop.

"It's your show," Venko called to McGhee as he headed to the passenger side of the car.

Venko gently tapped the passenger window with his flashlight. The female dropped the window down two inches. He quickly scanned the interior of the BMW and it's four occupants––well-dressed, and under 30 years old. He grinned as he thought of every generic cell phone commercial, where a rainbow of youthful hipsters rode sparkling clean busses and trains while transacting business and social conversations on sleek phones. The driver, Travis Anderson, had a tight brown bun on top of his head and wore a patchy, nearly full beard. His thin neck was accented by a light grey scarf over a black wool pea coat. He wore brightly patterned socks that were just visible at the bottom of his skinny blue jeans. The front seat passenger was an attractive blonde wearing, what Venko thought, was a bucket of expensive perfume that made his nose burn. Behind her was a tiny, college-aged Asian female, who was leaning forward intent on interrupting the conversation between Officer McGhee and the driver.

"I am a criminal justice major Travis, he has to tell you his probable cause for the stop. You do not have to get out of the car! You have rights!"

Oh boy, here we go, Venko thought. The interior of the car smelled of humid marijuana and stale beer, a stark contrast to the bitter cold breeze outside.

The passenger behind the driver was a thin, black male wearing a brown three-quarter length leather jacket, with a bright blue dress shirt under a V-neck beige sweater. He didn't say a word and nodded at Venko politely. His glance gave off a quiet intelligence and awareness.

Venko heard McGhee politely request the driver to step from the vehicle.

"You have no legal obligation to comply!" The backseat lawyer shouted.

"Sir," the driver began, "could you tell me what valid reason you had for pulling me over?"

Venko looked over the licenses he collected from the other three in the car, primarily to keep from looking at McGhee and laughing.

"Mr. Anderson, you turned in front of my police car, if I hadn't braked, I would have hit you. I can smell marijuana and beer coming from your person. Please step out of the vehicle." McGhee said in a restrained tone.

"I would disagree, I believe if you had not been speeding, you wouldn't have needed to hit the brakes," Travis slurred, and extended his pronunciation of "brakessss."

"That's right Travis, you tell him! He got no right to pull you out of a vehicle that you legally own," backseat counsel argued loudly.

"Sir, please step out of the vehicle," McGhee asked again, in his best de-escalation tone.

"Why - why don't you go back to your car and finish your box of donuts, and we will just head on home without filing a harassment complaint on you," Travis finished and looked to the other passengers for approval, as he snickered.

Truck 77 pulled up behind Venko's cruiser and activated the overhead lights on the wagon. Haystack stood outside the transport wagon door and looked at Venko. Venko gave him a thumbs up signaling that everything was okay.

Officer McGhee's patience had run out.

"Mr. Anderson, you may exit through the door or window, the choice is yours."

"Oh, hell no, he can't talk to you that way!" Street lawyer shouted, immediately understanding the implication of McGhee's statement.

Haystack had quietly moved to the rear of Travis's vehicle. Travis saw the fierce determination in McGhee's glare, and then looked back and saw Haystack nearly blocking out the light from the overhead streetlamp. Travis realized this would not end well for him if he pushed things and he exited the BMW. McGhee walked him to the back of the vehicle to perform a variety of sobriety tests. Venko returned to the cruiser and checked all the occupants for warrants on the computer. He looked up and saw

McGhee directing Travis to sit on the curb. Venko met McGhee just out of earshot of the car.

"What do you have?" Venko asked.

"He is borderline, I think he is over the limit. He obviously isn't an experienced drinker, and I know he smoked some weed, but he passed some of the tests, and wasn't horrible on the failures. He is also a spoiled asshole, and I think we should take him," McGhee finished and looked over at the seated driver.

Haystack walked over and quietly stood next to Travis, ensuring there would not be a peep out of him.

"So, if I'm hearing you correctly, the driver pissed you off and you're ready to throw out what you saw in the sobriety tests for some petty payback? Does that sum it up?" Venko smiled warmly at McGhee.

"Well," McGhee, visibly frustrated, paused before continuing. "I'm not comfortable with him driving."

"So, you would rather do two plus hours of paperwork on a DUI to get even, knowing someone else would have to cover our district in the meantime? Or maybe, you were thinking we could write a citation for the improper turn, and to be safe, see if we could find someone else in the car that might be sober enough to drive? I'm thinking that's what you meant.."

A flicker of recognition flashed in McGhee.

"Yeah, I'll write him a citation while you find a sober driver."

McGhee escorted the driver into the backseat of the cruiser as Venko approached the car.

"Anyone sober enough to drive this car? Officer McGhee is going to give Travis a citation for his traffic infraction but decided not to arrest him for DUI," Venko finished and glanced around the car.

The blonde burped and looked away. Venko glanced at the quiet man in the rear of the car for a split second before Miss Legal Aid began her onslaught.

"I can drive. I'll pass any fucking test you give me. I had one Heineken three hours ago, I know how long it takes for the body to process alcohol. This is still an unlawful detention."

Venko motioned for her to step from the vehicle. She nearly jumped from the back seat and was walking towards the back of the car briskly, continuing to look at Venko as she spoke.

"I know the only reason you're giving Travis a ticket is to cover your ass and make this stop appear legitimate," she was oblivious to the six-five tree standing in her path as she continued to stare down Venko.

The ensuing collision sent her sprawling onto her back near the curb, her left arm completely submerged in a pile of black slush.

"Jesus!" She shouted, looking up at the enormity of Haystack.

He pulled her up effortlessly.

"If you weren't paying attention earlier, I am Officer Venko, I'd like to have you perform a few short tests to determine your sobriety. Do not start until I have finished my instructions." Venko instructed.

Venko briefly looked at Haystack who shrugged before returning his gaze to the female. She was standing with her right leg in the air and her right index finger touching her nose.

"Do not start until I tell you to, put your leg down and your hands at your side. Please," he added for good measure.

Once she complied, he continued.

"The first part of this test is to determine your cognitive skills while impaired. The second part will measure your motor skills."

"I get it, I'm in college, not a GED flunky working as a cop on night shift," she said with an annoying edge to her voice.

"Well then, I'll begin."

Venko fired off three questions in rapid succession.

"What is the capital of Belarus? Most trees fall into two categories, name them. What famous Spartan general died in the battle of Thermopylae?"

The ersatz attorney stared blankly at Venko, in stunned silence. Haystack began to faintly hum the *Jeopardy* theme, ending with a flourish, *Dum, Dum!*

"Wait, what does this have to do with my driving skills? Uh, uh, I know these. Athens, Oak and Bamboo, and Leonardo?" She blurted out.

"No, sorry, the response I was looking for was Minsk, coniferous and deciduous, and Leonidas. Thanks for playing and Haystack, tell her about those lovely parting gifts," Venko said with a wink.

"Dan, I think you should give her a shot with your special field sobriety tests. I mean it's only fair," Haystack reasoned.

"Yes," she agreed, again standing on one leg and touching her nose.

McGhee, having completed the citation and overheard the random pop-quiz, rolled his eyes in disbelief.

"Okay, if this gets out everyone will think I'm going soft in my old age. Ma'am, are you familiar with Rock, Paper, Scissors?"

"The game?" She asked incredulously.

"Yes, it tests both your cognitive and motor skills simultaneously," Venko said logically.

"I'm ready," she replied.

"Haystack, I need a neutral party to count us in." He nodded in agreement.

"One, two, three."

The college senior shot out a palm down paper while Venko shot out all four fingers together in a horizontal blade shape.

"No! No, you didn't!" Haystack exclaimed at Venko.

"What is that? That's not scissors, and it's not a rock," she said shaking her head.

"Chainsaw. Chainsaw beats paper. I'll give you another chance," Venko offered.

McGhee walked over to observe the test and silently mouthed "there is no chainsaw" to Haystack. He winked at McGhee before counting them in, and this time, she shot out her first two fingers spread apart, scissors. Venko met her again with the formidable chainsaw blade.

"Chainsaw beats scissors," Venko and Haystack said in unison.

"Shit, you win, I am drunk. Jayden, in the back is sober, he can drive," she ran her fingers through her hair in frustration.

"Officer McGhee, go check him out," Venko ordered.

McGhee gave him a *I can't believe what I just saw* look and walked over to the BMW. A few minutes later McGhee gave Venko a thumbs up, Jayden was indeed sober.

As the BMW drove off, Haystack turned to Venko and McGhee.

"I always thought it was Galileo that led the 275 Spartans against the Puritans."

McGhee and Venko exchanged a quick look of amazement before McGhee added, "it was 300 Spartans."

"They were Persians, not Puritans, just a different continent a few hundred years apart that's all," Venko corrected dryly.

"It could have been 275 if, like you know, one of the wagons broke down or got a flat tire," Haystack reasoned.

Venko and McGhee nodded their heads emphatically.

"True, very true." They said in unison.

"I do know one thing for sure," Haystack started.

"What's that, Haystack?" Venko played along.

"You are the Zen master of Paper, Scissors, Rock. Game over! Marley, you listen to Mr. Magoo and learn something." Haystack finished with a backslap hard enough to jolt Venko forward.

"Mr. Miyagi you mean, Mr. Magoo was a different, blind, Zen master," Venko gently corrected.

They took three minor reports for damaged property, backed up two other cars on calls, and headed for coffee just past 3:00 a.m. Upon arrival, Officer Tim "Who" Stanley waved them over to his booth. Officer Keyshawn Carmen slid over and Venko sat next to him.

Carmen was a ten-year veteran of the 7th Precinct. A veteran officer on midnights was a rare commodity. Most officers bid to another shift or precinct around the fifth year when they accumulated enough seniority to successfully escape. Carmen enjoyed the action and still had cousins living in the precinct. Midnight shift permitted him to work side jobs in the early morning hours to support his growing family. The Carmens had three boys and one girl with a fifth on the way. An African American, he was born and raised in the heart of the 7th Precinct. He knew everyone and was frequently called to help other officers negotiate disputes. He had an uncanny knack for detecting lies. Often, it only took the threat of "Keyshawn is coming," to get to the truth. Fellow officers referred to him frequently as "Poly," short for polygraph.

"How goes it Dan? Marley towing the line?" Carmen asked, holding his mug out as Ebony filled it.

"Almost had a DUI. Found a sober driver. Bunch of rich college kids from the Wing-Lutz gone adventure slumming in the 7th," Venko explained, wiping his brow in mock relief.

"Hipster douchebags, I hate the type," Stanley added.

"It gets better, what's the worst type of college student?" Venko asked rhetorically.

"Criminal justice majors," Carmen and Stanley said together, before going through the list of standard mantras hurled by criminal justice majors.

"You didn't read me my rights."

"What is your probable cause for the stop?"

"I know my rights!"

"You need a search warrant to search me or my car."

"I don't have to tell you my name."

"I'm going to college to be a detective." Venko listed his favorite.

"That's a classic, I love it when people think they can bypass uniform duty and go straight to detective," Stanley said and paused. "No glory in uniform, I suppose."

Ebony brought the pot of coffee over and refilled the cups after setting down a piece of apple pie in front of Stanley.

"Keep eating like that Who, and you won't look like every other cop, and pretty soon, you'll actually have to answer for the complaints on you," Venko said with a smile.

"I know, but I gotta keep my strength up," Stanley said as he cut into the warm pie with his fork.

The conversation bounced between precinct gossip and sports until Carmen attempted to bring Marcus 'Marley' McGhee in.

"Marley, I hear you played some high school hoops."

"Mostly sat on the bench," McGhee responded with a smile and shrug.

Carmen could tell McGhee was uncomfortable in front of veteran officers.

"You were a west-sider? West High School, I'm guessing roughly five years ago, you like 22 or 23 now?"

"Yup," McGhee said with a nod.

"Me too! I was ten years ahead of you though. Coach Lincoln still there, or was he gone by then?" Carmen asked.

"Still there," McGhee said quietly, sipping his coffee.

"Good dude," Carmen added.

"What about you, Who, you ever catch a touchdown pass back in the day as a 140-pound flanker?" Venko chided Stanley in an attempt to deflect uncomfortable attention away from McGhee.

"I was 160, not the chiseled 172 pounds you see before you today. And yes, many touchdowns, they called me 'White Lightening.'" Stanley said with a grin.

"Bullshit," Carmen shot back.

"Seconded, but I can see at least one pregnant cheerleader your brother unfairly got blamed for back then," Venko remarked before draining his cup.

Stanley chuckled.

"Dan, did they have helmets when you played?"

"Yes, some experimental leather helmets, no face masks though. Remember boys and girls, this was the land before time. No cell phones, we made do with VCR's, land lines, answering machines and navigational aids called paper maps," Venko finished and smiled.

"Fucking medieval," Carmen said matter-of-factly, before dropping a few dollars on the table.

"Time for a bathroom break before resuming super-hero crime fighting."

Stanley tossed a dollar down before heading towards the bathroom.

"Good call," McGhee said and followed Stanley.

Venko tossed two singles down and had made it out the front door when Carmen grabbed his elbow.

"Something is off with your boy Marley. Coach Lincoln is my cousin. He quit coaching when Marley was in grade school. West is a basketball school, everyone knows that. You sure as hell would know who your coach is. Something isn't quite right here," Carmen finished in a low whisper.

"Poly, sometimes your radar may be a little off. Maybe he got kicked off the team, or hell, didn't make the team. Wouldn't be the first time someone exaggerated their high school athletic prowess. I get the impression he had some issues as a kid. Maybe he tells a few white lies to fit in. Maybe he was a complete washout as an athlete and was actually the star of the glee club. Who cares, I have to finish training him either way," Venko stopped abruptly as McGhee and Stanley walked into the parking lot.

"Watch your back," Carmen whispered after McGhee passed him and got in the driver's seat.

Venko pulled up waiting calls on the car's computer and saw the abandoned vehicle call was two blocks away.

"Advise dispatch we are gonna take the abandoned car at Clove Alley and Longfellow."

McGhee notified dispatch and put the microphone back in the holder before speaking.

"You want to take an abandoned vehicle?"

"Yes, for starters it's close. Second, we have been getting hit semi-regularly with break-ins over by the waterfront. More importantly, most burglars don't park their cars right in front of the place they are going to hit. They stash them and walk to the location," Venko added with sarcasm.

Two minutes later, McGhee notified dispatch on the radio that they had found the car parked in the alley just off Longfellow. The vehicle was an older rusted, navy-blue Chevy Tahoe. Venko and McGhee approached cautiously, the windows of the Chevy were heavily tinted. After determining that the vehicle was unoccupied, Venko opened the passenger door and noted the broken housing around the steering column.

"Column is peeled, it's stolen. You pull the VIN off the dash and run it. I'll start the inventory search," Venko directed.

Per the official procedure, every towed vehicle had to be searched and inventoried. This was to protect the officers from later being accused of theft. Officers were required to check the vehicle by the vehicle identification number or VIN, located on the door frame or the base of the windshield in addition to running the license plate.

Venko began the process of sifting through fast food bags and liquor bottles scattered on the floorboards. A siren blast startled him and he stood up suddenly, hitting his head on the interior of the Chevy.

"That never gets old!" Officer Stein said laughing from the driver's seat of Car 2.

Venko could hear the muffled screams of the female in the back of Stein's car. The front seat partition was pulled closed and the rear windows were up, but the woman was bobbing back and forth, obviously angry.

Stein and Fitzpatrick turned to the passenger and screamed in unison, "Shut up!"

This temporarily startled and silenced the woman.

Stein turned back to Venko and calmly asked, "What have you got there?"

"Column peeled, probably a fresh stolen. No big deal, just going to do the inventory and tow it. What transgression has your young lady committed?" Venko said and waved to the guest in the back of Car 2, setting off a wave of obscenities.

"Really, Dan?" Stein said and then back fisted the partition without looking back. A brief silence followed and she continued. "Stripper-gram came out of the meth house at 232 Parkwood, drove her VW right through a stop sign in front of us. Fitz saw her stuffing something madly down the front of her pants when we walked up to her car. She had an outstanding warrant for drug abuse and Sgt. Miller green-lit me to do a strip search on her at the precinct. I think she stuffed a gram or two up in her hoohaa."

Stein could see by McGhee's glance, that he wasn't fully versed in street parlance.

"Marley, you have not heard the term hoohaa? Money maker? Street purse?"

"Oh, right," McGhee said awkwardly.

"Yes, that's right, the vagina, preferred storage of female meth-heads everywhere. Dan, you only have a few more weeks to get Marley fully bilingual in 7th Precinct dialect," Stein finished.

"Baby steps, Rachel, baby steps," Venko shot back.

"Time to head in and put the claw to use," Stein made a clawing motion with her gloved right hand and cackled obnoxiously loud, before driving off.

Venko resumed searching the backseat area of the Chevy. He pulled a small shoebox out from under the driver's seat. He opened it and whistled. He quickly counted out $4,750 in cash and guessed the sandwich baggie contained about two ounces of tightly compressed marijuana. McGhee heard the whistle and walked over to Venko, who then handed him the box.

"I counted $4,750 in cash and I'm guessing about two ounces of weed. We can weigh it at the station. I need you to do a second count of the cash so we can tag it into found property."

Venko resumed searching the backseat area of the car. McGhee finished counting and nodded to Venko.

"I got $4,750 as well," he added.

Venko finished the inventory search and completed the tow report and was waiting in the car for the tow truck when his cell phone chimed.

"Who is texting you at 4:30 in the morning?" McGhee asked curiously.

Venko flipped open his phone and saw the message from Sarah.

Had a weird dream, hope you're ok, safe and warm. SS

"Sarah, uh, my lady friend, as you like to say. How do I respond to this?" Venko said, showing the message to McGhee.

"Well it better be something more meaningful than thanks," McGhee said with a chuckle, then watched as Venko struggled with the phone's numeric keypad. McGhee snatched the phone from Venko.

"Jesus, I can't watch you fumble your fat fingers into a one-word response. Let me do it," McGhee offered sincerely.

"No, I don't need any Cyrano to speak for me," Venko argued.

"Who?"

"Never mind, I realize you don't read anything on paper," Venko said, trying to snatch the phone back.

"Let me lay down some smooth chocolate charm," McGhee said and started typing.

"Uh, we are kinda vanilla folks, occasionally some butter pecan if I'm feeling crazy," Venko said nervously.

McGhee quickly finished the reply and hit the send key before handing Venko back the phone. Venko read the reply and sighed heavily.

"Really? That's chocolate charm?" He looked at the message again.

No worries Baby Gurl, I always come home to you.

"Well since she didn't immediately respond, we can assume she fell asleep and will get that little gem in the morning," Venko explained as the tow truck pulled up.

Twenty minutes later they were slowly driving along Birch Circle.

"Did you see that? Black male, dark hoodie, just tucked against the side of that duplex as we rolled by. Turn around and go over one block to Dogwood and sit at the corner. Let's see if he takes the cut-through and pops out. If he does, we'll stop him," McGhee complied with Venko's instructions and parked with the lights out at the corner of Dogwood and Hedges.

A few of the streetlights still worked and McGhee could see a figure a block up, creeping through front yards on Dogwood. The suspect was headed in the opposite direction and didn't see the blacked-out cruiser slowly approaching. With the snow starting to fall heavier, Venko knew they would be able to track him if he ran. The suspect continued at a brisk walking pace towards the boarded-up corner store.

"When he gets in the old 7-11 lot, stop him," Venko instructed.

A few seconds later, McGhee turned on the overhead lights and threw the car in park.

"Sir, hold up sir, we want to talk to you for a second," McGhee called out.

The man was an ex-convict and he stopped and turned towards McGhee who was forty feet away and closing. He did a quick mental appraisal of the situation.

The young officer would no doubt catch me if I ran. I can take him, but I'm not sure if I could shake him before the old guy caught up. The old cop is thick and still has suspicious eyes. His jacket is scuffed and worn, and he just put his ski cap in his pocket. He has thrown some punches. Definitely prepared.

The three-time felon decided to try and talk first, if that failed, well, he wasn't going back to prison on some chicken-shit parole violation.

"What did I do? What did I do? Why are you stopping me?" The felon shouted at McGhee, who was initially startled by the outburst. McGhee immediately put both of his hands in front of him in a calming gesture before speaking.

"Whoa, whoa, dude we just want to talk to you, and you will be on your way. I'm Officer McGhee and this is my partner Officer Venko," he said in a calm voice. The felon continued to step backwards as McGhee and Venko approached. Venko stayed to McGhee's left side, correctly assuming the suspect would be right-handed and likely to start any attack from that side. The suspect stopped backing up when he brushed up against the boarded-up window. McGhee and Venko stopped, leaving about six feet between them and the suspect.

"Jasper Williams, go ahead and run me. I ain't got any warrants, so leave me the fuck alone," the felon shouted at McGhee.

"Okay, Mr. Williams, just thought it was a little strange you were over on Birch Circle after 4 a.m. and cut through the back yards to Dogwood," McGhee explained in a soothing tone, never breaking eye contact.

Venko watched McGhee work and knew there was going to be trouble. He noted McGhee was doing his best to de-escalate the situation but in his zeal to maintain eye contact and develop a rapport, he wasn't watching the suspect's hands and failed to notice his body language. Venko knew this was symptomatic of many newer officers. The department, in the face of mounting pressure from a handful of high-profile violent encounters, began shifting recruit training to emphasize de-escalation techniques, at the expense, Venko thought, of officer safety.

Williams, while appearing to be listening to McGhee, glanced behind McGhee and over to Venko with short, nervous head turns. Williams pulled his hands from the front pocket of his hoodie and dropped them to his sides, clenching and unclenching his fists as he gave McGhee an address on Dogwood that Venko knew didn't exist. Venko quietly slid another foot closer to Williams as McGhee continued asking questions in a soothing tone, oblivious to Venko's maneuvering.

"Mr. Williams, you don't have any weapons or narcotics on your person, do you?" McGhee asked calmly.

Venko saw the almost imperceptible movement of Williams' right hand from his right hip, around to the small of his back.

It was done in a smooth, slow movement as Williams responded, "No I'm clean, I don't have anything."

With a surprising burst, Venko closed the gap and threw a straight left that connected with the side of Williams' face. A split second after the audible pop, the felon's knees buckled and he dropped to a kneeling position. Venko shoved Williams face-first into a prone position and handcuffed him.

McGhee stood in muted shock, his arms still frozen in front of him, palms out.

"What the hell, Dan? You just crack the dude?" McGhee said, and helped Venko assist the dazed Williams to a seated position. Williams slowly shook his head, attempting to lift the deep fog that enveloped him. His nose was starting to bleed from the impact with the concrete. The biting cold wind kept the blood flow minimal.

"Son-of-a-bitch, that - that was a punch," Williams mumbled.

"You're on your own on this one," McGhee said, stunned by what he saw.

"Well, let me explain something very important to you Marcus. This man has been down before. While you were busy de-escalating and making eye contact, you weren't watching his hands. He was looking at you, me, and behind us. He was calculating his exit route, and whether it went through you or me. He sized you up in a matter of seconds, he watched you, your hands, your eyes, listened to your voice and directions, and thought, social worker. In those seconds of interaction with you, you missed his right hand sliding behind his back."

McGhee's eyes grew wide as Venko pulled a partially rusted, small semi-automatic pistol from the back of Williams' jeans. Venko depressed the magazine release and removed the magazine. It could hold six rounds but only contained three. Venko worked the slide and ejected a live round from the chamber.

"Shit," McGhee mumbled, his shoulders visibly slumped.

"He would have shot you before you could get your gun out of your holster. Action is always faster than reaction," Venko stopped preaching to look at the knuckles on his left hand. Nothing seemed amiss.

"What if it wasn't a gun? What if he was pulling out his driver's license?" McGhee asked.

"Then I have to explain why I knocked a couple of fillings loose. But license or gun, we go home without any blood loss and our pictures stay off the precinct wall. I don't want the honor guard handing your mom a flag and the chief telling her what a great de-escalator you were. I don't know about you, but I want to go out swinging, not talking. I'm not worried about a punch, after twenty-two years, I've gotten pretty good at typing," Venko finished and keyed his mobile radio and requested EMS to his location and a sergeant.

"If you knew he had a gun, why didn't you shoot him?" McGhee asked, playing the last few minutes over in his head.

"I didn't know he had a gun. I did know, nothing good ever comes from someone trying to reach behind him without being ordered to do so. He wasn't reaching for a Snickers to share with us, that's for sure! Look around, we have no cover to retreat to, and we are too close to him to engage in a gunfight. If we all pulled our guns and started blazing away, he might have missed, then again, he might have hit one of us. At this distance, it's smarter to keep him from getting to the gun or knife or whatever he was trying to combat draw."

"Shit Dan, I'm sorry," A visibly shaken McGhee stated quietly.

"Marcus, understand that some people you can talk to and reason with. And by all means, talk and de-escalate the shit out of them. There are some people, like Mr. Williams who only see time, time to formulate a plan of action while you're talking. He is betting his freedom that you are new and soft and I'm old, fat and lazy. He guessed wrong," Venko patted the shoulder of the still woozy, seated Williams.

Car 1, with lights flashing and sirens blaring, began a sideways slide through the light snow into the parking lot. The slide stopped three feet from the back of Venko's cruiser. Bianchi and Martinez jumped out and ran up.

"What happened, Dan?" Martinez asked excitedly.

"We saw Mr. Willams duck by a duplex on Birch Circle as we rolled by. We figured he was up to no good and waited over on Dogwood with lights out. Sure enough he took the cut, through the backyards and popped out on Dogwood. Me and Marley thought we should talk to him on account of this bad weather. You know, see if he needed a ride or a hot cup of coffee. He decided to repay our hospitality by reaching for this piece of shit *pistola*. No worries, me and Marcus took care of things," Venko finished and held up the gun.

"Fucking sweet!" Bianchi whooped.

"Can you guys do me a favor? Backtrack his footprints through the cut and see if he dropped anything when he saw us on Birch?" Venko asked.

"No problem Dan," Martinez responded, and the pair began following the fresh footprints.

"Thanks Dan," McGhee said as he watched Bianchi and Martinez heading away.

"For what? There's no reason to embarrass you in front of them. They know what they need to know. One day, you'll be in my shoes.

I hope you remember this. And now the circus begins," Venko said as the ambulance arrived along with Miller and the omnipresent Haystack, filling the frigid air with a cacophony of sirens.

At 8:05 a.m. Venko and McGhee were into an hour of overtime to complete the paperwork on Williams. Bianchi called ten minutes after leaving the scene to tell Venko that he recovered a small pry bar, most likely dropped by Williams when he first encountered Venko's cruiser on Birch Circle. The duplex had fresh pry marks on the side window. They most certainly had interrupted a burglary in progress. This news somewhat alleviated Venko's growing fatigue. Just then his cellphone chirped. He opened it and read Sarah's message.

Dan, your phone has been stolen. SS

Venko looked to his left at McGhee, who was busy typing on the computer next to him, and sighed.

Chapter 6
Weasels and Rats, Oh My!

One week after the arrest of Jasper Williams, Officer Marcus 'Marley' McGhee strolled into the reception area of Internal Affairs on the 3rd floor of the modern Central Precinct building. Even after being off two nights, he still had difficulty functioning during the morning. He received a text message from Lt. Blake Tremblay last night, directing him to report to Internal Affairs at 10 a.m.

McGhee struggled the first couple of weeks on the midnight shift with his sleep patterns. If he left work on time, just before 7 a.m., he would be home by 7:40 a.m. It generally took him about two hours to unwind and fall asleep. On his days off, he might roll back by an hour or two, but he generally struggled to fall asleep by 5 a.m. A 10 a.m. meeting was brutal. On the two prior occasions he had to meet with prosecutors to discuss misdemeanor cases, he found it easier to just stay awake, rather than risk oversleeping. He found the shift to be exhausting so far and wondered how anyone would voluntarily remain working such miserable hours. Initially, the action and excitement were worthwhile. Lately, the desire for normal sleep was winning.

"Officer Marcus McGhee, here to see Lt. Tremblay. I have an appointment at ten," he stated in a courteous tone.

"I'll let him know you are here, please have a seat," Frannie Wright responded with a warm smile and motioned him to a row of soft leather-backed chairs next to a dark, wooden coffee table, covered with magazines. She quietly slid open the center drawer of her desk and took out her cell phone and sent a text message to Swanson.

FYI, McGhee is here to see the Weasel. I have the file you requested, but you have to come over to pick it up. ;)

Lt. Blake Tremblay supervised a team of Internal Affairs investigators out of the Central Precinct. Investigators were all the rank of sergeant and were handpicked for the job. The majority of investigators working for Tremblay were honest and hard-working. The old adage was still true, if you wanted to work for Internal Affairs, you probably shouldn't. Most of those assigned to the job were tapped on the shoulder by a captain or major that recognized their individual qualities of honesty, integrity and a deep commitment to the department. Most also realized that turning down such an offer was career suicide.

Tremblay shared none of the traits the majority of his subordinates possessed. Tremblay saw the position as a stepping stone to a captain's promotion, and openly lobbied for the lieutenant's position in Internal Affairs, commonly referred to by its initials, IA. His career to date, was wholly unremarkable. Tremblay spent his five years as a patrolman writing parking tickets and equipment citations. Cracked windshield citations were his favorite, and while he certainly increased city coffers with fines and fees, he did little to impact street crime.

Tremblay was promoted to sergeant and immediately assigned temporarily to Community Relations. This caused rampant speculation about how he avoided night shift patrol duty. The consensus was his participation in the summer golf league with several captains and three deputy chiefs. The temporary assignment lasted over two years. Sgt. Tremblay was adept at producing recruitment videos, speaking to various community groups, and supervising the background investigations of potential officers. He was a political animal by nature and could adroitly read the whims of the current administration.

It wasn't all smooth sailing for the sergeant. His irksome, overbearing micro-managing supervision style caused problems in Community Relations. Disagreements with his own background investigators caused three of them to request an early termination of their assignments and a transfer back to their precincts. Long-simmering disputes came to a head when Tremblay overruled the hiring decisions made on three police recruits. Investigators provided compelling evidence in two cases for dropping the recruits from the eligibility list and he overruled them and kept the candidates. In the third case, he dropped a candidate that had been overwhelmingly recommended. Rumors swirled around why the two candidates were retained, but nothing concrete ever materialized. The investigators' decisions were partially vindicated two years later when one of the disputed candidates was arrested for accepting cash payments to look the other way when two local bars remained open past 2:30a.m. The owner of one of the bars provided Vice detectives with a ledger, revealing the payments and the dates that the corrupt officer tipped off the owner, two hours prior to Vice raids.

Eventually, word leaked that the dropped candidate was the stepson to the political rival of Councilman Maury Rogers. Rogers was a longtime family friend of the late Councilman Walter Sellers, father of Captain Brian Sellers.

Tremblay was promoted to lieutenant at the relatively young age of 32. He spent his first year working in the Training Bureau, assisting in the operation of the police academy. A short time later, retirements created several openings and he was chosen for the IA post.. He was now tasked with investigating misconduct and policy violations mostly involving uniform patrol officers, a group he had no experience supervising.

Frannie knocked on the frosted glass of the door, just above Lieutenant B. Tremblay's silver and black nameplate. Without waiting for a response, she opened the door a crack. Sellers immediately stopped talking and shot her a disapproving glare.

"What is it Fran?" Tremblay responded tersely.

"Officer McGhee is here to see you," she said with her best fake smile.

"Tell him it will be a few minutes," Tremblay said with a dismissive flick of his wrist, indicating she should close the door.

Sellers resumed his conversation.

"What were the results of the integrity test?"

"I was able to pull up the evidence and found property reports for that night," Tremblay began. "It looks like Officer McGhee logged $4,750 in US currency and 1.8 ounces of marijuana into the evidence vault at the end of the shift the same night."

"Are those amounts correct?" Sellers asked, hoping they weren't.

"Well, yes," Tremblay responded knowing it wasn't what Sellers wanted to hear.

Integrity tests had fallen somewhat out of favor in the body worn camera age, where nearly everything was recorded. The tests were designed to see if an officer was honest. Normally the simplest test consisted of sending an officer out for a found property call, a purse, a wallet, or duffle bag. Any item could be used as bait. Generally, miscellaneous items of little value were included along with cash or jewelry, the real bait. The officers were then filmed during the call, and the evidence and found property reports scrutinized later. If the valuables turned up missing and not logged into the evidence vault, the officer was called in and questioned.

Tremblay brought integrity tests back with a vengeance under his watch. He knew exposing corruption, even at the lowest level, would raise his profile, his ticket to promotions. He also began to focus on policy violations, which in his opinion, were long neglected. In a lengthy, condescending memo, he instructed his investigators to also list policy violations while conducting quarterly, body-worn camera audits. These violations on midnight shift usually included the wearing of non-regulation ski-caps in the winter, as well as the use of profanity when dealing with the public.

Prior to Tremblay's arrival, his predecessors understood that a certain common-sense flexibility was necessary. Every precinct and shift dealt with a different type of citizen. Midnight shift in the 7th Precinct required a direct approach, one that included the use of some necessary profanity, in order to converse in an honest manner with the hard-scrabble residents of the 7th Precinct. Tremblay saw this as an opportunity to raise his profile within the current administration.

Profanity and uniform violations were an easy target. He was able to sell the sudden surge in violations as a way to make the department more professional and create a culture of integrity, especially on the younger, more impressionable night shifts.

Despite their age difference, Tremblay and Sellers were kindred spirits, both self-absorbed and consumed with irrelevant minutiae. When contacted by Sellers a month ago about his concern over the culture on the midnight shift in the 7th Precinct, Tremblay was eager to assist someone like-minded in their dogged pursuit of police professionalism. The meeting today was to assess the progress of the project, and explore the findings of the undercover source.

"Sgt. Lockesly videotaped the entire incident," Trembly explained, pointing to the monitor that was replaying the call Venko and McGhee took a week ago.

Tremblay clicked the mouse and stopped the video as Venko was searching the backseat area of the dark blue Chevy Tahoe.

"This is the point where Venko discovers the box with the money and dope. We can't see him count it, but we figure that's what he is doing. Here, he alerts McGhee to his findings. McGhee is in the car as instructed, giving Venko the space to make his own decision on what to do with the money and dope. McGhee did a nice job of staying clear. Venko hands McGhee the box and tells him to count the money, which he does. The seal we put on the dope was never broken, and it's the same packaging we use. We checked and Sgt. Lockesly's initials are still visible under black light," Tremblay finished and turned from the monitor to Sellers.

"Are we sure $4,750 is the amount we started with?" Sellers asked with a slight smile.

Tremblay grew suddenly uncomfortable when he realized the suggestion Sellers was making.

"Captain, Sgt. Lockesly and Sgt. Johnson counted out the bait money in my presence and they have already added it to the investigative report," Tremblay answered, subtly suggesting any falsification of the amount would require collusion beyond the current occupants of his office.

"Of course, of course, I'm just being thorough," Sellers remarked, in full backtrack mode.

"Let's bring McGhee in and see if he has uncovered anything significant," Tremblay suggested, and pressed the intercom to advise Frannie to send in McGhee.

McGhee walked into the office and was directed to a chair next to Sellers. They exchanged greetings before Sellers began.

"Officer McGhee, I appreciate what you are doing in my precinct. I am determined to change the culture on midnight shift in the 7th Precinct. In order to do that, I need boots on the ground intelligence to determine how to correct the supervision and identify the troublemakers. I know Venko is one of the de-facto leaders on the shift, and a known malcontent," Sellers paused and allowed Tremblay to speak.

"Marcus, walk us through what happened with the Chevy Tahoe and the drugs and money."

McGhee was handpicked for this assignment by Tremblay with Sellers' approval. McGhee was intelligent and social enough to blend in anywhere. At the initial meeting a month ago, McGhee was given a spectacular recruiting pitch. Tremblay knew if McGhee turned down the assignment, there was a good chance he would talk, and any opportunity to use a different undercover source would be lost. It was a gamble, but Tremblay was correct, he could appeal to McGhee's sense of integrity. He also understood that McGhee was new and most likely had ambition beyond working uniform patrol on night shift. This was another angle he would pursue. McGhee was told his actions would long be remembered as heroic, and that he could be the person that initiated long-overdue change; change that could remold the 7th Precinct. Tremblay stepped up his pitch, pulling out several folders filled with egregious police misconduct, all of which could have been prevented by one honest cop stepping forward.

Ironically, none of those incidents involved 7th Precinct officers, a detail that was intentionally left out. Tremblay explained that McGhee would be transferred to midnights in the 7th Precinct, where he would be assigned to Venko for his last phase of training. Sellers was present at the meeting and showed Venko's personnel file to McGhee, including a number of complaints and uses of force. Sellers correctly assumed that McGhee would not flip to the last page of the internal investigations and discover the majority of the complaints were dismissed and the uses of force were justified. Sellers used the volume of complaints alone to portray Venko as "out of control." The ploy worked. Sellers and Tremblay instructed McGhee to document unusual incidents and be prepared to discuss them when called upon.

Sitting in the same office again made McGhee uncomfortable. He quickly saw the midnight officers in the 7th Precinct for what they were, a group of hard working, under-appreciated street cops. Venko was a leader on the shift, and the person that had saved his ass. It didn't take a genius to see he had been sold a bill of goods and this charade was a slyly veiled personal vendetta. McGhee felt trapped and began to perspire. He recounted the handling of the drugs and money found in the Chevy Tahoe. Neither Tremblay or Sellers showed much interest and gave only an occasional nod. When asked about other incidents, McGhee paused nervously, then recounted the tale of the Rock, Paper, Scissors DUI that included a pop trivia quiz. The end result being a sober driver awarded control of the car and a moving violation for the original driver. Tremblay and Sellers looked at each other in total disbelief. Tremblay frantically started jotting down notes in his notebook. Sellers calmly asked for additional details.

McGhee explained that he had tested the driver himself and was not convinced that he was over the limit. He explained that Venko was right in not wanting to tie up a car for hours in a busy area plagued with burglaries. Sellers, obviously not interested in his opinion, asked him to talk about any other incidents.

McGhee began recalling the arrest of Jasper Williams. Tremblay stopped him a few minutes into the story.

"Officer Venko punched him? Without provocation? Did Williams do anything to instigate this assault?"

McGhee immediately grew concerned with Tremblay's use of the word assault. Although he was new to the department, he was well aware that terms such as use of force, subduing, or controlling were generally used when officers took justified physical action while making an arrest. The use of the term assault, instantly indicated to McGhee that Venko would not get the same courtesy other officers got in similar situations.

"Williams was reaching behind his back, Dan caught it, I didn't. The guy had a gun!" McGhee responded, becoming increasingly louder as his agitation grew.

"Neither of you knew that's what he had at the time," Sellers stated calmly, before continuing. "What was your probable cause for the stop of Williams?"

"We saw him duck behind a duplex on Birch Circle when we drove past. Dan guessed correctly that he would take the cut through the backyards and end up on Dogwood. Which he did. We stopped just to see what he was up to in a residential neighborhood after 4 a.m. He was very angry and seemed nervous," McGhee explained. "Turns out he was a burglar as well."

"Again, as Capt. Sellers stated, it's what Venko knew at the time of the stop, not what was found later. What I'm hearing is that Williams was stopped, gave you some attitude, and Venko exacted an immediate attitude adjustment on Williams, and then discovered the gun."

McGhee gave a look of pure astonishment, prompting Tremblay to continue.

"This is on Venko, we aren't blaming you, relax."

"Williams was reaching behind his back for the gun," McGhee said quickly.

"Did you see him do that?" Sellers asked, point blank.

"No, but I was busy talking to the guy, I missed the movement," McGhee was struggling between defending Venko and trying not to look incompetent in his actions that night. It was now apparent that Tremblay and Sellers only were concerned with Venko's activities.

Tremblay leaned back in his chair and rubbed his chin before responding.

"So Venko told you that he saw Williams reach behind his back. I think your recollection of events is clouded by the belief that Venko actually saw this phantom movement."

"For the purposes of this investigation, it might be better if McGhee just states he did not see any movement by Williams prior to being assaulted by Venko. It's cleaner if we just stop his statement there. It would be nice if we had body worn camera footage of this," Sellers interjected quickly.

"We just got four more in last week. Fran!" Tremblay shouted and Frannie opened the door seconds later.

"Yes," she responded in the doorway.

"Where are the four body-worn cameras that came in last week? I need two more over at the 7th Precinct."

"Captain Obermayer in the 2nd picked them all up yesterday," she responded coolly.

"What the fuck? Why didn't you tell me? Captain Sellers has been waiting forever," Tremblay snapped.

"Obermayer needed them all to outfit the extra reserve officers coming in for the anticipated protests at the abortion clinic over the next two weeks. The deputy chief emailed all of this information to you yesterday. Will that be all?" Frannie asked with a dripping sweetness.

"Fuck!" Tremblay exclaimed as Frannie closed the door.

He took a breath and started thinking aloud.

"Right now, I see several violations on the DUI stop, to say it was highly irregular would be an understatement. If my guys can get to the other passengers in the car, or to the bar where he was drinking, we might be able to show he was drunk and should have been arrested."

"Except, I gave him the sobriety test and I thought he might be close, but I didn't think he was over the legal limit based on my tests," McGhee interrupted.

"No offense Marcus, but you're new, no one expects you to be proficient at sobriety tests," Tremblay stated, blatantly dismissing McGhee before turning to Sellers and continuing.

"I think if we can get statements from the other passengers, or the bar, we can file charges on Venko for dereliction of duty. We can throw a bunch of policy violations at him for the clown show he put on with the female passenger. As for Williams, I need to see what kind of leverage we can get on him before trying to get his statement. I think we can go with a charge of excessive force on Venko if we can all maintain that Williams was just standing, talking with McGhee, when Venko punched him. The photo from Sgt. Miller's investigative package isn't very good. I need something with blood or copious amounts of swelling," Tremblay stopped when Sellers raised his palm.

"Sgt. Miller's investigation exonerated Venko's actions with Williams, he said the use of force was justified. That's going to be a problem," Sellers interjected logically.

"No, not a problem, Miller's investigation is based on Venko's statement. If we show that Williams was just standing there, and I think we can with McGhee stating he didn't see Williams move or reach," Tremblay was about to continue his thought when McGhee interrupted.

"Wait, just because I didn't see him reach for his gun, doesn't mean he didn't do it. Like I said, I was talking to him, I was focused on de-escalating the situation and his obvious anger," McGhee finished and glanced at both of them waiting for his comments to register.

There was a momentary pause and Sellers responded as if McGhee wasn't in the room.

"Could it be that Venko gave a false statement to Sgt. Miller? Is there a way to show that?" Sellers asked.

He knew Tremblay would realize the significance of that statement.

From day one in the academy, recruits are taught to be completely honest with Internal Affairs investigators. Lying during an investigation was a fire-able offense. A proven false statement was often much worse than the offense committed by the officers. Every officer knew this on day one and had heard of the names of at least three officers that were fired, not for the offense or policy violation committed, but for lying during the investigation. Tremblay thought about Sellers suggestion briefly.

"That would be really hard to prove without body-worn camera footage. I don't think it would fly. We can threaten to throw it on the pile at some later date if Venko's union representative starts to push back too hard on some of the charges," Tremblay finished and started scribbling additional notes in his notebook.

"Where does that leave us for now?" Sellers asked.

"For starters, I'll have a complaint typed up relating to the DUI and a separate one for the excessive force on Williams. I'll let you review them and then we will have McGhee sign it. Then we need to pull in Venko, interview him, and lock him into a statement. And obviously, without video, McGhee will need to be available, to give testimony and appear at any future discipline or appeals hearings."

McGhee had had enough. This was spiraling out of control. This was not what he was sold on in the first meeting. The time to speak was now.

"I don't need anyone to write a statement for me," he started, but was immediately interrupted by Tremblay.

"Marcus, we know you're an intelligent officer, but you lack experience in these matters. It's cleaner if we type up the statement, you just need to sign it, and affirm its accuracy at any subsequent discipline hearings."

"And that's another thing, I won't be testifying at any hearings, nor will I sign anything I didn't write," McGhee said and looked at Tremblay and Sellers for a response.

"Marcus, I'm sure Lt. Tremblay would look at any statement you draft and help you create one with the most impact," Sellers finished and Tremblay nodded emphatically in agreement.

McGhee knew bullshit when he heard it, and he was just tired enough to say it.

"What about the statement I draft, where I say Venko kept me from getting shot and is a good cop? Or the statement where I say, I wouldn't do things exactly the same, but the dude is an effective cop and actually cares?"

Sellers leaned forward and tried to remain calm in his response.

"Marcus, this is about changing the culture on midnights. In order to do that, you have to see the things Venko is doing are unprofessional, and influence a lot of young officers he works with. Would you want him to treat your sister like that poor young girl on the DUI stop? Would you want her humiliated and embarrassed like that? Is that professional?"

Sellers looked to Tremblay to move in with the heavy pitch.

"You were handpicked for this assignment. I believe you have the right moral compass to follow through. Being a change agent is tough, however, there are long-term rewards. Captain Sellers and I have already discussed getting you sent over to Narcotics or Vice when you complete your probationary period. Obviously, we would transfer you to another precinct during the investigation and any testimony we require from you. Usually, these things don't take long, once the officer is presented with all the evidence."

McGhee smiled.

"If you think Officer Venko will walk in here and resign or accept some long suspension, well, you don't know Venko at all."

Sellers had run out of patience.

"McGhee, just sign the statement and testify as needed. It's that simple. You have a college degree, a smart young cop like you can go places in this department. I can see to that. We have all invested a significant amount of time in this project. You can't just walk away now."

"I think when you got me to buy into this project, you honestly believed, and I sincerely mean it, you honestly believed it would uncover serious criminal offenses. When it didn't, you couldn't accept that. You wouldn't accept that. So, you're going to manufacture your own results. I will not sign any statement and will no longer be a part of this," McGhee finished and looked at Sellers, and now fully understood the depth of his vendetta.

"Just play ball," Tremblay pleaded.

Sellers had given up on the soft approach and started a different tactic.

"Officer McGhee, understand that you are in your probationary phase and as you are well aware, during this phase, the department needs little reason to terminate your employment. You are not fully protected until you complete your probation period. The 7th Precinct on midnights is not a fun place to be. As a matter of record, you are scheduled to go to the 2nd Precinct, on the afternoon shift. That was to be your final landing spot after you finish your training phase. Of course, the way things are going, and with the 7th being understaffed and all, I think I might have a say in keeping you in the 7th."

McGhee immediately understood the implied threat. His parents never wanted him to be a police officer anyway, they thought he was just going through some adventurous phase. They certainly didn't send him to a prestigious boarding school and four years in college to work as a civil servant requiring little more than a G.E.D. and a pulse. He knew he had options beyond the police department if they canned him. Like most twenty-two-year-old rookie cops, he was somewhat intimidated in the presence of two powerful supervisors. Knowing he had options gave him confidence, and he was a stubborn fighter. Sellers and Tremblay had somehow missed that quality when they were looking for a stooge for this investigation. His family had connections and he knew he would land on his feet, should things go bad. Today's meeting and what they were proposing struck McGhee as beyond dirty, he struggled to think of a term that would fit. Then it hit him, this was just *grimy*. He quickly crafted a response that would subtly convey his own threats in a way both Tremblay and Sellers would immediately recognize.

"Sirs, if you want to punish me for not agreeing to falsify my testimony, and let's call it what it is, you may do so. I realize I have little official recourse. If you do decide to fire me before I complete probation, understand that I will use the appeals process to the fullest, and this entire operation will be exposed in great detail. Granted, you may be believed over me, but it will be uncomfortable. As you are both familiar with my file and background, you know my father was the former attaché to the American Embassy in Jamaica. He has a lot of friends in this city, including a number of community activists that are deeply concerned with the racial disparity between the makeup of the community and the police department. They would most likely take interest in the dismissal of a twenty-two-year-old college graduate whose race is vastly under-represented in this department," McGhee stated.

He hated to use the race card in light of his privileged background, but then again, they got grimy first.

An uncomfortable silence hung in the air for nearly 30 seconds. In unique contrast, Tremblay grew pale, as Sellers turned crimson, in a muted fury. They both understood, very clearly, the message conveyed by McGhee. Sellers spoke in a slow whisper, hoping to contain the rage of a man who absolutely hated to lose.

"You little shit, who the fuck do you think you are? You want to stay in 7th? You've earned it! Understand if you were to mention this to anyone and it got back to the 7th, you would be persona non-grata. You would be a rat. You'd have no friends and getting backup might be difficult. Things might not only be difficult, but downright dangerous for you. Forget recommendations for any temporary assignments, you'll push a cruiser on midnights for as long as I'm captain and have a say. Optimistically, you might be able to bid to another precinct in five or six years when you have enough seniority. But something tells me staffing levels in the 7th won't permit losing anyone," Sellers finished and looked over at Tremblay who was closing his notebook and placing it back in his center desk drawer, in quiet resignation.

"Will that be all, sirs?" McGhee asked.

"Get out," Sellers responded before Tremblay was able to speak.

McGhee emerged from the elevator and quickly walked outside into the frigid blowing snow on the plaza in front of Central Precinct. He discovered he was sweating profusely. He felt confused, exhausted, nervous and something else. He took a deep breath and exhaled the frosty air. McGhee looked around the plaza and watched uniformed cops and plain clothes detectives scurry in and out of the building. Suddenly, he knew what he was feeling. Relief. Relief was washing over him. He couldn't tell Venko or anyone else in the 7th, but maybe, just maybe for once, he could finally be just a regular cop.

Chapter 7
Ducking Autocorrect

Sarah patiently explained the functions of the iPhone for the third time. She correctly assumed the only way Venko would come out of his technological cave, is if she dragged him kicking and screaming.

"Merry Christmas," she purred and kissed him on the cheek.

"It's December 5th," he replied grumpily.

"It's close enough, and a great way to start your work week tonight is with a shiny new smartphone! Now you can update your Facebook on the fly." She could barely get the words out without giggling.

Six months ago, she convinced Venko to create a Facebook profile. His effort consisted of posting a profile picture of Diablo sitting on the coffee table watching TV. His profile information was largely blank except for "occupation," where he listed City Trash Collector. Sarah, after much cajoling, convinced him to update his profile picture around Halloween. After holding out as long as he could, Venko posted another picture of Diablo, this time sitting next to a 3x5 notecard, with "Happy Halloween" written on it. This generated four thumbs up from random people that stumbled across the desolate wasteland that was his Facebook page.

"I can't believe you came all the way over here to give me a new phone. I appreciate it, but there really wasn't anything wrong with my old phone," Venko said sincerely.

"What else did I have to do on a Tuesday night at 9 o'clock? Oh! Before I forget, did I tell you I don't have to worry about prepping for a trial on Bishop?" She looked at him waiting on a flicker of recognition. None came.

"Wally Bishop, armed robbery, and most recently slapped with an abduction charge after the search warrant at his house turned up blood evidence from the Dakota Billings disappearance. Bishop turned up dead in his jail cell," she paused and Venko jumped in.

"Ah, suicide. Those kiddie snatchers don't do well confined," Venko remarked in a manner that Sarah knew indicated he was satisfied with that outcome.

"Yes, but the deputies at the jail are all puzzled by Bishop's level of determination, since he had twenty-six separate stab wounds," she watched as he slowly looked up from his phone.

"Uh, someone learned of his new charges I'm guessing, and they weren't gonna wait on a trial for a guilty verdict." Venko shrugged.

"Right, let's be honest, Bishop is no great loss to humanity. But I don't think he took Billings, and I'm not sure we will ever know what happened or find the kid," Sarah said in a somber tone.

Venko saw the look in her expression and measured his response carefully.

"Unfortunately, one day someone will run across Billings' remains. The likelihood that he is still alive after all this time is practically nil. I feel for his mother, that has to be brutal, just not knowing."

Sarah sat on Venko's lap and grabbed the iPhone.

"Let me show you how to use emojis!"

She looked at Venko and recognized his glazed-over, blank expression. The same look she received when she last offered him the opportunity to accompany her shoe shopping. Unfazed, she continued her lesson.

"Emojis are like shortcuts. See, little kissy faces, hearts, thumbs up, all ways to say 'Sarah, I miss you, I was thinking about you, can't wait to see you again,'" she cooed in his ear.

"Is there one that says I'm hungry?" Venko grunted.

"Ugh, there is a romantic buried somewhere in there," she responded, smacking his head playfully as she stood up.

Venko began putting on his uniform as she periodically stopped him to show him how to use various features on the phone. He assured her there was no reason to explain the different camera filters, because he was definitely not taking any selfies, and was pretty sure Diablo looked the same in portrait mode as in standard mode.

Sarah convinced Venko to let her drop him off at work instead of walking. Venko locked the apartment door and immediately felt an odd, sinking feeling. He put his keys in his jacket pocket and stopped. Sarah immediately sensed something was wrong.

"Dan, what is it, are you okay?"

"I, I think so, just felt odd for a second. I'm okay now," He lied and glanced down the hall. Everything was so quiet. A dull throb started in the pit of his stomach.

No, not quite, it's beyond quiet, it's still. Something is very wrong.

He didn't smell coffee and he didn't hear the faint strains of static-filled salsa music from a battered portable radio. The bistro table sat lifeless.

Sarah grabbed his hand and stopped him mid-stride.

"Are you okay?"

"Miss Rosales isn't sitting at the table tonight." He immediately realized how strange that sounded.

She wasn't always outside when he left for work. Most of the time, but there were lots of nights when she wasn't. But tonight, felt different.

Tonight was different. He knew. He felt it.

"She isn't out every night. Do you want to check on her?" Sarah asked, more concerned about Venko's look of confusion.

Venko took a step towards her apartment door, then stopped.

"No, I'm sure she is fine," he smiled and put his arm around Sarah as they headed down the stairs.

Sarah wheeled the grey Volvo in front of the crumbling steps of the 7th Precinct twenty minutes earlier than Venko normally arrived. He gave her a quick kiss and opened the door. She grabbed and pulled at his left arm, stopping him from exiting.

"Hey, please be careful tonight," she forced a smile.

Venko could see real concern flash from her green eyes. He felt himself flush under the attention. Venko squeezed her hand and smiled.

"Nothing to worry about. How about I meet you for a breakfast bucket of biscuits and gravy in the morning?" He saw her grin at the invitation.

"Sure," she responded with a warm chuckle. "Go now," She instructed and he closed the car door and drifted up the steps.

Venko walked inside and watched Sarah drive away from the window. He walked over to the bench and sat down. He realized his breathing was labored and he was starting to sweat.

Something is off, something isn't right.

Dex grasped him on the shoulder, startling Venko, causing him to jump backwards.

"Sorry man, I thought you heard me. You okay?" Dex asked.

"Yeah, just felt a bit off for a moment, I'm okay now, really. Anything going on?" Venko asked, changing the subject.

"You mean other than a major power outage in the 5th Precinct that hit about twenty minutes ago?" Dex stated as if Venko should know, then explained. "Bad snowstorm coming, wind has already picked up, I guess that could do it."

Venko nodded at this explanation.

Lt. Swanson walked through the door carrying a large manila envelope and stopped when he saw Venko and Mitchell on the bench. Swanson unwrapped his scarf and took off his gloves and shoved them in his pocket.

"Hey Dex. Dan, I need to see you in my office." Swanson continued up the stairs without waiting for a response.

"This can't be good," Venko whispered to Dex and headed after Swanson.

Venko walked into Swanson's office, closed the door and sat down. Swanson went to the door, cracked it open and peeked down the hall before shutting it again. Swanson hung up his coat and opened the large manila envelope.

"What's with the cloak and dagger, Cal?" Venko asked with growing concern.

Swanson took a deep breath.

"Frannie finally got me the file I was waiting on. Marcus McGhee is actually Marcus McGhee-Parker. McGhee is his mother's maiden name." Swanson paused to gauge Venko's reaction.

"What is this, Cal?" Venko asked, with a heavy sigh.

Swanson glanced up from the contents of the file to look at Venko.

"It gets worse, much worse. McGhee's online presence is completely fabricated. It's a front. Frannie showed me last night. Any online communication via Facebook or Instagram to McGhee's page is routed to computer terminal 6, Internal Affairs Office."

He let the last three words sink in. Venko felt the throb in the pit of his stomach growing.

"He is a plant? I'm being set up?" Venko asked with growing anger.

"I'm afraid so. Frannie warned me not to pull up his in-house employment file. Anyone doing that is automatically flagged in IA. I pulled Marcus's file up on the computer when I first heard we were getting him. That's no big deal, a supervisor getting a new cop would most likely do that. But if I do it now, Tremblay in IA gets an alert sent to his phone and I would most likely be answering questions at some time in the future."

"What the fuck is going on here?" Venko asked, throwing up his arms.

Swanson pulled a folder from the file cabinet behind him.

"Here is the page I printed out when McGhee first got here. Like every new guy that comes to the 7th, I start a shift folder. It tells us what they want us to know about McGhee."

He handed the folder to Venko.

"Now compare it to his real background," Swanson handed Venko the folder stamped "Confidential" in red ink across the front. "Look at his current assignment."

Venko opened the confidential folder and saw McGhee's photo at the top. He scanned down the page, starting at the top. McGhee was listed as temporarily assigned to Internal Affairs by Lt. Tremblay as of a month ago. At the conclusion of the investigation,

McGhee was to transfer to the 2nd Precinct, afternoon shift on a permanent basis.

McGhee's real background was radically different from what he had leaked out to the shift through casual conversation. He graduated from a prestigious east coast prep school where he was an honors student and an outstanding lacrosse player. McGhee went on to college and graduated with a major in Economics, and a minor in Sociology. He was the only child of Eralia McGhee and Addison Parker. Parker and McGhee met in Jamaica where he was an attaché to the US Embassy and she was a schoolteacher. They were married a year later and moved back to the U.S. at the conclusion of his assignment. His parents supported his decision to become a police officer, but were disappointed that he would be putting off law school.

A summary of the first meeting between Tremblay and Sellers was also included. This occurred prior to the selection of McGhee as the undercover investigator. In this summary, Sellers lists problems on the shift and believes Venko is the ringleader of a shift that, "devolved into a fraternity of thrill-seeking, violent, disrespectful adrenaline junkies."

The third page contained operational details of the investigation. McGhee's artificial background story, the creation and maintenance of fake social media accounts, as well as the creation of his fake departmental background file. Tremblay assigned two investigators to monitor all activity on McGhee's social media accounts and to flag anyone exploring his personnel file.

The integrity test was selected based on Venko's past assignments in Vice and assisting Narcotics. McGhee was to monitor that test and report and document any other incidents of interest. In the event of uncovering a major criminal act in progress or of imminent danger, an emergency extraction plan was listed in detail.

"That son-of-a-bitch," Venko mumbled and closed the file.

"I pulled up the evidence reports, although I hated to even do that, I'm paranoid and think any reports by you or McGhee are flagged straight to IA. Good news is, no issue with the Chevy

Tahoe or its contents; you passed, and it had to eat at Sellers and Tremblay. Anything else you can think of that might cause us concern?" Swanson asked and watched Venko as he ran his meaty hands through his salt and pepper hair.

Venko thought about his time working with McGhee, both the arrests, and the routine reports.

"Cal, I can't think of anything off hand, but then again, I'm not exactly a traditionalist in terms of police work. So, I'm sure there are things that would not be Sellers or Tremblay approved. It just depends on how low they want to go and what McGhee has added to the equation." Venko stopped talking but continued to process everything.

"That's the thing. Per Frannie, McGhee met with Sellers and Tremblay this morning at IA. There was a lot of shouting following McGhee's departure. No one is happy with him over there. And then, there is this." Swanson handed Venko an email he printed out that he received today from Sellers.

Lt. Swanson,

Effective immediately, per Deputy Chief Hawthorne, Officer McGhee has been assigned permanently to the 7th Precinct upon completion of his probationary period. Please add him to the midnight shift roster and see that he is scheduled for training updates and range qualifications as needed.

Captain Sellers

"That doesn't sound like much of a reward. I thought he was going to afternoon shift in the 2nd Precinct?" Venko asked, genuinely puzzled by the email.

"Frannie couldn't hear much of the conversation, but Sellers was definitely pissed off after McGhee left. I suspect McGhee's immediate permanent assignment transfer from the 2nd to the 7th Precinct is the result of that meeting. Either McGhee didn't come through or they didn't like what he gave them. I'm never an optimist when it comes to Sellers, but if he isn't happy then it has to be good for you," Swanson explained.

"How do we find out what they have up their sleeve moving forward?" Venko asked, involuntarily clenching his fists.

Swanson caught the movement of Venko's hands and commented honestly.

"Well first, we won't learn anything if you start raining down those meat hooks on McGhee. We need to take things slow. Look for opportunities to have real conversations with him. Slowly try to figure out his game. What does he get out of this? What's his angle? See if you can get him talking about Sellers. What does he know about him? If they had a blow up today and things went sideways, he may drop hints in his opinion on Sellers. Above all, be patient, try to act normal," Swanson finished and looked at Venko and could see him drifting away.

"Dan, do you hear me? Patience. Be patient and act normal. We will get through this, we always do."

Venko looked up at Swanson.

"Yeah, I got it Cal, just a little pissed, be cool, be patient. Got it."

"Head over to roll call and get ready for the shift. I'm going to try and grab Miller before the shift starts and give him a heads up," Swanson finished and Venko left, leaving the door open.

Chapter 8
Assorted Chaotic Sundries

Four blocks away from Venko's growing anxiety, Walter Niles is enjoying his second Budweiser on his day off.

Nuts and Bolts was still primarily a cop's bar. The clientele started to be more inclusive five years ago when Frankie Tomasino took over the business from his aging father and founder, seventy-nine-year-old, retired sergeant, Sal "Tommy" Tomasino.

Frankie washed out of the police department during his probationary phase for several indiscretions. The details of those activities remain largely unknown, however, most cops understood some deal was cut, and that Frankie was strongly advised to resign immediately. He spent the next five years driving a trash truck before becoming involved in local union politics and running for union office. His career as an elected union official ended nine-months later, when he broke the jaw of a reporter from the Port Isley News-Lantern who had the audacity to ask Frankie about being seen with a city labor attorney at a strip club. This was not unusual, Frankie enjoyed strip clubs regularly. However, being in the company of a city attorney and mysteriously changing positions on a labor contract being offered, raised eyebrows. Unfortunately for the reporter, Frankie had been answering questions on the subject all day after a photo had mysteriously been posted on-line.

Although Frankie inherited his father's pugilistic prowess, he was completely devoid of his even temperament. The elder Tomasino became involved, and lots of favors were called in. The end result, criminal charges were reduced to a single misdemeanor assault and Frankie resigned his post to run the family business. Now, the bar catered to not only cops and firemen, but local blue-collar folks as well.

Wallace Baxter Jr. felt welcome at Nuts and Bolts. He would certainly stay if Frankie did not call in his $137 outstanding bar tab. Today was a complete disaster for Baxter. He received his notice that he was officially terminated from the Ford plant where he had worked the last 16 years. His last appeal had been used up and to make matters worse, the lawyer he hired to handle his third DUI this year had quit over not being paid.

Baxter was an alcoholic that hadn't quite hit bottom, though signs that his elevator was nearing the basement were abundant. His two children lived with their mother out of state and showed zero interest in him. His brother had turned off the cash faucet two months ago, realizing his loans were not paying bills. He was also facing the very real prospect of actually doing some jail time for this DUI.

Baxter initially engaged in small talk with the frail cop seated next to him at the bar. In short order, despite Baxter's general aversion to cops, he saw nothing intimidating in the socially awkward Niles, and the two chatted about sports with a fervor. When the conversation devolved into the wickedness of ex-wives, the two were truly kindred spirits. Niles bought his new friend his second Jack and Coke and he ordered another Budweiser. Frankie broke Niles's twenty and put the change in front of the pair before pouring the drinks.

Back at the 7th Precinct, Venko threw his war bag in the trunk and climbed into the driver's seat. Roll call was short, and the majority of it was spent updating officers on traffic conditions and the number of accident reports waiting due to the sudden winter storm. This caused an audible groan to ripple throughout the room. Officers knew they would spend considerable time standing in the single digit temperatures and blowing snow, directing traffic around the various crash sites. Venko was seething and found McGhee's incessant small talk annoying. Getting through the shift in some sort of casual mode was going to be difficult. He took a deep breath and hoped for the best.

The wily veteran, Venko knew it was always good to drive on nights like this. The unofficial rule was the passenger officer took reports, and driving duties alternated each shift. Technically, it was McGhee's turn to drive, but Venko wisely jumped into the driver's seat and his glare was enough to keep McGhee from pointing out the obvious. By 12:25 a.m., they had taken two minor accident reports and McGhee was visibly shivering after the second.

"I could really use some hot coffee," McGhee stated, sounding more like a request than a statement.

"Yeah, I'm getting cold just watching you work," Venko remarked with a forced chuckle.

He had just completed a U-turn on the deserted street when they were dispatched to check an alarm.

"Shit." McGhee swore at his luck.

Three minutes later, Venko parked in front of the small brick structure that doubled for the office area of a closed steel mill. Dispatch updated them and advised it was a motion alarm coming from the front door.

"Gotta be the wind, no footprints in the snow," McGhee remarked glancing at the front door.

Venko put on his ski cap and gloves.

"Let's go check it out."

McGhee trudged through the snow and pulled on the front door as Venko shined his flashlight on the windows along the front of the building.

"It's open!" McGhee shouted to Venko over the howling wind.

"Figures," Venko muttered to no one, and headed to the door.

The pair spent the next five minutes exploring the three offices and the hallway. Convinced it was a false alarm, Venko whistled to McGhee. As McGhee approached Venko at the front door, Venko took a deep breath and looked up before remarking, "Sorry Cal."

McGhee barely had time to register the comment, when Venko caught him with a short right-handed punch just below his sternum. The compact, piston-like movement had the desired effect. McGhee immediately dropped to his knees, struggling to breathe. Venko placed his left hand forcefully on McGhee's left shoulder, effectively pinning him in place.

"First, you deserved that. We need to have a talk, and I wanted to get your full attention. You are going to listen," he looked at McGhee, who opened his mouth, but could not muster a word through his wheezing. McGhee finally nodded and slumped to a seated position on the cold concrete floor.

"Officer McGhee-Parker, I want to know what the fuck you are up to, and I'm not talking about your fabled lacrosse career. I told you about the importance of trust between partners. Let's just assume I already know everything, and you tell me what you, Tremblay and Sellers have cooked up."

Venko's blue eyes sparkled with malevolent glee as he smiled at McGhee. McGhee's expression slowly transformed from shock to resignation, and he held up a finger, indicating he would speak in a second.

McGhee caught his breath and explained how Tremblay had recruited him and misled him about the scope and nature of the investigation. He was told about serious criminal activity most likely occurring at the 7th Precinct and how uncovering it would bring about long overdue changes. Venko occasionally nodded in amazement. McGhee eventually covered what transpired at the meeting earlier.

"You expect me to believe that you just walked out and refused to play along? Just gave them the proverbial finger?" Venko asked.

"Sgt. Miller told me after roll call that I was now permanently assigned to the 7th, there will be no afternoon shift at the 2nd Precinct. Does it sound like a reward to you? Hell, I'm in the same boat as you now. I can't get out of here until Sellers dies or retires," McGhee paused as Venko nodded knowingly.

"Let me guess, you would be a hero, the person that finally changed the culture of the 7th Precinct. Did they promise you a spot in Narcotics or Vice down the road?" Venko watched as McGhee slowly nodded his head acknowledging the promises made.

"Of course they did, all you have to do is go along. Why didn't you just sign the statement?" Venko waited patiently for McGhee's response.

"It didn't take me long to figure out this is nothing more than some kind of fucked up, over the top vendetta. You guys do things different in the 7th, that's for sure, and I know I'm new, but it seems like good police work to me. I gotta say, Sellers wants you bad, he wanted to use the arrest of Jasper Williams as excessive force. Wanted me to swear that Williams did nothing before you punched him for no reason. Framed it as you giving him an immediate attitude adjustment," McGhee looked up at Venko.

Venko rubbed his chin.

"So, they can't leak word out that you are a rat because the details of this shitty little scheme might also get out. They know they can't rely on your testimony regarding Williams, and they can't risk not being able to control a statement from Williams. This appears to be a good old standoff. Well, except for the part where you're now under Sellers and stuck on nights in the 7th for a while. What are you going to do when they start coming at you? And they will. Payback is coming," Venko extended his right hand and helped McGhee to his feet.

"I'll walk, I have a degree and my folks would be overjoyed to assist me in finding a job they think is more fitting of my education. But not in the near future. I'm too pissed, you may not know the real me and I'm not sure how much of my background you know, but I plan to stay just so occasionally seeing my face pisses off Sellers," McGhee explained, brushing the dust off his pants.

"Marcus, if there are any other secrets I need to know about, tell me now. If I find out later, I won't be as nice next time."

"Nice? Nice? Seriously? Uh well, sometimes I secretly listen to classical music. My dad got me into it when I was a kid. How's that?" McGhee asked just in time to watch Miller pull the door open and enter.

Miller took in the scene with an all-knowing glance. He stood silently for a few seconds as his mustache twitched.

"Everything okay here?"

Venko knew Miller's question resonated between the two of them, on several levels.

"Yeah, all good here," Venko replied calmly.

Miller could still feel dissipating tension in the air and wisely decided against any follow-up questions. A good sergeant knew when to appear and when to disappear. Miller turned abruptly and headed to his running cruiser, cursing the blowing snow in his face.

"This stays between us. Trust me, if I say a word to the shift, you can't begin to fathom the problems you'll have. You've got some stones, McGhee-Parker-Smith-Johnson-Lewis or whatever the hell your name really is, I'll give you that much," Venko shook his head in amazement and continued. "Walked out on the big boys, just left them hanging. I love it."

"McGhee is my mother's maiden name, so yeah that's still my name."

Venko glanced over at McGhee and shook his head again.

"Copy that. Let's see if we can get to some pie and coffee without sliding into a ditch."

Venko dropped the shifter into reverse as dispatch interrupted the silence. Car 4 was being dispatched to a missing person call. Venko shoved the shifter back into park.

"Pull up Carmen and Stanley's missing persons call," he instructed and watched as McGhee typed on the computer.

"Rafael Espinoza, Hispanic male, 13 years old, per dad, left the house around 9 this morning has not returned. Last seen in the company of his cousin, Caesar Sandovar, Hispanic male 18. Uh oh, there are caution notes entered on Sandovar. Has a felony warrant for burglary, known to carry a gun. Gang member," McGhee finished and typed in the address of the call and retrieved information on prior calls before continuing.

"And Espinoza is no angel, habitual runaway, prior stops with known gang members last month. Expelled from school for fighting. Last time he ran away he was found at Sandovar's place on 14th Street over in the 2nd Precinct. Not our problem."

"Agreed, let's try for some coffee again," Venko replied, shifting the car into reverse and backing out of the small front lot.

By 1:45 a.m., Wallace Baxter Jr., had finished his fifth Jack and Coke. He felt energized and happy. He drank every day hoping to reach this point. Sometimes it required more, sometimes less. Niles had finished off four Budweisers when his new friend convinced him to down a couple of shots of Jack Daniels. Fueled with inebriated bravado, Baxter thought they should try and charm the girls in the corner.

The girls in the corner were a trio of blue-collar forty-somethings that arrived after their afternoon shift ended at the factory. They sat in the corner because they all recognized Baxter and wanted to be as far away from him as possible. Baxter turned his faded green John Deer ball cap backwards before sauntering up to their table. He practically dragged a very nervous Niles with him.

"Ladies, I'm Wallace Baxter Jr., and this here, is my friend, Walter. Walter is an officer of the law," Baxter shouted without realizing it. Niles smiled shyly, exposing his stained teeth.

The blonde at the center of the small round table visibly cringed at the sight of Niles. Baxter grabbed a chair and was in the process of sliding it next to the brunette when the blonde spoke.

"Wallace, you dumb fuck, we all know who you are. We work at the same plant. Take your sorry ass and your friend back to the bar and leave us alone," the blonde sipped her beer and resumed talking to the rest of the table as if Baxter and Niles didn't exist.

"They're all bitches! Fucking bitches!" Baxter shouted, loud enough to draw the attention of Frankie.

"That's enough out of you," Frankie said in a menacing tone.

"Another round for us Frankie and send the ladies a beer on me," Niles slurred in full peacemaker mode and dropped a fifty on the counter.

As Frankie delivered the beers Niles whispered to Baxter, "They are all fucking bitches." Niles's one hundred and fifty-six-pound frame was not processing the alcohol fast enough, and "bitches" sounded more like "britches." Niles knew he wasn't going to be able to drive home.

"Car 5, check the suspicious persons, 22 Waterfront, Morely and Sons." Dispatch instructed Venko as he and McGhee were exiting Molly's.

"Copy that, 22 Waterfront," Venko responded on his mobile radio as he climbed behind the wheel.

McGhee pulled up the details of the call on the computer.

"Two males, one possibly a juvenile, black or Hispanic. Both wearing red ski-caps. Adult wearing a black puffy coat, juvenile with navy or black puffy coat," McGhee finished.

"Shit, that sounds like Car 4's missing juvenile and felon. Pull up their call and see if the descriptions are similar," Venko said as the car started to slide into the turn. Venko skillfully counter-steered out of the slide and slowed as he approached the stop sign.

"Nothing on what Sandovar was wearing, but yeah, it sounds like our missing juvenile."

McGhee unbuckled his seat belt a block away from the Morely and Sons in the event a quick exit was needed. Venko killed the headlights two blocks from the location.

Venko saw the footprints before he saw the glass door had been shattered. They both saw the small figure dart inside the building. He stopped the car and grabbed the radio.

"Car 5, on scene, send me another unit, someone is inside 22 Waterfront."

"What the hell?" McGhee pointed as a tall, thin white male ran from the shadows into the building after the previous intruder.

McGhee broke into a sprint, Glock in hand. He covered the thirty yards to the door quickly. Venko had no time to dissuade or delay McGhee's pursuit. He knew waiting on backup and coordinating an entry would be safer and more prudent. Too late now.

"Shit," he cursed and un-holstered his Glock and ran towards the door, knees cracking with each stride.

Venko waited just inside the door for his eyes to adjust to the darkness. He took inventory of what he could see. There was some visibility from a streetlight coming in through a window about ten feet up. He could hear some creaking on the catwalk above him. There were metal stairs to his right that led to that level. As his eyes absorbed more of the dim light, he could see McGhee standing on the stairs. McGhee held up three fingers and pointed above him on the catwalk.

Venko and McGhee crept silently up the stairs. The catwalk led to two offices, forty feet ahead that overlooked the factory floor. They both paused at the top of the steps. Venko saw it first. A flashlight swept briefly across the glass windows of the farthest office. Venko lightly tapped McGhee's shoulder and pointed to the office. The pair progressed about fifteen feet forward. Venko on the left by the railing, McGhee hugging the wall. A skylight let in a small amount of light ahead, and Venko could see the railing was broken and gone.

Venko and McGhee crept closer, focusing on the farthest office. They saw a flicker from the flashlight again. McGhee glanced at the nearest office window, and then saw the muzzle flash, a millisecond before the window shattered.

The gunshots obliterated the silence, overwhelming the senses. McGhee fired twice reflexively at the source of the sound, before going down in a heap on the catwalk.

Sandovar darted out the office door ten feet in front of Venko and fired. Venko returned the volley with three quick shots from an instinctive crouched position. Sandovar stumbled backwards and fired again. Venko felt an immediate burning sensation in his left shoulder.

Another shot rang out from behind Venko, much louder than the previous volley. Sandovar fell with a lifeless thud to the catwalk. Venko spun toward the sound of the gunfire behind him, realizing too late that the railing was gone. He hit the concrete ten feet below him, flat on his back.

As he lay motionless, Venko could hear McGhee screaming into his radio.

"Shots fired! Shots fired! Officer down! Officer down!"

Disjointed thoughts filled Venko's head.

Is this it? No lights, no tunnel? What kind of pistol makes that kind of noise? Wow, that was loud. Sarah is going to be pissed if I broke the new phone.

The tall, thin stranger glanced briefly at his right wrist and ran down the stairs to where Venko lay. He placed two fingers on Venko's carotid artery and then ran towards the back of the plant and disappeared. Venko saw only a brief shadow and felt a light touch. He could hear sirens coming from every direction. Seconds later, flashlights flooded the inside of the building as officers searched the area frantically.

Haystack effortlessly lifted Venko.

"I got you buddy, I got you. You're gonna be okay," Haystack said gently as he carried Venko outside.

Venko felt the stinging cold as Haystack carried him through the blowing snow to the waiting paramedics. Venko glanced briefly at Haystack's panicked face before the darkness enveloped him.

"Last call! Drink em up and get the fuck out!" Frankie shouted at the five remaining patrons scattered throughout the bar.

"She - she digs you, you just gotta go be a man and tell this Rachael chick what's what!" Baxter said and drained his ninth Jack and Coke before slamming the glass down.

"I know, I know," Niles mumbled and dropped his Budweiser bottle on the floor, falling over when he tried to reach for it.

Frankie wiped the bar down and cleaned up a bit before approaching Baxter and Niles.

"It's 2:30, you need to pay up and leave. I'll call you a cab if you want," Frankie offered sincerely, after seeing the condition Niles was in.

"Nonsense. I'm good, I'll drive Niles home," Baxter said, glancing at Niles as he grasped the bar rail attempting to pull himself up.

"I, uh I, need to go to the bathroom first, Bax pay the tab," Niles mumbled, digging through his wallet and finding any cash was long gone. He handed Baxter his Visa and started an unsteady trek to the bathroom.

Baxter handed the Visa to Frankie and whispered, "Put my old tab on this too."

"You're a real dirtbag Baxter," Frankie stated, then ran all of the charges through without a second thought.

Niles climbed into the passenger side of the rusting Chevy S-10 pick-up truck.

"One for the road?" Baxter offered, as he pulled a flask out from under his seat.

"Fuck yeah," Niles responded with warm vomit still caked to the front of his jacket.

Six miles from Niles and Baxter's continuing party, Sarah was startled by the sudden frantic pounding noise. She glanced at the clock. 2:41 a.m. It took her a few seconds to realize the source of the noise was at her front door. She pulled on grey sweatpants and grabbed her sweatshirt from the laundry basket at the foot of the bed. She struggled through her sleepy haze to get her arms through the sleeves. Sarah stopped suddenly at the front door.

"Who is it?" She asked.

"Open up, it's Cal Swanson," he said, continuing to pound on the door.

Sarah opened the door and knew. It was written all over Swanson's expression.

"Sarah, it's Dan. He, uh, he has…" Swanson tried to get the rest of the sentence out, but Sarah interrupted forcefully.

"Where is he? Where is he!" She was screaming now.

"Memorial, I'll drive you," Swanson responded and reached for her arm.

Sarah slipped on her shoes, grabbed her keys off the hook by the door, and shoved past Swanson. He chased her down the steps, out the door and past his cruiser. She had the Volvo started and in gear as Swanson reached the driver's door.

"Wait!" He called as she sped off.

"We got, we gotta do this more often Bax," Niles said as Baxter bounced the tire off the curb and drifted into the center of the roadway.

"Yup," he agreed, then made a hard left that spun the truck a full 360 degrees in the heavy snow.

"Woohoo!" Niles yelled and took another pull from the flask.

The old Chevy picked up speed as it rocketed down the steep hill. Neither Baxter nor Niles noticed the red light at the bottom of the hill. The storm was now hurling snow with a blinding fury.

Sarah, heart racing and eyes misty with tears, never saw the rusty Chevy pick-up truck approaching the intersection. The impact occurred as she drove through the green light. The Volvo rolled twice. The second roll ejected Sarah.

The impact with the Volvo redirected the truck into a telephone pole. This secondary collision drove the engine block and steering wheel into Baxter, crushing his chest and shearing off his left leg at the knee. With a raspy exhale, he expired.

Niles felt the warm sticky fluid on his face. He tried to make sense of his surroundings. He opened and closed his hands. They were cold. He slowly turned his head left and saw the smoke, then the truck. He was on the sidewalk. Slowly, Niles moved his right hand to his face. Whatever was dripping on him, was now in his eyes. He gingerly moved his head. He could see the growing crimson smear on his snow-covered right hand. His head was bleeding badly. Instinctively, he wanted to get up. Niles was confused when his legs refused to cooperate. He glanced down and saw the jagged white protuberance that pierced his favorite Levi's just above the knee.

Hmm, so that's what my femur looks like. Strange. He thought just before he passed out.

Sarah wasn't cold, she found that odd. She watched snowflakes drift down on her face. She blinked once and felt nothing. Twenty feet from her smoking Volvo, Sarah Sterling died.

Swanson saw the crumpled wreckage as he approached the intersection. He pounded the dash and screamed.

Part II- Eight Minutes, Thirteen Seconds

Chapter 9

It's in The Details (Three days later)

Officer Danilo Venko woke again. This time the haze wasn't quite as thick. He knew he was in the hospital and it seemed flowers, balloons, and cards were multiplying every time he drifted back into consciousness.

The first conversation he could recall was with Swanson, and that was devastating. He learned Sarah had died in a horrific crash, racing to see him. Of all the memories the concussion had muddled, Sarah remained firmly entrenched in his subconscious. Her face was still smiling and her eyes still sparkled with unconditional love.

The fact that fellow officer Walter Niles was a passenger in the car that struck and killed Sarah, was stunningly surreal. Niles, now a paraplegic, would forever pay for his bad decisions that night. He also recalled a foggy conversation with McGhee, who was being released soon with some sort of cast on his arm.

On day three, the parade started. The deputy mayor, police chief, two deputy chiefs, a city councilman and Sellers came by for a brief visit. This had all the warmth of a staged photo op.

Venko had only met the chief once, when he came to roll call three years earlier to give a canned speech about improving morale and listening to the "boots on the ground." He quickly became angry and stormed off when two officers had the temerity to ask pointed questions about equipment, policy changes, and limited movement within the department. The chief's remarks were politely received at the other precincts with occasional nodding and the polite softball question lobbed by prepped precinct commanders.

Sellers had his list of pre-prepared questions interrupted by two officers in the front row. Without doubt, the officers were emboldened by the fact they could not be moved to a worse shift, nor a worse precinct.

Venko had never met the deputy chiefs nor the city councilman. He smiled shyly and nodded at their comments regarding his bravery and heroics.

Venko was also keenly aware that this parade was delayed two full days until the preliminary investigation into the shooting was complete, and the facts supported Officer Venko's actions. Therefore, the group's appearance would be politically palatable.

"Dan if you need anything, anything, just ask," Sellers remarked, more for the spectators than the patient.

"Thanks," Venko grunted awkwardly, and then smiled at the thought of how awkward it must have been for Sellers to take this entourage to visit McGhee in light of recent events.

"I have a spot for you and McGhee working cold cases in the detective bureau when you're ready for light duty," Sellers tapped the bed rail for emphasis.

Light duty was the department's way of utilizing officers that were physically unable to return to full duty due to injury or illness. Generally, it involved being restricted to the precinct and some relatively simple clerical duty or reviewing cold case files. It permitted the officers the necessary time to fully recover physically and kept them from feeling isolated. Additionally, it gave the public the perception that old, unsolved cases were not forgotten. But it was tricky, officers that had undergone a traumatic event, psychologically recovered at different rates. Some wanted to return to work as soon as they could stand, others needed more time to decompress.

Venko chuckled inwardly at Seller's use of "Detective Bureau" instead of the more common phrase, "DB." It was all part of a concentrated effort by Sellers to illustrate his rank at every opportunity by avoiding the common vernacular.

Venko looked past the foot of his bed and could see Swanson waiting just outside the door for the show to end. As if on cue, Dr. Ahuja entered and politely ordered everyone out of the room in his thick Indian accent. A silent resident shadowed the doctor. The VIPs could barely contain their relief at having this awkward show end, and quickly left. Venko watched as they passed Swanson without acknowledging his presence. Venko noted Sellers quickly strode to the front of the group next to the chief, chatting away.

"Mr. Venko, the last time we talked, you were somewhat sedated. Again, I introduce myself, I am Dr. Ahuja. Your condition has stabilized, which is good. I removed the bullet that fractured your clavicle near your left shoulder. The bullet spun and lodged in your scapula. We were able to remove it without too much difficulty. My concern is making sure there are no infections or other complications. You also suffered a nasty concussion and two fractured ribs. I'm going to keep you a bit longer, because I have some concerns about the head trauma. Do you have any memories of the incident?"

Venko thought about how his memory was returning in jagged fragments. The shooting returned in a full slow-motion loop that his brain replayed several times since waking this morning. What puzzled him was the loss of insignificant memories the day of the shooting. He knew he had a cat, but for the life of him couldn't remember its name. *Donald, Domino, Django? Damn it, it was something like that. He knew Swanson had keys to his place and would check on the cat, whatever its name was.*

"Doc, I woke up this morning and remembered the shooting in clear detail, but what I can't remember, is the name of my damn cat, or what I ate that day!" Venko finished and rubbed the stubble on his face.

"This is not an uncommon phenomenon. Do not trouble yourself. Everyone does not recover in the same way. You have a couple of staples in the back of your head. You may develop a headache or light sensitivity. These are all symptoms relating to your concussion," Dr. Ahuja said and pushed his gold wire-framed glasses up.

Dr. Ahuja began his medical examination of Venko. He dictated a barely audible stream of medical jargon to the resident, who was dutifully and frantically scribbling on an iPad. Finally, the doctor bid Venko a polite "Good day," and left. Swanson nodded to the doctor as the two men left.

"I suspect Haystack, Bianchi and the rest of the crew will be here shortly. I wanted to talk privately before they arrive," Swanson glanced down the hall before continuing.

"Frannie's son, Michael, his girlfriend, works at the medical examiner's office," Venko held up his hand and interrupted Swanson.

"Who works for the M.E.?"

"Michael's girlfriend, she is doing her internship at the medical examiner's office. The point here is she got access to the medical examiner's file on Sandovar," Swanson paused and let Venko digest that nugget of information.

"Before I ask the logical question, I have to say I'm totally impressed with the reach of Frannie's tentacles. Please tell her I am in awe. Now, what did they find besides I shot that piece of shit."

"Well, yes and no. You fired three times and McGhee fired twice. McGhee missed with both shots, high and left, those slugs have already been recovered by the Crime Scene Unit. You hit Sandovar two out of three times. Your miss went right of Sandovar, through the thin office wall and lodged in a desk. Your two hits were Sandovar's right shoulder and right side of his stomach area. That might have been fatal, eventually."

"Your point is?" Venko questioned and raised an eyebrow.

"This is going to sound weird. There is an entry wound almost directly over Sandovar's heart. No exit wound. Obliterated the ribs over the heart and shredded the top third of Sandovar's ticker. He was dead in seconds if not sooner. M.E.'s preliminary report linked the cause of death to the damage to the heart caused by a, yet to be determined, projectile or weapon. Does this make any sense to you?" Swanson looked down at Venko who was nodding.

"Yeah, it makes sense, no one has officially grilled me about the shooting yet, but I expect that very soon. It's simple. There was a third shooter in the building with us. When I was exchanging gunfire with Sandovar, I got hit. At that moment, someone behind me fired and Sandovar went down. I spun around, thinking I'm getting it next, lost my balance and fell to the floor below. Landed flat on my back. I guess I blacked out, kind of drifted in and out. I swear someone got within inches of me while I was laying on the concrete and ran off. If he wanted me dead, he had the chance," Venko pushed the remote for the bed and raised it to a slightly reclined sitting position before continuing.

"We saw someone small duck into the building. We were thinking, the missing juvenile from a prior call. A few seconds later, a tall white male raced in behind him. The white dude is the third shooter, and that gun was the loudest thing I ever heard. It was a cannon." Venko poured some ice water from the pitcher next to the bed into the plastic cup and gulped loudly.

"Well the M.E.'s report would agree with your assessment, it had to be damn near a cannon with the damage it did. But where is the round? There is no exit wound. Not that it matters in this case. Sandovar was a piece of shit, and no one can say he didn't fire at you guys. The shoot team should have no problem with this."

"How is McGhee? He stopped in earlier, but I was a bit out of it," Venko asked sincerely.

"Took a round through his left forearm, shattered his ulna, and had to have a steel plate implanted. He'll be fine. Did you guys have a talk about his Internal Affairs involvement?" Swanson asked after taking a quick peek at the open door.

"I think so, yeah, we talked," Venko remarked, then smiled as the memory resurfaced. "Cal, any chance that Frannie has pulled all the surveillance video from the surrounding buildings yet? I mean there isn't much she can't do."

"That's funny Dan, though you have to admit, she is highly efficient. Detectives already have it. I've seen it. The quality is shit, and it was during a snowstorm. The kid pops up a half block later on another business camera, so we know he got out of the building. No sign whatsoever of the white guy. We had some size 12 footprints outside the door and that's it, no sign of him after the shooting. We flooded the area with cruisers from every precinct. Couldn't find the shooter or the kid."

"What now?" Venko asked.

"Sellers is going to assign you and McGhee to cold cases for light duty. He has already cleared it with the deputy chief. Said you would be more comfortable remaining on midnights in 7th, instead of working day shift out of Central Precinct," Swanson said with a knowing shrug.

"That is mighty kind of him. Selflessly thinking of others as always," Venko said dryly.

"I expect IA will be in to get a statement from you soon, now that you are awake and alert. The shooting review board will eventually meet and rule on your shooting. I don't see any problem there at all. Unfortunately, you're familiar with critical incidents. You know you have to go see the department shrink before being released to light duty," Swanson finished and saw Haystack and Stein at the door talking.

"This third shooter isn't going to be a problem for the shoot team?" Venko asked.

"It makes things somewhat awkward, but it doesn't change what you did, nor does it impact what you did, which was, in my opinion, procedurally correct. I'm pretty sure that the third shooter makes things cloudy from a public relations perspective and that information won't be released. Oh, and by the way, the media already has your picture and it's been flashed all over the news," Swanson finished with a chuckle.

"A hopelessly outdated photo?" Venko asked as Swanson was already nodding.

"Yup, at least fifteen years ago, when you randomly decided to rock the flat top again. Oh, and I stopped by your place and fed Diablo, not exactly a friendly critter," Swanson said and motioned for Haystack and Stein to come in.

"Diablo! I could not remember her name! Thanks. Keep me posted on anything else you find out. And check on McGhee for me," Venko added.

Swanson warmly greeted Stein and Haystack before leaving.

"How you doing, bro?" Haystack asked, in a voice way too loud for a hospital, as he shook Venko's hand with a near crushing force.

Venko looked at the smiling giant in the bright red hoodie emblazoned with NEBRASKA FOOTBALL and returned the grin.

"I'm above ground, and everyday above ground is a good day. How about you Haystack? How are you Rachael?"

"I brought you some macadamia nut cookies, I know you're a sucker for sweets," she said and placed them on a side table with the other plants, flowers and cards.

She tried to hide her concern but knew Venko would see it. To officers in the 7th Precinct, Venko was immortal. He was a veteran that had been shot once before, and nothing phased him. He was the rock of the shift. The one constant they all needed, and leaned on from time to time. To see him connected to machines in a hospital, made him mortal and fragile. Officers like Stein and Haystack and the others in the 7th Precinct, were much younger, and pushed such real threats out of their heads in order to function as effective cops. Now they all knew, no one was immune, and a sudden end was only one call away.

"Bro, I brought you some awesome protein bars, I know the food here is bad and you need to keep up your strength. I've got a great shoulder routine that will help regain strength and flexibility. When you're ready of course, no rush," Haystack set the box containing a dozen protein bars down next to Stein's cookies.

"Thanks Haystack, I appreciate that. Might have to hold off on that workout routine until the collar bone heals," Venko replied, recalling silently the last protein bar he tried from Haystack tasted like vanilla, wet sand and Styrofoam.

The group chatted casually for the next hour with Haystack and Stein cautiously avoiding the mention of Officer Niles, knowing it would trigger memories of Sarah for Venko. They explained the entire shift had been by at various times over the last three days, though Venko slept much of the time. The other precincts were also well represented by flowers, cards and balloons on the table. The conversation stopped immediately and awkwardly when Lt, Tremblay and Sgt. Johnson entered the room.

"Well I guess we will be going now. C'mon Haystack," Stein stated flatly, without looking at the pair from IA.

"Bro, give me a buzz if you need more protein bars, I can blend you up my special energy shake and bring it up if you want. Don't forget I have a good shoulder blast workout we can start on when you're ready," Haystack said, with his ever-present grin.

"Dan, if you are busy, we can come back later," Tremblay remarked, without sounding believable.

"No, let's get this over with," Venko poured himself another cup of water and took a drink then said goodbye to Stein and Haystack.

"Officer Venko, we need to get an official statement from you regarding the shooting at 22 Waterfront Drive. I need you to start at the beginning and walk us through the entire incident," Tremblay instructed and then started the digital recorder. He recorded a brief introductory statement along with the time, date and location of the interview. He advised Venko that the statement was to be used for internal purposes only, and that he could have a union representative present, and that another statement would be taken by the prosecutor's office at a later date.

Venko began explaining where they were when they got the call and then walked them through the entire event up to the point where he blacked out. He was also well aware that IA would have already reviewed all of the statements by other officers on scene, and watched any and all video available. He correctly assumed they might have already interviewed McGhee and knew that Tremblay would seize upon any inconsistencies between his and McGhee's versions.

Venko also knew that Sgt. Johnson was an honest cop and would object if Tremblay veered off the path of a standard interview.

"Officer Venko, is there any reason for not delaying your entry into a building you knew was forcibly entered and occupied by multiple suspects?" Tremblay asked as a follow up to Venko's conclusion.

Venko quickly glanced to Sgt. Johnson, who was obviously uncomfortable with the implication of the question. Venko looked up at the ceiling and took a deep calming breath before starting his answer.

"I assume you already talked to Officer McGhee, and if he is as honest as I think he is, you already know he ran into the building before I could say a word. Of course, I wanted him to wait. I wanted to call additional units and set up a perimeter, choke off all the exits, and then talk about calling a k-9 unit or making coordinated entry. But rookies do what rookies do. He got caught up in the moment, like a dog chasing a rabbit. Yes, I called for additional units, but I couldn't stand outside and watch him go in alone," Venko finished and took a sip of water.

Tremblay cocked his head slightly and began to probe more.

"You were his FTO, his Field Training Officer," Tremblay emphasized the word "training" a bit louder than the other words before continuing. "I would think that McGhee would be better prepared for building searches than that. This lack of training is reckless, if not somewhat dangerous, not just to McGhee, but also to responding officers."

Tremblay stopped and made a few notes in his notebook, and looked over to make sure the digital recorder was still recording.

"I don't blame McGhee for either one of us getting shot. I don't feel the least bit sympathetic for a wanted felon getting killed. I'm not sure I could have done anything different, except maybe put a shock collar on McGhee and shocked him every time we got out of the car on a hot call. Rookies make mistakes, they learn, they don't make them again. McGhee has a steel plate in his arm that will remind him to think first for the rest of his career," Venko, now visibly annoyed, finished and sighed heavily.

"Maybe having you train McGhee was a mistake. I'll have to review the statements from you and McGhee to determine if there are any policy violations or what we can do to improve our performance in similar situations," Tremblay remarked smugly.

"Our performance? Our performance? Have you ever been shot at?" Venko found himself leaning forward towards Tremblay.

He glanced at Sgt. Johnson, who shook his head slightly, as if to say "*Calm down, he is pushing your buttons. We all know he is an asshole.*"

Venko took a drink and resumed in a quieter tone.

"Have you ever even been punched in the face? I'm sure you've gained immeasurable insight from reviewing written accounts of shootings and serious incidents. But I'm here to tell you it's a little different when you're actually being shot at, not just reading about it. Maybe I'm not the guy to train rookies. I'm sure there are lots of rookies that went through their probationary period without making a single mistake. Maybe if he was assigned to another precinct and dayshift, he could learn valuable skills like writing parking tickets and citing taxpayers for equipment violations. You know, a well-rounded approach," Venko remarked with obvious sarcasm.

"Tread lightly, Officer Venko," Tremblay admonished, pointing his finger at Venko, immediately recognizing his career was being mocked.

"Or I'll be moved to midnight shift in the 7th Precinct?" Venko asked with a knowing smile.

Sgt. Johnson reached over and wisely turned off the digital recorder.

"I think we have your statement Dan. Thank you for your cooperation," Sgt. Johnson sincerely offered his hand to Venko. Venko accepted and shook hands with Sgt. Johnson.

"Sgt. Johnson, would you wait in the hall for a second, I want to have a private word with Officer Venko."

Johnson shot a look to Tremblay that clearly communicated that it was a bad idea, but also knew that his boss was not asking.

Sgt. Johnson walked into the hall after packing up the recorder and his notebook. Tremblay opened his mouth to speak and Venko quickly interrupted.

"I have nothing to say to you. Do whatever it is you think you can do to me. Find some chicken-shit policy violation, see if it sticks. Understand that I will fight you every step of the way. I will make lots of uncomfortable noise. No matter how much you dissect this incident, the bottom line is someone shot at me and my partner and we returned fire. Even you must realize how bad it will look if you try to levy some petty discipline on me or McGhee. The deputy chief would kill it and you know it. I know you and Sellers are tight. And I also know you have tied your future to his wagon. You're going to have to make your bones with him some other way. I'm tired and I want you to leave now," Venko finished and pressed the button to recline the bed back slightly.

Sgt. Johnson, although just outside, heard the entire conversation.

"C'mon boss, we are done here."

Tremblay glared at Venko but left without another word.

• • •

Venko awoke to the disinfecting smell of pine cleaner. He saw the small cleaning girl furiously mopping her way down the hall towards his room. From a distance, her stooped posture made her look much older. He assumed he had been out for hours. His dinner sat on a rolling tray, untouched, next to the bed. He wasn't hungry and wasn't sure what he was feeling at the moment. The room was almost completely dark except for the light from the hallway and the eerie glow from the machines behind him. Then he felt it. He felt empty and alone.

He replayed the words Swanson told him.

"She wouldn't wait for me to drive her, I tried to stop her, she was racing to see you."

Venko's heart rate and breathing began to increase as he got choked up. He had entombed himself in solitude for so long that the weight of everything he felt for Sarah came out at once. Loss, regret and an overwhelming sense of blackness swept over him. All the words never spoken crashed down on him. He wiped the perspiration off his face with his gown then gulped down a full cup of water. His hands were shaking as he gripped the rails in an attempt to control his emotions.

Venko took a deep breath and watched the cleaning girl struggle to wheel the bucket and mop into the room. She stopped and retrieved a rolling trash can from the hallway. He heard her quietly humming as she dumped his trash can and replaced the liner. She stopped and looked at the table of balloons, flowers, and plants and seemed fascinated by a small plant at the end of the table.

"What is it?" Venko asked, after watching her curiously.

The sound of his voice pierced the quiet stillness, causing her to jump.

"I'm sorry, it is very pretty, I just wanted to look," the timid girl said through a thick accent.

She looked about 35, but the hard lines that edged her brown eyes indicated a life of back-breaking labor.

"Where are you from? You have an accent," Venko asked politely.

"Puerto Rico. I came with my children six years ago. I'm sorry I disturbed you. I shall go now," she added without making eye contact.

"Bring the plant over here please, I want to see it," Venko requested.

She did as Venko asked, cautious not to drop it. The plant had two large, reddish orange flowers. Each was the size of a small saucer in diameter.

"It is beautiful. Do you know what it is?" Venko asked.

"*Flor de maga,* it is the national flower of Puerto Rico. This is the first time I have seen one in the U.S., where did you get it?" she asked.

"Is there a card on the table where it was sitting?" He asked.

"No, there is nothing," she responded, scanning the immediate area on the table.

Venko thought for a moment, and a slight smile creased his worn face.

"I think I know."

Chapter 10
Beans And The One-Armed Detectives
(One month after the shooting)

Venko's alarm sounded briefly before he turned it off. He had been sleeplessly staring at his phone on the nightstand for the last twenty minutes. He had been at home a little over three weeks now and his sleep pattern had slowly drifted back to a day shift pattern.

Diablo crept over from the foot of the bed and climbed onto his chest and purred.

"First day back for me old girl. Not sure I'm going to like wearing khakis and dress shirts."

Diablo flicked her tail, as if shrugging noncommittally to his statement.

Officer Venko had been cleared to return to light duty three days ago. The doctor insisted he continue to wear the sling on his left arm to limit movement as his collar bone healed. He would be re-evaluated in three weeks and could most likely shed the sling. The prosecutor's office had not issued an official ruling yet on the shooting, but that wasn't unusual. There was nothing politically charged about the incident that required an urgent explanation. Unofficially through back channels, the police department was told that both McGhee and Venko could return to light duty status.

Evidence on scene indicated exactly what Venko and McGhee had revealed in their statements. The prosecutor's office as well as the police department were still very much concerned that both the mysterious white male and the juvenile had not yet been located. Neither agency was in a rush to release a statement on the incident. Both agencies were concerned with value or danger in the statements of two witnesses still at large. Venko was very much aware of this and was determined to find the pair. Swanson called him and warned that since it was his first day back, he could expect to see Sellers at the precinct. Venko knew that Sellers would personally oversee his assignments while he worked cold cases on light duty.

Venko winced slightly as he put his left arm through the sleeve of his light blue dress shirt. He managed to tuck the shirt into the waistband of his wrinkled chinos without too much difficulty.

By the fit of his pants, he knew he had lost weight. Looking in the mirror his eyes appear sunken and hollow. He pulled at the waist of his pants and guessed he had dropped nearly ten pounds. Venko slid his belt through the loops and attached his off-duty holster. He passed the well-worn notch at the second hole of his belt and continued to the fourth. *Definitely dropped ten pounds, maybe fifteen.*

Venko noticed the red Under Armor logo was showing on his white undershirt and buttoned the dress shirt up further to conceal the logo. Venko smiled and remembered all the times Sarah had urged him to buy some plain white t-shirts and start dressing like a grown up. *Logo wear is for the gym, not the office.*

Venko inserted his silver badge into the leather holder and attached it to his belt, just in front of his holster. He grabbed his handcuffs off the closet shelf and shoved them into the back of his waistband. He sat on the bed and tied his brown oxfords, stopping to scratch Diablo under her chin.

As he sat petting Diablo, he realized he was stalling. He could feel his stomach churning. Everything was different. A new uniform hung in his closet still under plastic, replacing the one that had to be cut away. He pulled his gun off the shelf and placed it in his holster. Venko took one last look around the room before putting on his coat and slipping the iPhone in his pocket. As he passed the desk, he grabbed his old flip phone out of the drawer and shoved it in his pocket.

He stepped into the hallway, locked the door and was immediately enveloped by the rich aroma of strong coffee.

"You're still losing weight. This is not good Danilo," Miss Rosales said softly, handing him a cup of coffee as he sat.

Venko had become accustomed to her unique sensitivity. Her remarks no longer surprised him the same way they once did.

"I'm going to be in plain clothes for a bit, I'm a lot lighter out of the heavy gear on my belt and uniform."

"You've lost your jangle," she remarked with a chuckle. "But it's also in your voice. It's thinner and doesn't resonate as much. How is Marcus?"

Venko was pretty sure she had only met McGhee once and was surprised she remembered his name…surprised, but not shocked. He had talked to McGhee a few times over the last month and saw him briefly when they met with the prosecutor's office and police department investigators assigned to investigate the shooting. Venko knew McGhee also had to meet with the department psychologist in order to return to duty. He assumed McGhee gave off no red flags or he would have been held back from returning to light duty.

Like most cops, Venko knew McGhee would be uncomfortable opening his brain to a stranger, and a non-cop at that. He suspected McGhee would be cautious and guarded in revealing his feelings. The goal would be to return to work as quickly as possible, repressing anxiety and apprehension or risk being labeled as weak or soft by his co-workers. Venko understood this process all too well.

"He is fine I'm sure. I'll see him tonight," Venko remarked confidently.

The pair engaged in small talk about the bitter, cold snap and the neighborhood. Miss Rosales sensed the anguish in Venko but knew he would not discuss anything personal.

"I guess it's time to head in and see how this goes," Venko stood and grabbed the thermos.

"Danilo," she started, patting his arm. "Put your mind at ease. Remember, nothing is ever truly lost," Miss Rosales slowly shook her head. "Nothing is ever truly lost," she repeated.

"Thank you. I know you believe that. Good night, Miss Rosales," Venko said softly, and started down the stairs.

• • •

Dex saw Venko enter the precinct and ran over to him, stopping when he saw Venko turn to protect his left arm and shoulder. He awkwardly pulled back from a hug and grabbed Venko's right hand and shook it vigorously.

"It's good to see you Dan," Dex exclaimed and released his grip.

"Likewise, my friend. I'll be up in DB until they release me to full duty," Venko explained.

"With Beans and Cassie? What will you be doing? Just a heads up, Sellers got here about five minutes ago."

"Yeah, I expected as much. McGhee and I will be working cold cases I've been told. I better head up to the fourth floor since Sellers is already waiting," Venko began his trek up the stairs.

"Hey Dan, forgot to tell you, they finally fixed the elevator."

"Oh, not for this guy, I'm not going to tempt fate on my first day back. I think the stairs are my safest bet," Venko retorted with a smile.

Venko entered the detective's cubicles on the fourth floor and immediately saw Sellers talking with Beans and Oliver by the coffee station. McGhee was seated at a cubicle just behind the trio, listening cautiously to the conversation. Sellers stopped talking when he saw Venko approaching. He managed a painfully contrived smile, and greeted Venko.

"Welcome back Dan. You can set up shop in the cubicle next to McGhee. Detectives Bledsoe and Oliver will help out when they can. They have the cases I'd like you two to take a look at."

Venko sat his thermos down and took in the sterile surroundings of his cubicle. A chipped coffee cup held a smattering of pens and pencils next to a worn mouse pad. The computer monitor was newer, and large enough to see clearly. The half wall of the cubicle had a hook and he gingerly took off his jacket and hung it up before putting his left arm in the sling.

"If there is nothing else, I'll let Bledsoe take over and fill you in. Oh, not that you need to be reminded, you two are on light duty so I'd prefer you not go into the field for anything without prior authorization. If you need something checked out or a lead run down, Bledsoe can do that," Sellers finished and patted Beans on the shoulder.

Oliver shot a look of pure daggers at Sellers.

The thirty-nine-year-old divorced mother of two, immediately felt marginalized by the good old boys again. She had been ignored or dismissed outright, ever since coming to 7th Precinct two years ago as a new detective.

Oliver was smart, ambitious and dedicated. She spent ten years in patrol with the singular focus of becoming a detective. She asked questions and would do extensive follow up on routine patrol calls, at times, to the chagrin of her patrol sergeants.

"Write the paper, and move on," she was told numerous times. Or they would say, "This is the assembly line, just put the widgets down the detectives will handle the rest." And on more than one occasion, a crusty detective would tell her: "Stay in your lane."

Despite being the niece of the legendary retired Sgt. Sal "Tommy" Tomasino, she never used his name. In fact, other than a few day shift cops and supervisors working out of Central Precinct, Tommy was already forgotten.

She loved Tommy, but knew he was part of an old system that believed female officers couldn't be crime fighters. Women were fine for interviewing sexual assault victims or children and were better suited to passing out coloring books in Community Relations.

After seven years working afternoon shifts out of Central Precinct, she reached her limit. She was burned out and frustrated with leering old supervisors, and being paired with lazy partners working affluent, boring districts.

Despite receiving advice to the contrary, she transferred to afternoon shift in the 7th Precinct. During her second week, she was officially welcomed via a broken nose while wrestling with a drunk. She still carried the small scar across the bridge of her nose as a reminder of "getting her feet wet," as Sgt. Connerly humorously referred to the incident. That incident gave her instant credibility that the arrests of numerous burglars, and even a serial rapist failed to provide.

Two years ago, she aced the exam and was promoted to detective. The reward for this promotion was a spot on the midnight shift in the 7th Precinct working with the infamous Beans.

As Sellers walked out of the room, McGhee looked at Venko and nodded.

Venko had noticed that McGhee's face had become rounder than he remembered. The extra pounds made him look even younger.

"So, what is the plan for us? What cases did Sellers drop on you to keep us busy?" Venko asked after sipping coffee from the thermos cap.

Oliver looked nervously at Beans before beginning.

"Uh, Dan, he wants you to put fresh eyes on two unsolved missing persons cases. Cody Michaels, white male, 13 at the time he vanished in 1990; and Dakota Billings, white male, 12 at the time he disappeared in 2017," She finished and shrugged.

"I remember Billings, the guy they had in custody for that one ended up quite dead awaiting trial," Venko remarked. He thought about the conversation he had with Sarah about the Billings case over breakfast. It seemed so long ago. He bit his lower lip, he missed her.

Beans sat on the edge of Venko's desk and explained what he knew.

"Well, the feeling floating around the PD is that it was a weak case, and a big stretch to even charge him with the abduction. And, if he hadn't up and died before the trial, no way a jury would have convicted him on such weak evidence. Damn near a fist fight between investigators on whether to charge him or not with the abduction. Still, no great loss, he would have kept robbing people and eventually shot someone. You are back to square one and these cases are cold, polar vortex, Siberian cold. Best of luck to you and your young lad," Beans patted Venko's shoulder condescendingly, and walked back to his cubicle.

"Great, thanks," Venko snorted.

Oliver walked over to Venko and pulled up a chair and sat between his and McGhee's cubicle.

"Beans is almost worthless, but you probably already knew that. I'll do whatever I can to help and I'll make Beans work if necessary. Honestly, no one expects you to solve these, just type up your perspective and chase anything down you think was left out the first time," Oliver finished and introduced herself to McGhee, who grinned nervously as she shook his hand.

"Cassie, go make copies of the Billing's and Michaels' files for Venko and McGhee," Beans shouted from his cubicle across the hall.

Oliver was filling Venko in on the latest precinct gossip and stopped talking when she heard Beans's request.

"Motherfucker," Oliver whispered and exhaled slowly before standing up and looking straight at Beans.

She tapped her gold detective's shield on her belt with her right index finger and began to shout.

"Beans, does this badge say armed secretary? Let me see. No, it does not! It says detective. Yes, that's right, just like yours fucking does. I know you have been here a long time, probably since Cain killed Abel, and without overtime, I'm sure your lazy ass would have gotten Cain acquitted. I am not a secretary, I do not get you coffee, copy files, mail your letters or, for that matter do your work. Get off your ass and make the copies yourself!" With that exclamation, Oliver headed down the hall.

McGhee leaned out to watch her walk and mouthed silently, "Wow," to Venko.

As if on cue, Oliver said without turning back, "McGhee, stop staring, I have kids about your age," before disappearing into the break room.

McGhee rocketed back upright into his chair and tried in vain to look busy as he mindlessly tapped at his keyboard.

"Somebody has PMS," Beans said to Venko with a shrug as he pointed down the hall to cue up the response.

"I heard that asshole!" Oliver yelled.

Beams emitted a deep raspy chuckle. "That girl hears things that dogs can't, you have been warned."

Venko began to wonder just how fast he could heal and get back to uniformed full duty.

• • •

Eventually, Beans made copies of both case files and gave a copy to Venko and McGhee. This occurred after the mini-tour of the detective bureau, complete with a twenty-minute review of his retirement portfolio, and his countdown displaying the remaining time until he retired. Venko knew that for all practical purposes, Beans was already retired, he just happened to take up office space, and would continue to do so until the clock struck zero or Oliver killed him.

Venko and McGhee reviewed their thick case files on Michaels for the first two hours.

"Where is Detective Foster now?" McGhee asked, breaking the long silence.

"The name doesn't ring a bell with me, let me ask Cassie."

"What is it?" She responded, overhearing her name from her cubicle.

"Detective Foster was the primary on the Michaels' case back in 1990. Do you know where Foster is now?" Venko asked.

"Hey Beans, you were here when the Ten Commandments were still misdemeanors, where is Detective Foster now?" Oliver shouted.

Beans barely registered the reference to his age, and continued to eat his chicken salad sandwich and watch SportsCenter on his computer screen.

"Retired," he mumbled, spewing crumbs and mayonnaise onto his plaid tie. He took a long gulp on his Dr. Pepper before he continued.

"Retired in '07 on a medical. Diabetes got him bad. In a nursing home now. I think he is in Serenity Vista."

"I'd like to talk to him. Maybe jog his memory, see if something isn't covered in his report or the follow up he did," Venko said and looked at McGhee, who was nodding his head in agreement.

"Not sure that's a good idea. I heard he isn't very sharp these days. Besides it's a forty-minute drive up there and Sellers was pretty clear on no overtime. And obviously we can't go up there during the shift," Beans explained and made it clear all his decisions were based on overtime pay rate.

"If you want to go on your own time, I'm sure Cassie can drive you up there. Still not sure what you would get out of him now," Beans added, now furiously working a bag of Cheetos and licking his orange fingers with a loud smacking sound.

Oliver was trying to contain herself, but the smacking sound and Beans's aversion to leaving the office was too much for her to take.

"Yes, Cassie is now armed secretary and armed chauffeur. Beans, you're saying Foster isn't lucid anymore? How the hell would you know from the safe confines of cubicle world? Is he still functioning? Is he a vegetable? Or is he the kind of vegetable that wears a dandruff-covered sport coat and Petri dish ties, while collecting a paycheck?" she asked and looked over at McGhee, who was rubbing his forehead. *Mom and Dad are fighting again.*

Venko worked hard to suppress the impending grin.

"I'll call up there in the morning when I get home and we can set something for Wednesday morning right after work," Venko suggested to the group.

"I have a lot on my plate right now, not sure that is the best time for me. Besides, I should probably run that by Sellers first," a very nervous Beans stated, clearly indicating he would not be accompanying the group on any field trips.

"You mention this to Sellers, and I tell your ex about your offshore accounts," Oliver said with a menacing glare.

Beans slowly took off his thick black glasses and laid them on the desk before looking up at Oliver.

"Have you not a shred of decency?

Chapter 11
The Buck is Back

Wednesday morning at 6:30 a.m. Venko finished the last of his coffee from the thermos. Normally, he would eschew caffeine so close to the end of the shift, but he knew he would be up for a few more hours.

He pulled his old flip phone from his pocket and powered it up. Several times over the last month, he would just scroll through old text messages from Sarah. The antiquated phone's storage was nearly full. Thankfully, he rarely took the time to delete anything.

He was smiling when McGhee startled him.

"What are you still doing with that fossil? I know you're using a new iPhone now," McGhee asked.

Venko snapped the phone closed before responding.

"Nothing, nothing," he paused reflectively, then decided to ask McGhee for a favor. "Marcus, can you take the text messages from my old phone and put them on my new phone?" Venko asked, holding up both phones.

McGhee immediately grasped the implication of Venko's request and regretted mocking the old flip phone.

"Absolutely. Give me a few minutes," McGhee took the phones and disappeared down the hall.

"You about ready? We can take my pool car. It's not pretty but the heat still works. You drive," Oliver said and tossed the keys to Venko, who caught them with his right hand.

"No problem. Give Marcus a few minutes, he is doing a favor for me. We need to make a stop on the way."

"We do?" Oliver asked.

"Yeah, I talked to a staff member at the nursing home. Foster can be a bit cantankerous but is lucid. I also talked to him personally, he has no problem talking to us about any of his old cases, but we have to bring him a pouch of Red-Man chewing tobacco. Which of course, is strictly prohibited as well as all tobacco products at the home. But he will not talk to us unless we bring it. He instructed me to put the pouch in a McDonald's bag in order to smuggle it to him."

"So, they are okay with a diabetic having a greasy cheeseburger and fries, but not chewing tobacco? Does the police department write their policies too?" She mocked with a laugh.

Venko looked over at Beans, and before he could respond, Beans started.

"I won't be able to make it, I have some errands to run after work. I won't say a word either."

Five minutes later, McGhee returned and handed the phones back to Venko with a nod.

"Thanks. Let's do this," Venko said, scooping up the case files and heading to the door.

The trio walked behind the precinct into the parking lot. Oliver pointed out a beat-up, white Chevy Caprice. It was obvious that at one time this was a marked police cruiser. The decals and overhead lights were removed but the rusting spotlight still was mounted to the driver's door. Venko unlocked the driver's door as McGhee stepped to the front passenger door. Oliver immediately noticed his movement.

"Not a chance rookie," Oliver quipped and watched McGhee sheepishly open the front passenger door for her, acknowledging his breach of protocol.

• • •

Just before 8 a.m. they pulled into the parking lot of Serenity Vista. Although it was an aging facility, the parking lots were plowed and the sidewalks were salted. The front desk was neat and highly organized with Muzak lightly playing in the background. Venko noticed the same antiseptic smell as the hospital, his stomach churning at the odor.

"Hello?" Venko called out.

A tall, thin, silver-haired woman strode briskly from the back office.

"How may I help you?" She asked, obviously annoyed at being interrupted.

Oliver stepped forward.

"I'm Detective Oliver," she started, and handed a business card to the woman. "And this is Detective Danilo Venko and Detective Marcus McGhee, we are here to see one of your residents, William Foster."

Technically, Oliver knew that Venko and McGhee were not detectives, just officers temporarily assigned to the detective bureau. Introducing them as "Officer" would be confusing and might make citizens reluctant to talk to them or question their qualifications. Oliver guessed correctly that no one would notice her gold badge was different from the silver badges clipped to the belts of McGhee and Venko.

"Hello, I'm Jeanette Seavers, Director of Resident Services," Seavers said, and shook hands with Oliver in a perfunctory manner. "Ah, Detective Buck Foster, as he likes to tell anyone within 1000 feet. He makes the other residents call him detective. He should have just finished breakfast. Check the dayroom straight ahead. If he isn't there, ask one of the staff members to direct you to his room," Seavers finished and curtly pointed to the dayroom. It was obvious she did not view Foster warmly.

The dayroom had three large screen TVs playing quietly. Old movies played on two of the TVs, with the third turned to a twenty-four-hour news channel. Nearly 20 residents were scattered about the tables and sofas.

After watching Venko and Oliver scan the room for several minutes, McGhee spoke up.

"Y'all don't know what Foster looks like, do you?"

Venko looked at Oliver and they both shrugged. McGhee looked over at the staff table and picked out the most attractive of the three women sitting there and approached her.

"Excuse me ma'am," McGhee began with his best disarming smile. "I'm Detective McGhee, myself and my partners over there are looking for William Foster," McGhee stuck out his hand.

She flicked her brown hair back before smiling and shaking his hand. McGhee noticed her sudden preening and his grin grew.

"I'm Sandie, that's with an i-e not a y."

McGhee figured her to be about 25, she was a little thinner than he preferred, and probably worked in food service. He correctly assumed she was slightly self-absorbed and would overstate her job classification into something important sounding like "Assistant Dietician," or "Nutrition Specialist," instead of "Cafeteria Worker II."

"Well Detective, see the white-haired gentleman in the wheelchair staring at the Fox News Channel? That's him. You'll also notice there isn't a female resident within thirty feet of him. Yeah, he has only one full leg, but his arms work just fine. I'd let your friend know," she pointed her thumb at Oliver as she finished.

"Thank you, Sandie," he said as he motioned to Venko and Oliver and pointed to Foster. He could feel Sandie's eyes upon him as he walked away.

Foster saw the group approaching him, and he spun his chair quickly towards them, causing his gown to flutter where his right leg used to be.

"Hello detectives," Foster said, holding out his hand, palm turned upward. Venko handed him the McDonald's bag.

Foster noted the look of surprise on the face of Oliver and McGhee.

"The only people that come in this early are doctors and lawyers, and they don't wear wrinkled khakis and scuffed shoes," Foster finished and worked his gnarled fingers into the pouch before stuffing an enormous wad of chewing tobacco in his cheek.

"Mr. Foster," Oliver started, before Foster interrupted.

"Buck, call me Buck," he corrected, before slowly appraising her up and down.

She suppressed her revulsion and continued.

"We would like to discuss an old missing person's case you worked on back in 1990. Could we sit at the table and chat?" She asked with an obviously forced smile.

Venko introduced everyone and Foster wheeled to the nearest table.

Foster spotted Seavers making her rounds. Seavers' hands were clasped behind her back as she meandered through the tables, her hawk-like eyes constantly scanning the room. Foster nervously hid the McDonald's bag behind him in the wheel chair as she approached.

"Mr. Foster, all residents are required to be fully dressed in the dayroom, no sleeping gowns," Seavers snapped, turned on her heels, and headed off.

"Yes ma'am," Foster mumbled. "Nurse Ratchet," he added once she was out of earshot.

McGhee and Oliver shot a puzzled look to Venko.

"Never-mind," he shrugged, realizing they were too young for the reference.

Venko opened the Michaels' folder and placed it on the table.

"What do you remember about this case?" He asked.

Foster reached into a small pouch attached to the side of the wheelchair and took out a pair of eyeglasses. He put them on and scooped up the folder and scanned the contents for a few seconds.

"I remember this one, chased down a bunch of leads the first couple of days, and then it went ice cold. No sightings, no rumors, nothing. Took the sketch of the suspect and showed it all over town. Like the kid, the suspect was a ghost. No one saw him again. We had a decent sketch of the suspect, but you got to remember, this was in the days before fancy computer programs could damn near create photo-like drawings. An actual person had to draw the suspect based on a description," Foster finished, and grabbed the Styrofoam coffee cup off the table and spit an alarming amount of tobacco juice into it.

"What about the kid? Anything you can remember that wasn't in the file?" McGhee asked.

"Not really, the kid had issues, he could be explosively violent at times. I think that is all in there. All his friends I tracked down back then were delinquents as well. They all became petty criminals as adults."

The group spent the next hour pouring over names in the file and jotting down notes from Foster's recollection of interviews. Venko looked at his notebook and sighed. He realized this was a dead end. He would type up this interview and add it to the file tomorrow.

"Anything else you can remember that might be helpful or we forgot to ask?" Oliver asked as the trio gathered up notebooks and pens.

"Well," he paused, "as strange as it sounds, I think the same suspect was responsible for two other attempted abductions years later," Foster finished and pushed his glasses up on his nose.

Venko, McGhee and Oliver, who had just stood up to leave, froze. All three wore the same incredulous expression.

"What?" Venko stated in surprise, as the three simultaneously sat down.

"Yeah the descriptions of the suspect in the two attempted abductions matched the physical description of the suspect in the Michaels case," Foster stated nonchalantly.

"What are the names? Where are the case files? The reports? Did anyone else work those cases?" Oliver asked excitedly.

"Whoa, slow down sweetie, there were no reports filed for those cases," Foster remarked and spit again.

"How is that possible?" Venko asked.

"Because the missing kids wandered home while I was on scene. If I remember right, and this was a while back. There were two cases. I got on scene within a minute or two of patrol officers getting the call. I had a real dick for a boss in those days, Sgt. Stafford. So, I spent as much time as I could in my car away from the office. I heard the calls go out and responded," Foster paused as if he lost track of the question.

"Buck, why were no reports done?" Oliver pressed him.

Foster became alert again at the sound of Oliver's voice.

"Because the kids returned home. Probably no more than ten to fifteen minutes after they disappeared. Just walked right in while we were on scene. Neither of the kids had any recollection of any attempted abduction. As a matter of fact, they couldn't tell us anything about the last 10 minutes. Patrol supervisors on scene just wanted their guys to get back in service and clear the call. They probably thought the kids took off on their own and didn't believe them or the witnesses that saw the white male lurking nearby," Foster explained.

"Dan! That sounds exactly like what happened to us. My first couple of weeks at the 7th Precinct, we got a missing person call and the kid walked right in while we were there. Detective Bledsoe responded to the scene as well. Cassie, can you call Bledsoe and see if he can pull up the report and give us the name of the kid?" McGhee asked excitedly. Venko nodded his head in agreement.

"Slow down, Marcus. First, Beans is home sleeping. Second, even if he was awake, there is no way he answers his work cellphone. We will have to talk to him at work tonight," Oliver replied.

"It would have been nice if someone had done the reports back then. That would have been a huge help," Venko said with a sigh.

"Would seeing my notes from those calls help?" Foster offered.

"Yes!" Oliver, Venko and McGhee shouted in unison.

"Come with me," Foster said and wheeled out of the dayroom and down the hall.

Foster's room was a stark contrast to his slovenly, disheveled appearance. The room was exceptionally neat and highly organized. A prosthetic leg, with a white tennis shoe attached, lay across the bed, the only item jarringly out of place. Foster opened his closet door. On the floor, neatly stacked in piles three high, were shoe boxes.

"I kept all my case notes in small notebooks. Every box contains a year's worth of notebooks. I went from patrol to detective bureau in 1988 and retired in 2007. The boxes are marked with the year facing outward. I can't remember the names of the kids. These days, I can only remember a few of the big cases. It would have been late '90s or early 2000's. There's a piece of paper taped to the top of each box. In red ink there might be notations such as *UA, UH, UB*. That will indicate which boxes contain notes on unsolved abductions, unsolved homicides, and unsolved burglaries. There are other abbreviations, but for your purposes look for those boxes that have *UA* on them. Technically, those two cases aren't unsolved since both of the juveniles returned home. But I felt strongly about making sure I kept the information because I believed something happened, and the suspect's description was very detailed."

The trio carefully removed six boxes and began to pour through the small notebooks contained inside. Occasionally, Foster would offer up tidbits on cases and suspects he had arrested over the years.

"Shawn Cole, white male, 12. Abducted May 4th, 2001. Returned," McGhee read the notation aloud, before skimming the rest of the notes on the page silently.

"Yes, yes," Foster agreed.

"Ethan Daniels, white male, 14. Abducted February 13th, 2006. Returned," Oliver read excitedly.

"That's the other one," Foster said nodding his head before continuing. "I noted the physical description of the suspect the witnesses said was in the area. Compare his description in both cases, and with the suspect in the Michaels' case."

"Daniels and Michaels were 18 years apart," Venko said, his voice full of skepticism. Foster just shrugged.

"Can I take these notebooks with me?" Venko asked.

Foster paused for a second as he watched McGhee and Oliver carefully stacking the shoe boxes back into chronological order.

"Yes, just make sure I get them back."

"No problem," Venko assured Foster.

Venko, McGhee and Oliver were almost to the front door when Seavers called after them.

"Detectives, I need to speak with you,"

The trio stopped just feet from the door and turned around. Seavers strode quickly towards them holding a Styrofoam cup out like it contained acid.

"Much like the police department, we have rules here. There are to be no tobacco products on the premises. Imagine my surprise at finding this, this cup of nasty tobacco juice sitting where Mr. Foster was sitting. I'm well aware of Foster's fondness for Red-Man. One doesn't have to be a detective to figure out how he came into possession of chewing tobacco, do they? Since he didn't have it last night, I'd say it goes beyond the realm of coincidence that he has it after you arrived." Seavers paused to hand the cup, still holding it at arm's length, to McGhee.

"Uh," McGhee started to speak but Seavers interrupted.

"Please dispose of that in the outside trash receptacle. Detectives, we don't have a search policy for visitors, but this makes me wonder if one is now necessary. Good day." Seavers turned abruptly and walked back towards her office.

"That was a little over the top," McGhee stated, as he stepped out into the cold air.

"You think?" Oliver added sarcastically.

Chapter 12

With A Little Help From My Friends

The trip to Serenity Vista drastically altered Venko's sleep pattern. He felt slightly disoriented when he woke up. There would be no time to slowly get into his pre-work routine. After a quick shower, he got dressed, fed Diablo and tucked his cellphone into his coat pocket. He paused and looked at his old flip phone on the table before grabbing it, not understanding why he needed to take it, but not wanting to be without it.

He locked the door and smelled the coffee that awaited him at the end of the hall.

"Hello Miss Rosales, how are you tonight?" He asked warmly as he sat down.

"I am fine, thank you for asking Danilo. You didn't shave today," she said, smiling as she sipped her coffee.

Venko grinned, knowing he only applied a moisturizing aftershave to his face on days he shaved. Today was just a splash of cologne. The two had distinctly different smells.

"Going for the rugged look. Besides I'll be buried in folders and paperwork at the precinct today, no one will see me. Not much chance of leaving the building."

"Maybe you should get out and have a slice of pie. You could use the extra weight and familiar places are comforting. What are you working on?" Miss Rosales asked with genuine interest.

Venko spent a few minutes telling her what he could about the missing persons cases. He admitted he had collected a lot of pieces but wasn't sure how they fit together.

"Sometimes it is best to put all the pieces on the table, so you can see them all at once. Once you do that, your eyes will know where they go," Miss Rosales explained, nodding her head.

Venko grinned, and silently wished such a simplistic answer would work.

"Well, anything is worth a try," he remarked, and capped the thermos as he stood.

"Danilo, the hard part is to believe what you see, believe what you feel," Miss Rosales said softly.

He stopped on the first step, her words inexplicably rattling him. Venko's stomach churned nervously as he looked back and caught her sightless gaze. As quickly as the feeling washed over him, it was gone.

• • •

Venko walked into the roll call room to a chorus of catcalls and whistles over his detective-like attire. He still had ten minutes before any supervisors would arrive. Venko sidled up to Officers Bianchi and Martinez.

"I need a favor; can you guys find Rafael Espinozo for me? He is the juvenile missing person that hasn't been seen since my shooting. I think he was a witness. I'd really like to talk to him. The kid had previously been found at Sandovar's 14th Street crib. That place was a de-facto hang out for gangsters. I suspect it still is."

"Sure, we can sit on that location for a bit when things are slow. You do know that is over in the fucking 2nd Precinct, right?" Bianchi answered.

"You know us Dan, we ain't no rule breakers, we would never sneak out of district," Martinez added, sarcastically and grinned.

"Internal Affairs is looking for him as well. I would like to talk to him first, before they mess things up. A case of your favorite cerveza if you find him and call me first. Spread the word through the shift," Venko finished, sweetening the pot.

"You got it, bro," Bianchi replied.

"Spray some WD-40 on your wallet, you're going to have to pry it wide open. Me and my amigo, we don't drink cheap beer," Martinez said.

Venko gave the pair a thumbs up before heading out of the roll call room.

Venko took the two flights of stairs to the detective bureau two at a time. He stopped abruptly when he saw Sellers walking towards Oliver's cubicle. Sellers spotted Venko as he was trying to duck into the bathroom.

"Venko, I need to see you as well," Sellers barked. Venko exhaled slowly and walked into the cubicle and pulled a chair from the hallway. He sat down and looked over at Oliver who gave a quick shrug, as if to say, *I have no idea what he wants.*

"Do you think I like coming here this late at night after already working my shift?" Sellers asked, rhetorically. "I came in tonight to talk with the both of you because of a phone call I received today from Jeanette Seavers, Director of Resident Services at Serenity Vista Nursing Home." Sellers paused and looked directly at Oliver. Oliver caught his glance and looked away quickly.

"She wanted to talk to the supervisor of Detective Cassie Oliver. She was extremely irritated that Detective Oliver and her two cohorts would smuggle chewing tobacco, a prohibited item, I might add, into the facility and give it to a resident."

"Uh, boss that one is on me; I talked to Foster on the phone and he requested a pouch of Red Man before he would be willing to review old cases," Venko explained in a voice just above a whisper. Sellers stopped staring at Oliver to momentarily glance at Venko.

"Did I ask for your explanation Officer Venko? No, I did not, as a matter of fact, I wasn't finished. If it's okay with you, can I finish now?" Sellers asked with obvious sarcasm.

Venko had enough of these conversations to know that any verbal response would not be welcomed, so he just nodded his head. Sellers turned his attention back to Oliver.

"I distinctly remember telling you to confine your investigation to shift hours, and there were to be no field trips without prior authorization. Since I didn't know and Lt. Swanson didn't know, one can assume your trip was not authorized. I don't like getting calls from angry busybodies at nursing homes. I don't like pretending to be aware of your travels just so the police department doesn't look totally incompetent. And why can't you just follow the rules?"

Venko started to speak and decided against it.

"Oliver, you're grounded, go back to your own caseload. Venko and McGhee can handle the cold cases with a phone and a computer. All I need is for them to slip on the ice and get hurt WHILE ON LIGHT DUTY!" Sellers realized his volume had increased substantially and took a breath.

"Detective Oliver, you are not to drive or facilitate in any way, transportation out of this building for Venko or McGhee. You'll find yourself back in uniform if you do. Is that understood? They are on light duty."

Oliver nodded while seething inside.

"Officer Venko, no one expects you to solve these cases. If the detectives over the years couldn't, what makes you think you are any smarter? Call up some old witnesses, review their statements, type up your efforts and be done. You'll be back in uniform soon enough and no one will give a shit, and we can all say we say we tried," Sellers finished, zipped his jacket and headed towards the stairs.

Sellers ignored McGhee and Beans as they passed him.

"So, what did the big man want?" Beans asked nonchalantly.

"Fuck off, Beans," Oliver snapped.

"Roger that," Beams stated casually, and continued to his cubicle clutching his Popeye's bag.

McGhee pulled another chair from the hall and sat down with Oliver and Venko.

"What's up?"

"The Sea Hag from the nursing home called and complained to Sellers about our visit, and the package we delivered to Foster. Cassie is grounded from assisting us and we have no car. We are just supposed to sit here and generate meaningless paperwork to add to the file. The phone and our computers are the only tools at our disposal," Venko finished with a shrug.

"Ah man, fuck that," McGhee said, throwing up his arms.

"Good, my sentiments exactly. I've got the files on the table in the conference room. Make copies of the notes we took from Foster and I'll grab the whiteboard and wheel it in there," Venko finished and looked over at Oliver.

"Sorry Dan, Detective Kelly in the 2nd Precinct is going to retire in a month or so, I have just enough juice seniority-wise to get his spot on afternoons. I can't risk fucking up my chance to get out of here. I'll do what I can to help from here, but that's it."

"I understand; not a problem," Venko responded as he headed to the conference room.

"If someone were to need a car, and they checked the driver's side rear wheel well on a rusted, gold Ford Taurus out back, they might find a magnetic case with a spare key. I'll deny I told you that, and I also didn't tell you the heat doesn't work in the car," Oliver shouted down the hall.

Venko shot her a thumbs up without looking back. He picked up a black dry erase marker. On the left across the top row of the white board, he wrote the names of the two cold cases they were given, Michaels, Billings, then he wrote the names of the two attempted abductions, Cole and Daniels.

Venko started the brainstorming session.

"What do we know about all of the victims?" He asked McGhee.

"All white males, between ages twelve and fourteen. Michaels and Billings were delinquents, there isn't enough in Foster's notes to determine if Cole and Daniels were also delinquent hoodlums. Since they were juveniles at the time, there is no way for us to determine if they had prior arrests, unless we can find a detective still working that remembers those cases," McGhee finished and watched Venko write "white male" under each name and "prior arrests" under Michaels and Billings. He drew big circles under Cole and Daniels.

"We have to find out any criminal history on them," Venko stated, tapping the black marker on Cole and Daniels. "I'll see if

Cassie can pull up current addresses for Cole and Daniels from the in-house computer system. Let's go to suspect descriptions." Venko created a column on the left side of the board and wrote "Suspect."

McGhee spent the next several minutes reviewing the suspect drawing from the Michaels case, the computer-generated suspect sketch in the Billings case, as well as the written description of the suspects in the Cole and Daniels case. The latter took some time to locate buried deep in Foster's detailed notes.

"The sketch and the computer sketch for Michaels and Billings are so much alike it is creepy." McGhee held up the two and Venko nodded in agreement.

He traced a line from where he had written "Suspect" on the left side of the board and wrote "same," under Michaels and Billings.

"The suspect description Foster has for Cole and Daniels is also very similar. Hair color, approximate age, height, weight is very close. Hair style and clothing are different. Oh shit! Our dude is a lefty," McGhee quickly grabbed the Michaels folder and began scanning through the pages.

"What do you mean?" Venko asked.

"Foster's notes on Cole and Daniels, witnesses in both files, have the suspect wearing a shiny metallic watch band on his right wrist. The same for Michaels. Damn!"

Venko wrote "lefty" under Cole, Daniels and Michaels.

"Keep reviewing those files, I'm going to get Beans's file on that missing kid we responded to a month or so ago. What was his name? Sullivan, Sanders?"

McGhee scratched his head in thought before blurting out, "Solomon!"

Venko threw the marker on the table and walked briskly down the hall.

"Beans, I need the file you have on Solomon, the juvenile missing person that returned when we were on scene last month," Venko blurted out.

Beans, with his feet on his desk and deeply engrossed in a documentary on Netflix, took a crunchy bite out of his chicken leg. Without looking up, he pulled open his bottom desk drawer silently and pointed. Venko scanned through four or five folders until he found one with "Solomon" written across the tab. He took the folder and looked it over as he headed down the hall. Venko dropped the folder in front of McGhee.

"Page three of the incident report, suspect description given by mom," Venko said with a smile.

He picked up the dry-erase marker and wrote "Solomon," across the top row on the far right of the board next to the other names. He traced a line from "Suspect" on the left side of the board directly under Solomon's name and wrote in "same."

"Maybe an inch or two in height variance, but hair color, build and approximate weight of the suspect are damn near the same. No watch on the right hand though. Wait, here it is, mom said he had some kind of shiny bracelet on his right wrist, well, she thought it was his right wrist, and it reflected light from the streetlight above, that's why she noticed it."

"We want current addresses on Cole, Daniels, Billings and Michaels if we can find one. That case goes back to 1990. I'm not holding my breath, but we can have Cassie check the in-house computer. Mom or dad would most likely be the reporting party for the reports," Venko finished and took a sip of coffee that went cold ten minutes ago.

"Heather Conway is listed as the mother of Cory Michaels, and the reporting party. She works at Morely and Sons Manufacturing." McGhee stopped when Venko interrupted.

"Worked. That place has been closed for a while now," Venko corrected. "Who were the reporting parties on Cole and Daniels?"

"Looks like Selena Walton, grandmother of Shawn Cole, reported him missing, according to Foster's notes. She lives or lived over in the 3rd Precinct on Derby Ridge Drive. For Daniels it was his mother, Frieda Daniels. She lives on Rossler. For Billings it was..."

"His mother, I was on that call," Venko stated flatly.

"That's odd," McGhee stated, bouncing from the case files to the copies of Foster's notes, flipping pages back and forth.

"What's odd?" Venko asked as he watched McGhee with increasing curiosity.

"According to the reports that were taken, and Foster's notes on the returned kids, the reporting parties all worked or formerly worked at Morely and Sons. Why wouldn't a detective have worked that angle before?"

"Because it wasn't a pattern. Remember, no one worked the attempted abductions of Cole and Daniels. No official report was taken. If it hadn't been for Foster's on scene notes, we wouldn't know either. That was a huge plant, lots of people worked there. Two cases, years apart, would be a remote coincidence, not much more in a huge plant like that. We need to get out and talk to some of these folks."

"Maybe, but everything is starting to sound a little off about these cases if you ask me," McGhee said as he stacked the folders and notes neatly.

"Ah, you've got a feeling, do you? As in the pit of your stomach? But you can't explain why just yet. Your brain is telling you it's just a coincidence the suspects' appearance are strikingly similar. After all, the Michaels case was 1990 and Billings was almost 27 years later. The suspect in the Michael's case was around thirty years old. The descriptions in the other cases are between twenty-eight to thirty-five. If it's the same suspect in all of the cases, he would have been near sixty at the time of the Billings abduction. And you're slightly confused now, because the description of the suspect in the Billings case isn't of a sixty-year-old man, but of someone that is twenty-eight to thirty-five. Does that about sum up your discomfort?"

"Yeah, it can't be the same dude, but the similarities creep me out," McGhee answered honestly.

"McGhee, you might just be developing good old fashion cop instincts. I think we might get a clearer picture after we talk to some folks related to the old cases. Let's hope they are still awake and don't phone in a complaint against us. You feel like some pie and coffee?" Venko asked, making it clear they were going anyway.

Chapter 13
What Mama Said

With only five minutes of furious keystrokes, Oliver discovered that Heather Conway had been the victim of a car break-in two months ago. She easily pulled up the report for the incident and gave Venko the current address of 455 Teakwood Drive.

"Ah, everyone comes home to roost in the Woods eventually," Venko remarked as he wrote down the address on the top of the case folder.

"The good news is, even in the projects, no one would try to steal the piece of shit you're driving. I'll text or call you when I can find current addresses on Cole, Daniels, and Billings. You should head out now, it's 11:40 p.m., not sure how late she will answer the door," Oliver remarked before resuming the computer search.

Thirteen minutes later, Venko wheeled the rusting Taurus in front of the small duplex at 455 Teakwood Drive.

"TV is on in the living room. That's a good sign," McGhee said, peeking through the living room window.

Venko knocked twice.

"Who is it?" A voice called out immediately.

"Port Isley Police," Venko called out, then added, "Detectives to talk to you about Cory." Conway slid the chain back and unlocked the deadbolt. She cracked the door and peered out.

"Did you find him?" She asked in a voice filled with despair.

Venko and McGhee were overpowered by the smell of marijuana and they both reflexively stepped back on to the stoop.

"No ma'am, we didn't. We are assigned to investigate cold

cases and wanted to ask you a few questions about Cory's disappearance," McGhee stated politely.

"I don't see much of a reason for us to rehash all this. Every few years a different detective pops up on my door to tell me they are reviewing the case. I get it. You haven't forgotten Cory, but no one has found him. I appreciate the effort and I'll say the same thing when two new faces show up in six months or a year."

Conway's appearance startled Venko. She was fifty-nine but looked seventy. She was rail-thin, with sunken, red-rimmed eyes. Her greying blond hair had fallen out in patches, and what remained failed to cover a large surgical scar on the right side of her head.

"Heather, we don't care about the marijuana, and I promise we won't take up much of your time," Venko explained in a calming tone.

Conway pulled the belt of her ragged robe tight and opened the door. She directed them to a small, tattered couch, while she gingerly lowered herself onto the recliner. Venko noticed countless pill bottles scattered across the coffee table. Conway caught his glance at the coffee table.

"I have cancer. The marijuana is the only thing that keeps me from throwing up twenty-four hours a day. No, I don't have a prescription. Arrest me. Dying here or dying in jail is all the same to me. I rarely sleep, and never very long. What is it you want to know?"

Venko opened the file and began.

"From the original incident report, you gave a description of a person you saw in the street around the time that Cory disappeared. A neighbor, across the street from where you used to live, also gave a description of a person we believe was involved in abducting your son," Venko handed her the report and pointed to the paragraph with the description.

"I've seen this man every night when I try to sleep for damn near the last thirty years. If he walked in right now, I would know him. But he isn't going to, and all the might of the police department hasn't been able to find him. Like my son, he has vanished. Poof! Gone off the face of the earth." Conway stopped suddenly and began a violent, wet coughing fit.

Venko walked into the kitchen and located a clean glass. After he filled it with water, he handed it to her. She took the glass and sipped it cautiously. A few seconds later, her breathing had slowed to a steady rattle.

Venko then opened the Billings file and pulled the computer-generated suspect sketch out. He held it up, facing her.

"Yes, that's him. I forget which pills I'm supposed to take in the morning and what to take at night, but I will never forget that face," Conway said, barely above a whisper. She held a blood-stained washcloth up to her mouth, expecting another coughing fit.

McGhee noticed that Venko used the computer sketch from the 2017 Billings case instead of the drawing Conway helped create in 1990. He started to speak up, and Venko shook his head quickly to stop him. McGhee realized that telling her the same suspect might have been involved in other similar abductions would be devastating to a woman in her condition. It would do nothing for her recollection of events.

"I see that you worked at Morely and Sons at the time Cory disappeared. When did you stop working there?" McGhee asked.

"About three years after Cory was taken. I couldn't handle it. I wasn't sleeping and couldn't function at the plant," she answered.

"Was there anyone at the plant that had issues with you?" Venko asked, looking down at the folder intentionally. He knew what cancer did to his mother, it was painful for him to see it again in this woman.

"That place was a regular soap opera. All kinds of shit going on all the time. I avoided it. I got along with most folks there because I kept my nose in my own business," Conway stopped at the message chime on Venko's phone.

Venko looked at his phone and the message that Oliver sent. It was Ethan Daniels' address. He spent the next few minutes getting Conway to confirm what was in the incident report before finishing with, "Is there anything else you can tell us that might help?"

"I know Cory is alive. I know that, and I feel that. A mother knows. That's why this has all been such hell. He wasn't a good boy. I know that. He had a lot of problems. But he deserved the right to change. Maybe he has changed, wherever he is." Conway began to cough fitfully again, as tears streamed down her cheeks.

Venko closed the folder, stood, and patted her shoulder gently. He knew she had maybe a month left. The usual platitudes would ring hollow, they had all been used up years ago. He headed silently to the door. McGhee nodded to her as they pulled the door closed and stood on the stoop.

"Cassie sent the address for Daniels, let's try and knock that out and then we can grab some coffee," Venko stated, before walking towards the car, rapidly putting distance between himself and the memories Conway invoked.

• • •

The Taurus pulled in front of a neat, brick bungalow at 12:35 a.m. The sidewalk to the door had been shoveled and salted.

Venko knocked several times before a light came on and a faint voice asked, "Who's there?"

"Port Isley PD, ma'am, just need to ask you a few questions about Ethan," McGhee stated loudly over the howling wind. The door flew open and an animated Frieda Daniels began shouting.

"What is it? Is Ethan okay? What happened to him?"

Venko quickly realized McGhee could have phrased his statement better.

"I'm sorry, we are here to ask some questions about Ethan's attempted abduction in 2006. We are currently assigned to investigate cold cases. We think the suspect in your son's case might have committed similar offenses. As far as we know, Ethan is fine," Venko and McGhee held up their badges as she opened the door.

A small, slightly plump redhead waved them inside. She was dressed in a full-length green robe. Plaid pajama pants hung down over her white slippers.

"Frieda Daniels?" Venko asked and stuck out his hand. She nodded her head and shook his hand. "I'm Officer Venko, and this is Officer McGhee. I apologize for the late hour, and I promise we won't take up much of your time."

"Would you like some tea or coffee? I'm going to make some tea for myself," Daniels asked politely.

"No, thank you," the pair said in unison as they sat in chairs across from a small couch. There were a few religious magazines and a Bible on a square wooden coffee table in front of them. The living room was tidy and the furnishings were modest. There were several pictures of Ethan and his mother scattered throughout the living room. As Daniels prepared her tea, Venko got up and walked around the living room, examining the framed photos. In the oldest photo, Ethan was maybe nine or ten, eating cotton candy at the county fair. Daniels was much younger and probably fifteen pounds underweight, her eyes were heavily lined and she had two visible sores on her face. *The meth monster had you back then.*

Another photo had a smiling mid-twenties Ethan in a cap and gown with a much healthier-looking Daniels. Venko sat back down as she entered the living room, cup and saucer in hand.

"What is Ethan doing these days?" Venko asked, breaking the ice.

"He is a genuine, board-certified veterinarian. He has two partners in a downtown animal clinic. I couldn't be prouder of him," she beamed. "He has a lovely condo downtown as well."

"I know it was a long time ago, and not a pleasant memory, but what do you remember about the day someone tried to take him?" McGhee asked while opening the file.

"It was a long time ago; it was a different life for both of us then. Ethan was playing in the snow outside. He was very upset. The police had just been over to talk to him about some horrible, horrible things that happened to the neighbor's cat." Daniels stopped, her voice pausing to let the emotion of the memory pass. "He had been suspended from school again for fighting, so he had been home. He was such a sensitive boy, he tended to lash out. After the fight at school, he was taken to the principal's office. The officer who brought him home said he attacked the principal with a stapler, but I don't think he was capable of that. Anyway, I happened to look out the window and saw Ethan talking to this man. It was late afternoon, and the skies were clear. I had an immediate bad feeling about that man, by the time I got a coat on and went outside, they were both gone."

Venko opened the Michaels case folder and withdrew the hand-drawn suspect sketch from 1990.

"Is this the man you saw?" Venko asked.

"Yes," she said after a brief pause.

"What about him?" Venko said and handed her the computer created sketch from the Billings file. McGhee noted the different sketch, and now understood that Venko was testing a theory that despite the years between cases, the suspect was the same.

"It's the same person, slightly different hair. What is this?" She asked, puzzled.

"Just being thorough," Venko said before redirecting the focus of the conversation. "What happened after he disappeared?"

"I panicked, I began screaming for him. I ran inside and called the police. A police car was here in two or three minutes. A detective showed up about a minute later. I began talking to the detective as police cars raced through the neighborhood looking for Ethan. Maybe ten minutes after he disappeared, I heard a commotion out in the side yard. An officer was yelling, and then Ethan just walked in the side door like nothing happened. He seemed confused and couldn't tell the officers or detective much of anything about the last ten minutes. He did not remember talking to the stranger in the front yard."

"Did you take him to the hospital or see a doctor?" Venko asked.

"No. Paramedics came and checked him out. They told me that apart from him being confused, and a small bump behind his right ear, he appeared to be fine."

"Bump?" McGhee asked.

"One paramedic said it looked like a bug bite or maybe an allergic reaction of some kind. The other said it looked like scar tissue. Well, I knew it wasn't a scar. I knew my son, I remember all his falls, cuts and scrapes. It wasn't a scar. I came to realize it was where our dear Lord touched him and everything changed," Daniels took a sip of tea and smiled serenely.

Venko and McGhee exchanged puzzled looks.

"What do you mean changed?" Venko asked as he scribbled in his notebook.

"It didn't just change him, it changed me as well. The devil had me in his clutches back then. I was well off the path of the righteous. I was dealing with the evils of addiction. I wasn't a good mother and had a hard time dealing with Ethan's behavioral problems. I was a single mother trying to work and raise a son. There never seemed to be enough hours in the day. I worked in a god-forsaken place full of liars and fornicators and they pulled me into their hell. I was weak. I admit it," she paused, again becoming slightly emotional at the memory.

Venko saw McGhee start to speak and knew he was trying to redirect her and shook his head. McGhee sat back and waited for Daniels to continue.

"When Ethan walked back in the house that day in front of the detective and police officers, confused and cold, he was changed. God had truly touched him. It was just like Saul's conversion on the road to Damascus. He was suddenly kind, considerate, and began to do well in school. I quit my job at Morely and Sons a year after the incident. I began to pray, and God guided me through rehab. He showed me my true calling. I went back to school and became a certified addiction counselor. About three years ago, the devil tested my faith, tried to pull me back. Breast cancer was my test. Through faith and surgery, I beat my illness. Ethan finished high school second in his class. His SAT score earned him a full college scholarship and he never looked back."

Venko and McGhee exchanged a quick glance when Daniels mentioned Morely and Sons. Venko was now obviously curious about Ethan's behavioral change.

"Tell me more about this bump Ethan had," he inquired.

"When he first walked back into the house all those years ago, it looked more like a bee sting. It was a small, raised bump slightly redder than the surrounding skin. Over the years it faded. The bump is still there, but no longer discolored. It's hardly noticeable. But it's still there. It is the mark of Ethan's salvation."

"Thank you, ma'am. You have been most helpful," Venko said, cueing McGhee that the interview was over.

Once they were back in the car, McGhee exhaled and shook his head.

"What the fuck was that?"

"You're not buying the whole divine intervention?" Venko remarked with a sly grin, as he started the car.

"It's been really, really strange. One thing I know for sure, Frieda Daniels most certainly believes it was the hand of God at work. What do you think?" McGhee asked, rubbing his hands together in the frigid car.

"I think we just stepped into an honest to goodness, black and white episode of the Twilight Zone," Venko said, as he made a left turn.

"My dad watched that. Forrest Whitaker was the host, right? Early 2000's? It's still on cable sometimes."

Venko sighed and briefly looked at McGhee.

"To call that iteration the Twilight Zone is blasphemy. I'm talking black and white, Rod Serling magic. Ah hell, just Google it."

Venko pulled to the curb.

"Pull out the Solomon folder. Look in the report and see if Beans put anything in there about the kid's condition. I know the paramedics were on scene. Not sure if there was anything worth noting or not."

McGhee studied the report for a few minutes, thumbing back and forth between pages.

"Nothing about Solomon's physical condition is noted at all."

Venko thought for a second.

"I have an idea," he dialed Haystack's number and the big man answered on the first ring.

"Dan! Bro, I was just thinking of you. I have a brand-new concoction, you're going to love. I have a fresh batch of Elroy's elixir."

Venko tried to cut in, but Haystack continued on.

"Creatine, whey, blueberries, celery and a clove of fresh garlic. Put it all in the blender with some skim milk and ice, and boom, power smoothie! Contains all the antioxidant features of blueberries and it fights the free tentacles in your body."

Venko pounced on Haystack's pause.

"Free radicals Haystack, not tentacles, free radicals. That does sound tasty and all, but I need a favor."

"Name it bro!" Haystack replied.

"Are you still cozy with that paramedic chick, the one that used to come to the station and work out with you?"

"Emily, uh, we fell on some dark times," Haystack responded solemnly.

"Like how dark Haystack? Like midnight? Or maybe just charcoal to medium grey? Because I need something important."

"Bro, I just couldn't trust her anymore. She doesn't squat. I tried to get past it, I really did. But how do you carry on a relationship with a woman who won't do squats? Was I supposed to just look past the fact that she ignored working out fifty percent of her body? I couldn't spend our time together watching her calves shrivel, and her glutes drop."

An exasperated Venko slapped his forehead.

"Haystack, pull over and listen. Take a pen and paper out and write this down. This is important. Gabriel Solomon, 344 Birch Circle. Paramedics checked him out after an attempted abduction last month. He was outside in the cold for maybe ten minutes. I want the run sheet. That's the document paramedics create showing what they did and what they found on the patient. Ask Emily for the document. Tell her important detectives need it. Uh, there might be some privacy issues with getting it. If that's the case, just sneak a picture of it on your phone and send it to me."

"I can try. I'll call her and lay down some Haystack charm. But, understand how hard it is for me to fake interest in a chick that just lets her legs go."

"Thanks Haystack. That's all I ask. Just give it a try. And by the way, McGhee is interested in your new protein smoothie, whip up a batch and bring it up to the detective bureau tomorrow. I'd love to try it, but my doctor has me on a no-garlic diet."

"Awesome, bro, let little Marley know that with some of my magic juice, he will get big like me, in no time. I'll let you know what I find out from Emily."

"Later Haystack," Venko said and ended the call.

McGhee was shaking his head.

"Not cool, Dan. Not cool at all. I am not testing anything created by that corn-fed mad scientist."

Venko's phone rang, interrupting McGhee's rant. Venko saw it was Bianchi and answered on the second ring.

"Dan, we sat on the 14th street hangout, lots of activity. Can you meet us at Molly's? Saw some weird shit."

"We can be there in five minutes," Venko replied and ended the call.

McGhee looked over, "What's up?"

"It was Bianchi, they were sitting on the 14th street hang out, trying to find Espinoza for me. They saw some weird shit and want to meet at Molly's."

"I'm starting to think weird is a relative term. But I am starving and would kill for a Molly's chili cheese dog and some onion rings," McGhee added, resisting the urge to look at his phone. Venko drove the remaining three minutes to Molly's in silence, mentally replaying the interviews.

"Well, look at these two important people, all dressed like real-life detectives," Ebony said with an inviting smile as the pair entered the diner.

McGhee shot her his most charming smile as the pair sat in the middle booth. Venko took his usual seat facing the door. Ebony filled their coffee cups and took her pad out.

"What would you like tonight? Eyes up here Marley," she said casually, while looking at Venko for his order. McGhee immediately felt himself getting flush.

"Cherry pie for me. Officers Bianchi and Martinez will be joining us shortly," Venko saw Ebony's smile fade slightly at the mention of Bianchi and Martinez. He knew their excessive bravado was not everyone's cup of tea.

"I'll have a chili cheese dog and some onion rings," McGhee added.

"Would you looky here? Marley developed a man-sized appetite," she said with a smile and walked away to put the order in.

Venko looked out the window and saw the familiar faces of Officers Frank Bianchi and Sal "Jesus" Martinez as they pulled into the snow-covered lot.

"E-girl, your boys are here!" Martinez boomed as the pair entered the doorway.

"Frozen crime fighters in the house. Bring on the coffee," Bianchi shouted to Ebony before taking a seat next to Venko. Martinez slid in next to McGhee.

"How's the arm?" Martinez asked giving McGhee's cast a light rap with his knuckles.

"All good, the cast will be off shortly," McGhee responded.

Bianchi noticed Venko wasn't wearing his sling.

"What about you Dan, how's the shoulder?"

"Not bad, almost ready for full duty I suppose. What did you find?"

"Check it out, me and Jesus are sitting blacked out in the alley with a straight view of the corner of 14th and Hemingway. We can see the front of Sandovar's crib. We see the usual suspects come and go. A few gangsters, a few good citizens stopping to make pharmaceutical purchases. I have Jesus dialed in on the mission, don't worry, we are just there to locate the kid." Bianchi paused, as Ebony filled the coffee cups.

"Anyway, Jesus has the binoculars out and is checking out the area around Sandovar's apartment. He looks up the hill on Hemingway and sees a car parked. The ride is probably a newer black SUV. No plate on the front. He dials in a little better and sees a white dude in the driver's seat with binoculars, watching us! He hands me the goggles and I verify the dude was watching us. Dude must have gotten nervous because he pulled off. We decided to stay on the apartment, instead of chase him down."

"What the fuck? He looks like a cop? Internal Affairs? Narcs?" McGhee asked, as Ebony set the giant chili cheese dog and onion rings in front of him and handed Venko his pie.

"Yeah, I'm thinking cop, or alphabet, DEA, FBI. But it gets better," Martinez grabbed an onion ring off McGhee's plate before continuing. "We get called back to our district for a bullshit report. So, we go knock out the report in a few minutes and start slinking back through the area. This time we come up behind the apartment on top of the hill on Hemingway and sit. A few minutes later, I'm peeking through the binos and I see the same dude from the SUV, but now he is out on foot, talking to two dirtbags on the corner. It looks like a heated argument. We decide, fuck it, were gonna go down there and make the guy badge us if he really is an IA ghost. They hate being fronted out, so why not. We roll down and jump out. The mopes start doing the mope shuffle, sliding back towards the apartment. The white dude gives us the hand up, and said everything is fine, no problems, and turns to walk away," Martinez paused for a sip of coffee and grabbed another onion ring. Like an old married couple, Bianchi picks up the story without missing a beat.

"So, I tell him, hold up dude, we need to talk. He continues to walk, so I put the fucking claw on his right wrist and spin him towards me. His watch starts to slide down his wrist under my grip. The dude reaches over with his left hand, pulls my thumb counter-clockwise smooth as silk, and puts me in a wrist lock and shoves me back. This is all so quick that Jesus doesn't even realize it until after the dude shoved me."

"So," Martinez takes over, "I'm thinking, hell no, you are not gonna disrespect my partner like that. This dude needs a little physical taxation penalty, and then we are gonna chat with him. I go to drop a short right hook on his chin, and the son-of-a-bitch ducks right under it and pops up behind me. He sweeps my right foot at the same time he shoves me. Quick and effective. I go down in the snow. He turns and you'll never guess what he says to me."

"Fuck off?" Venko said with a shrug.

"No, the dude said *sorry*. Then he turned and bolted. Dude ran like a deer, long smooth strides. Me and Bianchi ain't no slouches, we are on him ten, eleven feet back. He makes a sudden turn into the alley. We lose sight of him for a second, maybe two. He vanished. Or found the world's best hiding place. No noise. No movement. Gone," Martinez finished and held up his coffee cup as Ebony came over with the pot.

"What about the body cam footage? Pull it up on your phone. I want to see it," Venko asked.

"Well, that's where it gets strange," Bianchi started before McGhee interrupted.

"It wasn't strange before that?"

Bianchi pulled up the BWC footage on his phone and began to narrate.

"I activate my camera as we're coming down the hill, just in case I got to jump out and run. That's why you have the beautiful view of the passenger airbag. And about now is when Jesus asks, in his own colorful way, who this good citizen might be. I get out of the car. Right there, you can see the two mopes talking to our overdressed white dude. Two more steps and then," he stops talking as they all stare at the phone.

"Static, and no image. What the hell? What about your camera Martinez?" Venko asked.

"Same thing, once I got within five feet, nothing but static and no image."

"What did the dude look like? You think it was a cop?" Venko asked as he took the last bite of his cherry pie.

"Yeah, that's the vibe I got. Maybe thirty, fit, six-foot two, maybe a buck ninety, lean. Wore a nice dark grey wool coat, came down to mid-thigh length. Khaki pants and hiking boots. Short brown hair. Not sure on the eye color," Martinez finished and looked at McGhee's plate again. McGhee nodded and Martinez retrieved another onion ring.

"You didn't put anything out over the air? You didn't call in units to swarm the area? You just got punked and ate it?" McGhee asked, smiling.

Bianchi looked at Venko with total disbelief. Venko nodded to Bianchi as if to say, *Go ahead, school the lad.*

Martinez started first.

"Rookie please! We are out of our district, doing a favor for you and your partner. We can't call in an air strike as much as we would like to, because we would have to explain what we were doing, and possibly fabricate a solid reason to stop the white ninja. And even if we could maybe bend some reasonable suspicion to justify the stop, said bending would still be taking place out of the district, without authorization for said excursion. We only turned on the BWC in case shit got real, real crazy." Martinez looked at Bianchi for support.

"So, Jesus and I held a little conference and decided it would be best for now if we took the loss and drove off. You know, FIDO, Fuck It Drive Off. We, of course, reserve the right to fucking collect righteous back taxes, should the opportunity arise. The dude had skills. Could have snapped my wrist and didn't. Ninja-magicked my partner right on his ass. It was clear the white ninja just wanted to get away from us. And he did. And yeah, we looped the block several times. The SUV was gone as well."

Venko took out his notepad and had Bianchi and Martinez again describe the white ninja while he wrote it down.

"Gents, I appreciate all your help tonight. Leave the place alone the rest of the night. But something is going on over there. I got Haystack on a favor, hopefully I get something back from him tonight or tomorrow. We have a couple of interviews to do early in the shift tomorrow and then I'd like to sit on the place. I'll fill you in tomorrow if there is a specific game plan." Venko smiled and called for the check, as a simmering uncertainty swept over him. He could read it on McGhee's face as well. This was strange.

Chapter 14
Strange Days Indeed

The following night, true to his word, Haystack came lumbering into the detective bureau carrying a quart of blue-green liquid.

"Cassie, you want to try some of my home brewed protein smoothie? I use it right before the gym, but anytime is good for a little pick me up," Haystack asked, holding up the clear carafe. Oliver could see gooey chunks and could only guess as to their origin.

"Haystack, wow, uh, now isn't a good time. I, I have to sharpen some pencils," Oliver mumbled and headed rapidly to the women's bathroom, knowing she could sit in peace until Haystack had finished doling out samples of his gruel.

"I can't guarantee there will be any left later!" He called to her as she entered the bathroom. Venko and McGhee raised up partially to see over the cubicle wall.

"Oh shit! He really did bring in a quart of that motor oil he drinks," McGhee whispered to Venko as Haystack headed toward their cubicle.

"Take a drink or two. Tell him it's a nice change of pace from your usual protein drink and thank him for sharing it. You're going to have to drink some of it in his presence, no way around it. Say what I told you, and you'll be off the hook for a few months," Venko instructed.

"Mother fucker, you're the one that got me on the hook!" McGhee growled, tossing his pen onto the desk in frustration.

"Haystack, grab that chair and pull it in here. Good to see you," Venko said with a welcoming smile as Haystack entered. "Were you able to connect with Emily last night or today?"

"Yeah," Haystack's face grew flush, grinning sheepishly before continuing. "We connected for like seven or eight minutes right before work. It wasn't easy, you know how I feel about chicks that aren't well rounded in their workouts. I knew it was important to you Dan, and I have a copy of the paperwork you wanted. Bro, I wouldn't do that for just anyone."

"You are a true humanitarian," Venko said as he took the folded paper from Haystack.

Haystack set two plastic cups down and began to pour the smoothie into the first cup. The smell of garlic was overpowering, and the plopping sound of the blueberry and celery chunks made McGhee's stomach churn. Underneath the odor of garlic, there was a faint smell Venko couldn't place. He filled the second glass and set the carafe down.

"Down the hatch Rasta-man," Haystack said, tipping his own cup up and chugging the eight ounces in mere seconds.

McGhee took a sip and tried to maintain his composure. He shot Venko a look of pure hatred before taking a large gulp. This brought on a coughing fit, followed by some mild gagging. McGhee felt his eyes start to water. He took a deep breath, hoping everything would stay down.

"Thanks Haystack, that's a nice change of pace from my usual protein drink," McGhee could barely get the words out, he felt his nose starting to drip.

"You're welcome bro. When I was whipping up this batch, I thought it lacked a little punch, you know, like an underlying pick me up, a subtle kick. And then it hit me! Cayenne pepper flakes. The whey protein acts as a binding, thickening agent, then one whole clove of garlic, one stalk of chopped celery, a cup of blueberries, add milk and a tablespoon of cayenne pepper and blend!" Haystack said proudly.

"My hat's off to you Haystack, most people I know would never think of mixing garlic, celery, blueberries and cayenne pepper together. Still, something smells different. Did you use soy or almond milk instead of regular milk?" Venko asked, watching the color drain from McGhee's face.

"Well to be honest, I was out of regular milk and all I had left was buttermilk. But it's chock full of nutrients too," Haystack explained as McGhee bolted from his chair and sprinted down the hall.

Venko and Haystack stared at each other silently for a few seconds.

"He has to turn in a medical update form to Lt. Swanson, probably wanting to catch him before he hit the streets," Venko remarked matter-of-factly.

"Gotcha," Haystack responded cluelessly.

Oliver exited the ladies room to the distinct sounds of retching coming from the men's bathroom across the hall. She continued down the hall and glanced over at Venko and Haystack talking. Venko caught her gaze as she started to point, and he subtly shook his head. She smiled and continued past the pair, with the knowledge that a good story would come later. She purposely veered left before passing Venko and Haystack, not wanting to elicit another sample invitation.

Venko unfolded the report Haystack gave him and began to pour over it. Haystack took the cue in stride.

"I got to get in service, a good wagon man is always available," he said as he grabbed the carafe and stood.

"Thanks again Haystack," Venko said and quickly turned his attention back to the form.

For a few brief seconds the room was silent, until Haystack's booming voice pierced the stillness.

"Yo Beans, you want to try some of."

"No."

"You don't even know what I was going to say."

"That is correct my overly-concussed friend. And the answer is still no."

Venko watched Haystack head down the stairs. He sent McGhee a text that it was safe to come out. Venko picked up

McGhee's cup and poured the remaining chunky fluid down the sink next to the coffee maker. He threw away the cup as McGhee returned to the cubicle.

"Who does that? Who would mix blueberries, garlic and celery? No one!" McGhee said as he wiped his face with a damp paper towel.

"With buttermilk," Venko added, as he struggled to maintain a straight face.

"Asshole," McGhee said as Venko finally cracked, breaking into a full grin.

McGhee looked at the report Venko was holding.

"Anything good?" He asked.

"There is a notation of a small circular welt behind the patient's right ear. Slightly raised. Appears to cause no discomfort to patient," Venko finished reading.

"You mean the mark of God? Like Daniels?" McGhee questioned, somewhat sarcastically.

"Exactly. And now I'm going to call Wendy Fischer and see if young Gabriel Solomon has had a similar conversion like Ethan Daniels. Give me five minutes or so to talk with Fischer and meet me in the conference room, pull all the suspect descriptions from the files."

Venko walked into the conference room ten minutes later. Oliver was sitting next to McGhee explaining computer print outs she brought over from her desk.

"You look puzzled Dan, what's up?" McGhee asked.

"I just got off the phone with Wendy Fischer. Gabriel Solomon is doing quite well. He is attending and participating in his therapy. He started at his new school three weeks ago. No problems at all. He is bringing books home and reading. Fischer said that he never used to read anything. Oh, and he wants to try out for the soccer team next year," Venko said with a shrug.

"Well hallelujah," McGhee remarked.

Oliver gave the pair a blank look.

"Long story," McGhee added.

Oliver held up the paperwork she brought.

"You might find this interesting. I was trying to get a current address on Selena Walton, grandmother of Shawn Cole. I found nothing in our computer system. She wasn't a suspect, witness or victim of a crime. Remember, Foster said no report was done on Cole's attempted abduction back then. I checked newspaper sites online and found an obituary for Selena Walton in 2003. Said she died after a long illness. The article also stated she was preceded in death by her daughter, Sabrina Cole. I found an obituary for Sabrina Cole, she passed away in 1999. Also after a long illness. She was Shawn's mother according to the article. That would explain why Walton was the reporting party per Foster's case notes from 2001." Venko raised his eyebrows and turned his palms up, waiting for the rest of the story. Oliver and McGhee looked blankly at him.

"Well that sounds interesting and all, but I'm not getting the significance," Venko answered honestly.

"You will. Tell him the rest Cassie," McGhee requested.

Venko nodded and Oliver began.

"In Walton's obituary, listed among surviving family members were grandson Shawn Cole, daughter Scarlett Schneider and son-in-law, Robert Schneider. On a whim, I cross-referenced the names Scarlett and Robert Schneider on the in-house computer. I got an address over in the nicer section of the 2nd Precinct. I pulled up an old police report from 2005 for that address: bicycle theft. Victim was a sixteen-year-old male, Shawn Schneider. There were no children listed for Scarlett in the Walton obituary. I'm guessing Shawn Cole was adopted and is now Shawn Schneider."

"Interesting. The kid would be about thirty-three or thirty-four now. I'd like to talk to him if we can find him," Venko said and looked at McGhee, who was smiling.

"That won't be hard, Sabrina Schneider is also listed in our system as the emergency contact person for Detective Shawn Schneider. Promoted from patrolman to detective two years ago, currently assigned to the 2nd Precinct, midnight shift," Oliver finished and handed a printout that included a photo of the smiling, bespectacled Detective Shawn Schneider.

"Wow. That is impressive Cassie. I think a road trip is in order. Marcus, gather this all up and throw it in your bag," Venko directed.

"Good luck gentlemen. I've got to get back to my own cases." Oliver grabbed her cellphone off the table and left the conference room. McGhee watched the movement of her fitted dress pants with great interest as she walked out.

"You have no shot. None. And, she would most likely kick your ass as well," Venko stated, noticing McGhee's longing glance at Oliver's defined posterior.

"Can't a brother just appreciate fine art without a motive?" McGhee said, stuffing the files into his messenger bag.

"Yes of course. You're just a connoisseur. I get it. Call over to the 2nd Precinct and see if Schneider will meet us at Denny's a few blocks from his station house."

A few minutes later McGhee returned and informed Venko that Schneider agreed to meet them at Denny's.

• • •

Venko broke the silence as the Taurus drifted by boarded up buildings near the 7th Precinct.

"Do these cases bother you? Does it seem like normal logic doesn't apply?"

McGhee thought for a second.

"That's why they are cold cases. Logic doesn't apply, if it did, they would have been solved."

"Let's stretch what's possible and say the suspect is the same person in all the cases, not just the cold cases, but the attempted abductions as well. Suspend logic, let's say the dude that took Cory Michaels in 1990 is the same guy that took Dakota Billings in 2017. Let's say he is the same guy that took and then released Solomon, Daniels and Cole, or was sloppy enough to let them escape. He is methodical and intelligent. Do you know how hard it is to disappear without a trace? So why keep Michaels and Billings? And let's be honest, they are most likely dead. What's different about them? What are we missing?" Venko looked over at McGhee as he finished.

"I find it strange that someone connected to each case worked at Morely and Sons," McGhee responded.

Venko nodded his head.

"I'm going to do some digging into Morely and Sons when we get back. Listening to Bianchi describe the guy that got away from them, a cop or maybe a fed, that bothers me. And it bothered me a lot when he said he grabbed the guy's right wrist and he was wearing a watch. Yeah, I realize there are millions of left-handed people, but his description gave me chills. The guy is in the area where we believe Espinoza has been hiding? Espinoza is the same approximate age as all the others in our case folders. Is he planning on taking him as well? And why?" Venko finished as he parked near the door of Denny's.

"We need to find Espinoza first," McGhee replied.

Venko suddenly remembered what Rosales told him. *Put all the pieces on the table first, your eyes will know where they go.*

Venko scanned the restaurant as they entered. As the hostess approached, he caught a wave from the corner of his eye.

"Ma'am, we are meeting a party over there," Venko said and pointed to a booth along the back wall. She stepped aside, and the duo walked towards the youthful man in glasses. He stood as they approached. He was average height with a thin build. His wire-rimmed glasses and blond hair made him look much younger than thirty-four.

"Hello Dan, Marcus," he said, and shook their hands with gusto. "Damn near the whole 2nd Precinct stopped by the hospital after your shooting. How are you guys doing?" Schneider finished and sat down.

A waitress appeared and Venko and McGhee ordered coffee.

"We're on the mend, doing well, assigned to cold cases while on light duty. Not sure what Marcus told you, but your attempted abduction years ago might be related to our cold cases. If you're okay talking about it, we would like to ask you some questions."

"No problem, I still have no memory of the actual incident though."

"Please tell us what you do remember," McGhee directed as Venko took out his notebook and pen.

"I was mad at my mom and I had been grounded after being suspended from school again..."

"What were you suspended for?" Venko asked, interrupting Schneider.

"Fighting. I'm not proud of it, I wasn't a good kid. I ran with two other friends at the time, and that's what we did. We beat up other kids and stole stuff. The final straw with the school occurred when I hit Jeremy Stinson with my math book. He was just sitting there at his desk, and as I walked by, I took a two-handed swing with my book and hit him the face, breaking his nose. Again, I'm not proud of it, I had impulse issues."

Venko glanced at the file he had constructed from Foster's case notes. "So on the afternoon of May 4th, 2001, you were home?" Venko prodded and Schneider began.

"It was really nice out, and there was no way I was just going to sit in my room. I snuck out the window and headed down the sidewalk towards a friend's house. The next thing I can remember, is being back in the yard and just walking into the house. Cops were everywhere. I didn't understand what they were saying to me or why everyone was so alarmed. My grandma was yelling at me. She said she saw a man talking to me and we walked behind a house. We had disappeared by the time she caught up I guess. I don't remember any of that. To this day, I don't remember any of that ten minute or so of time."

"What happened after that?" McGhee asked, gently probing for more.

"Paramedics checked me out. They said I was fine and told my grandma she might want to drive me to the hospital to get checked out. I wanted no part of the hospital. I was a little freaked out. Every now and then after that, she would ask if I remembered anything about the incident. I never did."

"I know your mom passed away a few years before that. Did she ever mention issues or problems with neighbors or coworkers?" Venko asked, as he waved off the waitress with refills.

"Not really. I was nine or ten when she died. Things had gotten pretty bad right before she died. Both her and my grandmother worked at Morely and Sons. Mom got sick and started missing work. They fired her about a year before she passed. We moved in with my grandmother, who still worked there. She picked up a ton of overtime to support us. It still bothers me what a complete hellion I was then, it only made things worse for her, I'm sure."

Venko stopped writing and looked up from his notebook.

"Sounds like you got on the right track, you're a detective now. Could you have imagined that when you were eleven or twelve?"

"No way," Schneider chuckled before continuing. "After the incident, I don't know if it frightened me, but I just suddenly lost interest in those friends and what we had been doing. The headaches I used to get trying to focus on reading or schoolwork kind of went away. I realized it wasn't that hard when I actually tried. I changed schools. Well, not that I had a choice, but the new school was great. Mom died and I lived with my grandmother until she passed, and then my aunt Sabrina and my uncle Robert adopted me. I kind of started learning and helping him with his accounting business," he paused wondering if he was being helpful or just droning on. "I'm boring you guys; do you really want me to go on?"

Venko and McGhee both nodded.

"I spent a few years working for my uncle and going part-time to community college after high school. At twenty-one, I took the police test on a whim. I was bored and thought my background with numbers and computers would be a plus. I liked being a patrolman, but working cases as a detective, solving puzzles, I like it more."

Venko closed his notebook and made small talk with Schneider for a few minutes, then looked over at McGhee.

"I guess we should head out and get back to work."

The trio stood as McGhee and Venko exchanged handshakes with Schneider. Venko saw it, as Schneider turned towards the door, a small bump just behind Schneider's right ear. Barely noticeable. But it was there. He froze momentarily.

McGhee, already three steps towards the door turned back.

"Yo Dan, you alright? I paid for our coffees, cash is on the table."

"Yeah, okay," Venko responded as he snapped out of his trance. He shivered slightly, and then resumed walking to the door.

Venko started the car and pulled onto the street.

"Did you see it? Behind his right ear, he had the same small bump as Solomon and Daniels."

"No," McGhee responded and was vexed that he missed such an important detail. So much to learn, he thought. The pair drove silently by the apartment building at 14th and Hemingway, and then headed back to the precinct.

Dex waved to the pair as they strode up the stairs. McGee set his messenger bag down next to his desk and headed to the coffee maker.

"Let's start digging and see what we can find on Morely and Sons," Venko said as he opened the search engine page on his computer.

For 25 minutes, the pair scoured the internet for articles on Morely and Sons. Venko weeded through several stories with loose references to the company before McGhee found one of interest.

"Looks like the business ran into financial trouble in the mid-eighties. About the time Eugene Morely stepped away from the business and his son, Stan took over. Right after that Morely and Sons formed an LLC, and expanded the plant," McGhee explained and took a sip of coffee.

"Can you track down where that sudden infusion of cash came from? They must have brought in partners for that kind of expansion" Venko responded.

McGhee spent ten minutes searching various websites and registries.

"Nope, whoever they are, they don't want to be found easily. Checked state business registries, and nothing."

"This is interesting," Venko began reading portions of the article aloud. "In 1989, the county health department received a number of anonymous complaints about the plant, including unsafe working conditions and exposure to dangerous fumes. Jacob Eason, County Health Director, conducted a three-month investigation and found the plant was in compliance with health and safety regulations. The article states that he recommended minor changes and the plant complied." Venko paused and pulled up a related article before continuing.

"In 1997, the News-Lantern did a story on the plant. Esther Kennedy, age sixty-one, and Beverly Watkins, age fifty-three, died within a month of each other. Both had worked at the Morely and Sons plant over fifteen years, and both died after long battles with cancer. Their families, through legal counsel, were calling on the health department to investigate conditions at the plant."

McGhee scrolled down the page until finding an article on a lawsuit against Morely and Sons.

"Here is something, August 12, 2000. The lawsuit filed against Morely and Sons was settled with the Kennedy and Watkins families. Terms were confidential. The plant was permitted to continue expansion and the health department signed off on a new waste disposal policy. And right below that article, I found this nugget. About a month later, Jacob Eason left his position as the county health director to accept a post with the governor's office." McGhee looked over at Venko.

Venko sat back in his chair.

"That smells like local corruption," Venko said as he scrolled down the screen looking for anything that might jump out. He stopped and clicked on an article and began to read silently before commenting.

"Whoa, you gotta hear this, November 2008, it appears the EPA responded to numerous complaints about the plant. Looks like the feds finally got interested in what was going on at Morely. There is a press release attached to the article." Venko silently skimmed a portion of the article before reading aloud. "Investigators are requesting full cooperation from the local health department, which has not occurred to date." Venko whistled before commenting. "That's pretty harsh for the EPA to call out the health department publicly for its lack of assistance. Wow!" Venko finished as he opened another article and began reading.

"On December 4th, 2008, the EPA along with state and federal law enforcement agencies attempted to serve a search warrant on the residence of Jacob Eason. The warrant specified records and documents relating to Eason's handling of prior complaints about Morely and Sons while in his position as county health director. His personal financial records were also targeted in the warrant, and all of his assets were frozen. As officers approached the residence, they heard a single gunshot. Officers kicked in the door and found Eason dead from a gunshot wound to the head. The house had been set on fire, and officers scrambled to escape the rapidly spreading flames. The house and all contents were a complete loss," Venko finished, and continued scanning articles.

"See," McGhee began. "See, that I can handle. That isn't Twilight Zone shit. That stinks of good old-fashioned greed."

"Yeah, unfortunately my mother and many others died as a result of this greed. No telling how many bribes Stan Morely and the shadow figures from the LLC threw around to keep that death trap humming and bringing in cash. And like usual, a bunch of little people go down, and the big guys move on to other projects," Venko said with disgust.

McGhee continued scanning the computer screen silently for a few minutes.

"Looks like Stan was questioned in 2010, and nothing came of it. In late 2011 rumors began to surface that he was negotiating with developers to sell the property. There was considerable interest in turning the property into upscale condominiums as part of a complete makeover of the waterfront district."

Venko nodded his head.

"Yeah, I remember that. The sticking point was cleanup costs for the site. No one knew what was really there. Few were willing to write a big check for the property and then be saddled with millions in additional cleanup costs. They must have negotiated some settlement on cleanup costs, because the property was finally sold almost three years ago. The plant ceased operations about three months before the sale. The EPA came in and dropped a stack of violations on the place and levied heavy fines. The developer initially moved a bunch of equipment out, while maintaining the surveillance and alarm systems. Nothing has happened since; the building sits nearly empty. I think the hold up for the project rests with the developers being able to obtain other adjacent properties surrounding the plant. I'm guessing someone on the waterfront is holding out for a little better payday," Venko commented as he grabbed the stack of articles off the printer. He rolled up the articles, and tapped the wall as he paced back and forth, deep in thought.

"So, what do we have?" McGhee asked.

"We have a steaming pot of coincidence stew. That's what we have. We have two ice-cold cases, twenty-seven or so years apart, that appear to have very similar suspects. Both of the victims' mothers worked at Morely. The attempted abductions all have links to Morely as well. And then there is the nasty trail of death, dying and cancer that surrounds the plant. How and why that is directly related to our cold cases and attempted abductions, I have no idea," Venko replied, unrolled the printouts and placed them in the case folder.

McGhee took it all in for a moment before asking the obvious. "What's next?"

"Tomorrow we sit on 14th and Hemingway and hopefully find young Espinoza. The bonus would be finding this white ninja that shook off Bianchi and Martinez like a couple of flies. Honestly, Espinoza is a habitual runaway and is probably fine surviving from place to place. My guess he is already running with the 14th street crew. If so, he is already being schooled on burglaries, breaking into businesses and running dope to the customers on the corners. The bad guys know nothing happens to juveniles if they are caught. Hell, when I first came on, my FTO refused to chase a juvenile that ran from a corner. He figured it wasn't worth a low-level dope arrest on a kid that would be released to his parents in less than two hours. Not to mention if you did chase and tackle a twelve or thirteen-year-old, they always got injured, which required a mountain of paperwork. I learned pretty quick that every little corner group had a designated runner. It would always be the fastest kid in the group and nine times out of ten, he was just a decoy to get you away from the kid holding all the dope." Venko clasped his hands behind his head as he rocked back in his chair.

McGhee shifted nervously in his chair before speaking.

"What if we find the mysterious white ninja and he turns out to be a cop?"

"If he is, we are going to have a long talk. I'm going to find out what he is working on, that I can promise." Venko noticed McGhee glance down at his cast. He guessed McGhee could be apprehensive about the possibility of a physical encounter given both of their healing injuries.

"Marcus, have faith in my communication skills. I can exude diplomacy if needed. When we find him, we are just going to talk. Nothing can go wrong," Venko said with a smile.

"Damn it, Dan! You had to say that? We are so fucked now."

Chapter 15

These Aren't My Pants

Venko woke gradually as Diablo trudged heavily across his chest. Her indelicate habits were nothing new; he was accustomed to her routine invasions. Venko restlessly glanced over at the clock. Four in the afternoon was a little earlier than normal to start his day. Lately, he slept fitfully and woke up exhausted. He saw the stack of folders on his desk and realized he brought his work home, something he swore he would never do. Venko pulled on his sweatshirt and made a pot of coffee.

He was pouring over the Espinoza report when his phone alerted him to an incoming text message. Venko sipped his coffee, momentarily ignoring the text alert. He stacked the reports neatly and closed the folder, before picking up the phone.

Call me when you get up, Cal.

Venko knew it was something important if Swanson needed a phone call. He took another sip of coffee and called the number. Swanson answered on the first ring.

"Cal, what's up?" Venko could hear Swanson exhale before responding.

"Your name has cycled back up for promotion again. Sellers told me to call you and find out if you're still interested in remaining in the promotional process, or if you want dropped. You are still on the eligibility list for sergeant for three more months until that list dies. The panel interviews are coming up. I remember what Sellers did to you in your last interview. I told him I didn't think you would be interested in another interview, but I told him I'd ask."

Venko paused for a second before responding.

"Sure, what the hell, I'll do the dog and pony show again."

"Uh, you want the panel interview?" Swanson was stunned.

"Ah hell, we both know I have no shot at getting promoted. But if I drop out, it would give Sellers too much satisfaction. Let him rack his brain trying to find some obscure topic or long forgotten procedure to ask about. He will have to work hard and that's good enough for me. After the last go around I checked our contract. Unless the interview is during my shift, they have to pay me overtime to come in for the interview." Venko knew this might ruffle Swanson.

"Dan, I don't think that is a good idea. I realize it is covered by the contract, but no one does that. Turning in an overtime slip for a promotional interview will not sit well."

"Getting passed over doesn't exactly sit well with me, especially after other less-qualified candidates get softballs lobbed at them by Sellers," Venko chuckled briefly. "I'll buy you a beer with the extra cash. When is the interview?"

"In a week."

"Of course it is, because I am working the night before," Venko remarked sarcastically.

"It gets worse," Swanson responded quickly.

"How is that possible?"

"Sellers said if you're interested, the only remaining time slot is 11:00 a.m."

"That is an epic fuck over. I know they hold promotional interviews all day, from eight to four. Since I was passed over in the last promotions, I should be at the top of the list and should've gotten first choice. Eleven in the morning guarantees I won't get any sleep after working the night before. Eight in the morning or 3:30 p.m. would obviously be better. But then I would expect no less from Sellers. Go ahead and give him the good news."

"Will do, Dan. Catch you later," Swanson replied and hung up.

Venko spent the next two hours creating a list of all the suspect descriptions from the individual case notes, as well as similarities between all the victims. The suspect descriptions were then paired down to a single list. Venko forced himself to suspend logic and assumed the suspects were all the same person. Once past this mental hurdle, the descriptions across decades were remarkably similar.

The missing persons and the attempted abductions were also strikingly similar. All were white or Hispanic males, between the ages of twelve and fourteen at the time of the incidents. All had severe behavioral issues. Cole, Daniels and Solomon all exhibited drastic changes shortly after returning and their metamorphosis appeared to be long-lasting. Venko was having a hard time trying to understand the sudden personality changes in this group. The incidents were years apart, and it seemed statistically improbable that all three would undergo the same transformation, but his instincts told him that's exactly what happened. All the cases were linked to Morely and Sons. He could not come to grips with that being either a causative element in the disappearances and attempted abductions, or the remarkable transformation of the survivors.

Venko looked at the notes he just scribbled. He circled the names Cole, Daniels and Solomon. He wrote "HOW?" in large capital letters. Next to Billings and Michaels he wrote "WHY?" Venko already knew who was responsible, though he didn't have a name yet. Once he shut out all the excess noise, the case had come down to how and why. And then he heard the heavily accented voice of Miss Rosales again. *Put all the pieces on the table first, your eyes will know where they go.*

Venko managed a forty-five-minute nap before getting ready for work. He scarfed down a toasted bagel and Coke while jamming case files back into the messenger bag Sarah had given him. He ran his fingers along the leather seams and wished he had taken better care of it, and of Sarah.

Venko could smell the coffee as soon as he stepped into the hallway. He reflexively smiled as the aroma soothed him. He turned and stopped. He could hear the static-filled radio and saw the thermos standing in solitude on the empty table. As he approached the table, everything looked exactly the same as many other nights…except Miss Rosales was not there. The thermos was capped and placed about two inches from the edge of the table. *Take it and go.* Venko took a step towards her door and stopped. He could hear nothing from inside the apartment. The quiet was unsettling, but his gut told him nothing was amiss. Venko turned and grabbed the thermos, then headed down the stairs.

At the station, Venko waived to Dex as he trudged up the stairs towards the detective bureau, leaving a trail of slush and snow in his wake.

He pulled off his gloves and hung his coat on the hook next to his cubicle. After setting down his messenger bag and thermos, he plopped onto his chair and typed his password into the computer. Venko opened his email and saw the message forwarded to him by Swanson. It was a short, curt message from Sellers to Swanson.

Lt. Swanson,

Per our previous conversation, Officer Venko's promotional panel interview is next Thursday at 1100 hours. There are no other available time slots.

Capt. Sellers

Venko did not hear McGhee walk up behind him.

"Whoa. Hey Cassie, Dan might be a sergeant soon," McGhee yelled over to Oliver, who was now approaching the cubicle. Venko sighed and closed out his email.

"First, you shouldn't be creeping up on someone and reading their email. Second, it's more like I will be going through the motions. Sellers buried me in the last panel interview, and he made sure the only slot available is 11 a.m. next Thursday. So, if I could fall asleep as soon as I got home at 7:20 a.m., I would get only two and a half hours of sleep before cleaning up and coming back. If I just stay up without sleeping, I will be a total zombie. So, you see my predicament."

"No Dan," Oliver shook her head and continued. "This time you're going to nail the panel interview, Sellers can go fuck himself. You got it this time, I just know it."

"Wouldn't that be something! Sgt. Venko," McGhee finished with a salute.

"Let's all hold our horses for a minute and come back to the real world. Why would I ever want to leave midnight patrol in the 7th Precinct?" Venko smiled, opened the thermos, and poured himself a cup of coffee.

Venko's cell phone rang in a loud vintage tone, reminiscent of old rotary phones.

"I just discovered that ringtone today," Venko said with a huge grin before answering.

"Jesus, what's up?"

"Dan, I just had a source call me. Cheez-it is out again and back in town. Word is, he is supposed to take Espinoza to the country sometime in the next couple of days. About thirty miles north of the city, don't have an exact address. I just know they are going to be rolling north in the next couple of days."

"Who, exactly is Cheez-it?" Venko asked, interrupting a very excited Martinez.

"Shawntell Morgan. Black male, 18. He is a frequent visitor to the apartments at 14th and Hemingway. A dumbass wanna-be. He did a stretch in juvenile detention at sixteen for a burglary. Wasn't hard to catch. Seems he had a great love for Cheez-its and left a perfect set of neon orange fingerprints on the window of a house by the waterfront. When he was stopped a few days later, his fingers were still coated with that glow-in-the-dark orange powder. His people have been calling him Cheez-it ever since. If you see him out tonight, he always carries a little weed and a pipe. If you can stop him, you might be able to squeeze him for more information. Detective Oliver has arrested him before, talk to her."

"I will, and thanks Jesus," Venko hung up and looked at Oliver. "So, do you know a Cheez-it? Mr. Cheez-it, or maybe just Cheez to his friends?"

Oliver uttered a deep throaty laugh that got McGhee's full attention.

"What's that dumb fuck done now? Let me preface his stupidity by saying even Beans has arrested him. Of course, he was a juvenile back then, so no real time. He is a terrible burglar and thief."

"I'm twenty feet away. I'm old, not deaf!" Beans shouted from the confines of his cubicle.

Oliver shot a glare over to Beans who appeared unaffected by her comment, as he resumed scrolling through real estate listings in Florida. She turned back to Venko.

"Dan, I need a favor. I have to interview a robbery suspect, could one of you guys go with me? I really don't want to tear Beans away from his important work," Oliver asked, with pleading eyes. Venko saw the glint in McGhee's eyes as he wordlessly implored him to go along.

"Take Marcus, I'll be out trying to find Sir Cheez-it. If I need assistance, I'll grab a uniformed cop. Can you get me a photo and physical description?"

"You got it Dan, and thanks." Oliver smiled and headed back to her desk.

McGhee couldn't contain his grin as he put on his jacket.

"Try to look cool and get rid of that stupid, happy puppy grin you're wearing. Be helpful and do whatever she asks you to do. And above all, try not to stare," Venko instructed.

"Please Dan! I am the definition of suave."

"Well try being a detective, too."

Twenty minutes later, Venko wheeled the Ford out of the snow-covered lot, having committed the details on Cheez-it to memory. A few minutes later, he backed the car into a parking spot on Hemingway. He had a clear view down the hill and could see the apartment building and the intersection clearly. As he glanced down the hill, Venko noticed all of the streetlights were out except for one near the intersection. This gave him the stealth he needed to sit undisturbed.

At 12:30 a.m., foot traffic to the side door of the apartments began to pick up. Venko watched through binoculars as the zombies shuffled to the door and then disappeared quickly back into the night, illicit medicine in hand.

Venko instinctively leaned forward as a chubby, youthful looking black male exited the door and bounded down the steps onto Hemingway. Switching quickly between the binoculars and the photo of Cheez-it in the file, he realized his target was on the move. He assumed his target would run if he tried to stop him, and decided some assistance would be needed.

Venko dialed Haystack's number and waited nearly fifteen seconds before he answered.

"Dan the man, what's going on?"

"Haystack, you busy right now?"

"Just stopped by Emily's place for a little follow up. If you know what I mean."

"Roger that. Haystack, did they ever replace the body-worn camera you broke last December?"

"No, not yet, but it's been a while and I expect it any day. Thank the gods for the tight budget. What do you need Dan?"

"I'm on Hemingway watching a mope walk northbound on 14th, I need to stop him and talk to him about a case. He probably has a little weed on him and will most likely run. It's a little too cold for exercise, and I might need some help stopping him. I'd prefer unrecorded assistance since this will most likely be a non-traditional Q and A, if you get my drift."

"Bro, those are the best kind!"

"My target is a black male, 18, wearing a red stocking cap, a set of expensive headphones, and a green jacket. About five-nine, a buck ninety or so. Chubby little man, goes by the moniker of Cheez-it."

"Ah shit Dan, everyone knows Cheez-it. I've hauled him before. If he is heading north, he has about five blocks before he gets to the apartment of a cousin. That's probably where he is heading. I think the apartments are at the corner of 14th and Joyce, right on the edge of the Books."

The Books were a series of east-west streets named for famous authors, starting with Hemingway, then Poe, Twain, Fitzgerald and ending with Joyce.

"Haystack, if you can get to the alley just south of Joyce, I'll come up behind him and run him right into you. Remember, cell phones only, nothing on the air, if we lose him, we lose him."

"Roger that. Dan, I'm on the way," Haystack said before hanging up.

Venko slowly turned north onto 14th. He could see Cheez-it ahead of him, obliviously strolling to the music blaring in his ears. Venko turned off the headlights and pulled to the curb. The street was deserted and quiet. The few working street lights illuminated random patches of desolation ahead.

Cheez-it was approaching Fitzgerald, when Venko received a text from Haystack indicating he was in place. Venko drove the blacked-out Ford to within fifteen feet of Cheez-it before exiting. He jogged up behind the still oblivious male and tapped him on the shoulder. Cheez-it jumped and spun around, pulling his headphones down. Venko could hear hip-hop emanating from the little speakers.

"What the fuck?" Cheez-it shouted as he stepped away, trying to catch his breath from his sudden scare.

Venko saw the subtle step backwards and immediately knew where this was going.

"Police. I need to ask you a few questions." He pulled his coat back to reveal the badge on his belt.

Cheez-it sprinted north with amazing agility for his relative girth. Venko began a steady trot behind Cheez-it, cupped his hands and shouted, "Don't hurt him!"

The headphones had fallen off about ten feet into his sprint, and Cheez-it was both confused and concerned by Venko's statement. Just as Cheez-it began to pull away from Venko, a blue giant emerged from the shadows, just ahead of the sprinting bowling ball. Like a cow on ice, Cheez-it tried to get his feet under him and change direction on the snow-covered sidewalk. Haystack watched in amusement as Cheez-it went down hard, and slid on his back, coming to a stop a few feet from him.

"Don't even think about it bro, just stay right there," Haystack ordered with a grin.

Venko, slightly winded, arrived seconds later and handcuffed Cheez-it. Haystack and Venko pulled the prisoner to a seated position and sat him against the retaining wall near the sidewalk.

"I am Officer Danilo Venko, my friends call me Dan, you can call me Officer Venko. Can we stipulate that you know, understand, and have heard your Miranda warnings on one of your many prior arrests?" He asked casually.

"What?" Cheez-it responded.

"Since you have been arrested before and questioned, I assume you know your rights and I can dispense with such formalities," Venko asked before Haystack chimed in. "You know, your right not to be stupid, your right to turkey loaf at the jail, your right to avoid bodily harm by being truthful. That sort of thing."

Cheez-it glanced at the pair, confused.

"Yeah, I know my rights."

Venko winked at Haystack.

"Where did you sleep last night?"

"At my girlfriend's crib."

"How tall is your girlfriend? And how much does she weigh? Approximately. And for the benefit of Officer Hayslip, known to his friends as Haystack, please do not use the metric system."

Cheez-it was momentarily stunned by the seemingly random questions, then answered.

"She thin, maybe a hundred and ten, a hundred and fifteen. She is about three inches shorter than me, maybe five-five or so."

"You're doing great so far Cheez, may I call you Cheez?" Venko asked, looking at Haystack, who was struggling to repress a grin.

"You can call me whatever the fuck you want as long as I get to go home," Cheez-it answered honestly.

Venko resumed his inquisition.

"What is the first thing you did after waking up this morning?"

"I took a piss."

"And after that?"

"I got dressed."

"What did you put on?"

"What you mean, what did I put on? What I'm wearing now!"

"How much do you weigh and how tall are you?"

"About five-eight or nine, probably close to two hundred pounds. What the fuck has this got to do with anything?"

"It is very, very important. I'll explain everything in a second. So Cheez, if you are five-eight or nine and a weeble-like two hundred pounds, it stands to reason that you could not have put on your girlfriend's pants this morning. I mean that is logical, right? Since she is shorter than you and somewhere around eighty or so pounds less than you."

"What the fuck man? These are my pants!"

"BOOM! I heard it Dan," Haystack shouted.

Venko rubbed his chin, as if pondering the wonder of the universe, before continuing.

"So, we have clearly established ownership of said trousers. The items obviously jammed in your front right pants pocket, we can assume, are most likely a bag of weed and a pipe," with that, Venko removed a bag of weed and a small ceramic pipe from the suspect's front right pants pocket.

"PFM. Pure fucking magic, Dan," Haystack said with admiration.

Cheez-it realized things were going badly.

"Now Cheez, you understand that once you have admitted ownership of pants under my abbreviated Miranda warnings, you relinquish the right to transfer ownership of said pants, post arrest." Venko paused and stared at Cheez-it waiting for a response.

"What the fuck does all that mean?"

Haystack knelt down and leaned towards Cheez-it before speaking.

"What it means, for all intents and porpoises, is you're screwed."

Venko glanced briefly at Haystack in awe of his penchant for malapropisms.

"Yes, for all intents and PURPOSES you are fucked. The supreme court has already ruled on this. Since the dawn of time 'these aren't my pants' has been a traditional defense of last resort."

"That's right Dan, I believe the court ruled once you have clearly established ownership of the pants you are wearing, through a verbal or written admission, all contents in said pants, are lawfully yours. I think that was Levi Wrangler v. Utah." Venko shot Haystack a sideways glance.

That was a bit over the top. Haystack blissfully ignorant, beamed proudly at Venko.

"So," Venko began in hopes of no more assistance from Haystack, "I'm guessing you're on paper of some kind. They didn't just release you, you're on parole of some kind. I'm also guessing that conditions of your release include not using drugs. In addition to arresting you for the marijuana and pipe, I could call your parole officer and recommend a drug test. I think you would fail that test. But let's put all that talk behind us. Because? Because there is door number two. And that is a good thing, because it gives you an option instead of the powdered eggs and moldy toast the jail serves for breakfast."

"What do you want?" Cheez-it asked, cutting to the chase.

"Where is Rafael Espinoza? Word is you are taking him out of town very soon."

"I ain't seen him. Yeah, I was gonna give him a ride. Supposed to take him and drop him in the country, off Big Ridge road. Someone, and I don't know who, is supposed to pick him up and take him to his distant cousin's or some such shit."

"When was the last time you saw him? If you haven't seen him, does he know about all these arrangements?"

"Saw him a day or so ago. He knows about the ride. After I talked to him, he was in the wind again. Word is he stabbed some dude in a fight and does not want to be found. I don't know nothing about the stabbing, just a rumor I heard. Why all this sudden interest in him?"

Venko found that statement odd.

"What do you mean all this sudden interest? He is a runaway and listed as missing."

"You're the second cop that stopped me in the last two days to ask about Espinoza."

Cheez-it had Venko's full attention now.

"What did he look like? Did he give you a card? What did he say?"

"Whoa. He a tall thin white dude, dressed nice. He look like a cop, he walk like a cop, he talk like a cop. Don't need to see no badge. Tell you this much, you could learn from that dude. He dropped a hundred-dollar bill on me, told me I get another one if I help him pick up Rafael. Said the kid was in real danger, like serious shit."

"You have his phone number?"

"It was on some paper, I think it might be over at my girl's place or it fell out of my pocket. The way I see it, if he's gonna give me a hundred to find Rafael, you might need to outbid him for the rights to that information. I think two hundred is fair."

Venko ignored the transparent ploy, and pulled the computer composite drawing of the suspect from his inside jacket pocket.

"Does the dude look like this?"

Cheez-it studied the photograph for a few seconds.

"Yeah, that's him. That look more like a wanted poster drawing, so this dude not a cop? He a criminal?"

"I don't know. Where is the hundred-dollar bill he gave you?"

"Uh, it turned into that bag of weed right there, a pizza and some beers."

"As to your reference of a finder's fee, here's what I will do. In lieu of a cash payment to you, I will not send you to jail tonight. I will hold on to this pipe and if I don't hear from you tomorrow, I will hunt you down and arrest you. Is that understood? Here is my card, my cell phone number is on the back, call anytime."

Venko and Haystack stood Cheez-it up as Venko removed the handcuffs. Venko placed the pipe in his jacket pocket and grabbed the small zip-lock baggie of marijuana.

"Haystack, I think we have a real storm coming, wind picking up running north to south."

"Nah, I think it's coming from the north and then blowing east," Haystack said, as he started to grin.

"Well, let's be sure," Venko said, opening the bag and dumping the entire contents into Haystack's giant cupped hands.

"Fly little birdie, fly," he remarked, as he tossed the contents high in the air, the wind quickly scattering the marijuana.

"Bro, you are correct, it is north to south."

Venko smiled and took a half bow. Then he saw the stranger, almost a block north, standing on the opposite side of the street. Watching them.

"You're free to go Cheez, call me if you see Espinoza or the mystery man, and I mean immediately." Cheez-it went back and collected his headphones then headed towards the apartments at 14th and Joyce.

Venko waited until he was out of earshot.

"Haystack, don't turn around, there is a guy watching us almost a block north, opposite side of the street. I'm going to take my car north and turn towards him. I'm guessing if he is going to take off, it will be west on Joyce. If he knows the area, he will take the service alley halfway down Joyce and cut south. Take your wagon west on Fitzgerald, loop north on the next block and then come east on Joyce. He should run right into you if he doesn't take the alley. If he does take the alley, your wagon won't fit and you will have to beach it on Joyce at the alley."

"Roger Bro. Is this fourth and goal worthy?" Haystack asked.

Venko knew the code. If something was fourth and goal, it meant the gloves were off. Clotheslines tackles were fair game.

"Haystack, this is Southern California on the Nebraska one yard line. Six seconds left in the game. If the Trojans score, they win. Nobody remembers the runners-up in the Rose Bowl. We need this dude. I have to talk to him, so he needs to be breathing. I'd prefer no concussion, but do what you have to do to bring him under control. Now, are you a Cornhusker?"

Venko watched as Haystack clenched both of his fists and worked himself into a muted fury. He nodded, and through clenched teeth muttered, "No one is going to score on the Haystack."

Venko took a quick glance where the man had been standing. Gone. *Probably ducked back down Joyce.* By the time he reached the Ford, Haystack had already pulled off.

As the Ford crawled west on Joyce, Venko scanned the area ahead. No movement. He put the car in park just west of the service alley that ran south. He got out of the car and peered down the alley. Then he saw the footprints in the fresh snow. *Gotcha.*

The tracks led to the service entrance at the back of a closed tobacco shop. An overhead light illuminated the door. Venko knew the second floor had four ramshackle studio apartments. There were stairs leading up to the apartments in the front of the building, but he wasn't sure about the rear entrance. He heard movement inside and saw the door slightly ajar. He entered quickly and waited impatiently for his eyes to adjust to the darkness. He realized he was in a stockroom. Cartons of cigarettes lined the shelves as well as tins of loose tobacco. A small desk occupied the corner of the room near the door to the main store area. Venko was creeping toward the door when he heard the glass break. He ran through the doorway into the main store area and stopped. He saw the broken ashtray on the floor close to the front door. The door was still bolted and undisturbed. Then he knew.

"Don't do it, Dan. Don't reach. Leave the holster snapped down and raise your hands," The stranger said calmly.

"Do I know you?" Venko asked as he slowly turned to face the stranger, hands still held high.

From what little light entered through the front window and door, he could see the barrel of a large revolver pointed at him. The stranger was about ten to twelve feet away, far too risky a distance to lunge. Though shadows covered most of the stranger's face, Venko knew exactly who he was. The nose and jawline matched the drawing in his pocket.

"No, you don't," The stranger started. "I really don't want to shoot you but I will if I have to."

Venko quickly began to analyze the situation. The man was taller than him, probably about six-foot one, or two. He was no more than thirty-five. He weighed maybe two-hundred pounds and appeared to be in good shape. The stranger held the revolver in a two-handed grip, in a triangulated combat stance. Cop. He wore black cargo pants, and a black sweatshirt. He could see parts of a shoulder holster under a dark grey jacket.

The stranger, without taking his eyes off of Venko, switched to a left-handed grip on the pistol. With his right hand, he slowly closed the heavy wooden door to the rear office. He then folded the clasp over the door, dropped the padlock into the ring and secured the lock.

Venko knew his radio was in the car. If things went badly, he would be on his own until Haystack could find them.

"What's your name, friend? I don't think you want to shoot a cop, so why are we here? Why did you lock my exit?"

"My name is Brody Franks. We don't have much time. It won't be long before Officer Hayslip tracks us here, and this padlock will buy us some extra time. The door is fairly stout, but the big man should make short work of it. I'm the only one that can save Rafael Espinoza. You won't, and you can't save him. I thought I could get in and out. I regret underestimating you. I've read your file Dan. You're a good street cop. Still, I didn't think you were quite this cerebral."

Venko thought the name the stranger gave would not show up in any database if he was able to get out unscathed to check. Probably a fake name. He thought about the other cases.

"Are you going to help Espinoza like you did Cory Michaels and Dakota Billings? Where are the bodies? There are people that need closure. C'mon Brody."

"Michaels and Billings are alive, they're fine."

"Where are they?"

"They're fine. They're just not here." Franks heard the outer rear door open.

"Hayslip is here. I can explain everything, just not now. I'm going to need your help, Dan. I'm the only one that can save Espinoza. I'll contact you tomorrow," Franks finished and heard Haystack trying to open the inner door.

"Dan, are you in there? It's me," Haystack whispered.

Franks turned his full attention back to Venko. Lowering his voice to just above a whisper he said, "Dan, I have to go now. You might want to turn around, if you don't, you will get sick. Your brain can't process what you're about to see."

"Nah, I'm not about to take one in the back," Venko said, slowly trying to inch his right hand down to his holster.

"Have it your way," Franks said and released his right hand from the two-handed grip. He turned his left wrist slightly, careful to keep the pistol aimed at Venko. What happened next, Venko would replay endlessly in his mind.

Franks placed his left index finger on the face of the watch. A second later the watch face turned red. He tapped the now red watch face a second time. Venko felt the oxygen leave his body like a sharp gut punch. He doubled over and saw a swirling mosaic of grays and blacks in rapidly changing patterns. A whooshing sound filled his head. Franks rapidly faded from view before vanishing. The pressurized popping sound made Venko's ears ring.

Venko took a step and fell to the floor. Wave after wave of nausea battered him. He got to his hands and knees and felt his stomach convulse. He turned his head and began to wretch. Hot acid filled his throat as his stomach continued to contract. Two, possibly three seconds had elapsed from the time Franks tapped his watch, maybe slightly less, he was unsure. Venko could not logically process what he witnessed. Slowly, the room stopped spinning and his equilibrium drifted back.

As Venko got to his feet, the rear door exploded inward in a shower of splinters. Haystack stood in the doorway, holding his flashlight with his left hand and his Glock in his right. He swept the room with light from right to left, blinding Venko.

Haystack could smell the warm bile.

"Dan, you okay? Where is he?"

Venko realized he could not explain what just happened.

"I got fooled. Following the footprints, he must have gone another way when he got to the back door. I figured he was hiding inside, so I locked the back office door so he couldn't slip out."

"Bro, you blow chunks right there?" Haystack used his flashlight to highlight the steaming liquid mess.

"Yeah, I guess I shouldn't run after a Molly's chili cheeseburger. I'm fine, I just need some water.

"Let's get you out of here. We can go check up and down 14th if you want."

"No, I think he had a car nearby, probably gone by now. You get back in service. We can try again tomorrow. Thanks for your help."

Venko started the Ford and dropped the driver's window all the way down. He hungrily took in gulps of the frigid air, as Haystack drove by and waved. His heart rate began to slow as he tried to make sense of what happened. He knew Franks was the suspect, crossing decades in all of the cases. He had cleared that hurdle. But how could he make sense of what he just saw? How could he rationally explain this to McGhee? How could he put this in a report? He could not tell McGhee, and he damn sure couldn't write it up. He pictured himself being strongly assisted into the psych wing of Memorial Hospital.

He slowly drove back to the precinct, the icy wind soothing his frayed nerves, unconsciously shaking his head.

What the fuck just happened?

Chapter 16
The Great White Ninja

Venko sat at his desk, the eerie silence intermittently punctuated by the soundtrack of a Netflix movie Beans was streaming. Venko tried to process what just happened. As he reviewed the conversation he had with Franks, several things jumped out at him.

How does Franks know me? He mentioned Hayslip by name. How would he know him? What did Franks mean, only he could save Espinoza? If he really had Michaels and Billings, where were they? If Michaels is alive, how is it possible that no one has seen a trace of him since he disappeared in 1990? Michaels would be 43, 44 years old now, would he know what happened? Would Espinoza be saved like Michaels and Billings, never to be seen again? And what in the name of Gandolph was the gizmo Franks wore on his wrist?

Venko poured over the report on Espinoza. He was a habitual runaway and probably had a criminal record. It would be tough to find that information because of his status as a juvenile. He entered Espinoza's name in the system, hoping to cross reference any mention of him as a suspect, victim or a reporting party. Venko found three reports from the past year. He entered any name he found in the reports and looked for addresses outside the city or near Big Ridge road. Nothing.

Venko could hear the footsteps and the casual conversation of Oliver and McGhee as they came up the stairs and into the detective bureau hallway. Their jovial mood was a stark contrast to the dark uncertainty he felt. He forced a smile as they approached.

"How did it go?" Venko asked.

"He wasn't being entirely truthful. Nothing incriminating, but I did lock him into a statement. I'll do some more digging and then pull him in for a more formal interview," Oliver said with a shrug.

"He will crack. I know it," McGhee added.

"Well, I have to type up the interview. Thanks guys," she said with a smile as she headed toward her desk.

"She is smooth. Walked the dude right up to the edge of an admission. But he wouldn't jump," McGhee stated, with obvious admiration.

"That's called experience. That's why you aren't eligible to take the detective's exam until after you've worked for three years," Venko said, placing the Espinoza report back into the folder.

"You find out anymore, or locate Cheez-it, or the white ninja?" McGhee asked, dropping into his chair.

"I found Cheez. I was able to leverage the weed and pipe in his pocket for some useful information. Apparently, sometime in the next day or two, he is supposed to take Espinoza up north, somewhere around Big Ridge road. Cheez also mentioned the ninja dropped a hundred-dollar bill on him and promised more if he led him to Espinoza."

McGhee whistled at the revelation.

"Nothing softens a mope like U.S. currency. You think Cheez will come through or is just playing you?"

"I think if he doesn't want to go to jail, he will call when he sees Espinoza."

Venko thought about how much more he could reveal to McGhee and decided a limited amount of information was best for now.

"The white ninja was watching my conversation with Cheez from a block north. I tried to slink up on him, but he ran down Joyce and cut south down the alley. I thought I had him near the delivery entrance for the tobacco shop, but he got away."

McGhee mulled over Venko's explanation silently for a few seconds. Venko knew McGhee thought there was more to the story.

"What about other units or a K-9? The calvary couldn't find this dude?" McGhee leaned back in his chair and folded his arms across his chest.

"I had Haystack assisting. The Cheez-it encounter was off the books, cell phone only. I have to keep things low key, since we are only supposed to be out with prior authorization. Besides, I have the promotional interview next week, can't have shit go sideways right now."

"Uh huh," McGhee said with obvious skepticism.

"Yeah, okay, that was pretty weak. You know I don't care about the promotional exam. Honestly, I have a feeling we are really close. I think things are going to get dicey. You have to trust me. If I need you to do something, just do it. No matter what. I am trying to get this done with minimal risk."

"Dan, spill it. Remember I'm the dude that has already been shot hanging out with you. So, whatever you are holding back for my safety, tell me."

"Let's play it by ear and see if Cheez comes up with something. You'll be in play if I hear anything. I'm not dumb enough to try this solo. Trust me. If Espinoza is on the move tomorrow, we'll find him," Venko stated, hoping this would hold off his curious partner.

"Roger that," McGhee nodded.

"Can you get with Cassie and pull everything you can find on Cheez-it? Prior arrests, field interview cards, and reports. I want to know everywhere he might think of going for tomorrow." McGhee nodded while jotting down notes.

Around 5 a.m., Venko stopped in to talk with Swanson. The two talked casually, and eventually Venko got around to asking about the panel interview. It was obvious, despite Venko's denials, that he was going to make a solid effort to get promoted. Part of this was pride, the rest was a never-ending war with Sellers. Unfortunately, Swanson could provide no insight as to what Sellers was planning this go around. Sellers could pull questions from any number of current issues facing law enforcement or bury him with him minutiae extracted from some long-buried procedure.

Venko didn't feel good about the upcoming panel interview, but he wasn't going to stop looking for an edge.

At 7:25 a.m., Venko dragged himself up the stairs of his apartment building. The hall was quiet as he entered his apartment. He fed Diablo and sat on the edge of his bed. Venko slowly took off his shoes then fell backwards, exhausted. He managed to place his gun on the nightstand before collapsing into a dreamless slumber.

The sudden, shrill ringing startled Venko. It continued, as he tried to place the source of the sound. A few more seconds elapsed before he realized he forgot to silence his cellphone before going to sleep. He looked at the clock. One in the afternoon. Anyone that knew him would not call that early. Venko picked up the phone and saw "Restricted" on the screen.

"Officer Venko?"

Venko immediately recognized the voice of Brody Franks. Despite just waking up, he was alert enough to realize that Franks called him, *Officer*. When they met last night, he was in plain clothes and to most people that might infer he was a detective. Franks knew he wasn't, so he had good intelligence.

"Yes, that's me. What do you want?"

"I imagine you are quite curious after our meeting and that you have your doubts about my intentions. I'd like to suggest a meeting. I think I might be able to convince you to help me. I suspect we have a lot more in common than you might guess."

"I'm sure we do," Venko replied sarcastically.

"The Starbucks on N. Market, downtown, at five. If I see you have arranged a hostile greeting party, I'll be gone before you knew I was there. I will answer all your questions then."

Venko remembered Franks' vanishing act and was still stunned by it. He was certain he could do it again.

"I'll be there."

"See you then," Franks said, then abruptly hung up.

Venko placed the phone on the nightstand and lay down again. Sleep would not return.

• • •

Venko preferred walking to driving. If he needed to drive, he still had his late father's battered, blue Subaru. The sedan was badly rusting above the wheel wells but ran decent for having accumulated 187,000 miles. He made an effort to start the car weekly or take short trips to keep up the battery. Last week, when the temperatures dipped into the low teens, he moved the car to the street behind the apartment. The slight grade would make it easier to bump start the car if needed. This option was one of the few good things about having a manual transmission.

By 4:30 p.m., Venko had scraped all the ice and snow off the Subaru. He sat behind the wheel, depressed the clutch and turned the key. The engine slowly turned over twice, then clicked. *Of course.* Venko released the emergency brake and opened the driver's door and got out. With a firm right-handed grip on the wheel, he leaned forward and began to push the car. Moving down the slight grade, the Subaru picked up speed. At the point where he was nearly jogging, Venko jumped in and slammed the gear shifter into third gear. The car bucked slightly, then started. He revved the engine a couple times and slowly pulled to the curb, to let the car warm up.

A few minutes later, Venko sat across the street watching the Starbucks parking lot. He had about ten minutes to kill and was still uncertain what to make of this meeting. Venko scanned the parking lot and the building, unsure of what he was looking for. Sunshine momentarily broke through the dense clouds above. He glanced skyward, then caught himself. *This is ridiculous, the Enterprise is not hovering above.* He smiled nervously, then remembered watching Franks' swift exit the night before. *He was there, then he was gone.* Venko pulled the Glock from his off-duty holster tucked into the small of his back. *I should call McGhee and get some back up. And tell him what exactly? I need backup because I saw a man disappear right before my eyes?* He gently pulled the slide back a half inch or so until he could see the live round in the chamber. Venko knew the gun was loaded, but something made him want to check, one more time. Reassured, he re-holstered the gun, exited the car and headed across the street.

Warm humid air enveloped him as he pulled the glass door open. The steady hum of traffic was replaced with a cacophony of voices, laughter and the distinct sounds of coffee grinders. Much to Venko's chagrin, jazz music played softly in the background. The place was large, bright and spacious. The customers were an eclectic mix of boisterous college students, somber executives and a few of the local homeless population.

Venko scanned a portion of the room and did not see Franks. He walked to the counter and was immediately greeted by a bubbly girl in her early twenties, wearing the red face of a recent visit to a tanning bed. Her name tag read "Tiffani" in a self-printed font with a large smiley face dotting the last "I." What he thought he heard Tiffani say, seemed to be one long connected word delivered with an overly happy, sing-song cadence.

"Would-you-like-to-try-a-venti-of-our-new-pumpkin-peppermint-almond-spice-soy-latte?"

Venko wasn't exactly sure what she said, or what that beverage was.

"No, just a small black coffee," he said after a brief sigh.

Tiffani, still effervescent, and obviously only fluent in coffee house parlance asked, "What size would you like?"

Venko was quite certain he said small, but repeated, "small," and pointed to the small cup next to the medium and large versions.

"Which blend would you like?" She asked and pointed to the four blends behind her.

He took a deep breath, "Black coffee, with caffeine. The first one."

"Would you like room for cream?" She asked.

Venko sighed again. *Didn't black coffee explicitly imply no cream? Why do I need room to add nothing? Corporate scripting, no one listens anymore. This is why I enjoy going to Binders Book Store. Coffee comes in a mug. I don't know where the coffee comes from, I don't care if it is trucked down a mountain, on the back of a donkey, in environmentally friendly bags hand-stitched with unicorn thread by Keebler elves.*

"No room, just a small black coffee. That's all."

"Can I have a name for your order?" She asked with a dazzling white smile.

Venko looked at the coffee urn behind Tiffani. He estimated the distance to be roughly four feet. She could turn and take two steps and fill the cup. He could see no intermediate step necessitating a delay, hence the need for his name.

"Leonardo."

She cheerfully wrote "Leonardo" on the cup, converting both "O's" to smiley faces, before filling the cup.

Venko paid for his coffee and was leaving the counter when Tiffani added, "Have an awesome day, Leo."

Venko spotted Franks seated at a corner booth. As he approached, Franks put both his hands on the table top. A deliberate and obvious ploy to put Venko at ease. He immediately glanced at the watch Franks wore on his right wrist. It had a large rectangular face and currently displayed the time and date in a cool blue hue. It could be any number of smart watches currently on the market. Venko knew little about them and preferred the reliability of his analogue watch, whose functions were limited to the time and date. Franks stuck out his right hand as Venko sat down.

"Detective Brody Franks," he said.

Venko shook his hand and then leaned back in the booth.

"You mind verifying that?" Venko requested.

Franks withdrew a small black leather wallet from his interior jacket pocket. He opened the bi-fold wallet and laid it on the table. Venko picked it up and studied it briefly. The top portion held a police identification card with a photograph of Franks. A barcode ran the length of the card at the bottom. Next to the photo, a holographic image could clearly be seen. The bottom fold contained a gold badge embossed with "Detective" across the top. The badge was similar to the silver badge Venko carried. The photo ID was different; it looked newer. Venko expected that. He had only been issued two ID cards, one when he was hired, and one when the last chief took over. He assumed that younger cops and those recently promoted would have newer versions of the ID card. Venko realized the department was large enough that he might have never run across Franks. He doubted it, but it was possible.

Pushing last night's memories from his mind, Venko continued his general query.

"What district do you work out of? What unit are you assigned to?"

"I work out of Central Precinct, assigned to the Warrants Division. We actually have some things in common. I served in the Army as well. Army Intelligence, Cyber-Terrorism."

"So, you spent time inside an office, or in a bunker, pushing buttons? That's a little different than my Army experience," Venko said with a smirk.

Franks smiled at the insinuation.

"We all did our part. Computers and technology is kind of my thing."

"So then tell me Dumbledore, what kind of wizarding magic did you pull off last night?" Venko asked, before taking a small sip of his coffee.

"I forgot," Franks chuckled, "you are a fan of science fiction and fantasy novels."

"And how would you know that?" Venko asked, remembering the stranger knew his name and Hayslip's.

"Seriously Dan? How hard do you think it would be to hack your computer and view your browser history? Your purchase history on Amazon? Online orders at Binder's Bookstore? Would you agree any of those options would give me ample insight into what you like to read? And, by the way, 'fat Diablo' is not a secure password."

Venko was trying to maintain a poker face. He could feel his face getting flush with annoyance. It was all extremely plausible. But that did nothing to stem the feeling his privacy had been violated. He did not like the intrusion. He took another sip of coffee and tried to remain calm.

"All of those options would also require a search warrant."

"Which I was able to obtain for informational purposes relating to my larger case," Franks stated in a manner indicating he expected the question.

"Well, Detective Franks, what does Warrants Division want with a bunch of twelve and thirteen-year-olds?"

"Dan, you know as well as I do, Warrants Division just executes the warrants. Pick them up and drop them off. The why, isn't really my concern. Sure, I need to know enough to do my job safely, and I know a little bit more about the why, but you're not ready for that explanation yet."

"Oh, I don't think you give me enough credit. For some impossible to explain reason, I think you're the same guy that took Cory Michaels back in 1990. You also took Billings a few years ago. Last night, you said they were fine. Could you please share with me how they are fine? And where they are right now, at this minute? You also attempted to abduct Cole, Daniels and Solomon, but they escaped. That part I can't figure out since you were so effective with Michaels and Billings."

Franks reached inside his jacket, exposing the butt of a revolver suspended in his shoulder holster. Venko's right hand moved with instinctive speed towards the back of his waistband.

"Whoa, take it easy Dan," Franks said calmly, as he slowly removed his cellphone from his jacket.

Venko's shoulders relaxed as he released the grip on his Glock.

Franks placed his thumb on the phone's scanner, then swiped down twice. He then turned the phone towards Venko. A photograph of a much older Michaels took up most of the screen. He was seated behind a desk, wearing a nondescript grey sweatshirt. He appeared to be in his early 40's, a stubble of a beard and mustache filled out an angular face. A visible, one-inch scar ran just above his right eyebrow. Michaels appeared to be slightly thin, but otherwise healthy. He wore a blank, vacant expression, as if unaware he was being photographed.

Venko's face registered the photo with immediate shock. He had studied the file closely. He knew every inch of the photograph of the thirteen-year-old Michaels, down to the scar above his right eye. Venko was speechless. Franks turned the phone back to his direction and swiped down twice more. The next photo showed Dakota Billings, wearing a nearly identical grey sweatshirt.

Billings was essentially unchanged from the file photo Venko had. The hair was longer, and he now wore glasses, but it was Billings.

"How do I know this isn't Photoshop voodoo?" Venko asked.

Franks contemplated the question for a few seconds.

"I guess you don't. But you know it isn't. I can see it in your face."

"So where are they now?" Venko asked, doubting he would get a logical answer.

"In a medical institution." Franks answered.

"In an institution that no one knows about, or has ever heard of? I spoke with Cory's mom, I can assure you she doesn't know he is in an institution. That woman has suffered for decades. How do you justify that?"

"I can't explain right now. I need your help. I need to find Espinoza before it's too late. If I don't get to him, he will die," Franks paused and took a sip of coffee, letting those words sink in. "I know none of this makes sense. I have proof. Drive me over to the Wing-Lutz. It's where I am staying right now."

Venko took in the last few minutes of conversation.

"The Wing-Lutz? Is there a drastically different pay scale over at Central Precinct? Or are you just dirty?"

Franks smiled at Venko's questions.

"Just temporary accommodations. I know you have integrity, and aren't the grizzled, disgruntled veteran cop you want people to think you are. I'm going to ask you to trust your gut and believe what I show you. I'm going to do you a huge favor at the risk of my own career."

Venko raised a curious eyebrow at that comment.

"What would that be?"

"You'll see. Let's go. I assume you parked across the street and surveilled the lot for a few minutes before coming in."

Venko nodded at Franks' statement.

"I would have done the same," Franks remarked as he stood.

"Rusted, blue Subaru across the street. You may have to help push it if it doesn't start," Venko added, as the pair exited onto the sidewalk.

Chapter 17

Eloi And Morlocks

The car started on the first try, and the two rode in silence for the first few minutes before Franks spoke.

"Can you drive by a mailbox? I want to mail a letter."

Venko nodded and pulled to the curb a few blocks later. He thought it was a strange request, but everything about his contact with Franks was strange. He noticed that Franks did not remove the letter until he was out of the car. A ploy to keep its recipient secret, Venko guessed. With this task complete, the pair resumed the silent ride to the Wing-Lutz Apartments. He parked in the visitors' section on the side of the building.

Once inside, Venko stopped walking and took in the lobby's opulent luxury. Overstuffed leather chairs were arranged around gold-trimmed, glass coffee tables. A small counter along the far wall contained several high back chairs with charging ports and outlets. Three frantic businessmen were typing away on laptops, oblivious to the outside world. At the rear of the lobby, just past the elevators, was a full-service bar. Four well-dressed couples casually chatted quietly around the bar. A bartender in a grey suit poured refills. He scanned the lobby and quickly spotted the plain-clothes security staff. One by the bar, and two standing off to the side of the front door. All looked like linebackers stuffed into spandex blazers. Venko realized that Franks was waiting for him by the elevators and headed that way. He thought about texting McGhee, but figured he would wait until he got a room number in case anything went bad.

Franks used his keycard to open the door marked 914. Venko noted the apartment was tastefully decorated as he visually swept the room for threats. As he looked around the living room and office area, he noted the distinct lack of personalization. Decorative art hung on the walls, but he did not see a single framed photo. This was a furnished apartment. Franks motioned for Venko to sit in an overstuffed chair near the desk. Franks sat behind the desk.

"So, are you going to tell me the truth about Michaels and Billings? How is it you have pictures of them, but no one knows where they are? And about that fancy watch of yours? And how you beamed to the mothership?" Venko asked while removing his phone from his jacket pocket.

He started to text McGhee before Franks interrupted him.

"That won't do you much good. The entire apartment is like a giant Faraday bag. Your cell phone can't receive or transmit."

Venko looked at the reception bars at the top of his phone. No signal. *This isn't good.*

"Let's cut to the chase, where are Michaels and Billings?" He asked, leaning forward so his Glock would be quickly accessible if needed.

"I already told you, and it's not where they are, but when." Franks gave Venko a few seconds to digest that before continuing. "Physically, they are in an institution for medical research and treatment. They are less than two miles away, however, they are living seventy-five years into the future."

Venko froze in an expression of slack-jawed astonishment.

"Okay Gandolph, I'll bite for now. Why is it necessary for them to be institutionalized? Without parental consent I might add, in the freaking future?"

"Let me start from the beginning, then you might understand. I am assuming you did your research, not just on Billings and Michaels, but also on Cole, Daniels, and Solomon. So, you already know that there is a link to Morely and Sons Manufacturing. Research in the near future will tie chemical exposure at the plant to cancer. Something you, and many other people, long suspected since the 90's."

Venko grimly nodded his head at this. He remembered the pain his mother endured before passing. Franks looked at Venko momentarily. Venko reasoned that Franks already knew about his mother.

"Go on," Venko requested.

"The type of cancer was particularly devastating. Research showed it affected women almost exclusively. What was found to be particularly heinous, was the cancer triggered dormant genetic mutations. Meaning the cancer could lay dormant in the host for months or years without a single symptom. It could then attack rapidly without any warning. The altering genetic mutation would be passed down to some of the male children after onset in the host. We don't know why it was only the male children affected, and only a small group of them. As in five, possibly six, male children born to the mothers that developed cancer as a result of working at Morely."

Venko frowned.

"There were more than five cases of cancer related to the plant over the last forty years. I'm sure of that."

"That is correct. But I am talking about a specific type of brain abnormality caused by the recessive gene mutation passed on by the mother. Those five mothers that developed a particular sickness from the chemical exposure at the plant," Franks sensed that Venko was confused by the medical jargon. "Dan, like you, I am not a medical professional. This was explained to me and I was lost. I had to learn about the illness to understand what was going on. To put it bluntly, those five cases are Billings, Michaels, Cole, Daniels and Solomon."

"But Cole, Daniels and Solomon are fine. Hell, Cole is a cop now. You didn't take them. How were they affected?" Venko was struggling to process any timeline that involved the future. He knew from being a cop for over twenty years, that Franks was telling the truth. Specifically, Franks believed what he was saying, whether it was plausible or not.

Franks leaned back and realized Venko was both smart and cynical. He had much more to explain if he was to get assistance with finding Espinoza.

"Yes, they are fine. As with the medical profession now, or seventy-five years from now, nothing is absolute or clear-cut. These five represent the last of the cleanup efforts of the Morely plant. Not to get too technical, but all five developed a specific type of brain tumor that was genetically carried as a by-product of their mothers' cancer. This tumor creates severe behavioral issues, including bouts of extreme violence. Onset of changes occur starting around ten or eleven. The window for successful treatment is between eleven and fourteen years of age in the patients. We know what the results will be if they aren't treated, and they are catastrophic."

Venko rubbed his chin in thought. He knew from reading the files that Michaels and Billings had serious behavioral issues before they were taken. He also knew that Cole, Daniels and Solomon had issues as well. But after their attempted abductions, they had experienced a positive metamorphosis. Logically, he realized it had to be some sort of treatment to have achieved those results. Then he remembered the small bump the three had acquired. Hardly noticeable, just behind the right ear. Paramedics were unconcerned.

That's where our dear Lord touched him, Frieda Daniels had said.

"You're telling me, you know what happens if they aren't treated?" Venko asked, already aware that the treatment was most likely surgery.

Franks nodded his head and opened a drawer and began to reach into it. Venko sprung out of his chair and smoothly drew the Glock, leveling it at Franks.

"Stop right there." Venko was trying to process the impossible and this made him jumpy. Fear crept into his thought process.

Franks froze, and slowly withdrew his left hand from the drawer and looked at Venko.

"I'd feel a whole lot better if you would use your right hand and remove that canon from your shoulder holster," Venko ordered.

"Fine, no problem," Franks responded coolly. He unsnapped the gun and withdrew it carefully. He set it on the desk, with the barrel pointed away from Venko.

Venko picked up the gun with his left hand and stepped back from the desk. He tucked his Glock back into his holster. He stared at Franks' pistol. It appeared to be a revolver. Large caliber, probably a 357. But something was strange, it felt cold. The grips were some sort of black polymer with small ridges, in a checkerboard pattern. He could feel his palm tingle periodically, while gripping it.

Franks was visibly relieved and resumed exploring the drawer. This puzzled Venko.

"Stop, put your hands on the desk. I don't want to shoot you, but I will if you make me."

"You won't shoot me. For two good reasons," Franks paused. "One, I know enough about you, and your career that tells me you won't shoot me. Two, you couldn't shoot me if you wanted to. Go ahead, pull the trigger," Franks finished, leaned back in the chair and folded his arms.

Venko knew he couldn't shoot Franks without a perceived threat, and a grave one at that. He started this showdown because things being presented were beyond his control, and most likely beyond his comprehension. He understood that. Fear was winning the short-term battle with logic. Venko was not used to that. He tried to pull the hammer back on the revolver, but it would not budge.

"The tingle you feel in your palm is the handgrip sensor reading your palm print. It's not mine, so it continues to scan your palm. The hammer can't be pulled back, nor the trigger. As you have discovered by now, the gun feels colder than it should. That's because it fires a round made of a synthetic resin. Let's say for the purpose of simplicity, a wax bullet. The round, upon entering the human body, immediately starts to break down and melt. Any environment over seventy degrees will cause that, the warmer the temperature, the faster the round dissipates. The leftover, melted resins in the body are currently undetectable. If you are wondering: yes, I have to charge it overnight to maintain the battery that cools the weapon during the hours I carry it."

Venko thought about the weapon and immediately connected it to the Sandovar shooting. Now he understood why there was neither an exit wound, nor round fragments found during the post-mortem of Sandovar. He already knew the answer to his next question, but wanted to hear it from Franks.

"Were you at Morley when I got shot? Did you shoot Sandovar?"

Franks was nodding before Venko finished his question.

"Yes, I shot him, the world will not grieve his loss. I have limited rules of engagement per department procedures. I can use deadly force, to protect myself or that of my warrant. I stretched things in my report, indicating I believed Sandovar was going to shoot Espinoza. I am not going to stand by and watch a cop get killed. Period. The weapon you are holding is only authorized for warrants detectives. They have to be signed out and can only be carried while working a case involving a temporal fugitive. As you can imagine, a standard weapon might be problematic with all the forensic evidence it leaves behind. And while it's rare that a warrants detective is involved in a shooting, it does happen. The department obviously prefers we slip in and out quietly." Franks shifted his lithe frame in the chair, lightly tapping the armrests as he became more comfortable with Venko.

"Temporal fugitive?" Venko asked.

"Yes, fancy department lingo for serving a warrant in a non-current year," Franks said.

"I can't believe I am saying this out loud, time travel? You have a DeLorean parked nearby?" Venko sat Frank's pistol down on the arm of the chair and rubbed his forehead.

"How does that even work? Is that all contained in your watch?"

"Imagine being disassembled down to a molecular level and shipped from one magnetic field to another before being instantaneously re-assembled. And no, my watch can only take me to a fixed waypoint in the current time period. Which is quite handy when I don't want to hang around and answer a lot of questions from street cops like you. If you're wondering how I get home, I have to return with my target to LB, or local base, in plain English. That is a location with the necessary equipment in place, within my area of operation. From there I can go home, so to speak."

Venko's head was spinning more with each new revelation from Franks.

"How--how did this start?" He asked.

"I assume you mean my method of travel? Like everything else, someone was always looking for a faster way to travel. Horseback, cars, trains, plains, and jets were developed to get from point A to B faster. Two years from now, Wilhelm Anderson will be born. Many years into the future, he will be the first to research and invent a transportation system between enhanced magnetic fields. During the testing phase required by the U.S. government, his project failed miserably. That is to say, the items sent from point A never arrived at point B. In this case, they left Langley, Virginia, but never arrived in London, England. Anderson did not take the failure well and began researching historical references to magnetic field anomalies in and around London. That's when he discovered an archived article from The Times dated August 11th, 1997. This article detailed a farmer's discovery of a strange metal box containing several small computer-like devices that appeared in a field where his sheep were grazing. After the local police determined the box was not a bomb, they removed it from the pasture, and no further historical reference was made to this find. Anderson realized the test box did make the journey from Langley to London, it just arrived in the wrong year."

Venko sighed, and ran his hands through his hair. "Wait a minute."

Franks held up his hand to stop Venko and continued. "Realizing he would never be able to move forward with his project as a method of transportation, he began experimenting with time travel. Obviously, as always, the military had a keen interest in supporting the project. I'm guessing they wanted to somehow weaponize Anderson's findings. Once Anderson had a working prototype blessed by the newly formed regulatory commission, human volunteers began testing the device."

"Volunteers? Come on," Venko asked, skeptically.

"Does encouraged pioneers sound better? Some non-violent offenders were given an option of early release with participation. They were sent in pairs on a predetermined course to a specific year. They could not wander around and were automatically returned after a fifteen-minute stay. They all retrieved small, time relevant items as directed. A year after those successful tests, the first group of detectives from Warrants Division were sent to July 14th, 1980. This was to be an earlier intervention on Morely and Sons and prevent the horrific events that would transpire later."

"That obviously didn't work," Venko answered with sarcasm. "So you were sent?" he asked patiently.

Franks held up a finger, indicating things would become clearer once he finished the whole story.

"The previous control groups and prior tests went so smoothly, everyone became complacent. During the departure phase, there was a brief power outage. Backup generators were in place for just such an emergency. So, no big deal, right?" Franks shrugged for emphasis. "Wrong. Nobody had researched what would happen in those perilous milliseconds between the main power source failing and the backups kicking on. From the perspective of the mandatory observers present, everything appeared like a normal departure. A brief flicker of light was the only clue. The control panel indicated the power was temporarily transferred from the backup generators until resuming with the main power source again. It was such a brief swap it didn't trigger any warning lights. But." Franks slowly shook his head and sighed before resuming.

"Now we know just how precise the time pattern is. We didn't realize then the impact of even a brief power surge or outage. Those milliseconds without power, and I'm talking about a blink of an eye, were devastating. One detective never returned and the other three came back within a minute of departure. All were in terrible shape and died within two weeks. They returned severely injured, grotesquely disfigured and suffered from varying degrees of brain damage. The department can't officially list the missing detective as dead until the remains are found. There are protocols in place in the event a detective is lost. Detectives are trained to post a coded advertisement in the nearest newspaper for two consecutive weeks. The department's Intelligence Unit has a computer that continuously scans archived newspapers from all over the world, looking for the coded ads. If we find one, we will know where and when the detective is. So far, no luck. In reality, severely disabled and most probably dead," Franks finished, and neatly stacked the articles he retrieved from the desk.

"Cole, Daniels and Solomon, the small bumps or welts behind the right ear, injections or surgery of some kind? How was this done? They didn't go with you. They were gone for only ten minutes or so," Venko asked, glancing at the articles Franks placed on the desk.

"Eight minutes and thirty-seven seconds. They were gone eight minutes and thirty-seven seconds, to be exact. At least as far as time you could document. In actuality, they were gone for three weeks. Surgical procedures, specifically brain surgery, is radically different from what you know. Less invasive and very precise. After serving the warrants on the three, they were taken to the psychosurgical wing of Memorial Hospital. They were 3D scanned and prepped for surgery. After surgery, they were kept for monitoring and testing for another two weeks. The patients were kept in a state of semi-sedation during their stay. Once the doc cleared them, another 3D scan was taken and compared to the first taken upon arrival. This was done in case they needed a haircut or other minor cosmetic touch-up before returning. We had to return them in exactly the same condition as they were when taken. They have no memory of being gone. If the tumor was successfully and completely excised, well you know the results on Cole, Daniels and Solomon. I don't have to explain that. If you are wondering why we can't return them to the exact time we took them. Well, that's a glitch. Yeah, I know, not exactly a scientific term, but a glitch, nonetheless. Eight minutes and thirty-seven seconds is the closest we can get."

Venko immediately thought of the vacant expressions in the photos of Billings and Michaels.

"And what about Billings and Michaels?"

"Obviously, in medicine, like everything else, results are not guaranteed. Follow up and tests indicated that the tumor had spread and was uncontainable. They are currently being treated with experimental drugs. Further surgery is also an option, but right now the odds of them ever living outside the institution are slim."

Venko remembered the anguish on the face of Heather Conway. The pain of not knowing what happened to her son ate at her as much as the cancer.

"You're telling me you tore Cory Michaels and Dakota Billings away from their families at eleven or twelve years old based on what you think they might do in the future? What gives you, or any police department, that right? They have the right to live out their own lives and make their own mistakes. How are you better than the vermin I chase nightly? Badge or no badge. We are supposed to be the line between the Eloi and the Morlocks. What oath did you take?" Venko realized his voice had grown louder and more impassioned. He took a breath and sat back in the chair.

Franks started to smirk at Venko's classic literary reference, but stopped in deference to Venko's sincerity.

"It's not what we think they will do, it's what they will do, if we don't stop them," Franks picked up the first article, held it out, and recited portions from memory. "We know on September 22nd, 2004, a 27-year-old Cory Michaels wakes up and kills his wife and five-year-old son. Michaels had been working as a laborer for a construction firm contracted to build the new downtown arena and convention center. Nine months earlier, when support columns for the structure were being poured, Michaels had the ingeniously evil foresight to conceal an enormous amount of plastic explosive inside the base of the center column. Those explosives lay dormant inside the support column for nine months. No one ever discovered how he was able to detonate the recessed explosives. Twelve hours after murdering his wife and son he drove to the newly completed arena. Fifteen minutes into the opening band's set, he detonated the explosives killing 3,125 people. An additional 4,000 people were injured and maimed. Michaels had multiple priors for assaults and had been in and out of prison since turning eighteen. What was hard to fathom, was how a high school dropout developed such a knowledge of architecture. He knew exactly which support column to take out. The column he selected caused a partial collapse of the building, causing as many deaths as the flying concrete and debris from the explosion. Michaels was arrested after a lengthy investigation. It was determined he acted alone. He was convicted and executed eleven years later. Because I picked up Michaels in 1990, that event never occurred," Franks finished as he handed the article to Venko.

Venko scanned the article, his stomach flip-flopping as he read through the horrific details, sensationalized in grotesque detail by the News-Lantern reporter.

"So, there are two realities? How can a single person be exposed to two different realities?"

"I see your philosophical point, but it doesn't apply in this case. Michaels was removed in 1990, fourteen years before the bombing. The only time dual realities or dual memories if you like, become an issue, is when the past is changed. We altered Michaels' future. Our knowledge of the effects of competing memories is limited. In most cases, both the prior memory, and the altered final reality will briefly overload the senses. The new memories and the old memories will converge and compete in a swirl of the conscious and subconscious mind for roughly fifteen to twenty seconds. The old memories will fade and disappear, conceding space to the new memories, bringing the return of equilibrium. Trust me, you will know if your past is altered. Well, at least for the first fifteen to twenty seconds of becoming aware of the inconsistencies. Instant nausea, dizziness and light sensitivity. All this, while your head is full of 3D contrasting images and competing memories. You have about five seconds to process the old reality and the new, and then suddenly, it's gone. All that remains is the memory of the new reality. No trace of the former memories. I suggest if you ever experience those fifteen or twenty seconds, you find a place to sit before you fall, and drink water as soon as you can," Franks explained with a half-smile. The implication was clear, Franks knew what he was talking about. This terrified Venko.

"And what of Billings?" Venko asked, expecting an equally depressing version of the future life of Dakota Billings.

Franks grabbed another article and held it up. Reciting the highlights from memory.

"On May 5th, 2040, Dakota Billings was arrested and charged with the murders of fourteen women between the ages of 19 and 47. These murders occurred between 2034 and 2040. The bodies were all found dismembered along the interstate. Local media dubbed the killer, The Highway Hacker. Billings worked for the highway department in maintenance. He primarily worked maintaining rest stops. As you might have guessed, he was hidden in plain sight. No one suspected the quiet loner. If a state trooper hadn't stopped to assist Billings when his truck broke down, he would have continued killing. The trooper noticed several drops of blood on the rear bumper of Billings' pick-up truck. The trooper looked closely at the tarp, and noticed what appeared to be a single finger poking out from under the cover. At this point, Billings struck the trooper with a tire iron. Before Billings could hit him again, the trooper fired four shots, all center mass hits. Billings died on the spot. Under the tarp, were the right arm, legs and head of Sheila Simmons." Franks handed the second article to Venko.

"Holy shit," Venko mumbled as he looked over the article.

Franks passed several more pages to Venko.

"Here are the nefarious achievements of Cole, Daniels and Solomon as covered by the News-Lantern. That is to say, the prior reality before corrective surgery altered that landscape."

Venko shook his head reflexively, as he reviewed the articles.

"There is no article on Espinoza. Is there no future atrocity committed by that little hooligan?"

Franks opened his mouth to speak and stopped. He looked down for a second and then raised his eyes again. Venko knew whatever Franks was about to say had been discarded in favor of an honest approach.

"I was supposed to return tonight. My case is closed. All the loose ends from the cleanup of Morely and Sons are concluded.

I know in my gut that Espinoza has the tumor. His mother abandoned him and his father shortly after getting sick. Because she worked in the same area of the plant that Heather Conway did, I assume she was exposed to the same chemicals. She appears to have disappeared off the face of the earth. I suspect she died somewhere, but there are no records that I could find. She did not want to be found when she left.

Officially, Espinoza doesn't matter because he is going to die very soon and that will be the last of the Morely loose ends. My boss is okay with that scenario. Sure, it's neater, but not so much for Espinoza. I was told not to go after him and there is no warrant for him. Technically, as you can imagine, I could get in a lot of trouble for grabbing him. That's why there is no record of some horrible future crime. If I don't find him tonight, someone will take him to a deserted area off Big Ridge road and drop him off. He possibly will walk or get another ride a few miles further north. He will, however, be clipped by a car in a blinding snowstorm. By the way, the worst snowstorm of this decade will be hitting tonight. Espinoza will fall more than eighty feet down a steep ravine. The car won't stop or report the accident. Just a single piece of yellow plastic covering the turn signal will be found a month later. Just another unsolved fatal hit-skip accident. Espinoza's body will be covered under two plus feet of snow for a month or so, until an unexpected thaw in late February reveals his final resting place."

"Why don't you grab him off the side of the road along his route of travel before he gets hit?" Venko asked, wondering why this wasn't obvious to Franks.

"For a number of reasons. First, I know where he ends up, but not the path he takes to get there. Second, temperatures will stay near or below freezing for the next month. That, coupled with the amount of snow entombing Espinoza, will preserve his body. Forensically, it will be nearly impossible to determine a time of death in a window small enough for me to work with. What I do know is the last time anyone sees him alive, is tomorrow around 0025 hours. Confounding this process is the fact that Espinoza, unlike millions of other teenagers, has no social media presence. I can't historically track his plans. He has no Facebook, no Instagram, and he has already sent his last text message from his cell phone. I know where his body will be found, but no clear timeline with a logical point to intercept him." Franks exhaled deeply and rubbed his eyes.

"Why don't you work backwards from the discovery of the body. Just keep going back to the site of the body a day earlier each trip, until he isn't there?"

"That is the logical solution, except I have no warrant for Espinoza, therefore I am not authorized for temporal transit. And no, I can't just hijack the machine and go. The case is already closed, my boss is okay with the last remaining loose end dying at the bottom of a rocky ravine. I should be home by now, but like you, I occasionally have issues with supervision."

He has read my file! I wonder how much he really knows? He knows when I will retire, quit or get fired. This is just bizarre. Venko drifted back as Franks continued his explanation.

"If I can intercept him before he gets that ride, I can take him back with me, get him to the hospital and give him a shot at a normal life. So, I am asking for your help. I think Mr. Cheez is going to try and play both of us tonight, but I think one of us will get the real story."

Venko nodded his head in agreement with Franks' assessment of Cheez.

"I don't know your boss, but if he's anything like my captain, he isn't going to take you sidestepping his directives lightly."

"You are absolutely correct. He isn't quite the asshole that Captain Sellers is, but will not be pleased for sure. However, if I can grab Espinoza, get him treated, and bring him back here. There won't be any official fallout. My boss will be politically powerless to take any action. The optics would be bad. After all, his directive was to let Espinoza die, to close out the last of the Morely case. Finding a way to save the kid and return him plays out much better. No, it won't look good violating an order. But his hands will be tied if Espinoza can successfully be treated. Of course, I will be subject to his unofficial sanctions."

Venko nodded his head in agreement, he was all too familiar with unofficial sanctions over his career.

"That is assuming quite a bit. First, you're assuming Espinoza has the tumor, and he isn't just another kid going through a knucklehead stage. Second, if he does have the tumor and your wondrous medical advances can't save him, much like Michaels and Billings, then you have a lifetime of care to provide, and your boss will have something to hang you with."

"Yeah, I know. But something tells me this will work. And the only other option is finding his lifeless body at the bottom of a ravine. I'm asking you to call me if you find Espinoza tonight or you get a tip from Cheez."

Venko pondered his options. *What you conveniently left out was another option. I can find Espinoza and return him to his father. He gets to grow up. Besides, there is nothing definitive to prove his mother has the illness. Yeah, it's easy enough to prove she did work at Morely, but not why she got sick and disappeared. Espinoza could actually be just like thousands of other teenagers going through a phase of being a complete shithead. Doesn't he deserve a shot to outgrow it? Granted any option is better than lying dead. Then there is the problem if you find him first. I have to take him from you. I really don't like being hit with lead bullets, let alone some giant wax bullet fired from your hand-held musket. This would be a much easier decision if I knew where Espinoza's mother was. I don't think I'm going to have time to find her. I hope I don't have to shoot you, but there's no way in hell I'm letting you take that kid.*

"If I hear anything or find out where he is, I'll call."

As soon as the words came out, Venko saw the expression on Franks' face. Franks knew he was lying. Franks smiled and jotted his cell number down on a yellow Post-it note and handed it to Venko.

"I assume the number came up 'Restricted' when I called you?" Franks asked.

"Yup," Venko said as he tucked the note inside his jacket pocket and stood up.

"I'll see you tonight then," Franks said, extending his hand.

Venko shook his hand, pursing his lips into a false, close-lipped smile. Nodding at his comment, he said nothing.

Chapter 18

Knuckleheads, Cheez And Snowshoes

Venko sat in his recliner with Diablo perched on his lap. She always knew when he was deep in thought. She sat motionless, while he stroked her rhythmically. Her steady purring, the only sound in his apartment. His hand moved automatically over her back as he replayed his earlier conversation with Franks. Over the last twenty-two years, he had mastered the art of reading people. Vocal inflections, body gestures, eye movements, all painted a picture of whether someone was being truthful. Sure, he had been fooled occasionally, but it was rare. He knew Frank's fantastic tale was the truth. He tried in vain to logically debunk it. The investigation into the cold case abductions prior to meeting Franks, had several gaping holes. Venko had the answers now. Assuming everything he heard was true, what to do now?

Venko called McGhee and told him they were going to find Espinoza tonight. They discussed either staking out the 14th Street apartments for Espinoza or tailing Cheez. The best way to accomplish this was to split into two vehicles. McGhee and Oliver in one car and Venko in the other. McGhee wanted to use available, on-duty cruisers, depending on where Cheez led them. Venko was less enthusiastic but did not share his reasons. After some debate, they agreed to enlist the help of Officers Bianchi, Martinez, Stein and Fitzpatrick. He would speak to them before roll call in case he needed them later.

Venko knew he would not be able to nap. His body vibrated with nervous energy and his mind raced through several possible scenarios. *What was it that Warren Zevon sang? I'll sleep when I'm dead?*

He took a long shower, shaved and dressed. Venko tucked his blue shirt into his khakis and stopped. He stared at the wardrobe. Venko walked to the wardrobe and dug out the dusty box from behind a pair of tennis shoes. He lifted the lid off the shoe box and sat it on the bed. Venko stared at the old snub-nosed 38, laying it atop the padded ankle holster. The revolver looked archaic, a relic from a bygone era. It was the first gun he ever purchased. Twenty-three years ago, it was what every new cop did. He *needed* an off-duty gun. Something small and compact. Just in case. Venko remembered qualifying with it at the outdoor range the first couple years he owned it. Dependable accuracy was, at best, twenty feet or so. The owner of the gun shop told him the snub-nose five shot was for that up close and personal battle. *The gut shot gun.* He carried it off duty maybe a dozen times his first two years as a patrolman. Then he just stopped. He rarely went to places off duty where a gun was needed. It became a chore to put on the ankle holster, or stuff the revolver into a belly bag, the ubiquitous symbol of off duty cops that screamed, "Look at me, off-duty policeman here!" Over the years, he realized he preferred not to advertise that fact, and face the instant judgement that came with it.

Venko finished his second cup of coffee and could feel a slight tremble in his hands. He opened the revolver's cylinder and saw it was loaded with five rounds before snapping it shut, and sliding it into the holster. Venko pulled up his left pant leg and wrapped the Velcro holster around his ankle, snugging the strap down tightly. *Just in case.* He stood up and paced around the apartment. He could feel the extra weight on his left leg, it was noticeable, but not uncomfortable. It felt reassuring.

Venko grabbed the holster containing the Glock and the belt badge from the wardrobe shelf. He depressed the magazine release on the semi-auto pistol and locked the slide back. The ejected round flopped quietly onto the bed. Venko effortlessly disassembled the gun and inspected the parts. He ran a bore brush through the barrel and wiped down the parts with cotton swatches, moistened with a cleaning solution. The grime on the swatches indicated this was long overdue. He reassembled the Glock, placed a full magazine into the well, and racked the slide. He released the slide and removed the magazine. Venko grabbed the bullet off the bed, loaded it into the magazine before sliding it back into the Glock.

Realistically, he knew all this extra preparation was nothing more than a stall tactic. If he had to go to his backup gun, it meant he had burned through the sixteen rounds currently in his Glock, and an additional fifteen rounds in the spare magazine in his pocket. If things went that bad, he wasn't sure if a few hand grenades would make a difference.

He changed out of his brown dress shoes and into his waterproof hiking boots, remembering Frank's warning about the impending storm. He put on his jacket, gloves, and hat before stopping at the door. He looked at Diablo, comfortably situated in the center of the bed. Venko added more food to the uneaten portion in her bowl and filled the water bowl next to it. She flicked her tail and watched him with affection but remained on the bed.

"Just in case I'm a little late. That's all. No reason to worry." He felt stupid the instant he said it, but she seemed to understand.

He grabbed the spare key off the hook and placed it in his jacket pocket. It was the key Sarah used to have. He took a deep breath, repressing the emotional tide rising from within. As he stepped into the hallway, the familiar aroma of fresh coffee drifted to him. Venko locked the door and could feel Miss Rosales's presence.

She smiled as he approached.

"Your hip is bothering you again," she said, as he sat in the tiny metal chair.

"Just a bit, it always seems worse this time of year," he replied, and opened the thermos. He poured a cup and took a sip of the hot coffee.

"It's the coming storm, my knees always know first. Be careful tonight," she stopped and tilted her head curiously, briefly raising her gnarled fingers to her ears. "There is metal in the air again. It hasn't been this bad in many, many years. Oh, Danilo, do be careful."

"Don't worry, I will drive slow tonight, and I think I can get the service garage to put some chains on my tires as soon as I get in."

"Do what you must do. Nothing more. Everything else will fall in place."

Venko watched as she spoke. It chilled him. Instead of looking at him, she was looking just above his head. He glanced up, hoping to see whatever imaginary specter she was fixated on. Sensing his unease, she smiled and lowered her gaze.

"Nothing to worry about. I'm always cautious and prepared," He said, as he shifted his left leg, the extra weight suddenly noticeable. "Miss Rosales, I would like to ask a small favor," Venko stopped and retrieved the spare key from his pocket. "If anything should happen to me, would you take care of Diablo? I mean, until she can be resettled in another home?" He placed the key down in front her, with just enough force that she could hear it. She smiled broadly at his unnecessary gesture.

"Of course, Danilo, but you will return after your shift. Both stronger and wiser. You are the center, everything else is the orbit. You have much to achieve yet."

"Thank you," He replied and felt a gradual calming seep over him. "I think Diablo would like you." He drained the last of the coffee from the cup before putting the cap on the thermos. "Until tomorrow, goodnight." Venko stood and grabbed the thermos.

"Until tomorrow," she said.

He headed down the stairs and realized he could still smell the coffee, two flights down. Then a strange thought occurred to him, all the times he had stopped and chatted with Rosales all he *could* smell was the coffee. He never smelled lotion, soap, perfume, or a fragrance of any kind. She didn't smell like mothballs, as some of the residents at Serenity Vista did. She didn't have any smell. None. He pondered this as he walked into the teeth of gusting winds, towards the 7th Precinct.

Venko waived at Dex as he jogged up the stairs. He wanted to get into roll call before any of the sergeants arrived. He nearly ran over Miller leaving his office.

"Hey, Dan. Looking fit. You about ready to come back to full duty?" Miller asked.

"Oh yes, I am definitely ready for the wardrobe change and back to navy blue polyester."

"Hey, I heard your panel interview is right around the corner. You'll kill it this time. We could use you right here in the 7th. A sergeant with your experience would be respected and valued."

"Thanks, I appreciate that. I love the shift and the people here, it's the command that might be a problem for me. And let's not get too far ahead, I still have to pass the interview. Sarge, I could use a little favor. I'm working cold cases, and they might be related to an active missing person case. Rafael Espinoza. If the storm slows things down, I could use the help of Bianchi, Martinez and maybe Stein and Fitzpatrick later."

"Storm? We might get a little snow, but the bad stuff is supposed to hit east of the city by twenty or so miles. But okay, if they aren't tied up on calls, they can assist."

"Thanks, sarge, I'm going to run into roll call and give them a heads up."

Venko spent a few minutes huddled with Bianchi and Stein, knowing they would brief their partners later. He advised that one person from their car monitor radio channel 7. Channel 7, more commonly referred to as Chatter Channel, was a non-recorded channel only good for short distances. A group of officers working in the same building or within a half mile could pick it up. Outside of that, it was useless. It was primarily used for off-duty jobs where several officers needed to communicate inside a small area and did not want to tie up a main channel. While it was not a recorded channel, officers knew any other officer or supervisor in the general area could listen in. It was still a much faster option than cell phones.

He jogged up the remaining two flights of stairs to the detective bureau, buzzing with nervous energy. He could see

McGhee hovering near Oliver's desk, obviously fawning over her. McGhee's smile subsided as Venko approached.

"What's the plan Dan?"

Venko sighed at McGhee's attempt to sound cool.

"Cassie, can you help out tonight? I want to sit on two locations tonight, and hopefully come up with Espinoza. Can you take McGhee in your car and sit on Cheez's cousin's place, the apartments at 14th and Joyce? I'm going to sit on the apartments at 14th and Hemingway."

"Sounds good to me," McGhee responded instantly, trying to sound casual.

"Can we let Cassie answer?" Venko asked, prolonging the awkward moment.

"Yeah, sure," She responded with a knowing giggle.

"We need to get out there as soon as possible. One of you monitor chatter channel. I have Officers Bianchi, Martinez, Stein and Fitzpatrick also monitoring the channel. Per Sgt. Miller, they can help out if they aren't tied up on a call. Let's get moving." Venko turned and headed down the hall.

At 11:40 p.m., Venko found a parking spot on Hemingway that overlooked the apartment building on 14th Street. He removed the thermos cap and poured himself a cup of coffee. He sat the binoculars on his lap and sipped the coffee, preparing himself for the wait. He cursed as he heard Stein and Fitzpatrick get dispatched to a burglary call on the other side of the district.

"You copy that, Cassie? Stein and Fitzpatrick are out of the game for the next half hour or so," Venko asked, speaking into his hand-held radio.

"We copy. Nothing on our end so far."

"The A team is still with you Dan," Bianchi chimed in.

"Roger that," Venko responded, relieved that Bianchi's comments were expletive-free.

What had been light flurries ten minutes ago, had turned to squalls, with periods of complete white-out. Venko knew if the snowfall remained this heavy, driving was going to get dicey. *Gotta hand it to you Franks, you called that one correctly.*

At 12:21 a.m., Venko's cell phone rang. He didn't recognize the number but answered right away.

"Hello?"

"Yo, It's Morgan."

"Who?" Venko asked with a furrowed brow, still watching for any movement.

"Cheez-it."

"Right. What do you have for me Cheez? Where is Espinoza?"

"A dude that goes by the name Feets, is picking him up at my cousin's place, 14th and Joyce in the next ten minutes. Old Chevy pick-up truck. Lowrider. Green."

"Thanks. Hey Cheez, did you by any chance give anyone else this information?"

"Nah. We square on the little pipe you took off me?"

"Yeah, we're square." Venko hung up.

He knew Cheez was lying. Franks already knew.

Venko picked up the hand-held radio.

"Heads up. Cheez called. Espinoza is getting picked up in a green Chevy S10, sometime in the next ten minutes, at your location."

"Copy that, Dan," Oliver responded.

Venko glanced around. He had a sinking feeling that he was being watched. He picked up the binoculars and scanned up and down the block.

"Cassie, this might sound crazy. Do you have any counter-surveillance on you?"

A few seconds later, she responded.

"No, not that I can pick out. You gonna drift down our way?"

"Not at the moment, I want to make sure Cheez was being straight with me. Bianchi, you copy the location?" Venko could hear a muffled, static filled transmission.

"I can't copy you Bianchi. You may have drifted out of range. Cassie, try to raise them from there. Marcus, call them on the cell."

Venko heard more muffled static as he turned his wipers up to keep pace with the driving snow. At the bottom of the hill, he could see a small green pick up approaching the corner.

"Son-of-a-bitch!" Venko yelled into the hand-held radio. "The truck is here, it's here!"

"We can't raise Bianchi on the radio or phone. We are headed your way."

Venko pulled away from the curb and started down the hill. He realized the Ford was starting to slide in the heavy snow. He fought hard to keep the car going straight. Visibility was down to almost zero. He could see the truck's outline under the street light, at the bottom of the hill. Then he heard the first of four gunshots.

"Shots fired! Cassie, go to dispatch channel and put out shots fired at my location!" He yelled into the radio.

As he approached the bottom of the hill, he saw a black SUV race up 14th Street, northbound, coming right at you Cassie." He slid to a stop near the green truck and jumped out. Venko saw a Hispanic male on the other side of the truck near the curb.

"Police. Are you okay?" The male tossed a pistol behind him casually before responding.

"Yeah, I'm okay. White dude in the black SUV just shot at me and grabbed Rafael."

Venko jumped back into the Ford, ignoring the obvious gun toss. He slammed the shifter in to drive and gunned the engine.

"What the fuck man?" The male shouted, as Venko steered the Ford northbound.

"Coming right at you Cassie. We are north on 14th. He is about two blocks ahead, in this shit I can only see his tail lights. Black SUV." Venko felt the car starting to lose traction on the snow and slowed.

He took a deep breath, trying to slow the surge of adrenaline. The SUV took a sharp left. Venko realized it would be hard to keep up with the SUV's four-wheel drive.

"He just turned left on a side street," Venko barked into the radio.

He could now see Oliver driving towards him. As he made the left turn, the car slid and struck the curb. Dispatch channel put out the shots fired call, and he could hear several officers acknowledging the call.

By the time Venko got the car moving again, the tail lights were gone.

"He's gone. I don't see the tail lights ahead. You guys go north at the next block, I'll go south." Venko tossed the radio onto the seat and gripped the steering wheel tightly, with both hands.

He could see Oliver's headlights behind him. She turned north after he turned south, at the next intersection. The streets were deserted, and it would be a few hours before the snowplows could catch up. This was a nightmare.

"We got nothing Dan," Oliver said with a tone of resignation.

"Just keep crisscrossing east and west through the alleys as you move north, I'll do the same south-bound."

Venko heard two other cruisers report to dispatch, they were involved in accidents on the way to the shots fired call. No injuries, but the cars were out of service. Venko pulled to the curb and put the car in park. He reached into his jacket pocket and retrieved the note with Franks phone number. He dialed the number and listened to the rings. After a minute, he threw the phone down.

"You dick!"

He knew by the silence on the radio, Oliver wasn't having any luck.

Where did you go? Where would you go? Local Base is what you called it. Where would that be?

Venko picked up the radio, "Cassie, go to the Wing-Lutz Apartments and look for the black SUV."

"What? He couldn't have made it that far."

"JUST DO IT!"

Cassie Oliver looked at McGhee, who shrugged.

"Whatever," she said, as McGhee nodded solemnly.

With the radio quiet again, Venko resumed his analysis.

Franks, you're driving, so you have to get Espinoza to your local base. You called the Wing-Lutz a waypoint, so you can't get home from there. I'm hoping you weren't packed and ready to go just yet. So where is this Local Base? You said it was in your area of operation. What would be central to your area of operation? How big can that area be? What is central to this investigation? Fuck!

Morely and Sons Manufacturing! It's been closed for a while. You can get in and out, relatively undetected. It's the center of this whole fucking case! Gotcha!

Venko drove as quick as the snow-covered streets would allow. With no other traffic on the roads, he made it in three minutes. He saw the SUV beached on the sidewalk by the side entrance, across from the park. There were three fresh bullet holes in the rear quarter panel. Venko parked the Ford a few feet away. He shoved the hand-held radio in his jacket pocket and grabbed his flashlight off the seat.

He heard Cassie Oliver's muffled voice, "You find anything Dan?"

He ignored the radio and stepped through the partially opened door.

He froze, letting his eyes adjust to the low light, while listening for the faintest clues. Venko noticed there was no audible alarm, and the security lights next to the door were still green. *More of your voodoo, future-man.* Then he heard the footfalls. About forty yards ahead and off to the left. Venko swept the flashlight across his path as he ran towards the sound—the basement. Franks was headed to the basement. As he approached the basement door, he could hear a faint whooshing sound. Venko burst through the door and stopped at the top of the stairs. He caught a glimpse of Franks carrying what appeared to be an unconscious Espinoza over his shoulder at the bottom of the stairs. Franks broke right, and out of sight. Venko stumbled near the bottom of the stairs but regained his footing as he got to the last step.

"Stop! Don't do it!" Venko yelled as he caught sight of Franks approaching what looked like a full-sized TSA body scanner.

Franks was at a control panel next to the machine. The scanner had small LED lights running up both sides of the frame. The frame looked like a doorway, about seven feet high by three feet wide. The lights were slowly turning from yellow to green, as they climbed the frame on both sides. Franks was furiously working the control panel with his left hand, while keeping Espinoza balanced over his shoulder with his right. Venko, flashlight cupped under his Glock, had crept to within twenty feet of Franks.

"Damnit Franks, stop!" Venko ordered.

Franks ignored him and continued working at the panel. Venko fired a shot to the right of Franks and through the center of the opening. The concussive sound made Venko flinch. Franks slowly turned around. The frame lights were now all green.

"Dan, you won't shoot me," Franks said calmly.

Venko lined up the Glock's glowing tritium sights. He picked a point on the left side of Franks' chest. Venko knew he could hit him cleanly at this distance, but the slightest jerk or pull might put the round close, or into the dangling legs of Espinoza. The kid would survive that. Franks raised his left hand and slowly stepped back. Venko could see Franks hadn't drawn his pistol. There was no way Franks could get to his shoulder holster with Espinoza draped over him.

"I'm going to take him back to his father," Venko said sternly.

"No, you're not," Franks said quietly and took another step back.

Franks was now inches away from the lighted doorway of the machine.

Venko's hands were starting to tremble. He knew the trigger pull of the Glock to be roughly five pounds. Venko guessed his right index finger was already at two pounds. He took another breath and slowly exhaled, lining up the sights again. Venko raised his eyes above the sights and looked at Franks. The pair locked eyes. Venko knew he couldn't shoot Franks. Sweat trickled down his forehead, as he felt the tautness in grip slowly recede. Doubt crept back in fueled by the haunting photos of Michaels and Billings. Venko hoped that Espinoza would never share their hollow, vacant expression. As quickly as the feeling came, it was gone. Venko knew. He felt it. Espinoza would be okay.

Franks nodded to Venko, "I owe you one. You might want to cover your ears."

Venko lifted his finger off the trigger as Franks stepped through the threshold.

The lights all along the frame turned red as Franks and Espinoza passed through. The machine instantly pulled the surrounding air into it. The force of this sudden suction pitched

Venko violently forward, and onto the floor. An ear-splitting CRACK followed. He rolled onto his side and covered his ears in pain. The noise seemed to reverberate around the room for ten seconds. Then nothing. Venko's head throbbed as he looked up. The machine was gone. Venko slowly stood up. He swept his flashlight across the room--nothing but old crates and pallets. It was all gone. Venko coughed several times, as the dust around him swirled slowly before settling.

Three minutes later, Venko stood next to his car, the cold snow blowing across him. He realized he was sweating, and the cold air felt good.

"Dan? Dan? You there?" Cassie Oliver asked frantically.

Venko pulled the radio out of his pocket and replied, "Yes, I'm here."

"I've been trying to raise you on the radio. What happened?"

Venko exhaled slowly, the adrenalin receding.

"I was checking a couple of spots. I must have turned the radio down. You find anything?"

"No. You have any other ideas?" Her voice fraught with resignation.

Venko exhaled slowly and ran his hand through the hair, brushing the gathering snow out. "Maybe just a hunch. Drive over to Espinoza's house. Maybe his father has heard from him." Venko released the transmit button on the radio and knew what they must be thinking.

Oliver shot McGhee an incredulous look.

"Right, Dan, after all of this, the kid is just going to go home," McGhee mumbled to Oliver.

"All right. We'll give it a shot," she responded over the air, while nodding in agreement with McGhee.

Venko started the car and rolled the driver's window down. He poured the last of Miss Rosales's coffee from the thermos into his cup. He inhaled the rich aroma before taking a sip. Ten minutes later, he heard Oliver's excited voice screaming into the radio.

"He's here! He's fucking here! He's fine!"

Of course. Of course, he is.

There was a way to turn the white flag, and perhaps regret, rather interpret the card that would be one
thing. Captain self is going to eventually turn on a thing.

Chapter 19
Study Hall (Six days later)

By 5:30 a.m., Venko was exhausted and knew, with the
promotional panel interview in less than six hours, it would be a
while before he slept. He finished typing the second draft of his
investigation, closing out the cold cases. He expected his doctor
would clear him to return to full duty next week. As he read over
his draft, he was struck by the irony of it all. Venko was supposed
to just do a couple of interviews, document what he did and toss
the case back into the unsolved pile. Another detective would
pick it up in six months or so. Wash, rinse, repeat. Venko knew
exactly what happened to Billings and Michaels. He knew where
they were, but since he had no way of actually producing them, he
kept his narrative generic. There would be no mention of Brody
Franks, Morely and Sons Manufacturing, or any link between
the attempted abductions of Cole, Daniels or Solomon with the
Billings and Michaels cases. Venko figured he would never see
Franks again. That was just fine with him.

Satisfied with the draft, he printed out two copies.

"Marcus, read over this and let me know what you think,"
Venko said, handing a copy to McGhee.

McGhee spent the next twenty minutes reading over the
investigation, murmuring an occasional "Uh huh, hmm."

"Kind of glossed over the info we got at the nursing home
from Buck. There is no mention of Cole, Daniels or Solomon as a
possible link to the cold cases. Nothing on the white ninja at all,"
McGhee finished and leaned back in his chair, arms folded.

"If there was a way to find the white ninja, and get a documented, recorded statement from him, that would be one thing. Captain Sellers is going to eventually sign off on this. I can't put my gut feelings and conjecture in this report, or he will blow a gasket. Bottom line, we are both going back to full uniform duty shortly, and we can't find Billings or Michaels, so this will all be added into the cold case files," Venko finished and gave McGhee his most sincere look.

It was a fifty-fifty proposition that McGhee would buy this explanation of his report.

"Just so you know, when I make detective, I am going to reopen this case," McGhee said confidently.

"Have at it," Venko said with a shrug.

"What time is your panel interview?"

"11 a.m. Less than six hours."

"Shouldn't you be studying? Why are you still here? Go home."

"I'm not going to sleep anyway, and I wanted to finish the cold case paperwork first. I've reviewed some on-line articles and other materials Lt. Swanson gave me," Venko said, without sounding confident.

Oliver overheard the conversation and walked over.

"Good luck, Dan. Brush up on your community-oriented policing theories. That is still huge around here, at least on paper. I'd also take a peek at anything you can find on utilizing social media in police work."

Venko noticed McGhee staring at Oliver. He smiled.

"Why don't you just go in my place?"

"Nah, I like working in DB, even if my help has no pulse," she said glancing in the direction of Beans's cubicle.

A hand, middle finger extended, shot up above his cubicle's grey half-wall.

"Seriously, why are you still here? Go home and put on a pot of coffee and read a little, before you clean up for the interview," Oliver tried convincing Venko.

Venko paused for a second, then nodded.

"I think I will Cassie." He grabbed his jacket off the hook as he stood.

"You're going to kill it!" She shouted as he walked down the hallway.

"Do us proud!" McGhee added.

The streets around the 7th Precinct were eerily quiet this early. Venko reflected on the past couple of days as he trudged through the snow, the cold air clearing his head. He had completed the paperwork on the cold cases and done what he was supposed to do. It wasn't exactly closure. He knew where Billings and Michaels were. But that would be no consolation to those that still held out hope. They would, most likely, never know the truth. Venko thought of the horrific alternatives that Franks presented. This was probably the best option, and that son-of-a-bitch somehow was right about Espinoza.

Venko stopped on the ground floor of his building and retrieved his mail. When he reached his apartment, he was still shivering.

After making coffee and feeding Diablo, he sat at his desk and began to pour through the weeks-worth of mail. It was his habit to pile it on the corner of the desk, and then sift through the pile every couple of days. Venko opened bills and automatically placed them under his keyboard. That was his system for bills that needed to be paid soon. He generally paid them once a week…unless he forgot. Anything that resembled junk mail went to the trashcan next to the desk. All flyers were tossed first in this process.

Venko poured a cup of coffee and dug out another envelope. He opened it, removed the letter, and threw the envelope into the trash can. He scanned it quickly expecting it to be an invoice. After a quick glance, he realized there were no numbers. He started at the top and began to read. Halfway down, he paused.

Holy shit! This can't be what I think it is.

He continued reading and began to laugh. He pounded the desk with his right fist and let out a celebratory "YES!" Venko looked at both sides of the paper. There was no signature or handwriting on either side of the printed document. He pulled the trashcan onto his lap and fished out the envelope. It was *his* name and address on the envelope. He looked at the return address and smiled. A single word was printed in the top left corner of the envelope.

Hogwarts.

Chapter 20
Every Dog Has His Day (February 6th)

Venko knew he would need to leave by 12:15 if he was to make it to the ceremony by 1 p.m. That would give him enough time to push start the Subaru if necessary, and swing by Binder's and grab a coffee and cherry Danish for the short drive to Central Precinct.

He returned to full duty ten days ago. It felt good to get back into the swing of midnight patrol. He barely flinched when Swanson told him he would be keeping McGhee as a partner, full time. McGhee would be back to full duty tomorrow. Venko was sure he finagled his doctor into an extra week of light duty, to milk a few more days with Oliver.

Venko pulled the plastic sheet off the hanger that held his dress uniform. The creases were still crisp. He put on the white shirt and buttoned it. The gap in the neck indicated he lost a few pounds since he last wore the shirt. He clipped on the navy-blue tie and tucked his shirt into his uniform pants. Venko pulled on his Ike jacket and ran his fingers along the four light blue hash marks that adorned his left sleeve. One for every five years of service. In less than two years he would get his fifth hash mark. Twenty-five years of service. He would be eligible to retire. Venko had thought a lot about retiring over the last several months. He was still unsure of what he would do when he hit that milestone. He would be a sergeant after today and things would be different, same place, same people, but different. Venko sat down and applied a fresh coat of black polish to his boots. Today his future felt brighter.

He looked in the mirror and adjusted his tie. He tried to run a comb through his hair, then ran his hands under the faucet and fared better with his fingers. Diablo circled Venko's legs curiously, as if wondering why he was up so early.

Venko managed to start the Subaru with the key today, another sign that luck or the fates were on his side.

He jogged from the parking lot to the door of Binder's Book Store full of nervous energy. The smell of fresh pastries was comforting.

"Danilo, look how handsome you are today!" Mrs. Esposito greeted Venko and gave him a hug as he approached the counter. Giuseppe Esposito smiled and waved at Venko from the other end of the counter, as he filled a box with pastries.

"Could I get a small black coffee and a cherry Danish to go?" He asked, slightly embarrassed by her attention.

"To go? Why don't you stay? We never see you anymore."

"I'm getting promoted to sergeant today, otherwise I would stay, but I promise I'll be back tomorrow and grab a table." He watched her place two pastries in the bag, then fill a large Styrofoam cup with coffee. While her back was turned, he placed a ten-dollar bill on the counter.

"Congratulations on your promotion Danilo, your money's no good today. Take it, I mean it." Venko smiled sheepishly, and headed out the door.

Venko ate both cherry Danishes while driving a stick shift, and at various points, steering with his elbows as he ate. He parked in the lot just south of the Central Precinct. A large glob of cherry filling had landed on his white shirt, inducing instant panic. Venko sighed with relief, realizing that buttoning his Ike jacket would conceal the stain. He was twenty minutes early. Venko watched several officers in full dress uniforms walk into the auditorium side of the precinct building. Streaks of sunshine began to pierce the cloud cover.

• • •

Brody Franks prepared for a different trip. One that would change the past. He knew his computer skills would enable him to scrub the historical GPS data from the official record kept on the machine. It would show no evidence of temporal transit since his official return. He was still that good of a hacker, he hoped. What's the worst that could happen? He could get fired. Or get fired and arrested. Neither option sat well in his nervous stomach. He had bet on himself before and won. He kept telling himself that. Franks hit the departure button, and started his journey back a few months, to the fifth of December.

Franks exited the cab in the parking lot of Nuts and Bolts Bar. He paid the cabbie the fare and included a twenty-dollar tip. Franks stood in the light snow a few feet from the neon glare of the Budweiser sign in the window. He glanced at his watch, December 5th, 0145 hours––the day two drunk idiots killed Sarah Sterling. He would go in and observe for a while, then pick his spot.

Franks sat at the bar and ordered a Guinness from Frankie Tomasino. He nursed his beer and watched the very drunk Wallace Baxter Jr. and Walter Niles stumble towards a table of four women. Nothing in their expressions indicated the drunk pair was welcome to join them. Nevertheless, Franks watched with sociological interest, the train wreck that was about to unfold. He couldn't hear the golden line that Baxter opened with, but the results were as expected.

"They're all bitches! Fucking bitches," Baxter shouted as the pair slinked back to the bar. This drew the attention of Tomasino.

"That's enough out of you," Tomasino warned in a menacing tone. Baxter flinched slightly. Franks saw it and smiled.

"What the fuck you looking at?" Baxter shouted to Brody Franks, in an attempt to salvage what was left of his machismo.

"Nothing, just drinking my beer." Franks responded, and watched as Baxter sent a round of drinks to the girls in the corner, as a peace offering.

Franks was astounded at the amount of Jack Daniels consumed by Baxter and Niles. He surmised, correctly, that Baxter was an alcoholic and Niles would be throwing up very soon. Franks only needed a fifteen or twenty second delay--but a minute or two would be safer.

"Last call! Drink em up and get the fuck out!" Tomasino shouted at the five remaining patrons scattered throughout the bar. Baxter drained his ninth Jack and Coke before slamming the glass down. Niles mumbled something incoherently and dropped his Budweiser bottle on the floor, falling over when he tried to reach for it.

"It's 2:30, you need to pay up and leave. I'll call you a cab if you want," Tomasino offered sincerely, after seeing the condition Niles was in.

"Nonsense. I'm good, I'll drive Niles home," Baxter said, glancing at Niles as he grasped the bar rail attempting to pull himself up.

"I, uh I, need to go to the bathroom first, Bax, pay the tab," Niles mumbled, digging through his wallet and finding his cash was long gone. He handed Baxter his Visa and started an unsteady trek to the bathroom.

Baxter handed the Visa to Tomasino and whispered, "Put my old tab on this too."

"You're a real dirtbag Baxter," Tomasino stated, and then ran all of the charges through without a second thought.

Brody Franks held up some cash and watched as the muscular bartender walked towards him.

"Here's a ten for my Guinness and another fifty for your troubles."

"What troubles?"

Franks left the money on the bar and walked up to Wallace Baxter Jr. Without saying a word, Franks threw a perfect left hook that caught Baxter flush on the jaw. Baxter's green John Deer cap fluttered off his head as he fell. It would be a full minute or two before Wallace Baxter Jr. woke up. Plenty of time. Franks raised both of his palms to Tomasino.

"That's all, I'm leaving."

Tomasino, still bewildered by what he just saw, shook his head. He looked at the crisp fifty-dollar bill and stuffed it in his shirt pocket.

"All right then, rock on dude," he said as he casually wiped the bar down.

"What the fuck?" Niles exclaimed, as he walked out of the bathroom and spied his supine friend.

Tomasino looked at the fresh vomit dripping off Niles's shirt and onto the floor.

"Get him up, and both of you get the fuck out of my bar."

It was actually closer to seven minutes later, by the time Baxter got the rusting S10 started. As the pair headed down the snow-covered hill at breakneck speed, Sarah Sterling had already cleared the intersection below, en route to Memorial Hospital.

Baxter would not strike the grey Volvo. As fate would have it, the S10 bounced off the curb as it picked up speed down the hill. Then, as a result of a drunken oversteer, it slammed into a telephone pole. The impact drove the steering column into Baxter's chest, killing him. Niles was ejected through the windshield and would never walk again. Some things were just meant to be.

Franks felt exhausted. He had bounced to December 5th and home, then back again. He knew this would wrap things up, as he parked the rental car two spots over from a rusting Subaru. Franks knew what would happen at the promotion ceremony, and if he was honest, he wanted to see Venko get promoted. Despite their differences in age and backgrounds and living seventy-five years in the future, Franks could relate to Venko. Cops were cops and Brody Franks always paid his debts.

He took a seat in the back of the auditorium and nervously fiddled with the bottle of water he was holding. Franks scanned the stage and spotted Venko on the right side. From the uniforms, he could tell this was a mix of promotions for both sergeants and lieutenants. Franks listened as a deputy chief at the podium droned on about dedication and achievement. The front row was filled with precinct commanders. They would eventually come on stage and pin the badges on those promoted from their precincts. Much to Frank's displeasure, the 7th Precinct would be last. He listened to the smattering of applause as each name was called. Franks watched the forced smiles and awkward photo-op handshakes given after each badge was pinned on. Venko had to be the oldest of those being promoted.

Finally, Captain Brian Sellers introduced himself at the podium, and announced the promotion of Officer Danilo Venko to sergeant. He walked over to Venko and pinned his badge on.

"If I didn't know better," he whispered through gritted teeth, "I'd swear you had a copy of my questions in advance. But I didn't print them out for the committee until five minutes before you walked in."

"Yes sir, that would be impossible," Venko said as he shook Sellers' hand and turned towards the department photographer.

Franks saw the contingent on stage slowly moving down the steps towards waiting family and friends. He clutched the bottle in his left hand and strode briskly down the aisle towards the stage.

Venko was mobbed by Haystack and Swanson as he came off the stage.

"Thanks guys, I didn't expect to be here."

"You must have smoked the panel interview. Did any of the materials I gave you help?" Swanson asked.

"Yes, that and I must have just got lucky. I - uh, excuse me guys." Venko stopped talking and took a few steps away from the group. *It can't be. It can't be.* His brain would not let him process what his eyes clearly saw. Beautiful, smiling Sarah Sterling was walking towards him.

"I'm so proud of you Danilo." Venko threw his arms around her. "How? How are you here?" He took in the smell of her hair and kissed her cheek. Venko couldn't comprehend he was physically holding his best memories.

Sarah was becoming concerned as he squeezed her tightly. She could feel his tears on the side of her face. "Danilo?" He pulled his arms away from her and staggered sideways before mumbling "Thank you Brody Franks." Haystack saw Venko going to the ground and tried to catch him but was too late.

Venko struggled to get to his knees. The voices and sounds around him rose to a painful din. His vision blurred to mere shadows and shapes. Venko closed his eyes and saw swirling colors, then individual memories. At first, they were individual threads, the day in the hospital when he was told Sarah died in a crash. Then they came like a waterfall, confusing, violently overlapping, and continuously crashing down on him. He began to yell, a stream of consciousness and fear combined. Purple, red, gold and blue hues drifted in and out of his head. The spinning slowed. He suddenly remembered the day Sarah visited him in the hospital. The long walks they took after his physical therapy. He smiled and took a deep breath. Beads of sweat rolled off his nose and he watched in perfect clarity, as the droplets struck the carpet. Haystack and Swanson pulled him to his feet.

"Bro, you okay?"

"I think so, thanks Haystack."

"Electrolytes are out of balance, dude, I've seen it happen before," Haystack explained more to Sarah, than Venko. A tall stranger pulled a folding chair from a nearby row. "Have a seat and drink some water."

Venko sat down, opened the bottle and took a long gulp. He did feel better. Sarah looked into his eyes with genuine concern.

"Danilo, maybe we should take you to the hospital."

"Nah, Haystack is right. Wearing this full-dress uniform, no air circulating, and I probably am dehydrated. I drank way too much coffee. And I think I have had enough of hospitals for a while."

"Who is Brody?" Swanson asked.

"What?"

"When you went down, you said, 'Thank you Brody Franks.'"

Venko shot a confused look at both Swanson and Sarah.

"I don't know who Brody Franks is. I feel fine now, really guys." Venko saw Swanson lean over to Sarah. He knew she was being directed to keep a close eye on him the rest of the night.

Venko stood up.

"Really, I'm good now. As a matter of fact, I could use a good steak and a beer. Who is in?"

"Sounds good to me," Swanson seconded.

"Yes sir, Sgt. Venko," Haystack said, and clicked his heels together for emphasis.

Venko threw his arm around Sarah, pulled her close and kissed her again.

"Now I'm really worried about you," She said with obvious sarcasm.

As the four exited the auditorium, the tired stranger drove away.

Chapter 21
Time To Pay the Piper

Detective Brody Franks was finally going back to work. The first three days after his return from Venko's promotion in 2024 were spent in mandatory quarantine. He was poked, prodded, examined, inoculated and questioned. Internal Affairs spent most of a two-hour video conference challenging nearly every aspect of his report. Eventually, they relented when his story never wavered. He was able to wipe his last trip from the GPS storage on the machine. There were still some data fragments he couldn't delete, but he knew it would take a genius to find them and reassemble them. He felt safe.

As he maneuvered the Tesla through downtown traffic, he saw a message light on his rear-view mirror flashing. The one thing he disliked about modern technology: you couldn't ignore it. If a message was left on your phone's voicemail, it followed you everywhere until you checked it. After quarantine, he had two days off. He wasn't going to ruin them by answering his phone, or his TV. He decided to kick it old school. He sat on his deck and read a book. An honest to goodness, real, paper book.

Franks decided to end the mystery.

"Play messages," he directed.

The Tesla's control panel displayed the face of a very angry Lt. Murphy before the video commenced.

Detective Franks, Captain Russel has submitted your name for a commendation for the work on the Morely case. He found your solution for Espinoza to be courageous and humane. So, now you have me painted in a corner. It must be funny to you, that I can't touch you for disobeying my order. Because now, that order never existed. I can assure you one hundred percent, that I am not laughing. I told you from day one, this unit did not tolerate grandstanding hot dogs. It will always be about the team not the individual. Obviously, I can't shit-can you. But I think your days traveling are over for a while. The unit needs another good nerd in Records Research. So, I am transferring you. File a grievance if you want, the contract states I can transfer any detective based on an emergency need. And we need more library nerds. From the time your retinal scan is taken in the lobby, it should be a five-minute walk to my office. So, I will see you at 0805 hours, and your ass better be on time.

Franks replayed the message again, just to watch Murphy's face get red and listen to his voice grow more frustrated with each word.

• • •

He parked the Tesla in the underground garage and straightened his tie before exiting. Three minutes later he was in the lobby security entrance for Central Precinct. Several uniformed officers stopped and shook his hand, congratulating him on a job well done. A few older detectives patted him on the back as they hurried to their offices.

Franks approached the scanner and looked directly into the small screen. Two uniformed officers sat at small desks on either side of the glass door. They nodded to Franks as his picture and name flashed green on their screens. An electronic buzz followed, and the door was unlocked. Franks entered the atrium and turned right down the second hallway. "WARRANTS DIVISION" was posted above the hallway entrance in large blue letters.

Like most divisions in the police department, the Warrants Division had a memorial for fallen officers from the unit. Every time Franks returned from a temporal assignment his routine never wavered. Part of it was a way to honor those that sacrificed their lives in pursuit of justice. The rest was simply a superstition he could not overcome. Plaques lined the left side of the hallway.

The photos captured a single smiling moment, frozen in time. The narratives below the photos, contrasted the smiling faces with the grim reality of their end. Franks walked to the first plaque, stood at attention, then silently read the narrative. He touched the left corner of the plaque and moved to the next one. He repeated the process three times for each of those killed from the Warrants Division. Franks solemnly moved down the hall to the plaque standing alone. This one was dedicated to the lone detective still listed as missing. He read the inscription.

Sent to July 14th, 1980, to execute a warrant. Did not return. WE WILL NEVER STOP SEARCHING.

Franks knew the detective was probably dead and touched the left corner of the plaque. He took a few more steps towards Lt. Murphy's office and stopped. He turned and glanced at the photo on the plaque. Her clear brown eyes seemed to twinkle and the freckles across her nose arched with her smile. Detective Anna Rosales. Forever memorialized at thirty-two years old.

Chapter 22

Hope Springs Eternal

On the same day seventy-five years before Brody Franks touches the portrait of missing Detective Anna Rosales, newly minted Sgt. Danilo Venko locks his apartment door. He has no memory of what Detective Brody Franks did for him, or the repercussions Franks faces in the distant future. There is only here and now, and he feels good. Venko can smell the strong coffee and glances down the hall at Miss Anna Rosales. Venko sees her turn her head at the sound of his keys. She is humming along with the Salsa music crackling from a small radio. He approaches and pulls the chair out, pausing to check the chime on his cellphone.

Be safe tonight Sgt. Venko. Love you, SS.

"She worries about you, because she loves you," Rosales said as Venko eased into the tiny chair, no longer phased by her clairvoyance. She is frail and old, how old exactly, he doesn't know, but he senses an underlying strength that is astonishing.

"I know," he mumbled before quickly replying to Sarah's text with:

Luv u2.

Predictive text brought up several emojis and normally he ignored them. But tonight, he sent heart emoji after the text.

"Do you love Sarah?" She asked.

Venko took a sip of coffee before replying.

"Yes, I do."

"Good, you deserve a second chance." She smiled, and for a brief second her brown eyes appeared clear.

276

About the Author

T.B. Pasko is a retired police captain with twenty-seven years of law enforcement experience including command assignments in Vice, Narcotics and Uniformed Patrol. He was part of a multi-jurisdictional task force recognized by the Ohio Attorney General's Office for their work on the investigation, arrest and prosecution of serial killer Richard Beasley. Pasko also appeared on an episode of Investigation Discovery's Very Bad Men that featured the case. He holds a master's degree in police administration from the University of South Carolina and a bachelor's degree in criminal justice from Ashland University. He is a big fan of The Twilight Zone and other classic sci-fi TV shows and movies.

www.ingramcontent.com/pod-product-compliance
Lightning Source LLC
Chambersburg PA
CBHW010737130726
47899CB00015B/3300